"Blakeley's lively story is a rapid-fire series of thrills and suspense, and readers will want more of Plenty Man's (Greenwood's) escapades." —*Publishers Weekly*

"Mike Blakeley turns the horses loose in all our souls."
—W. Michael Gear and Kathleen O'Neal Gear

"Mike Blakeley writes with an authority and empathy about a people superbly suited to the land."
—Lucia St. Clair Robson

"Authentic in every detail, *Moon Medicine* is big medicine, a great novel and a compelling page-turner."
—*True West* magazine

"Blakeley seems to get better with each book, you can look forward to the sequel or sequels being progressively better . . . underscored with depth."
—*American Cowboy*

"A gifted storyteller . . . Blakeley has a remarkable eye and a feel for physical action and a striking ability to render the swift blur of violent confrontation."
—*Texas Books in Review*

By Mike Blakeley
from Tom Doherty Associates

MOON MEDICINE

MIKE BLAKELY

A TOM DOHERTY ASSOCIATES BOOK
NEW YORK

MOON MEDICINE

Copyright © 2001 by Mike Blakely

All rights reserved.

A Forge Book
Published by Tom Doherty Associates, LLC
175 Fifth Avenue
New York, NY 10010

www.tor-forge.com

Forge® is a registered trademark of Tom Doherty Associates, LLC.

ISBN 978-0-8125-8025-9
Library of Congress Catalog Card Number: 200123252

First Edition: August 2001
First Mass Market Edition: February 2003

Printed in the United States of America

0 9 8 7 6 5 4 3 2

*Dedicated to the memory of
my fellow novelist, mentor,
and friend, Norman Zollinger*

AUTHOR'S NOTE

Toward the end of my novel, *Too Long at the Dance,* an enigmatic character shows up. He calls himself "Plenty Man." Though I created the character, I knew little about him at the time. It seemed he was intended to lend mystery to the story, even from the author's point of view. I knew that Plenty Man specialized in finding and ransoming white captives back from the Indians. I knew that he played the violin and recited poetry. Beyond that, I knew little more than the reader about Plenty Man.

A few years after writing *Too Long at the Dance,* I became interested in the 1874 Battle of Adobe Walls as a possible subject for a novel. As I began to research the story, I became just as intrigued with the history of the Adobe Walls area going back decades before the battle. The area had been named for the ruins of an old adobe fort that had served as a Comanche and Kiowa trading post for the firm of Bent, St. Vrain & Co. in the 1840's. It seemed to me that the story of the place known as Adobe Walls should start with Fort Adobe.

I decided to create a character who could tell the story from first-hand experience. He would be instrumental in the founding and building of Fort Adobe. Years later, during the Civil War, he would participate in the "first" Battle of Adobe Walls with Kit Carson. And finally, in 1874, he would find himself embroiled in the "second" Battle of Adobe Walls with Billy Dixon, Bat Masterson, Chief Quanah Parker, and others.

But, who would this character be? For some reason, I remembered Plenty Man, and knew immediately that he would serve well as the protagonist and narrator for this

work of historical fiction. So, I began to get to know Plenty
Man, and to explain how a violin-playing poet came to be
a ransom negotiator among the Plains Indians. Plenty Man,
who goes by many nicknames and aliases throughout the
story (including Honoré Greenwood), is totally fictitious.
However, many of the characters with whom he interacts
are based on real historical figures, including Kit Carson,
William Bent, Charles Bent, Ceran St. Vrain, Lucien
Maxwell, John Hatcher, J. W. Abert, Jim Bridger, Thomas
Fitzpatrick, Lucas Murray, and many other extraordinary
frontiersmen.

As it turned out, I could not squeeze the entire story of
Fort Adobe and Adobe Walls into one novel. *Moon Medicine* leads Plenty Man through all the adventures and turmoil that accompanied the rise and fall of Fort Adobe. The
two battles of Adobe Walls will have to be told in the coming sequel, or sequels, as the case may be.

MIKE BLAKELY
Rancho Quien Sabe
Burnet County, Texas

ONE

The ghosts of Charles and William Bent spoke to me last night. The spirit of Kit Carson came to me in the same vision. This was not a dream, but a vision. I know the difference.

Kit said, "Come on, Plenty Man, I've marked the trail."

William said, "It's alright, Kid."

Charles added, "Better hurry, Mr. Greenwood, before you do something stupid and take the low road."

As I woke, the echoes of their voices faded and became raindrops tapping the windowpane. The pale light of dawn illuminated my one-room sod house. I got up and went out in the weather in my nightshirt. I say, *"Bah!"* to anyone who suggests that a man of ninety-nine years should not be trudging around in the cold rain. The rain won't hurt you. And if you breathe a smudge of fir needles, it will ward off attacks from the Thunderbird. The Comanche medicine man, Burnt Belly, taught me that decades ago, and I have never been struck by lightning.

The smudge? Simple. Place the fir needles on a hot coal, and breathe the pungent smoke. You will need a forked stick of chokecherry to lift the coal from the fire. Chokecherry is dense and hard and resists burning. A live chokecherry tree will tell you all this and more if you listen hard enough.

Anyway, this morning, I went out into the drizzle and walked through the orchard and up the gentle grade of the prairie, letting the raindrops fall on my bare head, and feeling the mud ooze between my toes. I stood over the vestiges of the last few sunbaked bricks—all that remain now of Fort Adobe.

The casual observer would not even recognize these as adobe bricks. They now resemble a mere bump rising from the prairie. Grasses have taken root upon them. It looks as if someone dumped a wheelbarrow full of dirt here and left it. Yet, I know what lofty dreams and desperate struggles those few decaying adobes represent.

"Ta'a ko'oitu," I said in Comanche. We are dying.

I was not really sad. I got over my sorrow long ago. I remembered things I had done here. The children I had ransomed out of captivity. The battles I had fought. The demons I had slain. Here I rode with trappers and traders legendary in their own time. Jim Bridger, John "Freckled Hand" Hatcher, Thomas "Broken Hand" Fitzpatrick. Old Gabe. And, of course, William Bent and Ceran St. Vrain. Here Kit Carson would become my friend. The Comanche chief, Shaved Head, would adopt me. The warrior, Kills Something, would become my brother. The shaman, Burnt Belly, would show me how to make medicine and listen to plants and animals talk.

But now you think you are listening to the fanciful ramblings of a senile old fool, for I have tried to tell too much at once. Bear with me. Hear my tale. It is strange, and so am I. Yet, my story is like yours—or his—or hers—or theirs. I have lived and seen and done the strange, the unusual. Haven't you? Think. Could you not amaze me with some memory of your own? Of course you could. Perhaps you shall. Let me share with you what I have experienced. My peculiar fate. My singular destiny. Give me time. I will try not to disappoint.

Shall I make you laugh? I hope I will. I welcome your laughter. My ego can withstand even your ridicule. Will you make me laugh? You can. Think. You can make me laugh. And I will. I will laugh well. I have earned it. You need to know my laughter as much as I need to know yours.

But that is only the beginning. After we have laughed together, with genuine mirth and tearful eyes, then we will have only started, each to know the other. As I tell you these things about my life that will test your utmost credulity, you must stop and think. I will wait, even though you may ponder silently at length. I will wait. Think. You possess the selfsame humanity as do I. With what true tale from your own experience could you arouse my suspicion and disbelief? My story, though strange to you, is no stranger than yours. Only different. I will begin at the beginning. But first, I want to tell you about the adobes. The ones I watched this morning in the rain.

I made these last remaining bricks by hand, eighty-two years ago, when I was a lad of seventeen. These were the first I used in building the fort. They have lasted the longest. They possess parts of my soul. When the grass roots finally split them, and when the rain melts the last of the old mud bricks back into the earth, and when the wind turns them to dust, I will die; for my life intertwines with all that is left of Fort Adobe. But this morning, standing there in the rain, I saw that there were still a few adobes left. There is time yet, and I will make it precious. If you wish, I will spend some of my remaining moments with you, telling my tale. That would please me.

Anyway, when the rain began to chill me this morning, I turned away from the crumbling adobes and hiked back toward my sod house. On the way, an airplane flew over me. It flew lower than usual. Because of the rain, I suppose. Some fellow carries the mail in that airplane, I have been told, and apparently likes to follow the Canadian River as a landmark. He always flies right over my sod house. The noise doesn't last long, but it irritates me. One day, having calculated his schedule through observation, I waited for him to fly over. I sent a warning shot across his propeller with my old Sharps buffalo gun. I don't suppose he ever knew.

This morning, I watched him fly over and disappear into the mist, and said to him, "Godspeed, lad," for I harbor no real resentment toward him. I read in the newspapers that men are attempting to fly the Atlantic in one of those machines. I crossed the ocean on a square-rigger once. A man would need to possess courage in amplitude to fly where I sailed.

After the drone of the airplane faded up the river valley, I went into my sod house and made a good fire in the woodstove. It was forty-nine degrees outside. *Oh, pshaw!* I won't catch cold! That doesn't happen. Germs cause colds. The Indians knew this generations before anyone knew what a germ was. Comanches make themselves go out in the cold. They swim in icy streams. I am part Comanche. Not by blood, by heart. A good walk in the cold rain braces the body and the spirit.

So, I dried off, got dressed, warmed up, and played a bit of Chopin's trio on my left-handed Stradivarius violin. I ate some pemmican I prepared just last week from dried venison and tallow and fruit from the native plum trees over on Bent's Creek. Now I am cozy and content and since you have come to visit I want to tell you the things I have seen here in this place that called my name far across the ocean a lifetime ago. I want to tell you about the buffalo. About the Indians. About Snakehead Jackson, the whiskey trader. The black-powder days. I want to tell you about the wilderness.

First, I must tell you about myself. Have I mentioned that I am a *genius*? The question is rhetorical. I know I haven't mentioned it because my memory is and always has been perfect. I'm not boasting. I simply am a *genius*. It's nothing to brag about, really.

I am also a liar, but I'm not lying about being a genius. I am also a murderer and a thief. That is the truth. But now I have tried to tell too much at once again. Allow me to begin at the beginning. If you don't mind, I will wash and cut some dogbane root while we talk. I keep it on hand to chew. It helps me sleep and wards off night terrors. I am afflicted with an almost intolerable sense of efficiency. I can't just sit here and talk. I have to be doing something with my hands while I talk lest I should toss and turn all night over the time I have wasted.

There. Now I can begin. Let me tell you a story. This is the truth, so you will find it difficult to swallow. Should I lie, you should believe every word, but I will suffer your incredulity and hold to the truth. The Gospel, as they say. Yes, I knew Kit Carson, but I cannot just start there. I will begin . . . well, at the beginning. . . .

TWO

They called me precocious. That is, perhaps, the first word I remember learning. "Oh, Jean-Guy is quite precocious," my mother would say.

I remember her well, but don't care to tell you much about her. I don't think she ever hugged me. I didn't see much of my father in my childhood, but I remember his voice as if it were as fresh to my ears as yours, as, just now, you spoke to me. My father never used his voice to speak *to* me, but to speak often *of* me as if I were some rare-blooded racehorse of outstanding lineage.

"Yes, Jean-Guy is precocious indeed," he would say. "He simply excels at everything."

When I was not yet a year old, so my parents would later claim, I scaled the sheer face of the piano bench in the music parlor and proceeded to play Chopin. That is balderdash, of course. My hands were not yet large enough for the keys. Here is the truth:

I was born in Paris, France, in 1828, with a rare affliction known as genius. My brain works too well. Scarcely anyone understands or loves a genius. Least of all, another genius. To make matters worse, I was gifted with agility, coordination, athleticism, and physical endurance. Luckily, I possessed two obvious imperfections. I was small and rather ugly. Had I grown tall and handsome, I might have become popular and well liked, whereupon I would have become the toast of Paris and wasted my intellect and talent on some trifling pursuit like politics or popular music. Worse yet, I might have become an artist, a poet, or—God forbid—a novelist. Fortunately, the Great Mystery blessed me with bantam proportions and homely looks.

In later years, the Mescalero Apaches would know me by the name Little Ugly White Man—but then, they always did want my scalp. My Kiowa friend, Little Bluff, who possessed a wonderful sense of humor, would dub me Not-So-Big-for-One-So-Ugly. Lucas "Goddamn" Murray would once tell me in the billiards parlor at Bent's Fort: "Goddamn, Kid, you got a face make a mud fence look purty."

Coming to my defense, Kit Carson would reply, "He may be ugly, but just think: If he was big, then there'd be more ugly to look at. I don't mind a little cuss bein' ugly. Don't mind it at all."

I am old now, and old people can blame homeliness on the ravages of time. As an ablebodied youth on the frontier, I could manage enough dash and swagger to compensate for my lack of pulchritude. But nobody likes an ugly child—especially a precocious one.

My disproportionately large nose grew crooked from my face. My eyes bulged not unlike those of the corpse of someone frightened to death. My hair grew porcupinelike from my scalp at improbable angles. I was ugly.

Someone put a violin in my hands at the age of two, and within five minutes I was sawing away at a Bach violin concerto. Music has always been a wonderful sort of auditory mathematics to me, and I do love mathematics. Unfortunately, I had to endure endless insipid violin lessons delivered by instructors far less talented than I, until I grew to loathe the instrument.

By the age of three, I could read and write my native French. At four, I mastered the basic concepts of algebra. At five, I became so frustrated with the stupidity of my Latin tutor that I threw an inkwell across the study, spewing its contents all over an expensive settee. The tutor administered a sound thrashing with a folded parasol he found nearby, and ordered me to march across the room and pick up the inkwell. I promptly obeyed, whereupon I turned and hurled the inkwell back at the tutor, hitting him in the left eye with such force that he stumbled back onto the fireplace tools and ripped his trousers on the poker. Presumably, he ripped some flesh as well, for he ran wailing from the room holding his left eye with one hand, and his right buttock with the other.

I was a troubled and violent child because my nurses and governesses attempted to make me sleep and eat and study and otherwise function in accordance with the rotations of the earth and the so-called risings and settings of the sun. I realized by the age of seven that my biological rhythms followed the moon.

Years later, the Comanche would herald me as some kind of priest or shaman and attribute to me powers known as "moon medicine." The new moon, you see, plunges me into exhaustion. The only remedy is a sort of human hibernation lasting two, three, or even four days. Throughout the other phases of the moon I am unable to sleep for more than two or three hours at a time. During the full moon, there are periods of two, three, and four days—sometimes even more—when I do not want or need to sleep at all. I once went six days without sleep on a trading expedition among the Kiowa with Thomas "Broken Hand" Fitzpatrick and John "Freckled Hand" Hatcher.

When I do slumber between moons, a strange phenomenon often vexes me. I start dreaming before I am actually asleep. Even before my eyes close. These dreams occur to me in the form of hallucinations—usually wild animals stalking or charging me. As a tormented child in Paris, I would see them right there in my bedchamber. Strangely, these wild animals were usually of the North American variety, though I knew of the New World only through books and newspapers. Grizzly bears would lumber through my *boudoir* door and gnash their teeth at me. Mountain lions would fix their frightful gaze upon me and stare, growling, for what seemed like hours. Whole herds of buffalo would stampede from my very walls, slinging saliva and menacing the night air with pointed horns. Even today, during these night terrors, I am unable to move any part of my body, except my eyes.

My somniferous torment does not end there. Around the time of the new moon, routine tasks occasionally lull me into irresistible sleep. The peculiar thing is that I am able to continue the task even while I sleep. I have been known to sleep with my eyes open like a dead man, washing camp dishes, or even riding a horse. I can carry on with any mundane chore as if I am awake, yet I have no recollection of my actions when I come out of my trance. One time, at Kit Carson's ranch on the Rayado, I fell asleep while splitting firewood. When I came to, I had just finished stacking the quartered billets, the pieces fitting so close and perfectly together that I must have spent an hour building the stack. Unfortunately, I had stacked the wood in Mrs. Carson's outhouse and had to move it.

On another occasion, while scouting for horse thieves with Lucien Maxwell during the dark of the moon, I suddenly woke up alone on my mount, having no earthly idea as to my whereabouts. I had to back-trail myself almost ten miles before I found the place where I had strayed from my companions. It is a miracle that I was never killed while in the throes of one of these trances during all my decades beyond the frontier.

I have learned to cope with my disorders by adjusting my daily schedule to the phase of the moon and by using various herbs like moccasin-flower root, dogbane, and fir needles. Is it so strange that the moon should wield such power over me? Does not the moon move tides? I am peculiar among men; but among wild and savage beasts, I am ordinary. I sleep, and hunt, and feed, and romp, and revel with the phases of the moon.

When I was a child, living in a society regimented by ever-circling hands of the clock, I was not allowed to adjust my schedule in accordance with the movements of the moon. At nine years of age, I tried to explain my peculiarities of sleep and my hallucinations to a good Christian governess who promptly accused me of satanism and sorcery and left my parents' employment.

By the time I reached ten years of age, I had become so rebellious and unmanageable that my parents sentenced me to a place of incarceration known as the Saint-Cyr Boarding School for Boys. This particular institution held a reputation—why, I have never quite determined—for high academic standards. Its faculty consisted, to a man, of frustrated underachievers.

The Saint-Cyr Boarding School for Boys encompassed one entire block in the city of Paris, not far from the Champs-Élysées. The gargoyle-infested architecture was dirty and depressing, and the cobblestoned courtyard included a frothy little fountain full of scummy water and unfortunate goldfish.

At this school, I became immediately disliked by the other boys—all of whom were older, larger, stronger and less intelligent than I—because I used dirty tricks when fighting. I mean, really dirty tricks. A boy has trouble carrying forth an assault with one hand covering his testicles and the other guarding his eyes.

So, one day seven of these boys ganged up on me outside of the chapel and beat me unconscious. When I had sufficiently recovered, I wrote each one of these seven boys a note stating that he had better go ahead and kill me if he ever intended to sleep again. I wrote these notes a few days before the full moon, when I knew I could remain wakeful for several days. Logic and an instinct for survival told me that I had better do something about my enemies before the next new moon, when I would again be thrown into helpless depths of slumber.

We boarded in pairs at the Saint-Cyr School for Boys. My roommate was one of the ringleaders among my enemies. The night after I delivered my threatening notes, my roommate rose quietly at midnight and let two other boys into the room. They thought me asleep, but I was only pretending. They came armed with sticks with which to beat me, but before anyone could strike the first blow, I tossed my blankets aside and doused them all with a cup of lamp oil I had taken to bed with me. They stumbled back in surprise, giving me the moment I needed to strike the match on the stone windowsill.

"I will burn you alive," my boyish voice growled.

They dropped their weapons and ran whimpering from the room.

I was diabolical in those days, for they would not let me sleep when I needed to. It is a wonder I did not commit more murder than I ultimately did. My roommate refused to board with me after this incident, so I enjoyed a private room for the rest of my stay at the Saint-Cyr School for Boys.

Four of the boys who had beaten me unconscious were yet unpunished, and the worst of these awoke screaming in the middle of the night, his nose broken and bleeding because a chamberpot had inexplicably fallen upon it. I was a ghastly, fearful thing in my troubled youth, lurking through the dark corridors and shadowed chambers of Saint-Cyr. I thought I was insane because of my night terrors and insomnia and blackouts. It seemed that ninety percent of my life I was unable to sleep, and the other ten, I was unable to stay awake.

My last three attackers came to me the day after I broke their comrade's nose. They apologized for having beaten me unconscious outside of the chapel, and promised they would leave me be forevermore.

I only smiled at them. "You had better kill me if you ever want to sleep again," I repeated. Mercy was not regarded as a virtue among the inmates of Saint-Cyr. Vengeance was the supreme rule. Sooner than I could have imagined, this understanding of revenge would stand me in good stead among the Comanche, the Kiowa, the Apache. . . .

All three boys in question transferred from the boarding school shortly thereafter, and I had no more trouble with bullies. Strange to say, I never feared these boys or any amount of pain their beatings might have inflicted on me. I have, in fact, never feared much of anything—a trait given more to foolishness than courage. Yes, I am a foolish genius.

About the time I turned thirteen, I began to dream of a strange place under the full moon. A place where a trail crossed a river. Where wind whispered through grasses, then howled through timber. Where sunshine bleached bones and blizzards split stones. Wild beasts populated this place in numbers unimaginable. Mountain lions, black bear, and wolves. Antelope, wild turkey, and deer. Geese, ducks, cranes, prairie fowl. And buffalo. (Bison if you insist on taxonomic propriety.) Oh, the buffalo . . .

I had read of these creatures, but had never seen them. Logically, I should not have dreamt of them, especially in such vivid detail. I had read of Africa, as well as North America, but never dreamt of elephants. Does a mind have the ability to dream of the future? Or, for some reason, has my brain erased my memories of my other dreams, selectively allowing me to remember only what it wishes me—and thus itself—to remember? The world seems more a mystery to the genius than to the simpleton.

I suppose it is not so unusual that this strange and faraway place should call to me across the ocean. I have seen sailors called to unknown mountaintops, and mountain men to sea. Wise men followed a star to find Christ. Christopher Columbus imagined a land beyond the edge of the earth. When first he came west, Kit Carson rode to his northern New Mexico home straightaway, and called it home through four decades. In my middle years, when I met a young Billy Dixon, I knew that he, too, had dreamt of the same place that called me. A place that would become known as Adobe Walls. A rather plain place in appearances, but a place of power beyond comprehension.

One Saturday afternoon, while walking along the streets of Paris, I noticed a crowd of people gathering around the window of a gallery. Muscling my way through the adults, I reached the glass and saw what had attracted all the attention. The owner of the gallery was displaying a painting from America. It depicted an American Indian warrior standing beside a horse. Immediately, I felt a connection with the image. I fancied I could see the feathers on his head move in the breeze. I could see the muscles of his bare arms and chest writhe under his skin. I felt his eyes trying to glance my way and lock with mine. What's more, this warrior stood surrounded by the place of which I had dreamed. I knew it.

"Is it authentic?" someone asked.

"Without a doubt," the gallery owner boasted, standing in his doorway. "The artist's name is George Catlin, an American. He has lived among the Indians. I have documents that prove this painting is a portrait of a typical Comanche warrior of the Great American Desert."

After this, my dreams of the strange place came ever more frequently. I told no one of these dreams. They came during the odd hour or two of sleep I sometimes managed to catch at night. Waking, I would be unable to move for several minutes; but, by blinking my eyes rapidly, I could eventually get my face, then the rest of my body to move. Then I would get out of bed and think about the dreams while I peered through the window that overlooked the courtyard. At my window, I would bide my time and study the movements of heavenly bodies.

Otherwise, I simply continued with my education. In spite of my problems with sleep, I excelled at mathematics, history, astronomy, the arts, foreign languages. . . . I excelled at everything. All my teachers bored me, and only my fencing master liked me, because I was unbeaten with a foil. My English professor would rail in anger when I answered a question in German, and vice versa. My mathematics teacher would redden like a beet when I solved algebraic problems using Roman rather than Arabic numerals.

My violin instructor, Herr Buhler, especially hated me because of my ambidexterity. I have always preferred playing the violin left-handed, though I play equally well upon either shoulder. My left eye is slightly dominant over my right, which causes me, all in all, to favor left-handedness, though I can shoot a rifle or bow and arrow with either hand. I can also produce an identical signature—even writing upside down and backwards—with my right or left hand. When you sleep only a few hours most any given day, you find ways to occupy your time.

Herr Buhler, the so-called virtuoso of the Saint-Cyr Boarding School for Boys, played a left-handed Stradivarius violin. "Antonio Stradivari built this violin in his later years, at the age of ninety," he once told me, in his thick Viennese accent. "It was the only instrument Stradivari ever built for a left-handed violinist."

I personally do not know that the great master built only one left-handed violin, but that was Herr Buhler's story. Buhler himself played left-handed, but insisted on teaching me right-handed.

"I think I should rather play upon the right shoulder like you, Herr Buhler," I told him one day.

He became unreasonably angry, leaned close to my face and, with rum-tainted breath, growled, "What orchestra would employ you? Your bow would angle the wrong way. Why do you think I am banished to teaching at this school for wretched boys? The orchestras discriminate against left-handed violinists."

"But I am a soloist," I replied. "I should think the opposing angle of my bow would contrast nicely against the bows of the strings behind me."

"You are *not* a soloist!" he roared. "You are a stupid, ugly boy!"

One day, when Herr Buhler turned his back on me to listen to my rendition of a scherzo, I switched my violin to my right shoulder and played the entire first movement left-handed, though I had to reach my fingers far over the strings to carry the notes on my right-handed violin. You see, I can play a left-handed violin, or a right-handed violin, but I can also play a left-handed violin right-handed, or a right-handed one left-handed.

Anyway, Herr Buhler turned around to offer a rare

compliment, when he saw my violin upon the wrong shoulder, my bow angled awkwardly over the strings, and my slender fingers groping unnaturally all the way over the neck of my instrument. I learned several profane words in German that day. Herr Buhler became so incensed that he turned a violent shade of purple and stormed out of the music parlor.

I sat there gloating for a while. Several minutes passed, and I grew bored. I saw the left-handed Stradivarius lying in the open case where Buhler had placed it. I went to it, approaching carefully, like a boy trying to charm a frightened kitten. When I slipped my hand under the neck, I felt the lifeblood of Antonio Stradivari, the master, course into my own veins. Wood, because it comes from a living tree, can absorb the energy of a living being, and store it as gunpowder stores the power of explosion. I felt charged with strange medicine when I placed the ebony under my chin. The bow was a fine one, made of imported pernambuco wood from South America. It is not even important what I played, but the vibrations of the instrument moved me to such euphoria that I decided at that moment to become a violin maker. Had not events beyond my control swayed me from this goal, I might be a violin maker yet. I have always felt that, given several decades to study the art and craft, I could have made a violin as fine as Stradivari's best. But alas, I was destined to become a murderer, a thief, an Indian trader, a ransom payer, a whiskey merchant, and a slaughterer of buffalo. . . .

Signor Giovanni Segarelli, the fencing master at the Saint-Cyr Boarding School for Boys, prevented my becoming a violin maker. All the other boys feared Signor Segarelli, and he seemed to detest them all. But he saw in me the same diabolical love of violence that he himself possessed. It was known that he had survived several duels to the death. Upon his face he bore numerous saber scars. In those days, the secret fencing societies held blood matches where the combatants wore leather collars to protect their jugulars. The swordsmen would slice away at each other with Italian sabers or German *schlagers*, until one collapsed from loss of blood. As their forearms were also protected, most of the cuts fell upon the heads and faces of the fencers.

Signor Segarelli thought his scars made him quite the ladies' man, and boasted often to his students. "Tonight, while you loathsome boys jerk at yourselves in your beds," he would claim, "I will sleep in the bed of a little French tart. Should her husband wish to duel, so much the better."

I always won my bouts with the foil against the other boys. This was partly because of my quickness and agility, and partly because all the other boys feared me. To unnerve my opponents, I had a habit of reciting aloud while fencing. My memory is wonderful, and I can read from it as if from a scroll. One day, while parrying the ineffectual lunges of an opponent, I was reciting from Coleridge's *The Rime of the Ancient Mariner*:

> Like one that on a lonesome road
> Doth walk in fear and dread
> And having once turned round walks on,
> And turns no more his head;
> Because he knows a frightful fiend
> Doth close behind him tread . . .

And I executed a wonderfully swift balestra followed by a killing *coule* that would have pierced the throat of my opponent had he not worn a fencing mask.

"Bravo!" shouted Signor Segarelli. "I must take you to Italy, Jean-Guy, and teach you how to kill. These other boys do not offer you enough of a challenge."

I might have gone to Italy as Segarelli's protégé. The thought of facing someone in a duel to the death caused me no more dread than killing would have caused me remorse, for in those days my insomnia made me quite absent of conscience or fear. Also, in Cremona, Italy, the best violin makers resided, including some protégés of some protégés of Antonio Stradivari.

But I never went to Italy. Everything changed for me that

year. The cause of this change was a girl. Her name, Nicole Beaumarchais. She was eighteen, and perfectly beautiful. I thought I was in love with her, though soon enough I would suffer the honest pangs of real love and realize that what I felt for Nicole was merely boyish infatuation. Nicole was a humble kitchen maid at the Saint-Cyr Boarding School for Boys. She lived in the servants' quarters across the courtyard from my room in the dormitory.

Sleepless nights at my window, I would sometimes see her sneak out. I had been an overprotected boy, but I knew stories of the Paris nightlife. Sometimes Nicole did not return until nearly dawn. Once I saw a young man return with her, and in the shadows of the alcove that led to her quarters, I vaguely saw them roll, half-dressed, on the ground. The courtyard spanned a hundred yards, but my eyesight was keen, and I know I glimpsed moonlight upon her breasts.

The mystery of Nicole's flesh became an obsession to me in my loneliness and friendlessness. One night I saw her slip away, and I, myself, slipped out of the dormitory. I waited for hours in the dark alcove, watching stars and reciting poetry to myself to pass the time. Finally Nicole came home. My heart pounded like hooves on cobblestones when I saw that she had returned alone.

"Don't be afraid," I said softly as she came to the archway of the alcove.

She gasped, then placed her hand over her mouth. "Who's there?" she demanded.

"My name is Jean-Guy." I stepped into a beam of moonlight.

She looked at me hard and stumbled to her right to catch her balance. Even dizzied by drink, Nicole moved with sensuous grace. "I know you," she said. "You sit alone in the dining hall."

"Yes," I replied, thrilled beyond reason that she recognized me, and hoping that the pale light from the courtyard softened the ugliness I felt.

"The faculty talk about you. They say you are very smart, and very difficult."

"I don't mean to be difficult," I said. "I am not here to be difficult with you."

"What *are* you here for?" she asked, tossing a loose strand of her chestnut hair over her shoulder.

"I—I simply wanted to—I saw you leave earlier, from my window, and . . ."

She smiled with utterly radiant beauty and approached me. "I know what boys your age want. Have you ever kissed a girl, Jean-Guy?"

I fell back against the cold stone wall in the dark corner of the alcove. "Oh, no. I have never even *touched* a girl."

"Do you want to kiss me?" She smiled with delight, moving with provocative ease.

I nodded.

She was slightly taller than me, and I could feel the warmth of her breasts, even through her tight bodice and my wool shirt, pressing against my upper chest. She smelled of liquor and smoke. She breathed warmly upon my face. "Put your hands here," she said, taking me by the wrists to place my palms against her trim waist. I dared not move. I let her lips come closer. Instinctively, I closed my eyes, which only increased the sensation of warmth against my palms, my chest. I had no idea that she would involve her tongue. When it slipped between my lips, I saw something that looked like fireworks against a night sky. Nicole leaned against me hard, trapping me between her steaming flesh and the cold stone wall of the alcove. Her ribs pressed into me. The solid curve of her hip locked against mine. The hardening in my trousers throbbed, and still she bewitched me with her tongue.

A breath of fresh air rushed into my mouth. I opened my eyes to find that she had pulled away from me.

"Did you like that, Jean-Guy?" she asked.

I could only nod.

"That is only the beginning. Go back to your room now and think about that. There will be more for you later. If you like to watch me so much from your window, then you will see when I signal for you. I will wave my scarf, like this." She pulled the scarf from around her neck and demonstrated. "If you speak of this to anyone, you will never touch me again."

I watched for many nights. Finally, Nicole appeared in the alcove and signaled. I sprinted past the room of Herr Buhler, who was the faculty supervisor of my wing of the dormitory. Buhler always slept rum-soaked, and never knew about anything that went on in the dormitory at night.

I burst out into a crisp Parisian night. When I stepped into the alcove, I heard Nicole say, "Good, you are here."

There are girls who, having crossed the threshold of womanhood, delight in introducing boys less experienced than themselves to the mysteries of the flesh. Nicole was the best teacher I had at the Saint-Cyr School for Boys. She initiated me by degrees. Each time I went to meet her in the alcove, she led me one step closer to the thing she knew I wanted. Finally, one night, she brought my desire into hers with an exultation of pleasure. We said nothing for a long time. We simply lay together, breathing, wrapped in a blanket she had brought from her very bed. She made me feel handsome, wanted, and loved for the first time in my life.

I know now that Nicole was never to have been anything more to me than a beautiful introduction to the ways of intimacy. But at the time, I wanted her every day, and always, and would have killed for her.

And did.

It happened so very suddenly and unexpectedly that it was as if a meteor had fallen upon me. My life changed to such a degree that even now I wonder how I survived it. It came with the new moon, which I always dreaded because the Saint-Cyr School for Boys forced me to carry on through my lassitude as if I were a normal person. It was night, and I was dreaming of the strange place that called to me, when I began to hear a voice in the dream. I knew the voice belonged to Nicole. In my dream, I looked all around the stark openness of the strange place, trying to find Nicole, for her voice cried out for help. I ran everywhere: from the brookside timber to the grass-covered hills, but could not find poor Nicole.

Then, for the first time, the dream turned into a vision. For the first time, I saw a person in this dream-place that had called to me. Not a natural person. A painted man. That is to say, the man from a painting I had seen in the gallery not far from my school—the one by the American artist, George Catlin, who had lived among the Comanches. The man in my dream-turned-vision was the Comanche warrior, lifted from the Catlin painting—the only way I could have visualized a Comanche at that time. Then, though he was only an artist's rendering, the warrior's eyes moved and he looked at me. He somehow assumed depth and motion, and came to life. He brandished a war axe and came to kill me as Nicole's scream for help joined his battle cry.

I woke with my heart pounding as if it would burst from my chest. My breath came in gasps and sweat drenched me. As usual, I could not move for several minutes; but when I regained control, I rolled from my bed and went to my window. There I saw Nicole waving her scarf from our alcove. But the signal had changed. No longer fluid and seductive, it twitched with excited distress.

I threw my clothes on and flew down the corridors and staircases as swift and as silent as a lion. I still recall every pebble and cobblestone I passed sprinting across the courtyard. Every star above and its exact position. Every wind-flaw. The odors of wood smoke and pigeon droppings. The tinkling of some draft pony's bell beyond the courtyard, and the clop of its iron-shod hooves on the street.

I found Nicole shivering in the corner of the alcove. Her left eye looked swollen almost shut. A rivulet of blood streamed from her nostril. Each sob sucked her lower lip into her mouth. When her eyes met mine, she wept uncontrollably and rushed into my arms.

"What happened?" I demanded.

She calmed herself as her fingernails clung like the talons of a falcon. "He beat me."

"Who?"

"He tried to take me, and I didn't want to go. He was drunk. He beat me, and—"

"Who?" I, shook her. I could feel the madness of the moon sweep over me. I feared nothing. I hated anyone or anything that would harm my sweet Nicole. "What happened?"

"He *raped* me!" The word came out like a horror to her, as though even to speak it violated her very soul. "The swordsman. Segarelli."

"Where is he?" I said, scarcely recognizing my own voice.

"He fell asleep, and I slipped away."

"Where?"

"In his room."

I looked across the courtyard, toward the gymnasium. Here, Signor Segarelli was quartered in a small room adjoining his study. I had seen his study once. Upon its walls were numerous dueling blades.

"I will take care of Segarelli," I said to Nicole.

"How?"

I loosed her clinging hands from my shirt. "I don't know yet."

With that, I tore across the courtyard, heedless of Nicole's voice calling my name. The doors through which Nicole had escaped still stood open. When I reached the gymnasium, I stalked past the rows of fencing masks hung upon the wall, and strode boldly into Segarelli's study. I padded silently to the door of his bedchamber and saw him lying on his back, his chest rising and falling in drunken slumber. I turned back to his study and chose an Italian saber from the wall. I walked, blade in hand, to the edge of the dueling master's bed.

I raised the hilt and positioned the point of the blade above the sleeping ogre. I will never know why I woke him first. I suppose I wanted him to know his murderer. *"Maestro!"* I said loudly, jabbing him with the saber tip.

He snorted, and his eyes opened. They focused on the blade and followed it to my face. "Jean-Guy?" he mumbled.

As his eyes widened, I made my thrust. His body lurched fantastically and made horrid sounds, but I drove the blade hard. Only a wooden slat under the mattress prevented the hilt from touching his chest. Blood darkened the bedsheet like a storm cloud building in a summer sky. Looking back on it—judging by memory the angle of the blade and position of his body—I know that I pierced Segarelli's black heart.

I heard a gasp, and turned to see Nicole at the door, her hands over her mouth. She turned away from the murder, keeping her mouth covered to prevent her own screams from escaping. I left the saber standing in the dead man's chest and went to her.

She calmed herself with remarkable swiftness, but would not turn back around to look at Segarelli. Instead, she took me by the hand, leading me through the study, and into the gymnasium. She shut the door that led into the courtyard. "They will call it murder," she said.

I had not thought it through that far, but knew immediately that she was right. "I will explain to them," I replied.

Nicole shook her head. "No. *I* will explain. I will tell them how you defended my honor. But, they will still call it murder. None of them like you. You must go away."

"But where?"

"Go get your things. Meet me in the alcove. Do as I say, Jean-Guy!" She opened the door and shoved me into the courtyard.

I ran to the dormitory and up the stairs. I heard Herr Buhler snoring as I passed his room. I trotted down the corridor thinking about what Nicole had said. I had defended her honor. Perhaps it was a cowardly kill, but logical. Though I was better than the other boys at fencing, I could never have taken Segarelli in a duel. Had I failed to kill him, Nicole would have remained in danger, and unavenged. He had deserved his fate, and I was proud to have been the one to run him through. I did not feel even a grain of remorse. I had but one concern. The time of the new moon was near, when I would plunge helplessly into fatigue. I could already feel it coming on, and it beckoned. Sleep. Wonderful, insensible slumber.

I reached my room, cast off a fearful desire to crawl into bed, and stuffed some clothes into a laundry bag. I grabbed my copy of Voltaire's *Candide,* and left forever my room at the Saint-Cyr School for Boys. I walked calmly down the hall, then down the stairs. I stopped at Herr Buhler's door when I heard him snore. Why I entered his room, I will never know. I suppose the soul of Antonio Stradivari called me there. I saw the violin case on Buhler's writing table. I opened it quietly to make sure it contained the left-handed Stradivarius, then closed it, and slipped it into my bag.

Nicole met me at the dormitory door and led me across the courtyard and away from Saint-Cyr. I did not tell her I had stolen the violin for fear she would hate me for the thief I was, though I am sure she must have laughed later when she figured out that I had taken the Stradivarius from the unworthy Buhler.

We walked for blocks, until we came to a jolly saloon. Laughter and crude piano music rang from within. She dragged me inside and made me wait at the door. At the bar, she found a young man she obviously knew. His eyes lit up quickly when he turned to find her there, but darkened just as quickly when he saw the effects of the beating she had suffered. She silenced his questions, had a few words with him, then pointed at me. He scoffed and shook his head. Nicole promised him something then—I can only guess just what. The young man smiled slightly, then turned to toss back the rest of his drink.

"Jean-Guy, this is a friend. Never mind his name. He will get you safely away from here. You must do exactly as he says." Then she put her lips against my ear, and I felt the words she spoke carried on the warmth of her breath. "You are a wonderful lover, Jean-Guy. You are beautiful. You are my brave protector. I will remember you always." She kissed me quickly and softly on the lips, then turned to run away down the street, leaving me with her friend.

This fellow, whose name I will never know, took me to

a stable and bid me climb into a dray filled with—of all things—chocolates. *Crates* of chocolates.

"Lie there behind the seat," he ordered. "Cover yourself with that canvas. Do you hear?"

I did as I was told. As my deliverer hitched a horse to the dray, I thought of Nicole; the saber standing in Segarelli's chest; my theft of the Stradivarius; the dream of the strange place and the vision of the Catlin warrior come to life.

Then I fell into a deep sleep.

The cart driver shook me violently to wake me. I saw faint moonlight, smelled the unfamiliar scent of the sea in the air, heard the creaking of vessels at anchor, and the shriek of unknown birds. "Wake up!" he demanded. "We are here."

"Where?" I grumbled.

"Le Havre. Hurry, boy, we have just caught the *Dover Star*."

I climbed groggily out of the dray and looped the drawstring of my bag over my shoulder. I looked around me to find a maze of wharves, moorings, and masts. I saw a man urinating into the harbor water from one of these wharves, and I went to do the same.

The driver called me back to the cart and handed me a crate of chocolates. "Carry these, and be good about it."

He shoved me toward a gangplank that led to a three-masted square-rigger. Up I went, glancing back to see the dray horse lathered with sweat. It wasn't the same horse I had seen the driver hitch to the cart in Paris, and I realized he had obtained a fresh horse somewhere. Le Havre was over one hundred miles from Paris, so I surmised I had slept some forty-eight hours.

A gull cried, and a longshoreman almost jostled me from the gangplank. The waxing moon loomed lustily over the spars. I stepped onto the deck, still trying to wake myself and focus on my plight. Sailors and workmen swarmed all over the boat, obviously preparing it for an imminent voyage.

"Down to the hold," the driver said, motioning me toward the open hatch. I set the crate of chocolates on the deck and swung down into the hold, which was crammed full of cargo packed so expertly that it almost made a level floor upon which to walk—so much cargo that little headroom remained under the timbers of the ship's deck. The driver came down after me, and we carried our crates to a dark corner created by other boxes, trunks, and crates. Shoving me into this nook, he stacked the three crates of chocolates in front of me within seconds.

"Stay quiet." He tossed a water flask to me. "Now you must take care of yourself."

"Where are you going?" I asked.

He smiled. "Back to Paris."

"Where . . . Where am I going?"

He was a good fellow, and must have heard the apprehension in my voice. He took the time to tousle my hair a bit like a brother before he slid the upper crate in front of my face to cover my place of hiding. "America," he replied. *"Bon voyage, boy."*

THREE

When I awoke again, I felt the roll of the ocean and heard the vessel groan around me like some restless she-beast who had protected me long enough within her womb. Though I yearned to stand and stretch, and though my stomach felt as empty as a pauper's wallet, I forced myself to lie still and think.

I felt utterly rested, perhaps for the first time since infancy. With this dearth of fatigue came things I had never felt. Normal things. Chief among them, fear.

I was a friendless boy somewhere at sea. I did not know how to swim. I had never been beyond sight of land. I had no money. I was a thief and a murderer who might spend the rest of his days in prison or have his head lopped off by a guillotine if returned to France.

I was a frightened boy. At Saint-Cyr, I had begun to think of myself as a young man, mostly due to the teachings of the intrepid Nicole. But let no one claim that manhood begins when virginity ends. Not even battle makes a man, for I have known some of the fiercest warriors to behave like schoolboys in the face of lesser adversities. A boy becomes a man when he learns to feed his soul above his stomach, his pocket, his lust. When he defies all else—be it father, mother, law, lover, brother, pain, or death—in favor of what is right and good. *That* is what makes a man.

I was a frightened boy on a merchant packet.

From my hiding place, I heard voices speaking the most profane English. I had always liked the English language because of its challenges, its illogical construction, its massive and expressive lexicon. I would have no problem communicating, for I knew I could wield the English tongue with more authority than a bunch of common British sailors.

As I lay there, I contrived my story. I was a runaway from a Parisian orphanage. My father, a Frenchman, had died before my birth. My mother, God rest her soul, had been English, hence my facility with either language. She had raised me to the age of twelve, when she died, virtually penniless. I had stowed away to escape the wretched orphanage and to seek my fortune at sea, or on some savage frontier of the New World.

While concocting all of this, I heard a thump and knew someone had dropped into the hold from the deck above. Rising from my hiding place, I peered over the crates that had concealed me to find a sailor extracting a bundle of canvas from a nook among the crates. He kept a close watch on the hatch he had come through as he produced from the bundle of canvas a copper flask with a cork stopper. He pulled the cork and tasted a minute portion of the flask's contents with obvious delight.

"May I have a drink of that?" I asked.

He flinched, then stowed the flask under his shirt. "Who's there?"

I climbed out over the crate of chocolates. "A stowaway."

"Bloody hell!" he muttered. "The cap'n ain't gonna like that."

I pointed at his flask. "He ain't gonna like that, either."

"Now, see here, boy—" he began angrily.

Then he took a good look at me, and I could see the compassion in his face. He was a man built for the sea. Rather small, lean, and wiry. He was seasoned, but still young enough to climb the rigging in the fiercest gale. Everything about him looked like energy and industry, and I knew the liquor was a mere treat to him, rather than a vice. The hair that hung out from under his sailing cap gleamed yellow like freshly shocked wheat.

"We're a day and a half out to sea, boy. What have you eaten?"

"Nothing."

He handed me the flask. "Just a sip, now, to warm you."

I took the flask, and his advice on temperance.

"Ha!" he said, his voice hoarse. He snatched the flask from me. "Now you're in it with me! What's your name?"

"Honoré," I said, assuming a name I had always admired.

He apparently mistook this for *Henri*, because he said, "Well, Henry, they call me 'Jibber.' " He wrapped the flask and stowed it back in the nook. "Now, you're in a bad fix, lad. A stowaway caught with a flask of the Irish. But Jibber's a fair bloke. He might overlook the flask for a lad who'd do the same."

I smiled. "I'm the lad," I said.

"Stay put. I'll talk to the first mate. There might still be a biscuit left in the galley."

Jibber sprang from the hold, and I returned to my hiding place to pry open a crate and sample a French chocolate.

Jibber came back with the first mate and a plate full of cold boiled potatoes and biscuits. The first mate, whose name was Hawkins, interrogated me as I ate. I have always been a marvelous liar, and I convinced him easily.

"You'll have to face Captain Robbins now," First Mate Hawkins said. He gestured ominously in the direction of the hatch, and I walked toward the light of day.

When I stepped onto the deck, a dazzling panoply of impulses electrified my senses. Having been raised in the city, and compelled to study all manner of bookish things, I had never spent much time outdoors. Now a boisterous spirit of freedom imploded on me, then just as suddenly exploded from me, making my heart race and swell as I had never felt. The salt air rushed into my nostrils as a sprinkle of spindrift tingled my face. I heard wind flapping the colors flying on the mainmast above me, and looked up to see several huge squares of canvas straining to carry the vessel seaward, the sun shining golden through them.

By now the news of my discovery had spread across the ship, and old salts gawked at me as if I were a menagerie animal as I was led aft and up to the poop deck to the captain's quarters.

The captain, a weathered man of stony visage, tried to frighten me. "The law allows me to put a stowaway in chains," he said. "We haven't provisions for an extra hand."

"With your permission, Captain," First Mate Hawkins said, "the lad can't eat much. Perhaps Jibber could share a crumb with him, since he found him. I'd do the same. Provided he earned it, of course."

"I don't eat much, Captain," I said.

"Speak when you're spoken to," the captain warned. "I've had men flogged for such insolence as yours." He glared at me long enough to convince me that he told the truth. "You'll pull double your weight before you get so much as a snip to eat. I'll hail the first ship we cross that flies the colors of France or England and have you taken back to your orphanage. In chains, if need be."

"If I may speak, sir . . ."

He frowned. "Well, what is it?"

"I'm seventeen years old, Captain, and right strong for my size. I'll work hard." I lied about my age. I was really only sixteen.

"You look all of twelve." The captain clasped his hands behind his back and paced about his tiny cabin, crowded by his three underlings. "You, Jibber. What do you say should be done with the stowaway?"

Jibber sighed and sucked his teeth. "Give me a crack at him, Cap'n, with permission. In a day, I'll have him dousing the royal. With luck, he'll slip and dash his brains out on the deck, and we'll be done with him."

"Very well, but he's to eat in the hold where you found him, and only what crumbs the crew collects by charity. He's to pull every bit the weight of a full-grown man, or he'll be punished accordingly." With this, the captain scowled at me. "There'll be no wages for you. None. Not a bloody farthing, do you hear?"

Jibber shoved me out of the captain's quarters and started schooling me in the manly arts of the sea. I excelled, of course. I, too, was built for the sailing life. I could climb the ratlines like a monkey. Having once seen a knot tied, I could duplicate it, tell its use, and give its name. In a day I knew the names of all the masts and sails and the terms for all the rigging. This was child's play for a genius.

Jibber was a man of common intelligence and very little education, but he was a good fellow. He had a knack for teaching by example and explaining things in plain terms, unlike any of my teachers at Saint-Cyr. The first time he took me aloft to bend the main royal to its yard, he warned me to keep my eyes on my hands and off the deck, some seventy feet below.

"One hand for the ship, one for the sailor," he said. We hooked the heels of our shoes over the rope that spanned the breadth of the spar, leaned over the spar, and hoisted the canvas into position, always keeping a grip on something with one hand, as Jibber had advised.

"I'm not afraid," I boasted.

"That'll kill you, lad."

I joined the starboard watch, under the charge of the first mate. In those days, the crewmen of a sailing vessel were divided into two watches, one called starboard, the other port. We worked four hours on and four hours off, except between the hours of four and eight o'clock in the evening. Then, we worked two hours on, and two off. In this way, no man worked the same hours today that he worked yesterday, and every man had to work an equal number of midnight watches, which most of the sailors disliked.

They tried to catch me asleep on my midnight watches, but failed. After my long slumber in the dray and in the hold, darkness meant nothing to me but a chance to study the stars. And such stars. Such air. I could feel the elements charging me with new vigor and heartiness. My face and hands became burned by the wind, salt, and sun, my palms blistered by manual labor. But I toughened quickly, and I actually gained weight, thanks to the charity of the sailors and my private stock of chocolates. Much to the consternation of the crew, I never knew the meaning of seasickness. The hard work helped me sleep some, and the four-hour watches were tailor-made for an individual who could catch his winks only in spurts of two or three hours. Gone were my frustrations and violent brooding at Saint-Cyr. My mind, body, and soul felt free and at peace. Within a week, I was a mascot among the sailors, and even the captain let a French schooner sail by without hailing it to put me aboard, though I'm sure he only wanted to save time.

Our packet, the *Dover Star*, was a merchant vessel designed for the American cotton trade. She measured 1,000 tons, and 170 feet from stem to stern. Her mainmast stood 90 feet, her hold reached a depth of 20 feet below the deck. Jibber told me that cotton packets like the *Dover Star* had been designed with flat bottoms in order to sail up the Mississippi River to New Orleans—a primary cotton port. It seems that the flat bottom reduced drag and added speed. In some ways, the cotton vessels were the precursors of the swift clipper ships that were just beginning to be built in

New York. The *Dover Star* could make 80 miles a day in light airs, and had been known to fetch 250 a day with good winds.

I learned from the crew that the bottom of the hold was filled with coal and salt, which provided good ballast and could be sold in New Orleans. On top of these had been stowed all manner of goods and merchandise for the American trade, some from England, some from France. After off-loading her cargo at New Orleans, the *Dover Star* would take on hundreds of bales of cotton and return to its home port of Liverpool. Captain Robbins had once held the record for sailing from Liverpool to New Orleans in sixty-eight days. However, his record had been beaten, and his obsession was to win it back. Depending on the winds, he would pile on canvas until the masts and spars came within a hairsbreadth of splintering. He kept the crew constantly busy either reefing or adding sail to get the top speed out of his ship without dismasting her.

Two weeks out to sea, the winds failed as we entered what Jibber called "the Calms of Cancer," and we found ourselves adrift. The ocean stretched like a sheet of glass as far as the eye could see, only an occasional fin marring its surface. In this interim, Captain Robbins ordered the crew to paint the ship. Yes, we painted the entire ship. After that, he put us to work sealing the cracks between the planks of the deck by hammering in oakum. Between watches, the men would write letters if they knew how, tell stories, sleep, and sing.

Jibber played a harmonica, much to the enjoyment of the crew. He would play along with the men singing "Grog and Girls" and "Yo, Heave Ho," and other such sailing songs, while some of the sailors danced lively little jigs on the forecastle deck. It was all I could do to keep the secret of my violin. You see, I didn't know any common tunes and didn't know how to explain my familiarity with Chopin and Beethoven, since I supposedly had come from a lowly orphanage. I thought it best to keep my Stradivarius concealed from the crew. But after a day or two of listening to Jibber's harmonica, I knew I could find the notes to his common songs on my violin. I could feel the tunes played out through my fingertips and the strokes through my bow hand. Even without holding the instrument in my hand, my muscles were memorizing the melodies.

On the third day of the calm, when the men had about exhausted their repertoire of songs, I took the risk of speaking out. "I can play a fiddle," I said.

A moment of silence was followed by a great roar of laughter. I happened to look aft and see the captain standing at the weather rail on the poop deck, the smoke from his pipe hanging around his head like a perfect cloud.

"I can," I said. "My mum gave me one before she died, and I learned how."

"Pray, did ye stow it aboard with you?" Jibber said. The men again laughed at my expense.

"I'm sure I did," I said. "It's my only possession. It's just an old one, but it plays well enough."

Jibber scowled at me. "Fetch it then, lad, and be quick about it. But mind you, we shan't listen to any bad fiddling!"

By that time, I was already in the hold. I finished tuning the Stradivarius as I approached the crew. I chose a tune I had heard Jibber play earlier that day; one the men sang to called "Tom Tough." I can say without boasting that they were astonished to utter silence by my talent. Even the captain came forward from the poop deck to listen and watch. Before long, Jibber was playing along, and the men were singing and dancing. As I played, I noticed that the captain looked suspiciously at me and my violin.

During the calm, some of the crew would strip once a day and plunge into the sea for a quick bath in the cold water. I didn't bathe in the ocean, of course, because I couldn't swim. On our fourth day becalmed, Jibber caught me hauling up a bucket of water to wash with and asked why I didn't just jump in.

"I never learned to swim," I admitted, trusting in his discretion.

"Oh, I'll teach you to swim, lad. Me and the men."

Before I could speak, Jibber had called half the crew around him and told them I required the benefit of swimming lessons. They ushered me amidships behind the deckhouse, sat me down on a coil of rope against the mainmast, and began my lessons.

"Now, swimming is the easiest thing in the world," Jibber began. "Why, a puppy can swim. A horse, mind you. A snake can swim without a leg!"

"Nor an arm," someone added.

"Of course, without an arm," Jibber growled over his shoulder, "it's a bloody snake, ain't it?"

"Aye," the first mate said, watching from the poop deck above, "it's the easiest thing there is, Henry. Swimming, I mean. Mind what Jibber says."

"Now, there's just three rules to swimming," Jibber continued. "Can you remember three rules, lad?"

"Of course I can, but—"

"Then here's rule number one. You don't breathe the water. You breathe air, not water. See?"

"Sure, Jibber, but I don't want to learn out here in the deep—"

"Now, shut your mouth, Henry. Listen. Here's the second rule. Cup your hands. You push against the water like a bird pushes air with its wings. Try it."

They made me practice my swimming strokes with cupped hands pushing against thin air, and all of them gathered around me made the most serious demonstrations.

"You use your legs, too," said a burly sailor named Big Willie. "Show him, Jibber." With that, Willie hitched his arms around Jibber's chest from behind and lifted him off his feet. Suspended, Jibber made the arm and leg motions of a man treading water, all the while holding the most pleased look upon his face, as if truly enjoying a tepid swim.

"Now, you, Henry," someone said, and I was suspended

above the deck like Jibber and made to practice my swimming strokes.

"Now repeat the first two rules," Jibber said when I found my feet back on the deck, "so's we know you've got them good."

"I'm not to breathe the water," I said, "and cup my hands. But—"

"Good," Jibber said, interrupting me. "Now for the third and final rule. Listen carefully, lad. Come closer."

Jibber beckoned me with his finger, so I leaned toward him as if he were going to tell me a great secret.

"The third rule is this," he whispered. "Mind the sharks."

In an instant, the men had caught me by my arms and legs. I writhed in fear, but they pulled off my shoes, carried me to the gunwale, and threw me over, fully clothed. Vaguely, I heard the whistle of a steam kettle. Then I screamed bloody murder until I hit the water. It was now that I disobeyed rule number one, tormenting my lungs with water. I thrashed in terror until I felt my head emerge from the sea. I tried to breathe, but I got very little air. I can still hear the crew laughing, jeering, and shouting advice.

"Don't breathe the water! Cup your hands, lad! You've forgotten the first two rules."

I *did* cup my hands, and found that I could keep my head above water. I gasped again, this time managing to get some air past the water I had inhaled. I coughed and fought the sea.

"Slow down!" Jibber shouted. "You're not drowning! Take slow strokes with your arms and legs. That's it! Better!"

I finally caught enough air to speak. "Get me out, Jibber. It's cold. I've learned now. I can swim enough."

The crew howled with laughter.

"You're forgetting one thing," Jibber said.

"What?"

"The third rule. Mind the sharks!"

I glanced over both shoulders, learning to turn myself about in the water.

"There's one!" the first mate said, pointing at nothing. "And another!"

"Another!"

"More behind you! A whole bloody school!"

They laughed and laughed, and Jibber threw a line down to me. I climbed like a wet squirrel and landed among them like a rabid dog. The men only laughed and dodged my fists, some slapping my back in congratulation. I was too exhausted to carry on long, and the first mate soon brought me a cup of hot tea the cook had begun preparing about the time the others sat me down for the three lessons.

Now I could swim. I was angry, but the thought of vengeance fell away from me with each droplet of salt water I shook off. In their own rough way, these men of the sea, had taken me in to their fraternity, making me one of their own. There was no time for coddling or hand-holding out here on the open water. A man learned quickly, or he perished, perhaps taking a fellow crewman with him. I sipped my tea, and swallowed my pride. Some genius I was! I could speak Latin, French, English, German, Spanish, and Italian. I could play Mozart, recite Shakespeare, and solve quadratic equations—yet I could scarcely swim, sail, or look out for myself. These simple men humbled me. *Me! A genius!*

Another realization struck me. My fellow crewmen liked me, not because they knew me, but because they thought I was just like them. They didn't know that I had employed geometry and triangulation to calculate, in my head, the area of canvas the Dover Star could carry at full sail. They didn't know that I had figured the length-width ratio of the vessel at four-to-one and ciphered the cubic area of her hold. They didn't know that I had recited the entire third act of Shakespeare's *Macbeth* to myself on my watch last night. They didn't know that I could play Chopin's piano, violin, and cello trio backward, debate politics, or outline the factors contributing to the fall of the Roman Empire. Had they known of any of these things, they would have treated me like another species.

I resolved to let no one know about my affliction. I enjoyed being liked. More importantly, a boy genius would be wanted in France about now for murdering his fencing master. I was better off acting out the charade in which I was no more intelligent than the next fellow. Already, I was beginning to regret having revealed my violin. The captain had taken particular notice of it. Did he know music? Did he know musical instruments? He was suspicious of me. What if some ship overtook us from France, with news of the fantastic murder of a renowned swordsman and the theft of a Stradivarius violin? Becalmed as we were, some vessel could even now be gaining our beam in windier waters. The violin would give me away. I was a fool for having revealed it, but now all I could do was to stick to my fabricated history and hope we hailed no vessels from France.

After four days of calm, a breeze rose from the northeast. We soon had the *Dover Star* under full sail from spanker to jib and went plowing happily through the gentle swells. It was during this run that I happened to find Jibber on the forecastle deck between watches, juggling three limes for his own entertainment. We carried limes on board because the fruit prevented scurvy, which was why English sailors were so often called "limeys" in those days. They made good juggling balls on top of all that.

"Can you show me how to do that?" I asked, and within the half hour, Jibber had me juggling as though I had been born to the carnival, but of course my powers of dexterity and agility had always been highly refined. "Where did you learn to juggle?" I asked as I practiced my new pastime.

Jibber smiled his snaggletoothed grin, and his eyes drifted across the water—toward England, I presumed. "I come from gypsy stock, lad. Street performers, we were, ranging from London to Liverpool. My whole family could juggle and tumble and do magic. And, pray, pick a pocket or two. The magician and the pickpocket use many of the same skills."

"You can do magic?"

"I'm quite sure, lad. Let me show you." He took one of

the limes from me and held it in his open palm. He covered it with his other hand, gesturing ostentatiously in the style of the classic prestidigitator. Now his hands separated, flying outward and upward, no sign of the lime between them anywhere. Before I could ask, he was reaching for my left ear, where he found nothing. Then he reached his other hand for my other ear, and I realized he must have misdirected my attention, for I knew he was going to produce that confounded lime. And he did, tugging my lobe as he withdrew his hand, as though he had plucked it from my very head.

"Alright," I sneered. "How?"

"Why, it's magic, lad."

"Right," I groaned, for I was annoyed at having been fooled.

"Aye, really, it is," he said, touching his forefinger to his head and looking at me, eye to eye, in a way that, for a moment, made me think that maybe Jibber was a posturing genius like me. "The magic's in the mind. In knowing how it works. Knowing how to lead it just far enough down the wrong path before snatching it back where you want it."

"Alright," I said. "So show me how it's done."

"How it's done? Lad, I've just told you."

"But, show me a trick, I mean."

He hooted up the mizzenmast. "Just like that? Show you a trick? Give you my magic?"

"Come on, Jibber. I'd like to fool somebody like that."

"Fooling people just makes them mad at you. You've got to amaze them. You've got to entertain them, lad."

"That's what I meant," I explained. "I want to amaze them all."

He put his hand to his chin and looked at me as though he was really pondering hard. "Here's what I'll do, lad. I'll show you one trick, and you're to practice it until you can do it blindfolded. If you can make it work with the first mate, I'll teach you some more."

I agreed, and thus began my instruction in the discipline of legerdemain. Jibber showed me how he had vanished the lime and then produced it again. He would let his audience

see the lime in his right hand, then curl his fingers around
it, turning the back of his fist to the onlookers. Then he
would grip the whole lime in the hollow of his palm as he
extended his fingers, giving the appearance that his hand
held nothing. Then he would drop the lime down his sleeve,
which he had expertly shaken open to catch the object, and
turn his palm to the audience, revealing nothing.

Making the lime reappear involved nothing more than
dropping his right arm so that the lime would fall out of his
sleeve, into his waiting palm. But this move would make a
skeptic suspicious, so Jibber misdirected the drop of the
right hand by reaching the left hand over his head—or behind my ear—as if to pluck the lime from nowhere with his
left hand. He would fail, of course, but now the lime was
back in position, palmed secretly in his right hand. As he
had said, the only magic was in misdirecting the mind, but
that was magic enough, for I respected the powers of the
mind.

"Now, look," he told me, "it's all about what the other
fellow sees. "The easiest fellow to amaze with a magic trick
is a one-eyed man because he don't see as much. The toughest fellow to amaze is a blind man."

For days I spent my spare moments on the *Dover Star*
juggling limes and practicing my one sleight-of-hand trick
with a coin Jibber had loaned me for the trick, because it
was easier to palm and conceal than a whole lime. Between
watches, I would be found in my nook down in the hold,
palming the coin over and over, dropping it down my
sleeve, shaking it back out. I decided to learn the trick left-
handed as well, and would practice it both ways.

My practice became so routine that one day, just after
coming off a morning watch, I fell asleep, in my peculiar
way, while continuing to practice the deception. I must have
practiced in my sleep almost two hours, repeating the con-
juration hundreds of times, for I was awakened by Jibber's
voice shouting down from the hatch.

"Lad, we're about to go back on watch. Come show Hawkins the trick if you're ready."

For days the winds had mounted and the seas had grown so gradually into larger swells that the change had been almost imperceptible. Now Jibber, Hawkins, and I stood amidships for my first attempt to amaze as a magician, leaning with each pitch and roll of the deck as I flawlessly executed the deceptions that made the coin vanish, then reappear. The first mate, if not amazed, at least raised an eyebrow and said, "Not bad, Henry, not bad. Now, be a good lad and furl the mizzen topgallant."

"Yes, sir," I said, happily nudging Jibber with my elbow as I sprang aft to ascend the rigging. I climbed the ratlines like a squirrel, all full of magic and freedom. It wasn't until I reached the uppermost spars that I realized how much the wind and seas had risen while I had been consumed with sleight of hand. I heard the first mate shouting orders for other men to douse the main and fore topgallants as well, reducing canvas to keep the topmasts from snapping off. I reached for the line that held the high starboard corner of the mizzen topgallant when suddenly the *Dover Star* plunged into a swell. The swell wasn't any bigger than any others we had plowed over the past couple of days, but now I was fifty feet up the mast, and the leverage associated with such height came near flinging me from the rigging. My feet slipped off the rope on which I had been standing, and I held on only by one hand to the rope that ran along the top of the yard. I went flying like a popper at the end of a whip.

"Hold tight, Henry!" I heard Jibber's voice shout from below.

Recovering quickly, I got one leg through the rigging and, with my free hand, grabbed the line I had been reaching for all along. The moment I took hold of the line, I felt the mighty tug of the wind coursing into my palm and wrist, and there I stayed, transfixed. The power in that topgallant sail suddenly awed me, and yet it was among the smaller sails on the mast. It was a mere speck on the ocean, catching an infinitesimal fraction of all the howling winds that crossed the wide seas. I literally could not move a muscle, trying in vain to absorb the magnitude of it.

And there was something else, as well. This wind was blowing me westward. I was hurtling into my own predestined future. With neither star nor compass, I knew the heading of this wind. It bore down on a lonely river crossing in one of the last wild places left on Earth, where timber moaned in a gale, and frosty grass sparkled in the dawn, and beasts lumbered and thundered the valley. A sacred place protected by Comanches.

Jibber was beside me in a flash. "Let go, Henry. Get below. I'll douse the sail myself."

The sail was tugging at me as if it lived, and I felt as ignorant and as insignificant as an insect. "Here's the real magic, Jibber," I said.

"What?"

"The wind. Where does it all come from?"

"Let's talk about this on deck, lad."

I broke away from the power of the sail, but I was charged. "I came to douse the topgallant, and I'll douse the topgallant," I boasted.

I stepped up on the spar rigging and began gathering sail as the men below loosened the sheet. Jibber took in the other end and we tied the canvas fast to the spar so it wouldn't flap itself threadbare in the coming gale.

"Good lad," he said. "Now, get below before she flings you into the sea."

We sailed through a roaring good gale that night, but without the loss of a man or any serious damage to the vessel. I spent all night on deck as did every man aboard, holding to something all the while so the waves wouldn't sweep me into the deep. A few times, I thought the sea and the storm would simply swallow our little ship, and I feared drowning. But when I observed what the other men were doing, I would find them carrying on through the wind and waves as if nothing out of the ordinary was going on.

It was odd, but comforting, to see men shrugging at such danger. This was a characteristic of courageous men that I would see many times in the future, with Indians, trappers, frontiersmen, and buffalo hunters. This "little blow" as Jib-

ber called it, was my first glimpse at indifference in the face
of sheer peril. I was happy that my face couldn't be seen in
the dark, for I am sure my fear must have been stamped in
my expression.

⚜

After the gale blew by, another problem beset me. I had
been at sea almost a month now, sleeping no more than a
few hours a day, and I was beginning to feel my exhaustion
mount. I could sense the strange dark powers of the new
moon creeping upon me. But how could I get the sleep I
needed with so much work to be done on board, and as
much expected of me as the next man? With the new moon
looming, a solution came to me. I spent my watch that night
drinking seawater. This wasn't easy, but I forced myself to
swallow a cup of it every few minutes. Before too long, I
felt sick as a sea monster.

Coming off the watch, I stumbled into the forecastle,
where Jibber was just crawling into his bunk. I shook him
by the shoulder.

"What's the matter, lad?" he said, looking at my pale face.

About that time, I vomited all over the forecastle.

Jibber sprang from his bunk and forced me into it. "Why
didn't you tell somebody you were sick, Henry?"

"I can't stay awake," I said. "I get the shivers, and chills."

"Hope it ain't cholera. Bundle up there, lad. I'll get the
first mate to doctor you."

After some prodding and questioning, Hawkins decided
that I had either eaten a piece of fish gone bad or had con-
tracted malaria or cholera or scurvy or all three. They let
me sleep two days, waking me only once a day to spoon
feed me a little broth, after which Jibber secretly gave me
a "nip of the Irish." When I awoke, I ate a hearty breakfast
and went to work about the ship, happier than I had ever
been in my life, and determined to make up for my laziness
of the last two days.

Only one thing interrupted my joy. I went to fetch my

violin one afternoon to play some ditties for the crew. When I opened the case, I could tell that someone had taken the violin out and put it back. A victim of obsessive ritualism, I have always done routine things one certain way, and I could tell someone had spread the velvet cloth over the bridge differently than I habitually did.

Reading the expression on my face, Jibber said, "The cap'n had a look at it while you were sick."

"The captain?" I said, feeling my anger rise. "This here's my property, Jibber."

"The cap'n's got a right to search anything on his vessel. He might have confiscated it if he wanted to. A cap'n's like a king aboard his vessel, lad."

Not long after that, the captain called me into his quarters, and ordered me to bring my violin. He told me to play something, so I lit into a Scottish hornpipe I had learned from Jibber.

"That's fine," he said, stopping me after one bar. "Now play something you knew in France."

"At the orphanage?"

"Yes, wherever."

"They never let me play at the orphanage."

"Then play something you learned before. You've obviously had some lessons."

"My mum taught me a little," I claimed. "Before she died, I mean." I put the violin under my chin and started Beethoven's Violin Concerto in D, taking pains not to play perfectly. I glanced at the captain's face as I played, and saw him smiling, staring at the wall, enjoying the rich, sweet sound of that wonderful instrument.

"Well done," he said, when I had finished the first movement. "Your mother must have been a woman of some culture and learning. Henry, have you ever heard the name Antonio Stradivari?"

I looked at the floor as if to search my memory. "I'm sure I haven't, Captain."

"He was the maker of your violin."

I looked at the instrument and shrugged.

"I should like to purchase that violin from you, Henry. When you get back to France, you'll need funds to take care of yourself. Since you've worked hard, I'll forget the passage fee you owe me for stowing away aboard my ship. And I'll make you a fair offer on the instrument."

"Oh, but, Captain, this was my mum's violin. It's the only thing I've left that was hers."

"Your mum would want you taken care of, wouldn't she?"

"Yes, sir, but she told me to look after her violin."

"What better way to look after it than to let a gentleman purchase it. A gentleman who appreciates its value. We'll fetch New Orleans in a week. When we do, I'll have a draft drawn up for you at the bank. I'll find you a vessel that's sailing back to France, and you'll have some money to finish your schooling at a better place than that orphanage."

"But, Captain, I hoped I might continue to sail with the *Dover Star*." I said, trying to change the subject.

"I haven't a place for you, lad. You're extra weight aboard this ship, though I'll admit you've learned well. You can go to sea after your schooling's done. I don't take on stowaways. Now, about the violin..."

I had to think quickly, for I could tell that Captain Robbins had his heart set on my Stradivarius. I remembered what Jibber had told me. He could simply confiscate the instrument if he wanted to. "Well," I said, "might I keep it until New Orleans, Captain? I mean, until you purchase it? I'd like to play it a time or two. My mum would like that."

"Very well." He smiled in his self-satisfied way.

I never had liked Captain Robbins, in spite of his leniency in my case. He was arrogant and pretentious; and if he thought he was going to get his hands on my stolen violin, he was underestimating me.

FOUR

My first glimpse of America sobered me. The call of "Land ho!" had rung from aloft, and I had scrambled up the rigging to get a view of the new continent. It was to be my first sighting of land since leaving France, for we had sailed through the Caribbean in squally weather that had obscured any island we might have neared. I climbed level with the first yard and looked. Even from this distance, at which America appeared as nothing more than a long dark line low on the northwestern horizon, it warned of savage danger. It looked wild.

I suppose I had expected to see hills with villages perched upon them, fields dotted by haystacks, harbors with fires burning, and all manner of civilized enterprise coursing through cobblestoned streets. I searched my memory for a map I had once seen in a book—a map of the coast along the Gulf of Mexico. Now I realized that I should have expected this line of nothingness on the horizon. My memory is perfect, as I have already explained, and I could remember the chart depicting undulating rivers and meandering estuaries, all of which spoke of a broad, marshy, virtually flat coastline. I knew the city of New Orleans lay somewhere up the twining channels of the mouth of the great Mississippi River. The city itself probably would not be visible until we sailed almost into it.

As we approached the delta of the Mississippi, I saw a flare go up from shore.

"That's from Pilottown," Jibber explained. "Now the pilots will race to see who gets to us first. The cap'n will pay the winner to guide us up the channel to New Orleans."

The sails of three sloops soon appeared; but as one took

the lead, the two others changed course and tacked back the way they had come. Nearing the *Dover Star,* the sloop furled sail and dropped a skiff into which two men climbed.

"The one wearing the top hat's the pilot," First Mate Hawkins said.

The oarsman of the skiff rowed the pilot to our packet. Our crew hauled up his valise and a bundle of newspapers the captain and crew could peruse to catch up on such accounts as had reached New Orleans. Soon after the pilot climbed the rope ladder, a steam-powered tugboat appeared at the mouth of the Mississippi. Catching a line tossed from the tug, we tied on and began to plow up the channel to New Orleans.

Captain Robbins had two men from the port watch lash themselves to the rigging and stand on the gunwales on either side of the ship. With a weighted line, each man continually sounded the channel and called out the depth, making sure the pilot had not strayed from the ever-shifting channel of the Mississippi. On both sides of the river, as we traveled farther inland, I saw towering cypress trees, moss hanging from their branches. The domelike crowns of colossal live oak trees mounded the skyline between stands of cypress. These were new species of flora to me, and they made me look for creatures I might not have seen.

First, I noticed the many birds new to me. I watched huge white pelicans with black wingtips swimming in small groups on the water, scooping up fish in their beaks. I saw brown pelicans, smaller than the white ones but more fun to watch because they would skim the surface of the river while flying and occasionally would swoop, wheel, and plunge into the water for a catch. I saw loons, gulls, cormorants, and herons. Cranes, swans, geese, and many different species of ducks. I saw one flock of flaming pink birds with spoon-shaped bills. There were sandpipers, dowitchers, and curlews. Snipes, gulls, and terns. Ospreys, hawks, harriers, and eagles soared over water, marsh, and delta.

I saw a small herd of deer turn from the riverbank and run from the noise of the steam tug, their waving white tails disappearing into a thicket of trees tangled with vines. And, more than once, along the sunny mud flats, I witnessed the torpid lumberings of alligators, so large and wicked that I fancied them monsters. Even decades later, after having faced grizzlies, mountain lions, and charging buffalo bulls, nothing would make me shudder like the memory of these horrid amphibious beasts, and I would suffer nightmares in which I tried to swim but could not move, while cold-eyed alligators came to crunch my limbs and drag me swirling into an agonizing underwater death.

Oh, yes . . . Once, when the channel veered quite near to the shore, I spied a lone coyote that I am sure the other sailors missed. He lowered his head to peer under a palmetto frond at me with amber eyes. He did not merely look at the tug or the packet. He searched both vessels until he found my eyes looking back at him, and then he stared at me hard, like a wary child. As the boats slipped by harmlessly, he tossed his head at me slightly, as if to say, "Fare thee well."

After so many weeks at sea, the land, wild and marshy as it was, beckoned to me. I began to watch over the bow-sprit for the first signs of civilization in America. The crew had told me quite a lot about New Orleans and now began to build my anticipation.

"They speak French as well as English, lad," Jibber said. "You'll get along right well if the cap'n gives you shore leave."

"The streets is named for grog," Big Willie added with a smile on his face.

"Well, a couple of them," Jibber corrected. "Burgundy, Bourbon."

"I'm afraid the captain won't let me go ashore, Jibber. He only wants to take my mum's violin and send me back to France. Back to that orphanage. That wretched, horrible orphanage. You blokes have been more a family to me than anyone at that place."

Silence hung along the starboard gunwale, except for the call of shore birds and chug of the steam engine on the tug.

"It's a pity, it is," Jibber said. "Too bad a lad like you—

who speaks French and could ask about the wharves—too
bad such a lad couldn't jump ship and see about a riverboat
steaming upstream. Pray, a riverboat to St. Louis, lad.
Wouldn't that make a bloody smashing passage? A lad
could buy a ticket on the first riverboat steaming upriver, he
could. And the cap'n . . . Oh, the cap'n might not know a
thing about it. Gone to visit that fancy brothel on Canal
Street, you know. They say the madam there plays a concert
violin. D'ye hear, Henry? A fiddling whore, pray! A lad
could be on his way upstream before the cap'n got his boots
off. The cap'n hasn't got the time to fetch some orphan
wretch who's jumped ship. Not with a cargo to unload, and
another to load, and get back out to sea. Pray, not with a
record to beat and four days of calm on the downhill run to
make up for. Chase a bloody little orphan wretch to St.
Louis? Ha! That's why it's such a pity, lad. I mean that
you've got to stay on board like a good lad and go back to
that bloody wretched orphanage." He made clucking sounds
with his tongue and shook his head. "Aye, a pity, indeed."

I smiled at Jibber with one side of my mouth. "Pity a lad
couldn't vanish himself like a bloody coin," I said.

Jibber only shrugged sadly and pointed at another big
alligator sliding into the river.

For hours we plied upstream through delta country, until
finally I asked Jibber when we might see the port of New
Orleans.

"The morrow, Henry. Try and get some rest. Tonight's
your last midnight watch."

I was disappointed, for I had hoped to see New Orleans
on this day. I knew I was too excited to even wish for sleep,
so as the sun sank, I went below decks and practiced magic.

The next morning, the port of New Orleans finally hove
into view along a bend in the river. I found the city a welcome change of scenery after the seascape I had endured
for seventeen weeks. The levees and wharves teemed with
longshoremen and workmen from every vocation imagina-
ble. I had not foreseen that so many of the citizens would
be black people, though it shouldn't have surprised me. I

had seen Africans in Paris on occasion, but here they made up a large portion of the workforce and went about dressed for every walk of life, from the dockhand's dungarees to the silk waistcoat of a cotton broker.

"Are they slaves?" I asked First Mate Hawkins.

"I don't think so," he said with a look on his face that told me he had never really thought about it or didn't really care. "New Orleans has been home to free Negroes for a long time, by the looks of things. I've seen them own shops and whatnot. Your French ancestors have mixed with them for generations."

"Aye," a sailor named Bill added, "there's plenty of pretty Creole whores about this town, lad."

This excited my memories of Nicole, but I doubted I would have the time or courage to patronize a New Orleans bordello.

"You'd probably get on right well here, Henry," Hawkins said. "They call New Orleans 'the Paris of the Americas.'"

This made very little sense to me. Paris was, and had been for centuries, surrounded by civilization. But this place bordered all that was wild. Instead of earthen levees and houses built up on stilts, Paris boasted grand monuments and classical statuary. If this was as close as America could come to Paris, more was the pity. But, for my own purposes, Paris was no longer to my liking, anyway. Even New Orleans was too civilized. I knew where I was going. I was a fugitive on my way to the frontier. That Comanche warrior from the Catlin painting called me to battle somewhere west.

I was rather egocentric in those days of my youth. I thought always of myself, and assumed everyone else thought always of me as well. I just knew that, back in France, a house-to-house search must still be under way; that my trail had led to Le Havre; that someone must have seen me board the *Dover Star*. I fancied that detectives were even now crossing the Atlantic to apprehend me and bring me back to stand trial for the murder of Segarelli.

Later, among the Indians, I would learn to look inside my own mind and soul, know my own heart, and shut out any

care of what another human might think of me. Then I
would learn to look with fresh eyes upon the people around
me, and actually care about them. Up to this point in my
life, I had cared only for individuals who had done me some
kindness—like Nicole, or Jibber. Later, I would learn to care
about people I did not even like.

Oddly enough, my God-given genius applied only to my
intellect. I had no genius for humanity, friendship, or love.
But I would learn. The Comanches would see to that.

Perhaps you think it odd that I would seek out the Comanches. Had I not been attacked in my vision by that
painted Comanche rendering come to life—the Catlin portrait? Had the vision not frightened me almost to the point
of seizure? This is true. But think. Have you never turned
to face something that frightened you. When you come to
a great precipice, do you turn tail, or do you creep nearer
and nearer to the brink, knowing all the while that a single
slip might send you tumbling to your death? You know why
I wanted to encounter Comanches. Even if you are not
aware of it, or won't admit it. You know.

The harbor pilot directed the tugboat as it nudged us to
an empty wharf. All the while, Captain Robbins strode from
starboard to port along the weather rail, looking after the
flanks of his precious vessel. When finally we docked, we
still had hours of work to do before setting foot on land.
Toward evening, the *Dover Star* was finally secured and
ready for off-loading. As the mates directed the last chores,
Captain Robbins went into the city to draw wages from a
bank account. When he returned, he called the crew on deck.
He wore a clean navy blue jacket and a crisp captain's cap
with a shiny leather bill. He had tied a silk scarf about his
neck, and his pipe stuck out from between his teeth.

"That's the getup," Jibber whispered to me. "Where do
ye think the cap'n's going dressed like that?"

Captain Robbins did not bother to thank his men. He simply told them they could draw their wages and enjoy a
thirty-six-hour shore leave before sailing back to Liverpool
with a load of cotton. The first and second mates handled

the payroll chores as the captain caught my eye.

"We've business to attend to," he said. "You won't be collecting any wages, anyway."

"No, sir," I said. "I mean, yes, sir."

He pulled an ornate gold watch from his vest pocket and glanced at it. "Where's the violin?"

"In the forecastle," I said.

He motioned, and we walked forward to enter the forecastle as the men collected their wages merrily and stomped down the gangplank one by one. I wanted to look over my shoulder to bid Jibber farewell, but that would weaken the illusion I was about to employ, for I had orders to stay on board and therefore might be expected to see the crew again before Captain Robbins put me aboard some French vessel.

But as I entered the forecastle, I heard Jibber shout, "Hey, Henry!"

I stopped, turned, and found him at the top of the gang-plank, about to descend upon New Orleans. He and I both knew we would never see each other again.

"*Bon voyage*, lad! Godspeed!"

I caught his eye, waved, and watched him sink out of sight.

"I don't suppose I'll see the crew again," I said.

"Not likely," Captain Robbins said. "You'll be sailing for France before they sober up. Now, let's get on with it."

"Yes, sir."

We entered the forecastle. I had placed the violin and its case in Jibber's bunk, which was shadowy. Turning my back to Captain Robbins, I opened the violin case, knowing that he would hear the noise of the metal latches. When I turned back around, I held the violin. I touched the bow to the strings and tripped up the scale. "I tuned it," I said.

"Good lad. That's fine. Put it back in the case. I've got the purchase fee in my pocket."

I turned my back to the captain again, returning the violin to the shadows of Jibber's bunk.

"I sought out a music shop today and priced violins," the captain said. "Twenty dollars ought to satisfy you, for that's the going rate. It's more than you would have earned in wages on this voyage."

I fastened the latches on the violin case and turned around with it in my hands. He took my violin case. I took his silver coins.

"Remember, you're not to leave the vessel tonight with the men." He tucked the case under his arm. "Is that understood?"

"But, Captain, if I might just—"

"Is that understood?"

I sighed as big as a whale. "Yes, sir."

"You're still a stowaway, and a runaway to boot. I've found a French vessel down the wharf. It will sail in the morning, and you'll be aboard. If you like, before you leave in the morning, I'll pen a letter of reference describing the skills you've acquired under my instruction, and stating your desire to sail when you've finished your schooling."

I stifled my desire to scoff at his arrogance, and tried to look grateful. "That would be most appreciated, Captain, sir."

"Very well. Until the morning."

And with that the captain turned his back on me and left the forecastle. He walked aft and stepped onto the gangplank. "Under your instruction, indeed," I said beneath my breath. I watched him disappear, then calmly slipped my Stradivarius into my drawstring pouch. "Twenty dollars is a fair enough price for a good violin case," I said to myself. I wondered how long it would take Captain Robbins to reach his bordello and open that case in order to show his violin-playing whore his new acquisition. When he did open that case, he was going to be angry at me, so it was well that I should be on my way upstream. Of course, the Stradivarius wasn't in the case. It was in my bag. But the vanishing of the violin hadn't happened as simply as you might think, for I had taken no chances on Captain Robbins's discovering my illusion before I was on my way out of New Orleans. Here is how I did it:

After I astounded First Mate Hawkins by making a coin

vanish, Jibber had taught me some more simple tricks. I
could now palm a playing card, making it seem to appear
and disappear with a flip of my wrist. I had even mastered
the so-called "backhand palm"—a logical oxymoron—
through which I concealed the card on the back of my hand
by gripping one corner between my thumb and the base of
my forefinger while gripping the opposite corner between
my little and third fingers. In this way, I could show my
audience the palm of my hand, to assure them it held nothing. Then, with a flourish of my hand to disguise my digital
manipulations, I would make the card appear out of nowhere.

Jibber could switch from the palm to the backhand palm
with such practiced ease that he could show both sides of
his hand, twisting it in midair, and you would swear that he
held nothing, when actually he was whisking the card clev-
erly from the back to the front of his hand all the while,
with every twist of his wrist.

But not all illusion was visual, I had learned. Sometimes
it involved heft and sound. Jibber performed a trick in which
he would cut a slit in a lime, tie it up in a sailor's handkerchief, and ask the sailor to squeeze the juice out of the
lime. When the sailor squeezed, he found that the lime had
changed to an egg, which would, of course, break open in
his handkerchief, much to the enjoyment of the rest of the
crew. We carried several chickens on board the *Dover Star,*
you see, kept in coops behind the deck house, but the important thing is that the weight and balance and shape of an
egg was close to that of a lime.

This was important to me in making my Stradivarius vanish. Captain Robbins understood things like weight and balance. He had to provide sufficient ballast for his vessel, and
load his cargo in such a way that the ship rode level in the
water. If I were to hand him an empty violin case, or one
balanced improperly, he would immediately suspect my deception through pure instinct. Also, if he picked up the case,
and felt its contents shift, or heard them make some non-
musical sound, he would likewise discover my artifice.

So, in preparing my illusion, I first balanced the violin case, with the violin in it, on a belaying pin to find its center of gravity. Next, I made a dummy violin, actually sort of a violin doll. I made it by bundling up and tying some sailcloth in a shape that would fit in the contours of the case. To make the dummy equal the weight and balance of the Stradivarius, I used chocolates. First, I made the weight match by holding the violin and bow in one hand, and the dummy in the other. I added chocolates like little weights until I could not tell the difference in weight between the real violin and the dummy even if I held the two objects in my hands for a full minute. Next, I tucked the chocolates into certain folds of the sailcloth, and secured them until the case balanced on the belaying pin at precisely the same place whether holding the violin, or the dummy. I did all of this between watches in the hold of the vessel where I slept. The rest of the trick would rely upon sleight of hand, which I practiced at every opportunity.

Perhaps by now, you have surmised how I did it. Jibber's bunk, where I had stashed the violin and the case, was shadowed. The captain, who had just entered the forecastle from the bright sunshine, could not see into the bunk. Even if he had been able to see, I had shielded the place where the violin and the case lay, standing in front of it, with my back to the captain.

He heard me open the case, and that, I knew, would make him assume that I was removing the violin, giving the impression that the Stradivarius had emerged from the case and would therefore return to it. In reality, the dummy violin was already in the case, and the real Stradivarius was simply lying beside it. Like a magician, I showed Captain Robbins the object that would later vanish, and then returned it—he assumed—to the case. In reality, I simply laid the Stradivarius to the side and covered it with the corner of a blanket. All this took about the same amount of time that I would have taken to place a violin and bow into a case. I then latched the case loudly, again giving the impression that the instrument had just been placed inside, and handed the case to Captain Robbins. I could tell the moment he took it that he suspected nothing, and that my illusion had succeeded. He wouldn't open that case until he arrived at the bordello. Why would he? His mind was completely satisfied that the violin was in there.

Now Captain Robbins was turning a corner onto some street down the waterfront, and I knew my time to disembark had arrived. I have wondered for decades now what ever became of the *Dover Star*. I have fondly remember my friend and mentor, Jibber, all these years. I have heard much of New Orleans and regretted that I didn't have more time to explore it. But I was, a fugitive from justice, just beginning to pay for my crimes. I would carry the burdens the rest of my life. Fate had announced my sentence. I would hide, lie, assume false identities, and forever lament the lost tranquillity of truth.

When I disembarked from the *Dover Star*, I slung my bag over my shoulder and walked casually up the wharf to the place where the riverboats docked, exulting in my recent ocean crossing, yet feeling the very dirt beneath my shoes embrace me like a mother. Though the firm footing felt strange, I knew I would never go back to sea.

Within the hour, I found a stern wheeler preparing to cast off and move upriver, for there were dozens and dozens of steamers plying the Mississippi in those days. There were, in fact, sixty-four in view when I counted, at a glance. I paid two bits to board the squalid lower deck of the one casting off, and wondered what might become of me in America.

FIVE

I had learned from my experience with Captain Robbins not to draw attention to myself, so I did not reveal my violin to anyone, even though there were musicians of several nationalities on board the riverboat who played lively tunes in relays, day and night. All manner of happy, poverty-stricken people rode the lower deck of this steamboat. Above, on the upper deck, a few finely dressed ladies and gentlemen enjoyed a parlor and private cabins. Those of us below simply slept on the deck. I managed to catch a few hours of sleep that night by crawling onto a burlap bag full of coffee beans, curling myself around my drawstring bag, and letting the steady chug of the steam engine lull me.

I woke from my tenuous slumber when the sun rose over the eastern riverbank and winked at me through passing treetops. Squinting my eyes, I found a man staring at me. Emerging from sleep, I felt paralyzed, as I often do, and so I simply stared back at the man staring at me, for when I am in this stage of waking, I simply cannot move until my brain receives some auditory stimulus, like a person speaking to me, or a sudden noise, at which time I am able to use my muscles as if someone had turned on an electric switch to activate them. I stared, paralyzed, and mortified at my own disorder. But at least this provided me an opportunity to observe the man before me.

He wore spectacles on the end of his nose, but looked at me over the lenses, giving me the impression that he needed the eyeglasses only for close-in purposes. He wore a fine beaver hat several years old. His clothes were also old, but neatly kept. The buttons on his jacket did not match, as if he had sewed new ones on. His clean hands were draped over the handles of a leather case. His nails were immaculate.

"I can mend those garments," he said finally.

This comment did three things. It jolted me from paralysis, told me that this man was a tailor, and also identified him as a Frenchman, for his accent gave this away. Moreover, his offer was one to consider, for I had left Saint-Cyr with only two suits of clothes, both of which were now rather tattered from the rigors of my ocean crossing. I sat up and rubbed my eyes. "I have little money," I said, groggily.

"Perhaps we will make a barter. What is your trade?"

I thought for a second. "I am a sailor."

He laughed as he pointed toward the stern of the riverboat. "The ocean is that way," he said.

I smiled, for something about the jovial manner of this fellow Frenchman appealed to me. I also liked the way he addressed me as if I were a grown man, though my youth must have shown through my sailor's tan. After crossing on the *Dover Star,* my accent had taken on a decidedly British lilt, which so far had prevented this tailor from pegging me as a Frenchman. We conversed in English.

"I seek a change of vocation," I said.

He stroked his chin. "You have a gift with words. Perhaps we may strike a deal. Like you, I am nearly penniless. I have just visited my mother in New Orleans, where I left my wages from the entire last year. I kept only enough to get back to St. Louis. But I will mend your clothes for nothing if you will bring me a customer or two during this passage. Word of mouth, they say, is the best advertisement."

Immediately, I pulled my spare shirt from my traveling bag. "I am Honoré Dumant," I claimed, having already concocted my story. "I've been sailing with an English packet, the *Liverpool Moon,* but now I intend to explore the American frontier."

"Trés-bien!" he exclaimed, shaking my hand as he shifted his speech to French. "I am Louis Lescot. I am born

American, but my parents came from France. It is always good to meet a fellow Frenchman, *non?*"

"*Oui.*" I fell back into my beloved native tongue. "That shirt has three buttons missing."

"Yes, I have three that will match quite well." Looking through his spectacles, he chose a button and threaded a needle with hands as steady as the sun rising in the sky. "Perhaps I can help you with your aspirations to find new work and explore the frontier. I am employed by the firm of Bent and St. Vrain."

My perfect memory sang a recollection of a newspaper article I had once read, mentioning the firm of Bent and St. Vrain as a leader in the fur and Indian trade of the American wilderness. "What do you do for them?" I asked.

"I am employed as a tailor at Bent's Fort, on the Arkansas."

"Indeed? A fort? On the frontier?"

He looked up suddenly from his needle and thread. "*Bon Dieu!* How green!" he said.

I cocked my head quizzically.

"Bent's Fort is the grandest outpost in the western territories. It is more than just a fort, Honoré, and far beyond the frontier, as well. It borders Mexico, on the wild Arkansas River, within view of the Great Rocky Mountains. It is the most extravagant post ever erected for the Indian trade. A marvel of civilized architecture in the midst of savage nations. I sew buckskins there for mountain men and Indian traders."

Whether by destiny or chance, a tailor had come to pattern my future. I had hoped for an Indian fighter, or perhaps a guide, or trapper, or a *coureur de bois*. But my introduction into the ways of the wilderness would come through a humble tailor. "I would be pleased to accompany you to Bent's Fort," I said boldly.

"Of course you would, until the savages peel away your scalp." He laughed in a mighty burst. "Then you would not be pleased at all, would you?"

"I am not afraid of Indians," I said.

"You will be." Louis Lescot laughed again, then resumed his repairs on my shirt. By the time the riverboat docked at St. Louis, I had still acquired only a general idea of what Bent's Fort was, and how we would get there, for I had spent most of my time on board drumming up business for Louis.

"Thanks to your recommendations," the tailor told me, "we have earned two dollars and forty-five cents, a twist of chewing tobacco, three roasting ears, a live hen, and a knife with a broken point." Louis then handed me a beautiful little scabbard made of golden fringed buckskin. "You may keep the knife, Honoré. I made, for you, a scabbard in which to carry it. *Joli, oui*?"

"Yes, it is pretty." I held the unexpected gift in my hand. *"Merci."* I drew the bartered knife. One half of the bone handle was missing, and the tip was indeed broken off. Still, I felt like a frontier explorer when I threaded my belt through the little scabbard and felt it against my hip.

Louis handed me the tobacco and the three ears of corn. "Carry these in your bag, *mon ami*. Perhaps we can trade the tobacco to a stagecoach driver in lieu of our fare. That will be quicker than riding a steamer up the Missouri," He picked up the chicken, which lived in a makeshift crate of string and wooden slats, and we stepped onto the St. Louis docks.

I asked few questions, not wanting to make myself a bother to the man who had agreed so readily to take me on as his traveling companion. I knew only that we would take a stagecoach from St. Louis to a place called Westport, Missouri, where we would join the Bent and St. Vrain caravan as it embarked upon the Santa Fe Trail. By some mysterious route, this would lead us to Bent's Fort. Vague as the prospects seemed, I found them splendid. A view of the Rocky Mountains! The tailor's warning about Indians had already fluttered from my mind. I *wanted* to see Indians. And I would. . . .

At St. Louis, my companion had to make a number of purchases for his employers and other residents of the fort.

I followed him through the shops as he bought medicine for the trading-post apothecary, needles and thread for his own use, five decks of playing cards and a set of dominos, a pair of scissors, three tortoiseshell combs, and a large bottle of ink. In all the shops, the owners and employees recognized Louis Lescot and welcomed him warmly. He paid cash for nothing, signing for all his purchases on behalf of Bent and St. Vrain. The shopkeepers kept him busy all the while with questions about names I squirreled away mentally for future reference.

"How are Charles and William?"

"Well. Waiting for me at Westport."

"And Carson?"

"Married and trying to start a *rancho,* but he is forever sought out to guide parties and carry dispatches."

"How about Fitzpatrick?"

"Broken Hand? Trading this winter, as usual."

"Where is Ceran?"

"He is in Taos with his new wife, but it is tense there. I fear for him. And Carlos Beaubien, as well. This trouble from the Texans, and talk of war with Mexico puts them at great risk. There are plans for escape, however. You can count on that."

"Smith?"

"Which one? Peg Leg or Blackfoot?"

"Both."

"Blackfoot will hunt meat for the caravan. Peg Leg? Stealing horses in California, of course. He is indestructible."

"How about Jim Bridger?"

Louis shrugged. "Lord knows where Old Gabe goes."

We ended our shopping spree in a bookstore where Louis found several titles requested by various residents of Bent's Fort. While browsing the bookstore with Louis, I happened to notice a dusty volume on magic called *The Art of Prestidigitation.* Thumbing through the book, I noted that the last chapter described a well-known illusion in which the magician would apparently catch a bullet fired from a pistol.

He would sometimes catch it in his hand, sometimes in his teeth, sometimes on the edge of a knife. Knowing there would be bullets and knives where I was going, I purchased the book myself, intending to broaden my repertoire of illusions begun under Jibber's tutelage aboard the *Dover Star*.

We carried our packages and our live chicken to the stage station just as the coach prepared to trundle west. Louis explained to a sour-faced, bewhiskered driver that Bent and St. Vrain would pay our fares. The driver spat a stream of tobacco between his wheel horses. "I remember you," he said to Louis. "The tailor, right?"

"*Oui,*" said Louis.

"Get aboard. I don't know about the kid."

I reached into my bag and offered the driver our twist of tobacco. He took it and grunted, gesturing with this head for me to climb in after Louis.

"You might have saved that for the Indians," Louis said sternly when I got into the coach. "At least half of it."

I thought about apologizing, but decided against it. Instead, I shrugged and said, "*C'est la vie.*"

While the stagecoach racked toward Westport, I opened my book on illusions and turned to the chapter describing the pistol trick. The moon was half full and my eyesight has always been very keen even in near-dark, rather like a deer or an owl. I have always read with remarkable speed, as well, so I learned how to perform the illusion while Louis Lescot and the two other passengers slept during one of the smoother stretches of road.

Here is how it is done. The magician pours gunpowder into the muzzle of the pistol and tamps down the powder with the ramrod. Before dropping in the pistol ball, he marks it with some sign and allows witnesses to see it. He drops the marked ball into the muzzle.

The ramrod holds the key to the illusion. It is not an ordinary ramrod. It has one hollow end just large enough to slip over the pistol ball and extract it from the pistol barrel when the illusionist uses the ramrod to, ostensibly, seat the projectile. The magician removes the ramrod, and by slight of hand, palms the bullet. Now he stuffs wadding down the barrel, supposedly to hold the bullet in place, though he knows very well the bullet is no longer in the pistol. This wadding he stuffs in with the *other* end of the ramrod which is not hollow. All that is left is to ask a volunteer to fire the bullet past the magician. When this is done, he makes a grand flourishing production with his hands as if he is actually catching the bullet, though, of course, it has been in his hand all along. In other versions, he "catches" the bullet in his teeth, or on the edge of a knife blade.

The book also said that several magicians had been maimed or even killed by the stunt, because the volunteers who fired the pistols for the magicians were forever dropping bits and pieces of things down the muzzle of the gun. There are people, you see, who detest a magician because they can't stand not knowing how every little thing is done, and will make statements like, "Oh, that's just some sort of a trick!" or "Just let me look under your coat, if you don't mind," or "Just let me fire *my* pistol at you, you son of a bitch!" thereby ruining the fun for everyone else.

Anyway, as I lurched westward with two complete strangers and a frontier tailor on my quest for that strange place I had dreamed of, I began to consider how I might alter a ramrod so that it would retrieve a ball from the barrel of a gun rather than seat it in the powder.

First I needed a pistol.

SIX

The sounds of hammers ringing against anvils sang through the dust as our stagecoach stopped at Westport, Missouri. Piling anxiously out of the vehicle, I visually explored my surroundings as I stretched my legs and pushed my spine back into alignment.

A mule brayed as if just lanced, and I looked ahead of the jaded coach team to see the wild-eyed beast making impossible tangles in the rigging of a freight wagon. The stage driver spat a brown stream past my face. Hot iron sizzled in water as a wheelwright cooled a glowing red wagon tire tight around a spoked hardwood wheel. Two men dressed in a mixture of white men's clothing, blankets, and buckskin, trotted by on shaggy ponies. I took them for Indians—or at least half-breeds.

Louis piled out beside me. "Come, Honoré. The Bent brothers will be waiting." We retrieved our packages from the boot on the rear of the stagecoach and walked briskly amid the energy that surged through the dirt streets of Westport. A steam whistle wailed from the landing on the nearby Missouri River.

Huge freight wagons loomed here and there along the street, parked at odd angles, some with canvas wagon sheets arching, others with bare bows that moaned in the wind like the ribs of a carcass. In front of a grogshop called "The Last Chance," I saw a man with fantastic whiskers standing in blackened buckskins that looked as if they might stand on their own. He wore a fur cap with the face of a fox over his own and held a tin cup of some sort of grog in his hand.

Walking beyond the acrid smell of wood smoke, coal, and hot iron, I found an open field littered with wagons, hacks, buckboards. Herds clustered. Oxen stood stupidly in their yokes. Men bartered for horses, rode them at every gait. One flew from the back of a lithe pied pony that had suddenly humped and bucked with all the fury of a whirlpool and a tornado combined.

"The oxen, they are the best for this trail," Louis said, out of nowhere. "Better than the mules. Charles himself discovered this."

"What makes them better?" I asked. "I would think the mules would pull faster."

"*Oui*, the mules pull faster at first, but tire faster as well. The oxen, they plod along. The Indians don't like to steal oxen—at least, not as much as mules. And when the trail is cold, or dry, and beasts die from freezing or thirst, and men are starving, which beast do you think is better to eat?"

"I've never eaten mule meat," I said, "so I have no experience on which to base the comparison."

Louis Lescot stopped in his tracks and looked at me with a puzzled grin. He shook his head and started walking again. "I recommend the beef."

Soon we came to a string of fine-looking freight wagons, each so large that the hubs of their wheels stood over my head. Unlike the vessels at the wagon yards behind us, these stood in a perfect row. Around these wagons, the other freighters had left five acres of open space, as if to give respect to the possessors of the vehicles. This, I knew, had to be the caravan of the brothers Bent—Charles and William—who, by this time, I had gathered held boundless respect across the frontier. They had amassed a fortune and structured a dynasty around trade with Mexico and various Indian nations.

"I have never seen such huge wagons," I commented.

"The Mexican government levies an import tax on each wagon. Would you rather pay the duty on many small wagons, or just a few large ones?"

As we approached the caravan, Louis angled directly toward two men standing in front of one of the wagons. They stood shoulder to shoulder, looking at a wagon, talking without facing each other. As we came very near, I saw the family resemblance in each man's countenance. One brother looked older and wore the apparel of a townsman. He was growing just paunchy enough to leave the lower two buttons of his vest unfastened. I judged his age at forty-five. The younger brother, whom I took for about thirty-five, wore golden buckskins with fringes long and fine enough to resemble hair. He looked as lean and as weathered as any man on the grounds, and his eyes hit me with a glint as Louis and I came near enough to speak.

"Ah, Louis," said the man in city clothes.

"Charles," the tailor said, shaking hands with the elder brother, then the younger.

"Hello, Louis," said William in a dry tone that betrayed no emotion. "How was your mother?"

"Well, thank you."

Louis had set his packages on the well-rutted ground, and I did the same, happy to do so because the strings binding the package of books were beginning to hurt my palms. In one hand I had carried the bundle of books purchased in St. Louis. In the other, the chicken in the makeshift crate. My old laundry bag was still slung over one shoulder, the violin and bow inside.

"I've brought a cavvy boy along with me," Louis said, nudging me in the shoulder with his elbow.

Charles Bent looked directly into my eyes. I will never forget what he said. "Another genius."

Louis laughed. "He's a good French boy. Never complains. He has sailed the ocean, and now he wants to see the elephant."

William turned and walked away without a word, the fringe of his buckskins shaking like the mane of a mustang. How could I have known, at that moment, what friends William and I would become?

"I see he's brought his own provisions," Charles said, sneering at my chicken.

"He carries that fowl for the company," Louis said, "for we have struck a partnership. He owns exactly half of that chicken."

Charles Bent, in his business suit, said, "Let me have a look at your knife," speaking directly to me for the first time.

I drew the weapon and offered it to him, handle first, thankful that I had put a keen edge on it on the riverboat with a whetstone borrowed from a fellow passenger. Charles Bent frowned at the broken tip and the missing half of the handle, but raised an eyebrow approvingly when he felt the razor edge. He handed it back to me.

"Have a blacksmith file the end back into a point," he ordered. "How are you going to gut something with that thing? Get yourself a gun and you can come along. I don't guess you can ride a horse?"

I shrugged.

Charles sighed. "What do you have in the bag?" He pointed to the laundry bag slung across my shoulders.

"A couple of books," I said.

Bent looked at Louis, his very expression speaking volumes of sarcasm, as if he held less than little use for any man of letters.

"He learns quickly, Charles. I will teach him what he needs to know."

Charles Bent looked back at me, and sneered with a contempt that would take me years to understand, "Well, if you break both your legs," he said, "don't come running to me."

And with that I became an employee of the Bent, and St. Vrain Company.

⚜

Louis and I stowed our things in the shade of a wagon and walked back toward the village of Westport. In my pocket I carried Captain Robbins's money from the Stradivarius caper. I had decided to buy a pistol and a horse with this money, though I had no direct experience with either. I was, in fact, ignorant about a lot of things.

"Louis, what's a cavvy boy?" I asked.

"You'll herd the cavvy—the loose livestock that follows along with the caravan." He laughed. "I hope you'll like breathing dust like once you breathed sea spray. It's dangerous, too, so you'd better go running back to civilization with your tail between your legs if you're afraid."

"Why is it dangerous?"

"The Indians, they like to steal the livestock. Mules and horses to ride. Cattle to butcher for their feasts. You'll be apart from the caravan most of the time, and vulnerable. They'll attack the cavvy first, out of nowhere, and you'd better protect yourself, for there will be no one else about."

"I want a pistol," I said.

"Then you shall have one, of course. I know a gunsmith who barters with me. You can pay me back when you are able."

"I have some money."

Louis stopped suddenly and looked at me with the quizzical expression that made him so easy to like. "You little rapscallion," he growled, feigning anger. "You have held out on me."

We started walking again, striding along like soldiers into battle.

"This money has been earmarked for weaponry and transportation," I claimed, as if following some plan to my life. Even in my youth I was a marvelous liar.

Louis grabbed my ear. "Here is your earmark," he said, laughing as he nearly yanked my ear from my head.

I was still rubbing my ear, but grinning, when we burst into the log cabin owned by the gunsmith. The man inside looked up from a homemade wooden workbench across which were strewn bits and pieces of a Colt revolver.

Louis and the gunsmith, whom the tailor addressed only as "Joe," went through the usual frontier small talk.

"William needs a gunsmith at the fort," Louis said casually during the course of this conversation.

Joe laughed. "Git scalped and tortured? No, thanks."

"Joe, if you were meant to get killed by Indians, it would do you no good to move to New York City. You would still get killed by Indians."

"I haven't lost no Indians, and I don't see the need to go huntin' any."

"You're going to miss it all, perched right here at its doorstep."

"You go not miss it for me, will you? You and that kid there."

Louis sighed at the gunsmith's disregard for adventure. "That kid wishes to purchase a weapon," the tailor said. "Do you have a reliable revolver?"

"This one here might be if I git it fixed."

"What's wrong with it?"

"Fired off all six loads at once't. Ol' boy lost a finger. Buggered it up pretty bad."

"I need a muzzle-loading pistol," I said. "One with a ramrod."

The two men looked at me as if shocked that I could speak.

Joe got up and opened a trunk, throwing back the lid as if setting something free. "Take your pick. You can have any one for two dollars."

I looked into the trunk, finding it filled with single-shot horse pistols of all makes and calibers. Most of them were percussion weapons, but a few old flintlocks lay in the bottom. Louis helped me line out the half dozen most serviceable specimens on a wooden counter made of old wagon lumber.

"This one will be heavy to carry," the tailor said, hefting a stout pistol. "Forty-four caliber. But, it will take a charge powerful enough to pierce the lungs of a buffalo if you get close, and it is sturdy enough to use as a club."

I took the weapon from the tailor and read the inscription stamped on the rust-pitted barrel: "E. Remington and Sons, Ilion, New York." I pulled the ramrod from the sleeve under the barrel and studied it. It had a brass fitting on the end that I thought could be hollowed, or perhaps reversed on the end of the wooden dowel, or otherwise modified to retrieve a bullet from the barrel, as needed in the illusion where the magician catches the projectile. I nodded at Louis and started to leave my two dollars on the counter, but the tailor grabbed me by the arm and forced my money down and out of sight.

"Unfortunately, the lad has only one dollar to spend on such a pistol. It is a good pistol, Joe, but old. Look at the rust!"

"You don't like the rust, pick another one. Two dollars."

"Would you send a lad to the wilderness without a gun?"

"Would you send me to the poor farm? Two dollars, Louis. Take it or leave it. Besides, I ain't sendin' the damn kid anywheres. Ought to send him back to his mama."

"Ah, Joe, Joe, Joe," the tailor lamented. "You must need something mended. Perhaps a scabbard made for a knife you wish to sell. Two dollars for such a pistol? There is a chunk of wood missing from the grip!"

By now I had had time to look all about the gun shop and had noticed that Joe also sold knives in addition to firearms. And, in the corner, I spied an old dragoon saber, much like the blade I had used to kill Segarelli, leaning against the overlapping notched log ends of the cabin.

"Well, I got a pair of britches ripped," Joe said.

"A dollar and the mending, then, for the pistol."

"Lord, you're a tight Frenchman. Dollar-fifty, Louis. Man's gotta eat."

Before Louis could counter, I boldly slapped my two dollars down on the old wagon lumber. "Two dollars for the pistol and that sword there in the corner," I said.

Both men looked at me, then at the saber.

"And the britches?" Joe said.

Louis rolled his eyes and threw his hands in the air. "Joe, Joe, Joe, you make a hard bargain. All right, and the mending, then. You get the upper hand every time. Always, I leave here shaking my head. How can a man make such deals?"

Joe was so impressed by this tirade that he threw in a tin flask full of gunpowder, a handful of bullets, and a pouch containing several percussion caps. And, of course, he fetched and handed over the torn trousers. As we walked back toward the caravan, I tucked my new pistol under my belt, and then tested the heft and balance of my new saber by jabbing it about as if in a fencing match.

"Don't go flashing that thing about like that," Louis said. "Someone will think you're begging a fight, and there are no end to the misfits who will oblige you here."

"Louis, will you make a scabbard for this saber?" I asked. "One that will match my knife sheath?"

"Ah, but now I know you are a wealthy little urchin. It will cost you six bits."

I walked on silently for a few steps, then said, "Five bits, and no more."

Louis Lescot stopped in his tracks, doubled over, slapped his palms against his knees, and laughed until his eyes sparkled with tears. "How green! Multiples of two, Honoré! There's no such thing as one bit! For one as innocent as you, I will charge only four bits—one half dollar."

We made it back to the caravan in time to fill our stomachs with fried beef, eggs, potatoes, and sourdough biscuits. This was my first taste of frontier camp cooking, and it suited me like nothing I had ever consumed. It far surpassed the meager helpings rationed aboard the *Dover Star* and attempted no culinary pretenses like the fare at Saint-Cyr, with its asparagus sprouts and cold soup. I had almost starved aboard the Mississippi River steamer, and had taken in only a couple of fleeting meals with Louis, as he had seemed in a great hurry to meet the caravan. Now, I found myself devouring great heaps of fried things, buttered, salted, and peppered beyond reason. Along with the grub, the Bent–St. Vrain cook served coffee so strong that he claimed it would "float a saddle blanket."

After "dinner," as the frontiersmen called the midday meal, Louis took me beyond the caravan to show me how to use my new pistol. A pack of dogs followed us part of the way, hoping for handouts. I tossed the smallest one a half biscuit while the larger dogs weren't watching. We passed a band of Mexican muleteers coaxing the third member of a four-mule team into harness. All the beasts heaved in fear and fatigue, for Louis told me they had been tied without food or water for a day, to weaken them into submitting to this ordeal so foreign to them. As I watched, the third mule went suddenly wild at the touch of a trace chain along his flank and reared up over the mule beside him, sending the other animals into fits of panic. Through all this, the muleteers stood just beyond the reach of hooves and teeth and struggled to gain control of the beasts. At least at that moment, I was glad I was a cavvy boy instead of a muleteer.

Walking far enough away to keep from frightening some skittish mule or horse, Louis found a creek bank suitable for a pistol range. He placed one of my lead pistol balls in the palm of his hand and poured gunpowder over it slowly until the ball was covered with a cone of powder.

"This is the rule of thumb, Honoré. Cover the ball with powder. In time, you will learn to judge this amount without having to go through this little exercise, and can just pour the powder directly into the muzzle; but for now it is a good way to train yourself."

He removed the bullet from the pile of powder, and poured the powder carefully from his palm into the muzzle. Now he produced a small square of linen cloth from a pouch on his belt, placed it over the muzzle, and pushed the bullet down on top of it, forcing the linen patch into the barrel, and holding both linen and bullet there tightly.

This concerned me, because my book on illusions had said nothing about cloth patches. "I thought a wad of *paper* was supposed to hold the bullet in," I said.

"That's one way, but where are you going to find paper in the wilderness? The temptation to use it in starting fires is too great, and soon it is all burned up. These oiled linen patches are easier to carry, and if you run out, you can use patches made from rabbit or squirrel skins." While he was explaining this, he used the ramrod to force the patched bullet down the barrel, seating it firmly on the powder.

"But, a fellow could use paper wadding if he wanted to, couldn't he? I mean, he wouldn't be thought of as peculiar, would he?"

"Not peculiar, just green. Now, pay attention, Honoré. You must make certain the bullet is seated. If there is space between the powder and the bullet, the whole gun blows up in your face." He showed me how to make sure the bullet was seated firmly. Drop the ramrod down into the barrel. If it bounces when it hits, the bullet is seated firmly. If not, there is that dangerous bit of space between the powder and the bullet.

Louis went on to show me how to place the percussion

cap on the nipple where the hammer would fall on it, how to cock and aim the gun, and how to fire it. He then watched me reload the pistol, and had me shoot at a rotten log across the creek bank. I missed with the first shot, and was surprised by the recoil of the pistol bucking in my grasp; but it allowed my powers of visual observation and my meticulous thought processes the chance to calculate exactly how my weapon aimed and hit home. My next two bullets smashed into the middle of the log and sent wood chips flying.

"Bravo!" Louis cried each time. "Now listen carefully. You know how to shoot the pistol now, but there is something more important."

"What's that?"

"Knowing when *not* to shoot. Even with much practice, how long do you think it will take you to reload that pistol?"

"I don't know. Ten seconds?"

"Ha! Perhaps twenty, with luck. Do you know how many arrows an Indian can shoot into you in twenty seconds?"

"No," I admitted, "but I assume even one might prove fatal."

"Only if the Indian intends it to be fatal. He might prefer to wound you so he can drag you home for his squaw to torture over a slow-burning fire. This is not just idle talk, Honoré. The savages know ways both wonderful and horrible. Do not let yourself be surrounded by the warriors of a hostile tribe. And if you do, you must save your one bullet. They will harass you, just out of range, trying to get you to spend that shot. Yet they are not fools. No one of them will rush upon you only to die with a bullet in his brain, just so his comrades can kill you. They have been known to taunt a man for hours, but you must hold your fire. It is better to use that bullet on yourself than on any one of them."

Louis was looking at me with an expression so earnest that it seemed to suggest more than a hypothetical acquaintance with the subject. "Has this ever happened to you?" I asked.

"Yes," he said, "it has. I went fishing some miles from Bent's Fort one day. Foolishly, I went alone. Returning from

my outing with a stringer of fish, I happened to cross paths
with three young Comanches. I suppose they were looking
for Utes or Cheyennes to scalp, but they found me. In an
instant they surrounded me. I dismounted, got my back
against a cottonwood, and cocked my pistol, keeping them
at bay for three hours. Luckily, a band of trappers happened
along, and I hailed them. The Indians fled, but I will never
forget how terrified I was for those three hours. Had I pan-
icked and fired my pistol, I would not be here to tell the tale.
Unless Colt can improve his revolver and make it more reliable, a man in the wilderness must save his bullet to the last
possible instant. That sword you are wearing will be useless
against Indian arrows."

The next question seemed so obvious to me that I almost
didn't want to make a fool of myself by asking, for I thought
I must certainly have missed something. "Why don't you
learn to shoot a bow and arrow like the Indians?"

Louis looked at me curiously, glanced about as if for an
answer, then snorted. "Find an Indian who will teach you.
It is more than just a skill to them. They attribute great
medicine to the making and care of the bow and arrows.
They won't share it with a white man. Anyway, they make
it look easier than it is. They learn from childhood, and they
practice all the time."

I didn't want to belabor the question with my only mentor, but the archer's skill didn't seem so mysterious and
complicated to me. I knew one thing for certain. I was going
to learn to shoot a bow and arrow. Aside from being the
only logical course for self-defense, it seemed that it might
also be fun.

As we walked back to the Bent and St. Vrain caravan,
Louis asked if I had ever ridden a wild western horse before.

"No, but I've gone aloft to douse the topgallant in a gale."

After a moment of reflection, the tailor replied, "A fair
comparison."

For the next three days, I watched, worked, listened, and
learned. I slept under a wagon anytime I wanted to. I seemed
honor bound to report to no one. While I slumbered an hour
here, or two there, no one bothered me, with the exception
of the little dog to whom I had thrown a scrap of biscuit
the day I shot my first pistol ball. He would curl himself
near my ankles, and seemed to respect me too much to stick
his nose in my face. I began to make a habit of saving scraps
for him, and he began to stay within earshot of me at all
times. I named him Jibber, for he reminded me of my former
companion aboard the *Dover Star*. He was mostly terrier, I
believe, with coarse hair that stuck out everywhere. He was
white except for a misshapen brown spot on his rump.

Anyway, this life of the Santa Fe caravan seemed to lend
itself to my peculiar needs for sleep, for I could catch a few
winks whenever I wanted, so long as I made myself conspicuously industrious for the good of Bent and St. Vrain
at all other times. Accordingly, I spent much time loading
freight wagons with all sorts of goods bound for Santa Fe.
I helped the freighters pack this merchandise with the same
painstaking deliberation the longshoremen had used loading
crates and boxes aboard the *Dover Star,* for the trail to Santa
Fe would cover more than 700 rough miles, and the merchants could not have their goods shifting about in the wagons.

When I wasn't loading wagons, I was mending harnesses
or wagon sheets with Louis, or cleaning skillets and Dutch
ovens with the cook, or greasing axles with the bullwhackers. Once a day, Louis and I would walk down to the creek
for more marksmanship lessons. He would bring along a
Hawken rifle so I could learn to use a long arm as well as
a handgun. I soon became a better marksman than Louis,
though the tailor claimed no particular genius with a gun.

To me, the art of marksmanship provided a study in
minute degrees of mathematical computations involving trajectory, windage, gravity, cause and effect, action and re-
action. This understanding, coupled with my gifts of muscle

control, concentration, and keen eyesight, made me a marvelous hand with a firearm.

My little dog Jibber didn't like the noise of the guns, and would wait on top of the creek bank until Louis and I had finished our practice. Then he would rejoin us for the walk back to camp, his tail wagging in time with his diminutive steps. Jibber was the first pet I ever owned, and a bond formed between us the likes of which I had never before conceived. His antics made me laugh, his fearlessness toward larger dogs filled me with admiration, and his loyalty toward me touched my cold, calculating heart to the point that I felt almost human.

With the Bent and St. Vrain caravan, I was getting more rest than I had ever managed in my life, for no one accused me of sloth or indolence for indulging in a nap, nor did anyone attempt to deprive me of the pleasure. While awake, I was never bored, for I had many practical things to learn. I was eating like a ravenous wolf, and felt healthier than a mule.

And, yet there was an impatience seething beneath my contentedness. I sensed that this caravan wanted to go westward, as if it were, itself, a living thing that felt an uncontrollable urge to migrate with the coming of spring. I was a part of this living caravan now, and I yearned to make it move, like a muscle in its belly that would cause it to crawl, snakelike, toward a mysterious destination. I found myself looking west sometimes and wondering. . . . Something called. Something awful and wonderful. Something hidden beyond the campfire smoke, the dust, the mist, and the veils of riverbank timber. I had felt this call come and go before, across the ocean, but now it tugged relentlessly, like the song of the siren of the southern plains. Had I only known the agonies into which this song would entice me, I would have fled back to St. Louis to become a store clerk. Had I but known the splendors it would reveal to me, I would have charged recklessly ahead of the languishing caravan, right into doom or destiny.

But now I am monopolizing this exchange. Certainly you,

too, have heard your own call from places far and times to come. Did you answer the call? Might you answer it yet? Think about it, and share. I would like to know. And when you have had your say, I will tell you about Fireball the Half-Blind.

SEVEN

The first time I saw Fireball, I admit that I thought none too highly of him. Tufted all over with a shedding coat of coarse winter hair, he looked like the unfortunate result of an impossible mating between a black sheep and a buckskin nightmare. He stood perhaps fourteen hands at his withers. His hocks turned in like a cow's. His knees seemed about to buckle outward. He had no fewer than seven different brands burned into his hide, including one ornate configuration of Spanish origin. His left ear was split from the tip, about halfway down to the base.

"The owner wants fifteen dollars," Louis said, "but of course that is ludicrous. He can be had for five."

I walked dejectedly around to Fireball's off side and noticed his right eye clouded over like some gypsy's gazing ball. "He's blind on this side," I groaned.

Louis leaned forward and squinted, as if he hadn't noticed. "So he is. He has half as much trouble to look for."

"Why is he so fat?"

"He's been well fed on winter hay and spring grass. He'll burn that grass belly off by the time we reach Council Grove. I've been told he's remarkably fleet."

I laughed involuntarily as I walked wide around his rump. I had little experience with horses, but knew they could kick.

"He'll never kick in a million years," Louis said, grabbing

Fireball by the tail and pulling it to make a point of the beast's docility.

Fireball merely craned his neck to get a look at the tailor with his good eye.

"What happened to his ear?"

"Ah, that is a good sign. This horse was captured by a Mexican soldier after a battle with Comanches. The Comanches split the ears of their best ponies so that they can locate their finest mounts by touch even on the darkest night. A Comanche pony with a split ear is truly a fine animal, for the Comanche are the greatest of horsemen."

"Maybe somebody just split his ear to fool us."

"Honoré, your mind is devious to think of such things. He's a good pony."

"He looks tired and lazy to me."

"He is a proven mount, Honoré. Twice he has been to Santa Fe and back. He will know the trail where you do not."

I threw up my arms in stubborn consternation. "You don't really expect me to ride this thing, do you?"

Louis looked at me harshly, as if insulted. *"Oui. Pourquoi pas?"*

"Why not? Because . . ." I looked across the grounds and spotted a sleek black steed tied to a stake driven into the dirt, prancing about his tether like royalty. "Because I want to ride something like that black horse. I do not care to be the object of ridicule."

"That black, there?" Louis said, following my gaze of admiration. "Well, then, if that's the sort of horse you like, why didn't you say so?" He dropped Fireball's lead rope on the ground and the little hay burner just stood there. Louis motioned for me to follow, and marched off in the direction of the horse trader who owned the black, and several other mounts for sale, including Fireball the Half-Blind.

The horse trader's name was Thomas Boggs. He was a young man of twenty-five, built like a bulldog, with a glint of intelligence in his eyes. In spite of his youth, he possessed much trail experience. Later, I would learn that he was a great-grandson of the legendary Daniel Boone, and that he would marry Charles Bent's stepdaughter as soon as he reached the village of San Fernando de Taos in New Mexico. But for now, I knew him only as a horse trader.

Within a minute or two, Louis had explained to Thomas Boggs that I wished to purchase the black, but wanted to ride him first. Boggs looked at me, then at the little terrier at my feet, then at the black. He grinned, and pulled an old saddle from the back of a buckboard wagon.

When the black saw the saddle coming, I knew from the way he lunged and twisted violently at the end of his rope that I had made a rash mistake. The tailor and the horse trader had to dodge flailing forefeet just to get hold of the black's halter. The excitement attracted Jibber's fighting spirit, and he leapt into the fray and began snapping at hooves. The horse snorted and fought like a crazed and cornered beast, but the two men managed to hold its head still long enough to tie a handkerchief around its eyes as a blindfold.

Still, the skittish steed trembled and kicked at the saddle rigging that tickled his flanks. Louis looked back at me as Boggs reached cautiously under the heaving barrel of the bronco to catch the girth dangling on the off side.

"Are you sure you want to test this beast?" the tailor asked, with a wry smile and a devious glint in his eye.

It was plain that I had allowed myself to be led foolishly into this trap, but I sensed instinctively that I would suffer much scorn and ridicule if I did not at least attempt to ride that black beast. "Yes." I looked at my bold little terrier for inspiration, for the dog was still darting and snapping at those deadly hooves. "I'm no more afraid of him than Jibber is."

Boggs laughed as he tightened the cinch around the prancing pony. "Jibber don't gotta ride him."

In a minute, Boggs had found an old bridle with a tremendous spade bit that he forced into the black's mouth, buckling the headstall tight behind the pony's ears.

Louis motioned me into position. "Mind the hind hooves

as you mount," he said. "The bloody bastard can rake you right out of the stirrup if you swing too far aft."

Vaguely, I appreciated Louis's usage of the familiar nautical term for my benefit. I was charged so completely with horrific anticipation that I actually lifted the wrong foot to put it into the stirrup.

"Other foot," Louis groaned. "You don't want to mount backward, do you?"

"Ain't gonna make no difference," Boggs chuckled.

When I mounted the black—the first horse of any kind I had ever straddled—a long, rattling snort rolled from his nostrils. Louis handed me the reins. The grinning horse trader reached for the blindfold.

"Try to keep his head up," Louis advised.

"And try to keep him from kickin' yours off your neck," said Boggs as he whisked away the blindfold, turned tail, and ran.

With the possible exception of Nicole, I had never before experienced such a sudden rush of excitement between my legs. At the risk of belaboring the metaphor, I must confess, in fact, that my attempt to stay aboard the black didn't last much longer than my first ride with Nicole.

The beast twisted in an instant and powerful contortion that blurred the scenery around me. Suddenly I was simply sailing through the air, quite harmlessly at first, until the bronco jerked the slack out of the right stirrup leather. As my right foot was still in the stirrup, the yank wheeled me face-first into the sandy ground the black had pawed bare. My face slammed into the dirt. I heard my nose break and felt a wave of pain engulf my whole head. Then I tasted dirt and blood. Vaguely, I heard laughter and hoots and hooves pounding the ground. I sat up and blinked away enough dirt to see that I had narrowly missed jobbing an eye out on the stake pin to which the black had been tethered. Jibber trotted up and sniffed the blood on my face. Louis was holding the horse, who was still bucking at the end of the long stake rope.

The laughing horse trader grabbed my hand and helped

me to my feet. "I'll give you one thing, kid. You sure got sand in your craw!"

I coughed and spit out enough dirt to speak, then replied, "I'll give you five dollars for Fireball."

"I ought'n to take no less than ten, but, hell, the show was worth five!"

With that, I became the owner of Fireball the Half-Blind. I bought the horse trader's saddle for a dollar and could be seen for the next several days, practicing newly acquired riding skills with two black eyes and a nose swollen as big as Jibber's.

For a few days, the muscles on the insides of my thighs ached with every step; but after Fireball got me trained to ride, I would spend so much of my life on horseback that I would never again become saddle sore. For the next seventy-seven years, I would straddle some form of equine almost daily. I am ninety-nine now, and haven't ridden in six years. The pounding of the saddle simply became too jarring for my old bones. But, between the ages of sixteen and ninety-three, I put in enough miles horseback to circle the globe more than six times. That is no idle estimate. I kept a running tally quite accurately in my head.

EIGHT

The day began with specks of light strewn across a dark blanket, as if the Big Dipper had spilled an impossible infinity of stars as it turned over slowly in the sky. I watched the movements of the constellations all night. I was unable to sleep for the anticipation.

The call of "All rise," from the husky voice of Charles Bent himself, virtually rocketed me from my blankets. The cook defied me to walk upwind of his fires and vessels, as

I started the line and got an ample breakfast slapped onto my plate.

The east was just beginning to glow a cool shade of cobalt when the Mexican muleteers roped the first beast from the nearby corrals owned by William Bent. I had studied this artistic and practical business of snaring animals with a thrown noose, and had found an old Mexican muleteer agreeable to teaching me a few of the many throws he was able to make. He seemed surprised that I could speak Spanish, though he ridiculed my Castilian accent, especially the lisping sound my Castilian Spanish instructor had drilled into my head at that awful place of long ago and far away—Saint-Cyr.

"Don Turo!" I shouted to the old man as he chose a mule from the herd in the corral. His name was Arturo, but he liked the nickname. "Allow me to make a throw at one!" I suggested as I climbed up on the corral rails.

"*P'alla!*" he growled, sending me away. "This is business now, boy. No time to practice."

Dejected, I climbed down from the corral rails, and happened to spy a familiar character riding by on a good horse. The man carried a long double-barreled shotgun across his thighs. It was Joe, the gunsmith.

"Godspeed, boy," he said. "You'll need it out there. Keep that pistol you bought from me handy, you hear?"

"I hear you," I said. "Where are you going?"

"Doin' a little huntin' up the trail before your damn caravan spooks all the game away. It's turkey gobblin' time. Farewell, boy. Mind the Injuns!"

I waved at Joe and watched him ride away.

I gathered that my cavvy-boy duties wouldn't begin until the caravan actually moved, though no one had detailed my tasks to me. I went back to the wagons, helped the cook clean up, and watched the men hitch animals.

There were six huge Bent–St. Vrain wagons, two pulled by mule teams, and four drawn by yokes of oxen. I had been told that this was a small caravan compared to the twenty-odd wagons that often made the trip in years of booming international trade. All the mules had been in harness three or four times by now, but some still rebelled, and the curses and tangles that resulted were almost comical. I heard the Mexican muleteers growl many words strange to my ear, and took them for profanities.

The oxen lumbered into place with much less difficulty, six yokes per wagon. Most of the bullwhackers who drove these beasts were of American or French-Canadian ancestry. Generally I could differentiate between the two at a glance, for the Americans preferred clothes that were drab in appearance compared to the colorful calicos of the Canadians. All of them used long whips fastened to the tops of tall poles, and could make them crack like the report of my cap-and-ball pistol. With these they could literally flick a fly from the rump of an ox. They could just as easily cut an ear from the head of a hatless man.

The sun shot orange beams through distant treetops as the last of the surplus animals were herded out of pens and corrals. I had cinched my old saddle around Fireball's barrel by now, and swung handily into the seat to begin gathering the stray herd—a thing strange to me, but seemingly simple enough to accomplish. Jibber ran circles of joy when I mounted, for he loved to trot alongside Fireball.

A veteran of this trail, Fireball knew what was happening. He pranced with enough excitement to steel my nerves against some impending wreck. He had seemed so lethargic for the past several days that now his snorting and head tossing made me respect Louis' claim that Fireball possessed impressive speed.

I saw Louis climbing up onto the second wagon in the caravan. I rode toward him to gather last-minute instructions before our string of wagons began to move, and Charles Bent rode by the other side of the wagon about the time I got there.

"Louis, let's go," Charles said. He slurred it in such a way that the suggestion came out sounding like the French tailor's name: Louis Lescot.

Louis laughed loudly at the pun, then saw me. "What are

you doing here?" he demanded. "Get to the rear and keep the cavvy bunched. Don't push them too hard; they will follow the caravan."

Too hard? How hard was too hard? I had never herded so much as a flock of chickens.

About that time, Charles Bent's voice boomed: "Stretch out!"

<hr />

I swear Fireball knew the meaning of the command, for he all but bolted toward the head of the caravan, the opposite way I needed to go. I pulled hard on one rein and got him turned, but I had to hold tightly to keep him from running headlong. I made my way toward the rear of the caravan, saw the loose animals milling. One extra mule was heading back toward the corrals, so I swung around the beast to turn it back to the cavvy. My maneuver worked. The mule rejoined the other beasts and my heart swelled at a job so well accomplished. Fireball was still huffing and slinging his head, but I held him. The power I felt through those reins reminded me of the line I had held atop the mizzenmast of the *Dover Star,* when I gathered in all the great energy of the winds of the world through a tangled topgallant. Now those winds seemed to surge within Fireball, stoking him to white-hot heat. I felt like the novice horseman I was, barely managing to control my steed.

Then the bullwhackers' whips began to crack, and Fireball lunged out of control. He stormed right into the cavvy, scattering oxen, mules, and horses. I ordered him to halt in three different languages, then tried a few of the Mexican profanities I had heard, though I had yet to learn their definitions. Nothing worked. Animals stampeded everywhere, including the two teams of mules pulling the first two wagons.

After a run of a quarter mile or more, Thomas Boggs, the horse-trader, overhauled me on his sleek black bronco. "Stop spurrin' him!" he ordered.

This confused me for a mere second because I had never worn spurs in my life. Then I realized that in my panic I was nervously clenching Fireball so tightly with my heels that he took it for a signal to charge forward. At the same time, I was pulling on the reins, confusing him and quite probably enraging him with my ignorance. I relaxed my legs, and immediately my mount began to slow down. I reined him to a stop, but he continued to sling his head and acted as if he would rear and fall over backward on me.

"Give him rein!" Tom bellowed.

I did, and Fireball finally stopped fighting me.

"Goddamn, don't tell him stop and go all at once!"

The horse trader peeled back toward the rear and began gathering the beasts I had scattered. Men on horseback had managed to restrain the runaway mule teams. I circled around, keeping the scattered cavvy in view on the side of Fireball's good eye, and taking great care not to send any more mixed signals. When I saw William Bent's scowl from the back of a buckskin Indian pony, I almost wished that I had gone blind on that side, like my horse.

Things went smoothly the rest of the day, or seemed to from my point of view. One wagon got mired in mud while crossing a creek, and required two teams of oxen to extricate it. All I had to do was keep the grazing cavvy gathered as I watched the laborious process of unhitching the oxen from one wagon, hitching it in front of the other team, and driving the beasts at the ends of whips.

Motion was the thing of highest import. With every plodding step, I eased farther away from apprehension by the bounty hunters I fancied on my trail, in earnest pursuit of the price on my head for the murder of Segarelli. I will not brood on the remorse and horror I felt for having taken another man's life—even a man like Segarelli. Especially in such a cowardly fashion—running him through while he lay in a drunken stupor. I will not brood on it now, but I did then. No matter how many times I reminded myself that I had been forced to kill Segarelli to protect Nicole and defend her honor, I still felt like a cowardly murderer. The motion of the caravan helped ease this guilt. I was moving ever farther away from Saint-Cyr. I suppose I had some misconception that I could somehow leave Saint-Cyr behind. I could not. It is with me even now. Can a man run from himself? He can try. In the end, he must face himself and all he has done. But enough of that.

Toward noon, the caravan stopped to prepare a meal and to rest the animals. Scarcely had the cook fires flared when Blackfoot Smith called out from the woods nearby the stopping place. Blackfoot was one of the hunters for the caravan, and had gone looking for game signs.

"William!" he shouted. "Better come look!"

Both Charles and William Bent grabbed their rifles and trotted toward the woods. Louis Lescot fell in behind them, as did I and some others. The old trapper-turned hunter was standing among some trees and the edge of the woods, looking at something on the ground.

The Bents got there first.

"Oh, God . . ." Charles's voice trailed off.

Louis was in front of me when he stopped suddenly in his tracks. I stepped around the tailor and saw a man's body on the ground. I took a moment gathering the horror of it. Then I groaned involuntarily and stared stupidly, unable to tear my eyes away. It was Joe, the gunsmith. Three arrows protruded from his chest. His throat gaped grotesquely where some blade had slashed it. Blood stained his skin, his clothes, the grass, the ground. The top of his head looked as if it had been torn away by a beast.

Charles Bent looked at Blackfoot John Smith. "Ride back to the settlements and tell somebody, John. We'll wrap him in a blanket and leave him by the trail where they can find him. Tell them to come quick, before the wolves get him."

Blackfoot nodded and turned back toward the caravan.

Charles spoke to his brother, William, who was studying the arrow shafts. "Pawnee?"

"Naw," William said, "looks like some half-breed Delawares maybe. Probably comin' off a drunk and stumbled on ol' Joe."

Louis pushed me away. "Go get an old blanket or something," he said.

I remembered well what Louis had told the gunsmith in his shop. If it was his destiny to get killed by Indians, he would be killed by Indians even if he moved to New York City. I also remember the last words Joe had spoken to me that very morning: "Farewell, boy. Mind the Injuns."

A daily ritual soon became ingrained in my personal routine as the days toiled on, usually at the rate of no more than twelve miles from sunrise to sunset. We would rise before dawn, eat a cold biscuit, hitch the beasts, and start. With the sun five hours in the sky, we would stop, unhitch the beasts, and let them graze. Now we ate a light meal they called breakfast, made various repairs, accomplished sundry chores, and rested into the afternoon. Our main meal of the day came next, consisting of fresh meat killed by one of the hunters, fresh-baked bread, and perhaps a roasted ear of corn. Then we would hitch up, stretch out, and drive westward until we fetched the next campground, usually right at dusk, for Charles Bent had made scores of trips across the plains, and knew how to time our arrivals with relative precision. He was as awed and respected on this trail as the rare sea captain who had crossed the Atlantic one hundred times.

The campgrounds were fixed and recognized sites established through twenty years of merchandising on the Santa Fe Trail. Arriving at camp, we would circle the wagons, with the tongue of each vehicle slanting outward and the front wheels of one wagon pulling abreast of the rear wheels of the one in front of it. This done, the teamsters turned their animals loose to graze.

The caravan crew soon came to realize my peculiar sleep habits. As cavvy boy, my duty was to guard the herds all day. At night, I slept if I could. But many nights, I knew the futility of my attempts to sleep, so I would wander out and relieve one of the night guards. The night guards had to stay with the herds all night, and would sleep in a swaying wagon by day, so they appreciated the occasional chance to sleep on the quiet ground in the dark.

On the seventh day of the journey, I fell asleep in the saddle, presumably for several miles. Apparently, Fireball knew his job well enough to keep the cavvy bunched and moving, along with some help from Jibber, who liked to nip at the heels of any beast that strayed from the herd. It was Jibber's barking that woke me from my trance. He was urging a lame ox back into the herd after it had attempted to stop. To prevent the monotony from lulling me to sleep again, I borrowed a lariat from my friend, old Don Turo, and began practicing throws from Fireball's saddle. I didn't realize it at the time, for I was still ignorant to horsemanship, but Fireball had obviously had ropes thrown from his back before. A horse untrained to the skills of the roper will twist off like a dust devil in mortal terror of a thing as strange as a noose whirling above and around his head. Fireball seemed completely unconcerned.

The crew of the caravan included a Mexican guitarist and a Missouri banjo player. At night, they would entertain themselves and others for an hour or so with songs from their homelands. At Council Grove, eleven days on the trail, I finally revealed my violin from my possibles sack. When I carried it into the firelight where the other two musicians were plucking and strumming away, the dozen or so listeners (they numbered fifteen to be precise, but I don't wish to belabor my facility to remember every minute detail) looked at me as if the violin were growing out of my head.

I had heard some fiddling around the camps of Westport, and had committed three of the tunes to memory: "Cripple Creek," "Chicken Reel," and "Boil Them Cabbages Down." I had never played them before, but I have already explained how music can flow into my ears, through my brain, and escape via my fingers. Soon the crowd of listeners had about tripled. Even Charles and William Bent came to listen. Charles smiled with appreciation of the music, but William scowled suspiciously. When I ran out of American fiddle tunes, I played a couple of hornpipes I had learned aboard the *Dover Star*. Charles Bent then ordered me to play one more song on the violin, so the crew could turn in. The first thing that came to my mind was "The Rose of Avenmore." Louis Lescot actually wept when I played it, and William Bent's scowl turned to a look of amazement.

The next day, I expected someone to grill me about my knowledge of music. No one ever said a word. This, I would later gather through long experience, was the code of the frontier. I was not the only fugitive to have gone west on the Santa Fe Trail. You didn't ask a man whence he hailed. If he wanted to tell you, he would. Otherwise, you were better off not knowing. Often, your very life depended on your ignorance.

NINE

I slept a whole day at Council Grove, where Charles Bent called a halt for rest and repairs. The night herders watched the herd for me by day. It was strange how everyone in the caravan seemed to sense my fatigue and make allowances for my day of indolence. They covered for me. It felt good. I knew they did it more for the good of the caravan than for me, but it still felt good, for I was a part of the caravan.

After I awoke and wolfed down a huge breakfast, Louis Lescot nudged me and said, "Come along." In one hand, he carried a saw. With the other, he handed me an axe. Intrigued, I went with him, Jibber padding happily at my heels. We walked from the circle of wagons, down a trail, and into a dense and beautiful grove of large trees. A stream ran among the roots of the largest trees, and sunlight flashed on spring green leaves that twisted in the breeze.

"Do you know what kind of trees these are?" Louis asked.

I admitted that I did not. Though I possessed a fair understanding of botany, my field-identification skills were woefully lacking.

"Hickory. The last we will see. The Indians make good bows from hickory, but they can't get it west of this grove. If you will help me cut a few limbs suitable for the bows, we will strike a partnership and enter into the Indian trade.

"That suits me fine." My face beamed as I fancied myself an Indian trader. We spent most of the day chopping, sawing, resting, talking, and stacking our raw product in one of the Bent–St. Vrain wagons.

The next day I spent greasing wagon wheels. We had long poles that we used as levers to lift each wheel from the ground. This required the weight of several men piling onto the pole. I didn't weigh much, so I was on the crew that removed the wheel, applied the grease, then replaced the wheel. This took us almost all day.

We left Council Grove the next day. The old hands wore somber expressions on their faces, as if the travails of the journey really began here, rather than back in Westport. This proved the case. Things got hard.

It started with rain, mud, and cold. Men, beasts, and wagons slogged through quagmires of oozing slop. One of the Mexicans gave me a wool poncho—a blanket with a hole in the middle through which I stuck my head. This turned some of the rain and kept me somewhat warm, but could not prevent a drenching that would last for days.

At the Little Arkansas, we had to halt the caravan and wait for the floodwaters in the stream to recede. The sun finally broke through, but the stream was still running fast when we plunged into it. I thought Charles Bent had lost his mind, that the wagons would be swept downstream and lost. Each of the big vessels floated, and the oxen and mules had to swim; but each made the crossing in tact.

The fifth wagon held my Stradivarius and all the hickory limbs Louis and I had cut for trade. My heart sank as I watched the wagon carry my total net worth into the swollen

river. I had tied the violin up high and had managed to keep
it dry throughout the rainstorm, but I feared all my fretting
would go for nothing as the wagon began to list in the current. But the bullwhackers doubled their oaths at their
beasts, righted the big trade vessel, and pulled it to the western shore.

Then came my turn to cross. The prospect frightened me
even more than the idea of being thrown into the ocean by
the crew of the Dover Star. Luckily, William Bent swam
his pony back over to my side to help me with the cavvy.

"Ever swim a horse?" he asked. These were the first
words William had ever spoken directly to me.

"No, sir."

"That horse knows what he's doin'. When he gets in, take
your feet out of the stirrups, hold the horn, and give him
his head. Just float alongside of him. Don't try to help him.
He doesn't need your help."

"Yes, sir," I said.

Some of the loose animals attempted to bolt upstream
rather than swim, and I had to go after them. Turning them
into the Little Arkansas, I had to enter the water behind them
where the bank was steep. Fireball slipped and slid in behind
the herd, but maintained his balance. He hit the edge of the
water with a splash, went under almost to his head, then
began to swim, forcing great blasts of air from his nostrils.

I did as William had instructed as the frigid water surged
quickly up to my face, making me gasp in protest to the
cold and danger. In spite of my swimming lessons aboard
the Dover Star, I knew that the current and my clothing
would drag me under in a second if something went wrong.

My sole morsel of confidence came from Fireball. He
stroked powerfully for the opposite shore as I clung to the
saddle horn with a steel grip. Halfway across, I knew we
would make it. I just knew. I began thinking about what I
would do when Fireball found his footing again. Get your
scrawny ass in front of the cantle, I thought. Find your stirrups. This I managed to do.

William Bent rode by me as Fireball caught his breath on

the western shore. "Good," William said without looking at me. This was my first glimpse of friendship from a man whose compassion, courage, and wisdom would overwhelm me many times in the years to come. But for now, I was just beginning to gather, from talk throughout the caravan, the impact the Bent brothers had made on the frontier.

That night, in camp, I asked Louis about the Bent brothers. By now they had earned my admiration, and I wanted to earn theirs in return. Louis must have sensed this, for he told me in some detail about his employers' history as we tried to dry out near a roaring fire:

"Charles made his first trip to Santa Fe some twenty years ago, when the trade between Mexico and Missouri had only begun. William soon joined him in the enterprise. They took a man named Ceran St. Vrain as their partner, and still maintain the partnership. The firm of Bent–St. Vrain has evolved into two divisions: trade with Mexico, and trade with the Indians. Charles developed the trade with Mexico through the markets at Santa Fe and Taos. He married a señorita and lives now in Taos. Ceran St. Vrain also took a Mexican wife, and lives in Taos, too. Charles spends most of his time freighting goods back and forth between New Mexico and Missouri. Ceran manages the company's retail stores in Taos and Santa Fe."

"And William?" I asked, fetching a coal from the fire so my friend, the tailor, could light his pipe.

"While Charles and Ceran were establishing the Mexican trade, William developed ties with the tribes of the plains and mountains. He oversaw the construction of Bent's Fort, which took no less than three years. The fort is sometimes call Fort William because of this. He married a Cheyenne squaw and has become an adopted member of that tribe."

"William must live in constant danger at the fort," I said, listening to Jibber crack an antelope bone he had found somewhere.

"Not at all. The fort has never been seriously threatened. It is a strong post; but, more importantly, William has much influence over the Indians. They respect him. A few sum-

mers ago, he managed to forge a treaty between the tribes
north and south of the Arkansas, and so he has brought
relative peace to the southern plains."

"Which tribes were at war?" I asked.

"The Cheyennes and their allies, the Arapaho, to the north
of the river were at war with the Comanches, and their allies,
the Kiowa, to the south. But since the treaty, even the Comanches have carried out some trade with Bent–St. Vrain,
though they are very troublesome."

"Troublesome?" I asked, leaning closer, so as not to miss
anything. I had been yearning to hear something of Comanches since the day in Paris, when I saw the Catlin portrait.

"They like to kill and scalp people. Four years ago, they
got Robert Bent, William's and Charles's younger brother.
He was only twenty-five. He strayed from the caravan on
the way to Santa Fe."

"And yet, Bent's Fort is safe?"

"Relatively. A man must watch his own back, of course.
I fear more for the safety of Charles and Ceran in Taos, than
for William's scalp or my own at Bent's Fort."

"In Taos? Why?"

"The trouble with Texas."

"I don't know about much of that. Only bits and pieces
I've read in newspapers, or overheard from conversations. I
know Texas is a republic that won its independence from
Mexico nine years ago."

"Yes, and there has been skirmishing between the Texans
and the Mexicans ever since. Those crazy damn Texans
think they own Santa Fe! They think their damn republic
extends all the way to the headwaters of the Rio Bravo.
They have even sent military expeditions across the Comanche country to conquer New Mexico; but, of course,
they have failed. Now they have a new strategy."

"What is that?"

"They attack the Mexican caravans on the trail to Missouri. They have looted and raided. The Mexican army has
had skirmishes with them. In one battle, the Texans killed
eighteen Pueblo scouts who were riding with the Mexican

soldiers. The Pueblos haven't forgotten. They make no distinction between a Texan and an American. To them, a white man is a white man. I fear they will rise up one day in Taos and murder some white men to avenge the eighteen scouts killed by the Texans."

"But they would be killing the wrong men."

Louis shook his finger at me. "You must understand the Indian mind. They think of themselves not so much as individuals, but more as members of their tribe. They think of us the same way. If a white man kills an Indian, the Indians must kill a white man to avenge the murder."

"It doesn't matter whom?"

"If I ride into a Comanche camp, kill a warrior, and get away, the next day the Comanches may happen upon you. They will kill you, and the matter will be closed, though I— the real murderer—remain unpunished. That is Indian justice."

"So I may be killed for something some Texan did? Days ago? Miles away?"

"We *all* may be. There is talk of making Texas the twenty-eighth state. The treaty has already been signed between the United States and the Republic of Texas. All that remains is to make it official, with some mysterious ceremony or something. When that happens, the trouble between Texas and Mexico will become trouble between the United States and Mexico. War will break out from Texas to California. You may be riding into the most troublesome of times this frontier has seen, Honoré."

I shrugged off the suggestion. "How many times a day must I be told of my impending doom?"

Louis sat quietly for some time. "The veterans tend to taunt greenhorns; that is true. But this is no idle warning, Honoré. Do not let yourself get caught far from the protection of friends."

Daily, I rode. I became like a part of Fireball, and I don't
mean only when on his back. Even when he was out of my
sight, I knew what he needed, what concerned him, what he
wanted. When not riding, I kept him tied to a wagon, or let
him graze with hobbles on his forelegs. I would be going
about some task, and suddenly realize that Fireball was
thirsty; so I would untie him and lead him to water. He knew
what I needed as well. In the morning, I would find him
near my bedroll, wherever that might be. He would not shy
away when I lugged my saddle toward him.

Meanwhile, I watched other riders—American, Canadian,
Mexican, and a Delaware Indian hunter—and learned from
them all by observation. The Mexicans and the Delaware
hunter mounted and dismounted from the right side of their
horses, while the Canadians and Americans climbed on and
off from the left side. I learned to mount or dismount from
either side. The Americans called the right side of the horse
the "off" side, which made no sense because they got off
on the left side, the same side on which they got on. I finally
came to understand that by "off" they meant the "away"
side. The frontiersmen made the strange English language
stranger still by their colloquialisms.

By the time we reached the Great Bend of the Arkansas
River, I felt that Fireball and I could read each other's
minds. He began to trust me to watch out for his blind side,
and we seemed able to handle anything along the trail. His
grass belly had drawn up with exercise, and his winter hair
had slicked off to reveal a smooth, glossy coat. And, he did
possess unexpected speed, especially with a rider as light as
me in the saddle.

When we reached the Great Bend, Louis Lescot invited
me to ride with him to the banks of the Arkansas.

"Look at this water flowing past," he said to me in
French. "It has come from snow melting in the Rockies—
the Shining Mountains, as the old voyagers call that range.
This water has flowed right past Bent's Fort. Would that it
could tell us what goes on there. Ah, but we must go see
for ourselves."

"How far away are we now?" I asked.

"We have only come about a third of the way. Now the hardest part comes. Indians. When we divide ranks, both parties will be more vulnerable."

"Divide ranks?" I asked. I had heard nothing about the caravan splitting up.

"You have a choice to make. In a few days we will reach the Cimarron Cutoff. Then, you can go up the Arkansas with me and William, directly to Bent's Fort. This will be a small party, with two wagons. Vulnerable to attack."

"Or?"

"Or you can go with Charles and the other wagons to the Cimarron River, and on to Santa Fe. This will take you through Comanche country, but you will have enough wagons to circle. You may thirst to death before you reach the Cimarron. It is very dry after you leave the Arkansas. But you will see Santa Fe and Taos if you survive the trail. Then again, if war with Mexico breaks out, you will be in grave danger there."

I watched a whole melted blizzard run past before I responded. "Can I get to Bent's Fort from Taos?"

"Of course. If Indians don't get you."

"I want to see the buffalo," I said.

"Then go south on the Cimarron Cutoff with Charles. The great herd will be migrating up from the *Llano Estacado*. Just remember. Where you find buffalo, you will likely find Comanches."

The next day, we reached Pawnee Rock, a famous landmark along the trail. It stood a couple of miles from the timber that clung to the steep banks of the Arkansas River. The old Santa Fe Trail ran between the river and Pawnee Rock, but closer to the rock. It loomed as we approached, and I studied it through the dust the cavvy raised. It created a bluff that faced the river, the only outcropping of its kind in sight. Upon seeing it, I wanted to ride to the top of it, for I could tell that it would lend a splendid view of the valley and the open grasslands beyond. I could also tell that I could easily ride Fireball onto the top of the bluff by riding up the gentle slopes that fell to either side of the rock bluff. The vertical bluff face was only about fifty feet high, but seemed stark and impressive in this land where everything wanted to spread itself out flat.

We made camp within hiking distance of the rock, so I left Fireball hobbled to graze and stretched my own legs toward the landmark. For decades, I had been told, travelers had carved their names in the blackened sandstone face of the bluff. Louis Lescot and others had suggested that I might do the same. William Bent said that the stone yielded to a knife blade, and that I could scratch my name into the bluff before the cook rang his dinner bell.

I thought about this. My birth name was Jean-Guy, a name I would never use again. I still feared that detectives from France forever hounded my trail, and I did not want to leave my imagined pursuers any clues. Perhaps these same investigators were now aware of my alias of Honoré. For that reason, I declined to carve any name in the rock. Anyway, it seemed senseless to spend any amount of time carving a pseudonym into stone. No man criticized me for not leaving my name at Pawnee Rock, but I could tell that my failure to do so caused much suspicion.

Perhaps you can imagine how a fugitive feels. He must deny and reject all that he ever was. He must distance himself from himself. He is less than nothing.

I walked to the west of the bluff, ascended to its summit, and took in the view. To the south lay the river valley, clustered with stands of timber like spots on a long, torpid snake. It wound away to the ends of the earth, eastward and westward. Beyond the river, great grasslands bounded to the horizon. Then I turned around and looked northward. Here, atop Pawnee Rock, I stood on the surface of the greatest open sward known to humankind. I must admit that I did feel like a speck. A few minutes of looking across those interminable plains proved too much to take. I felt the vast expanse sucking everything I possessed right out of my pores. I know now that the land was purging me, taking all that was corrupt and wicked, leaving the morsel of integrity

I had managed to cache away somewhere in my soul. But, at the time, it made me feel like the most useless individual in the history of human beings. Should Comanches kill me tomorrow, the caravan would scarcely pause to dig my grave. Then I would be forgotten forever.

I climbed down huge stair-step ledges along the face of the bluff and tried to entertain myself by reading the names others had left in the rock. The Bents were there, of course. Four brothers—Charles, William, George, and Robert. Robert was dead, as the tailor had told me previously, but seeing his name, which he himself had carved, struck me with a nebulous dread. Ceran St. Vrain's name was there, as well, along with his brother, Marcellin. Then there was my friend Louis Lescot, and some other Bent-St. Vrain employees I had met. Now I began to see names of mountain men I had heard repeated in stories since joining this caravan.

Jim Bridger. Joe Meek. Lucas Murray. Lucien Maxwell. Jim Beckwourth, whom I had gathered was a renowned Negro, or half-Negro mountain man and an outrageous storyteller. Tom Smith, who I knew went by the handle of Peg Leg, and had once stolen my own one-eyed horse from far-off California. Tom Boggs, from whom I had purchased Fireball, and who I had also learned was engaged to marry Charles Bent's stepdaughter this very summer. Thomas Fitzpatrick, whom I had also heard referred to as "Broken Hand." Dick Wootton, whom everyone called "Uncle Dick."

Then I came to the name of a man who was always spoken of with awe and respect by the men of the caravan. The name came up at least once every day on the trail. So many were the stories of this man's exploits that I had begun to think of him as some sort of alpine myth. But I was made to understand that he was real. His name in the rock was small and neat. Though unassuming, it rang almost like a sharp knell, through my eyes rather than my ears. KIT CARSON.

I reached my hand toward it to touch it, though I had felt compelled to touch no other inscription. Just then, I sensed someone at my elbow.

"Hey, cavvy boy. That's me below Kit."

I turned to see one of the bullwhackers I had noticed in camp and on the trail. His name I did not yet know. I looked at the name below Kit Carson's, and saw only the word "Blue."

"Oliver Wiggins," he said, jutting his stonelike bull-whacker's hand at me. A young man in his prime, perhaps twenty-seven or so, he stood about as tall as me, but weighed a good twenty pounds more. He beamed with pride at the word "Blue" or at Kit Carson's name—I couldn't tell which.

"I am Honoré," I said, shaking his hand. "Why does it say 'Blue' if your name is Oliver Wiggins?"

He chuckled. "My nickname. You can call me 'Blue.' I was a cavvy boy on this trail once, like you. Back in thirty-eight. I had run away from home. Sixteen years old. I wouldn't give my real name for fear they'd send me back. I wouldn't give a name at all. Well, I was wearing my only pair of trousers—made of blue denim—so Kit Carson took to calling me 'Blue.' He took me under his wing, Kit did." He laughed. "I was still so afraid they'd send me back that I wouldn't carve nothin' but 'Blue' on this-here rock."

"I don't suppose I'll be carving anything at all," I said.

Blue Wiggins shrugged. "Man makes up his own name out here if he wants to." He pointed to another name etched into Pawnee Rock. "Look here. Sol Silver. No tellin' what his name was when he was born."

"You know him?"

"You'll likely meet him yourself, if you live long enough. Sol was born in Mexico, but he was carried off by Comanches when he was just a runt. They sold him to some mean Kiowa buck who used to whup up on him. Once he got growed, Sol run off and throwed in with the Osage. He become a brave and led a war party on the Kiowa camp that had held him a slave. He got to kill that mean bastard Kiowa buck that'd whupped up on him so. Sol was real proud of that. He left the Indians finally, and throwed in with white folks at Bent's Fort. Kit kind of took him under his wing, too. Called him 'Solomon Silver' on account of Sol wore silver earrings in both ears. I don't know how Kit come up with 'Solomon.' "

"It's biblical. Solomon was king of Israel in the tenth century before Christ. He was famed for his wisdom."

Blue Wiggins looked at me skeptically. "Like I said, I don't know how come Kit to come up with that part." He pointed at the names on the rock again. "Look here. Jed Smith. Old Jedediah. Now, there went the greatest explorer of all times. Crossed the continent twice, from ocean to ocean. Some said he was the first to ever do that."

"What happened to him?" I could tell somehow that Blue Wiggins was speaking of the dead.

"Got lost somewhere below the Arkansas. Separated from Broken Hand and some others. Comanches got him."

"The greatest explorer of all times got lost?"

"Well, he didn't know where he was. That's lost, ain't it? Anyway, you ain't explored much if you ain't got lost a time or two. Broken Hand told me about it. Him and Jedediah was leading a little caravan to Santa Fe. They tried a shortcut to the Cimarron, got lost, and run out of water. So Jed and Broken Hand scouted on ahead horseback. Broken Hand's horse give out, so they drunk the blood, and Jed rode on alone. Nobody ever seen him again, but some Indians told the tale. About six Comanche bucks surrounded him and shot him dead. That was the end of Jedediah Smith. I don't think he ever intended livin' long as he did, anyway."

"Broken Hand is Thomas Fitzpatrick?" I pointed to Fitzpatrick's name in the rock.

"Yeah, you know him?"

I shook my head. "I've only heard his name. And his nickname. I had gathered they were one in the same."

"You'll know him when you see him. His hair's all white. You heard the story?"

"Vaguely."

Blue Wiggins sat down on a rock to tell this one. "Broken Hand—that's what the Indians call him—he come to the mountains as a young man. Like Kit. Like me. Hell, like you. Story was he went out with some old hands, and the Blackfeet ambushed 'em. Kilt everybody in camp except him. He hid out in the rocks for days, scared out of his mind, while the Blackfeet scouted around. Nothin' to eat, no help, no way out. Finally, them Indians left, and he made it back to some fur trapper's fort. When he got there nobody hardly knew him. His hair had gone white as an old man's and stayed that way." Blue Wiggins chuckled. "Hell, he wanted to come west."

"What about Kit Carson?" I asked, shifting my gun belt on my hips. "What's the story on him?"

"Hell, there's no end to the stories on Kit." Blue Wiggins touched Kit's name, as I had felt compelled to do earlier.

"Well, where is he nowadays?"

"He's tryin' to settle down. Been married two years to a Mexican lady in Taos. With all this war talk, though, they ain't gonna let Kit be. He'll be scoutin' and guidin' when the fightin' starts. He knows every trail from St. Louis to California."

"Do you think the fighting will start soon?"

Blue Wiggins chuckled. "Hell, yes, the fightin' will start. The Texans will see to that."

"Who will win?"

"Oh, Mexico won't be that hard to whip. New Mexico will be the easiest part, but some good men are still gonna die. It's the Indians that worry me. Git us Americans busy fightin' Mexicans, and them Indians will raid every ranch and settlement from San Antonio to Santa Fe. A man's gonna have to fight for his scalp with both hands." He seemed to welcome the prospect.

"I want to go live among them," I blurted. I had been thinking of this for weeks. I would be hard to find among the so-called savages. If I gained their confidence as a trader, I would be safer than if I lived in a frontier settlement or on a ranch that might be raided. I would not invade their territory, I would enter with their blessing and bring them things they wanted. I would not scatter their game, nor trample their ponies' graze, I would pattern my career after that of William Bent.

But there was something else, too. That place that had appeared to me in vague dreams at Saint-Cyr. The river. The crossing. The tall grass. The timber. I felt it somewhere to the south. I cringed every time I heard the name "Comanche," for I would remember the vision I had seen, where the warrior Catlin had painted came to kill me. I was going to live among the people who had murdered Robert Bent. Perhaps my hair would turn white like Thomas Fitzpatrick's. Perhaps I would die alone like Jedediah Smith. Like Blue Wiggins said, I wanted to come west.

"What have you got to trade?" Blue asked, matter-of-factly.

"So far, just some hickory wood for bows."

"That's a start. William will likely give you a try. He's tried for years to maintain some kind of trading houses on the Canadian, but the Comanche keep harassin' his traders and burnin' the houses down."

"That's where I want to go."

"Well, you're either brave or crazy, cavvy boy."

"I'm neither. I'm simply predestined."

Blue Wiggins turned away from Pawnee Rock. "You sound like that superstitious tailor, ol' Louis Let's-Go." He grinned, pulled a watch from his vest pocket, and looked at it. "Shit!" He thumped the face of the watch with his knuckle. He wound it a turn or two, then held it to his ear. "Shit!" he repeated, shoving the timepiece back into his pocket. "Well, if you ain't gonna put your name on that rock, you can come help me make a cinch ring out of somethin'. I busted one yesterday, and I hate to walk or ride a damn wagon."

"Alright," I said, and I spent the rest of the afternoon heating and bending a used horseshoe into the shape of a cinch ring for Blue's saddle. To test the cinch ring, we had a horse race, which I won aboard Fireball. As my prize, I collected Blue Wiggins's watch, which didn't work.

TEN

West of Pawnee Rock, the old veterans of the trail began to talk of buffalo. Herds they had seen, bulls they had killed, cows they had skinned, calves they had roped. One evening, while leading Fireball to a creek to drink, I saw William Bent leaving camp with his rifle. From the edge of the riverside timber, I watched him. He walked about a quarter mile from the wagons, lie down on the ground, and pressed his ear to the dirt. He stayed a long time, listening to the earth. At last, he rose. He didn't even bother to dust his clothes off. I could not tell from his actions whether he had heard anything.

The next day we camped near a clear spring that issued into a creek. The tall grass around the creek bottom served to keep the cavvy close to the caravan. Blackfoot John Smith and our Delaware hunter had managed to kill two deer, and the cook was making venison stew. The weather felt fine. A southerly breeze bowed the stalks of grass. An afternoon thundershower had settled the dust and cleansed the air. In spite of all this, a certain moodiness settled in over the camp. Tomorrow we would reach the Cimarron Cutoff, and the caravan would divide. Weakened, each new party would ride into the haunts of restless redmen. Our last night of relative security had come. Even here, Blue Wiggins told me, we were vulnerable to attack by Osage, Kiowa, Comanche, and Pawnee.

I played my violin that night and showed the bullwhackers how I could juggle sticks of firewood, and make Blue Wiggins's former pocketwatch vanish from my hands. This lightened the mood for a while, but not long.

I didn't sleep that night. My eyes stayed as round as the

full moon above me. I went to relieve a grateful night guard, and Jibber went with me. I heard the hoots of owls and the songs of wolves and coyotes. I had heard that Indians made many of these noises to signal one another, so I stayed alert, with one hand on my pistol and the other on my saber. The wind had died completely away.

I began to get the strangest feeling. It was as though I could *almost* hear something. Jibber seemed to sense it, too, though he may have only gathered and assumed my apprehension. My hearing is still keen today, but in my youth, I was like a hare. I took the risk of removing my hands from my weapons to cup them behind my ears. Now I could hear the river rushing along its course, almost a mile away. I held my breath. Ever so faintly, I heard something beyond the normal sound of the river. It was as if a great throng was splashing into the water miles upstream.

You may doubt me. What man can hear something so far away? It is true that my sense of hearing ranked above average for a human being, but you must understand something else about that time and place. When the wind died out on the plains, only the rushing of streams and the movements of creatures made noises. There were no railroads, no machines. The wagons were at rest that night. The beasts of burden had grazed and gone to lie down. In those days, out on the open prairie, the smallest peep could carry a mile. My ears *felt* something that they couldn't quite hear. Whatever it was held power, mystical and awesome.

I couldn't hold my breath forever, of course, so I put my hands back on my weapons and waited the long night through. As the moon sank low, I went to collect Fireball and get an early start at bunching the cavvy. I led my mount to the river, as I had some ten hours before. The moonlight and the grey glow of dawn illuminated the stream. I gasped at what I saw.

The Arkansas had turned muddy overnight. It had run clear at dusk. Now the red and brown stains of stirred silt painted it, visible even by the moon. The level of the river had not risen, for I stood upon my own tracks from watering

my horse the evening before. No rain had caused this mud-
dying of the waters. Something had crossed upstream.
Something I had almost heard in the night. The river was
trying to speak to me like a stranger, or a friend; a savior,
or a seductress. My heart pounded, and Fireball snorted at
the river, blasting dimples into the surface of the water with
his breath. He refused to drink.

I mounted and rode to the brink of the riverbank. The
camp had begun to stir. I wore my pistol under my belt and
my saber in the buckskin scabbard Louis had made for me.
Still curious about what went on upstream, I rode west, to
the first divide. Reaching the high ground, I scanned the
new terrain. Fireball flinched. I saw it. On the next rise, a
half mile away, the outline of a single buffalo bull stood
only slightly darker than the dawn sky behind it.

For a moment, I knew not what to do. Some kind of
hunter's instinct gripped me, but I knew better than to light
out after that lone buffalo by myself. I turned toward the
caravan—then back toward the bull—then back toward the
caravan. I gathered my senses. I needed to tell someone
before I went chasing buffalo.

Fireball did not want to leave that buffalo, but I made
him gallop back toward the camp. When I came within
shouting distance, I reined in my mount and cried out with
a single word: "Buffalo!" Then I turned back toward the
place where I had seen the bull. Looking over my shoulder,
I saw several men scrambling for their best ponies.

When Fireball and I reached the divide, the buffalo had
vanished from the next rise. Undaunted, we galloped on. I
knew what I had seen. Surmounting the place where the
bison had stood, I saw the young bull trotting away about
a quarter mile ahead of me. He had angled into Fireball's
blind spot, so I reined to the right until my mount spotted
the buffalo again. I only thought I had felt Fireball run. Now
he bolted ahead with a fury and a purpose I had never imagined. Glancing back, I saw a line of men streaming over the
crest behind me, yelling and waving with joy.

It was obvious to me that Fireball knew his business, so

I gave him his head and drew my pistol. It seemed simple enough. Fireball would get me close enough for a shot, I would aim for the beast's vitals, and pull the trigger.

The gap between me and the buffalo closed ever so slowly, but my mount would not relent. My innate feel for space told me that I had run over a mile from camp. The men behind me were falling farther behind, but were still coming on. I began to feel the same surge the lion feels when making a kill. The madness of all the world's carnivores consumed me, making my spine tingle as if I possessed hackles. Some kind of primordial growl escaped my throat, and to my astonishment, Fireball found new speed.

As we came nearer, my mount crossed behind the fleeing bull so that he could keep the bull in view with his one good eye. We came through the buffalo's dust trail to the tune of hooves pounding sod and soil. I saw the tongue lolling out of the bison's mouth on the right side. His eyes seemed devoid of expression. I tried to aim, but realized I must get much closer, for the sights of my pistol lurched all around the galloping beast. My heart was beating furiously and my legs were tired from absorbing the shock of the long run. The beast was so large and shaggy, and its black horns so menacing on its huge and powerful head, that I could not deny some fear.

Suddenly Fireball angled in on the beast. I aimed my weapon and pulled my trigger, more out of self-defense than any hunter's instinct. The shot roared above the hoofbeats, and a tuft of shedding hair seemed to explode along the flanks of the doomed creature. I enjoyed a mere second of pride, knowing I had made a good shot, before things twisted into unexpected chaos.

The wounded bull made a marvelously agile attack, springing suddenly to his right. Fireball was ready for this, and dodged with equal agility, wrenching me almost out of the saddle. I held on to the mane and found myself pressed against the left side of my mount. I twisted my neck and found the glassy-eyed brute charging right at me, his horns prepared to rake me out of my saddle and gore the life from me. Fireball carried me farther aside and kicked at the attacker just as the buffalo coughed a spray of blood on my face as a final insult. The bison stumbled, jarring the earth when he rolled. I lost my hold on the saddle and mane, and landed not far from where the buffalo had fallen. Fireball came slowly to a halt, and I sat up, spraddle-legged, to see several riders charging me.

The riders looked strange. I felt disoriented. Someone was yelping at the top of his lungs. The dust blew away and an arrow appeared in the ground with a thump, inches from the organs vital to the perpetuation of a family name I no longer employed.

An instant, overwhelming terror engulfed me and launched my reflexes into action. I sprang to my feet as three more arrows flew by like hornets, one tearing a sleeve. Gunshots came from behind me as I drew my saber. I had dropped my pistol, but it was empty anyway. The riders in front of me scattered suddenly. Only one continued to ride directly at me in a mad, screaming assault, a battle-axe held overhead. I assumed a defensive stance Segarelli had taught to me, and deftly parried a downward blow from the Indian warrior galloping by me, the steel of my saber ringing against the iron of his tomahawk. He continued galloping by me, into the weaponry of the white men who had come to rescue me.

I turned and watched as the young warrior charged crazily into the ranks of his enemy. Blue Wiggins fired a pistol almost point-blank, but the Indian's pony threw his head up at the very same instant, and took the ball. As the pony dropped, Louis Lescot delivered a vicious blow with the smoking barrel of his rifle to the warrior's shoulder. As his dead pony collapsed, the young Indian rolled and twisted over backward, landing on his feet and running right back toward me with his tomahawk.

Everything around me became dust and battle cries, horseflesh and gunshots. George Catlin's portrait had come to life again, this time in reality. The other warriors had imploded on the scene of this small struggle and engaged my friends in hand-to-hand battle to rescue their comrade. Again my saber tasted the iron of the tomahawk as my eyes met those of the warrior. He seemed no older than I, and appeared thrust into this fracas as surely as I, for I detected no particular malice in his eyes, even though he was trying to kill me. This was destiny.

The battle of the mounted men spilled in between me and the young warrior. Through the dust and yells, I saw my combatant vault miraculously onto the rump of a pony ridden by one of his friends. A horse stamped on my foot, causing me to yell in pain. Suddenly the Indians were gone, and my friends gave brief pursuit, as if they had repelled and driven away the attackers. Hopping on my good foot, I noticed that the Indians were leading Fireball away with them, and my heart sank into my guts with a nausea I will never forget.

About this time, Jibber showed up out of nowhere, barking at the dead Indian pony lying not far from the dead buffalo on the ground. Beyond, more mounted men were coming from our caravan.

"Quiet, Jibber!" I shouted, though I don't know what difference his barking made. At his feet, I saw something dropped by one of the Indians, probably the one with whom I had done battle. Limping to it, I found a quiver filled with arrows, and a long sleeve holding an unstrung bow. For whatever reason, the young warrior had chosen to make battle with his tomahawk rather than his bow and arrows. Picking up the captured weapon, I theorized that the warrior had lost the quiver when Louis Lescot knocked him backward from his dying horse.

I found myself surrounded by men from the caravan.

"You alright?" someone said.

"Horse stepped on my foot."

"Good!" I turned to see William Bent's scowl as he rode by.

"They got your horse," Charles added. "I hope you're happy."

"No, sir," I replied.

"At least you killed the buffalo," Louis Lescot said. "But it was a bad idea to chase it alone. The Indians, they think the buffalo are only for them. The saber, however, that was a good choice. You used it well."

"Lucky somebody ain't dead!" William said, not even bothering to look at me. He was dismounting at the buffalo carcass.

Blue Wiggins rode up to me, leaned from his saddle, and said with a grin, "William's sore."

I looked the way Fireball had disappeared. "They got my horse."

Blue shrugged. "There's more horses out west." He handed me my pistol, which he had found on the ground. I blew the dirt from the machined parts, but knew I would have to take it apart and clean it.

I noticed an arrow sticking up from the ground nearby as the men stood guard or studied the carcasses of the buffalo and the horse. I hobbled over to the arrow and pulled it from the sod. I gathered four more on the battlefield, all tipped with long iron points and fletched with bird feathers. For some reason, their fine workmanship made me think of Antonio Stradavari. I added them to the arrows in the quiver I had found.

Louis Lescot walked up to me, leading his horse, having dismounted to reload his rifle. "They intended only to hunt, not to make war."

"How can you tell?"

"The arrow points. No barbs. You can pull them from a dead buffalo and use them again. War points have barbs so you can't pull them from your chest when they shoot you. You have to push them through."

"Oh," I replied.

"Look." Louis took an arrow from my hand. "When this hunting arrow is notched on the bowstring, the flat blade of the point is vertical. They believe this will make it go between the ribs of a buffalo, though I think the arrow must spiral in flight. Now, when a war arrow is notched, its point is flat—horizontal. The Indians believe this will make it slip between the ribs of a man standing upright."

"Oh," I repeated, still feeling shaken from the battle and the chaos. "What tribe were they from, Louis?"

"Comanche."

"How can you be sure?"

"Their manner of dress. Their weapons. Their horsemanship. Look at the dead pony. See the rawhide cord woven into the mane."

Limping closer to the carcass for a better look, I saw the cord tied into the mane and looped under the dead pony's neck. "What is that for?"

"An Indian will thrust his arm into the loop, right up to the elbow. That way, he can ride along clinging to the side of his mount, using his horse for a shield."

"I must try that."

Louis laughed. "With what?"

I frowned, for his point was well taken.

"Well, you lost a horse, Honoré, but you killed a buffalo and captured a weapon. Luckily, neither friend nor foe died in battle, so we don't have any messy revenge killings to look forward to. Just the same, you'd better prepare for more trouble. Now the Indians know where we are."

"I don't even know where I am."

The tailor laughed. "Is your foot broken?"

"I don't know. I've never had a broken foot."

"If it was broken, you would know."

"I don't think it's broken."

"You'd better get over there and help them gut that buffalo. It was your kill, after all. They're going to take the tenderloin and a few other choice cuts."

I didn't know anything about gutting a buffalo, but I held a hind leg out of the way as Tom Boggs tore the bloody offal out of the steaming body cavity. I did my best to choke back the gagging that all those intestines and bullet-torn organs lumped in my throat, and managed not to puke right there in front of everybody.

Blackfoot John Smith pulled a purplish mass from the gut

pile, and held it toward me, dripping with blood. "Want it, kid?"

I sneered. "What is it?"

"Liver."

I shook my head.

Right then and there, Blackfoot John took a bite out of that raw liver, leaving blood all over his beard as he grinned and chewed and swallowed and took another bite. I turned away as men laughed.

The shadow of a vulture passed over me as the bird circled low between me and the rising sun. A coyote prowled on a rise downwind, sniffing the air greedily.

What kind of land was this, where rivers spoke to men in the moonlight? Where horses knew more than their masters? Where sport could turn to war with the glint of sun on steel? Where men ate raw meat and slaked their thirst with blood? Where even the tailors fought like caged lions? How had I come to this? How would I survive it? Why did I love it so?

ELEVEN

I must have presented the quintessence of misery. All day long, I trudged haltingly behind the cavvy, herding the animals on foot. I had expected no one to offer me a horse, and no one did. No one told me I must continue my duties afoot, but I knew I must. Only Jibber had made my work possible, for he nipped happily at the heels of the strays and laggards. Each step shot pain up my leg, but after walking a mere fifteen minutes, I had decided I would rather bear the pain than the chiding of my fellows. In addition to the pain, I had to endure my own fears of attack. I was pitifully exposed on one lame foot at the rear of the caravan. If the

Indians attacked again, I would have to stand and fight with saber and pistol.

I distracted myself from pain and fear by attempting to practice my newly acquired skill of archery. I tried for half an hour to get the bow strung. I bent it over the back of my shoulders by pushing down on it with both arms. I stood in the middle of it and attempted to bend it up that way. I sat down, hooked it over one knee and under the other.

Finally, Blue Wiggins left his oxen and rode back to instruct me. Leaping from his pony he said, "Let me see that there bow, Orn'ry." He had taken to calling me this because he had trouble with the French "Honoré." It had caught on, and many of the non-French caravan employees were now calling me "Ornery," which in the frontier vernacular, of course, came out "Orn'ry."

I handed Blue Wiggins the bow. "I think the bowstring is too short."

"Naw, they string 'em tight. I've seen 'em do it." He put the tip of the bow with the string already attached to it in front of his left ankle. Stepping over it with his right foot, he let the grip in the middle of the bow fall against the back of his right knee. Now he used his ample strength to bend the bow forward with his right hand as he looped the loose end of the bowstring over the upper end of the bow. Thumping the string a couple of times, he handed it back to me. "Bet you can't hit the side of a barn with that."

I looked around the plains, as if I might find a barn. "Not from here," I replied.

He laughed.

"Where are all the buffalo?" I asked. "I expected to see a big-herd today."

"Them Comanche probably stampeded 'em to keep us from killin' any more. When buffalo smell Indians, they get nervous, anyhow. White man's smell don't spook 'em as bad."

With that, he made a circle around the animals to bunch the cavvy for me, and rode back to his wagon.

I took errant shots with my captured weapon until the

bowstring made my fingers as sore as my injured foot. When I limped into the Arkansas River campground behind the cavvy, I was wincing with every step.

You need moccasins," Louis said. He was right. My left shoe was rubbing layers of skin from my swollen foot. The heels of both my shoes were run down anyway, both the soles flapping, all the seams unraveling. "I need my horse back," I said.

"I can't help you there, but I can fashion a pair of moccasins for you, though it is not my specialty."

"What'll that cost me?"

"Two hickory limbs."

"I'll give you one."

"One hickory for two moccasins? I can't work that cheap, Honoré. I have my pride."

I had my pride, too, but my foot was sore. "One hickory and one of these captured arrows," I said. The one I offered was slightly bent, anyway, and didn't fly true.

Louis faked a frown that turned into a smile. "You bargain like a Comanche. Alright, I'll make your moccasins for that price. But only because you are my friend, and I cannot bear to watch you hobble along anymore."

As we went into camp, I began to miss Fireball terribly. He had helped me kill the first buffalo I had ever seen. I had ridden him into the unknown, and lost him. Blue Wiggins had said that more horses waited out west, but I could not imagine one like Fireball. I lay down that night sore and dejected. I refused to play the violin, but I had eaten well, and I did sleep a few hours.

When I awoke, I found a new pair of moccasins staring me in the face. The uppers were made of deerskin, the soles of tough buffalo hide. I pulled them on immediately and went to help the night guards round up the mules and oxen. The moccasins made walking bearable, though my foot seemed even more swollen and tender than the day before.

The morale of the caravan lay stagnant like a brackish creek, barely even trickling. We would divide ranks this morning, most of us crossing the Arkansas River to take the shortcut to Santa Fe. The dry shortcut that sometimes caused men and beasts to die of thirst. The dry shortcut that had led even the great voyager, Jedediah Smith, to his death at the hands of Comanches. While Charles Bent led this prong of the caravan, William Bent would take two wagons on up the Arkansas to Bent's Fort. My friend, Louis Lescot, would go with William. I would go with Charles. Since the skirmish the day before, my fascination with Comanches had only grown. I even entertained the notion that I might explore the haunts of the men who had tried to kill me and find Fireball among them, whereupon I would ransom him back into my possession with all the trade goods I had yet to acquire, excepting a few hickory limbs.

This was pure fantasy, of course, and my rational brain knew it. Fireball was gone.

Crossing Charles's portion of the caravan over the river took most of the morning, for the teams had to be doubled and tripled to pull the wagons through the mud and silt. I didn't have to cross until the cavvy swam over, so I had time to say my farewells to the men heading upstream.

I knew William Bent had forgiven my stupid buffalo chase of the day before when he said, "Bring that fiddle 'round to the fort sometime."

Louis Lescot shook my hand and said, in French, "Listen to Charles. Look for water. Conserve strength in every endeavor until you find it."

"I will see you at the fort," I promised.

Blue Wiggins used his horse to force the cavvy across the river, and I felt stupid that I couldn't help, for I was afoot. I climbed onto the back of the last wagon bound for Santa-Fe and made a dry crossing of the Arkansas, not even getting my new moccasins wet.

On the other side, I waved, and began to bunch the loose animals as I limped. I had gathered and pushed them almost to the brink of the southern riverbank when some commotion attracted my attention. Whistles and shouts reached my ears, and I feared that the Indians had chosen this moment to attack. I took my pistol in my right hand and my saber in my left and charged up the bank for a better view, suddenly heedless of my injured foot.

Hoofbeats drummed the earth below me as I gained the brink. Then I saw a familiar horse charging directly toward me. It was Fireball, his sweat lathered all over him like sea spray. He looked as though he had run a hundred miles, but he came sliding to a halt in front of me, as sound as ever.

Suddenly, both sides of the river valley erupted in cheers as men threw hats and waved kerchiefs. Fireball pranced around me, heaving like a steam engine, then came face to face with me. I threw one arm over his neck and patted him vigorously. How he had escaped his captors and found his way back was a mystery I didn't even care to ponder. He was back. Don Turo brought me a horsehair bosal with long reins. I slipped it over Fireball's head and mounted bareback. Bullwhips cracked and bullwhackers sang curses like sailing chanteys. I made my mount cool down before I took him to water. He drank his fill; then we ambled back to the caravan. Riding my pony bareback, new moccasins dangling, and a captured quiver strapped to my back, my spirits soared like a hawk over the prairies and I felt well-nigh invincible.

Certainly you have experienced similar moments of pure unfettered rapture in your own time and circumstance. When the world seems to revolve to your advantage. When even your troubles resolve themselves to your benefit. When angels cast lucky stars into your very pockets. If so, you know exactly how I felt as I rode my pony back to the caravan. I truly believed in my own indestructibility. I was indomitable.

The Cimarron Cutoff would cure all that.

Two days down the Cimarron Cutoff, a water barrel strapped to the side of a wagon developed a leak from the jolting of the trail. This didn't concern me much, for it was only one of our eighteen barrels, but Charles Bent called an immediate halt until the barrel could be drained, its contents carefully moved by buckets to other half-full barrels until the leaky cask was empty.

The next day, some fool—luckily, it wasn't me—let his gun go off and shot a hole in the worst possible thing: a water barrel. Men scrambled as if under attack. The first to reach the damaged vessel used their hats to catch the water gushing from the bullet hole. They carried the brimming hats to favored mounts until someone showed up with a bucket. Scarcely a gallon hit the ground, but it seemed as if we had lost a river of water.

That evening, we found Middle Creek completely dry, where ordinarily it collected a few pools of stinking water suitable only for beasts. This meant that much of the water in the barrels would have to go to the draft animals and mounts.

By this time, I had gauged the amount of water that men and beasts required daily. Allowing a margin of error of about five gallons a day, I calculated by extrapolation how far we could go with the amount of water we carried. From listening, I knew how many days' travel we had left before we reached the Cimarron. It didn't take a genius to tell that we weren't going to make it there before our water ran out. The draft animals had to be doled water by buckets, and they were draining our barrels, yet they needed more. Their lack of water had caused them to move more slowly every day. We began to fall short of the campgrounds at the end of each day.

At noon on the fourth day, Charles called a halt. One of the oxen had died in its yoke. The men stood in a circle and listened to our captain.

"It's drier than usual," he began. "And hotter. Even if we cut rations back, our water won't last more than a day. We've got two days of trail left to the Cimarron. There's no guarantee it will have water in it where we strike it."

Suddenly I felt very thirsty, though I had fared well under the rationing system. I was small and had an easy job, and a horse to ride. I had conserved energy, as Louis had advised. I knew that some of the other men were suffering leg cramps due to lack of water. A few had to suck on pebbles all day to keep their mouths moist. One bullwhacker was unable to speak because his tongue had swollen; yet he refused all offers of water from those like me, who were better off.

"I need two mounted volunteers to go ahead with kegs on pack mules and find some water to bring back." He looked at me. "Honoré," he said, calling me by name for the first time, "you might loan your horse to one of the volunteers."

Every man cast a glance my way. "If my horse goes, I go," I said.

"Alright," Charles continued. "Who will go with the cavvy boy to the Cimarron?"

I could not, of course, back out of the corner into which Charles had led me, and didn't want to. In fact, the prospect elated me. I was going to ride ahead instead of drag behind.

"I'll go," Blue Wiggins said.

This suited me, and everyone else. We took two strong mules, each with two empty kegs strapped onto a packsaddle. Blue had a good horse, and I rode Fireball. Taking Jibber seemed unnecessary, so I ordered him to stay in one of the wagons, and he obeyed, whining piteously. We rode ahead at a long walk that verged on a trot. We did not speak. Opening our mouths would only rob them of moisture.

We rode through the day without stopping, following the well-rutted trail. We sipped water from our canteens only once. It seemed like a mistake. Though I knew my body needed moisture, the sip I took only made me want to drain the entire container. Fireball forged ahead, his reins swinging like parallel pendulums in a perfect cadence. My horse and Blue's were favored mounts and had been given a little extra water every day. The mules held up well for a while, but then the lack of drink started to tell. One mule stumbled, caught himself on his knees, and struggled to his feet.

"We'll have to slow to a walk," Blue said.

I nodded.

We rode right into the night. I must have fallen into one of my trances, because when I came out of it, the stars, and my internal sense of time, told me that it was just past three o'clock in the morning. I grunted, took another sip from my canteen, and said, "Do you know where we are?"

"Not exactly." Blue looked up at the stars. "Headin' southwest."

When dawn came, I noticed Blue's eyes sweeping the horizon. Years later, experience would teach me that he was looking for birds. A dove winging across the prairie in the distance could lead a man in the direction of water. We saw no doves on this day. In fact, we saw few signs of life. Three coyotes followed us for a while, either out of curiosity or hopes that one of us was going to die, which seemed increasingly likely.

Dawn revealed another thing to me. I saw no signs of a trail. Years of travel on the Santa Fe Trail had left unmistakable traces on the prairie from thousands of wagons. Now I saw no such evidence. We had lost the trail in the dark, I presumed.

Halfway into the morning we began to descend a long grade through dead, stunted grass.

"Somethin's wrong." Blue's dry voice was cracking.

"What?"

"That's the Cimarron valley ahead. The wind's blowin' right at us. The horses should be smellin' water by now."

"How do you know they're not?"

"I can tell. They'd be all het up if they did. It's dry down there."

The pit of my stomach felt dusty and sick. The prospect of a dry, lingering death scared me worse than the sudden Indian attack days before. We rode down into the valley and found it cracked and sandy. The animals stood with their heads low in the scant shade of a shriveled cottonwood.

Blue Wiggins squatted on his heels and opened his canteen. He tried to drink his last swallow slowly, but could not help turning the canteen upside down. I did the same with mine. For a minute, neither of us spoke.

"We drifted off the trail somewhere last night," Blue Wiggins said finally.

"I figured that out."

"Thing is, I don't know if we drifted north or south of it."

"What difference does it make?" I hated the way these words coated the inside of my mouth with glue.

"If we drifted south, this is sure 'nough the Cimarron, and we're in trouble, 'cause it's sure 'nough dry."

"What if we drifted north?" I asked.

"This could be the North Fork of the Cimarron. It joins the main fork north of the trail. The North Fork goes dry before the main fork, usually."

"Then, maybe if we follow it back to the left, we'll hit the main fork, and it'll have water."

"Maybe so. *If* we sure 'nough drifted *north* of the trail last night," Blue said. We both thought for a while, then stood up. Blue nodded down the stream's dry bed. We were betting our lives that this was the North Fork of the Cimarron.

※

When the first mule fell, Blue Wiggins slid calmly from his horse, drew his knife, and cut the throat of the beast. Then he caught the blood from the knife wound in his canteen. He drank some of it, looking like a ghoul as he handed me the canteen, his mouth all bloody. I had never dreamed that I would get thirsty enough to drink something as vile as the hot blood of a mule. I drank, feeling perfectly horrible, and miserably desperate.

We left the dead mule with two barrels and the packsaddle, and rode on. I wanted to gather my own sweat and drink it. My tongue was swelling in my mouth for want of water; my mind trying to beg a pool from the dry riverbed. Thirst will make a man contemplate the most unnatural prospects. I resisted. We rode on.

The second mule gave out. Again, we collected its blood,

but did not drink it. My stomach felt too ill. My head had begun to ache as if I had hot rocks inside my skull. We took the packsaddle with the two oaken casks from the dead mule, and strapped it onto Fireball. We left my riding saddle in some brush near the mule's carcass. We trudged on downstream, taking turns riding Blue's horse under the broiling sun.

My eyesight seemed to go bad. Everything looked bleached and blurred, though through concentration I could focus my eyes. My mind wandered, taking me mercifully away. Then I would snap back to reality from some night-marish daydream and realize that I was still on the road to death. My tongue was so swollen that I could barely close my mouth. My throat and mouth and guts felt the same need for water that your lungs feel for air when you hold your breath too long, except that the agony went on and on.

Blue's horse stumbled. Blue stepped down from the saddle and led the poor beast for a while, but soon the animal could go no farther. The gelding had so much heart that he refused to fall until his organs ceased to function. He practically died before he hit the ground. Blue did not collect his blood. We pulled Blue's saddle away from the mount, and hid it in some brush. Through all of this, Blue Wiggins seemed better off than me. I felt clumsy and confused. We trudged, and I drifted into thoughts so peculiar and bizarre that I cannot even remember them.

The next thing I knew, Blue had grabbed me by the shoulder. He motioned for me to stay low in the riverbed. He seemed to have a wild look in his eye, and I wondered if he had gone mad, as I knew I soon would. He took his canteen and his rifle, and slipped away down the riverbed, staying low. When he disappeared, I doubted I would ever see him again. I hoped he had spotted Indians who would come and kill us quickly. I placed my hand on the handle of my pistol.

I am not sure how many minutes had passed when the shot startled me. My usual facility for tracking time to the second in my head had oozed out through my suffering pores, but the report brought me back from some rambling dream. I climbed out of the riverbed, leading Fireball. I saw Blue waving at me down the course of the dry stream, and I hastened that way, hoping he had found some sort of salvation for us.

When I reached him, I found him cutting open the belly of a buffalo. "The Lord's with us, Orn'ry," he said. "I seen this buffalo. His belly's about to bust, full of water. He just got him a drink somewhere around here. Within a few miles, I'd say."

I knelt beside the carcass and watched Blue with an instinctive understanding. There was water inside that dead beast. With his bloody hand, Blue raked out intestines until he located the distended stomach. He opened his canteen and poured out the mule blood. With his knife, he carefully punctured the buffalo's stomach, causing a fountain of fluid to arch from the hole he had made. The pressure from the stomach died quickly, so he pushed on it to keep the stream shooting from the puncture.

When he had bled as much fluid as he could from the stomach of the slain buffalo, he handed the canteen to me. He gave it to me first. This courageous act of friendship, I would never forget. This was like being trapped in an underwater cave, with one small passage to the surface, and Blue paused to let me swim through first.

"Careful," he said. "Don't spill none."

I drank. Despite my swollen tongue, I swallowed the putrid water from the stomach of a buffalo, tainted with the blood of a dead mule. I drank without hesitation, and had to force myself with all my powers of discipline to stop drinking before I had drained the whole canteen. I handed it to Blue. He drank the rest.

The effects seemed miraculous. Within minutes, my thoughts cleared. The hot rocks inside my skull cooled. My stomach still felt queasy, but the ache in my chest and throat eased. I could stand and walk a straight line again.

"Let's back-trail the bastard," Blue said.

Less than three miles down the dry bed of the North Fork,

we found the main stream of the Cimarron River. It carried a gossamer trickle of water that collected in green, stagnant pools. We had approached through a crosswind, so Fireball couldn't smell the water until we were almost upon it. When he did, his head jerked upward like a bird taking flight, and I lost my grip on his lead rope. Fireball loped right down into one of the shallow pools and plunged his muzzle into the water. I fell to my belly just upstream and stuck my face into a fairly clear stream. I drank until I thought my belly would burst, and listened to the beautiful sound of my pony sucking water into his own belly.

When I could drink no more, I vomited, tasting the vile blood and acid I had swallowed before. This was a blessing, for now I could fill my stomach again—this time with water that was fresh, though somewhat tainted with the taste of alkali. When finally I quit drinking, I looked around and found Blue sitting on the ground, smiling at me. He had fared better somehow, and that made me respect him and loathe myself for a moment.

Blue Wiggins could have made the main fork of the Cimarron even without a buffalo stomach full of rancid water. I could not have. Perhaps Blue could have reached the water and brought some back for me before I died of thirst. I would never know. I think I should not have survived. Otherwise, why would God have sent that lone buffalo?

On the other hand, why didn't God just send rain? Maybe He needed that rain somewhere else. But, He's God, so why didn't He just make some more rain? Maybe God figures that if you go west, this is the kind of thing you're looking for.

This is the problem with explaining the Great Mystery. It doesn't make sense, until you begin to understand the infinite complexities of the universe. I am a genius, and even I can't make sense of it all. At the time it didn't matter anyway because I didn't believe in God back then. That would come later, through visions and dreams. At the Cimarron, all I knew was that I was saved, but the caravan was still in deep trouble.

"Should we go back and get the other barrels?" I asked.

"I don't think that runt pony of yours can carry more than two," Blue said. "Anyway, that'll take time, and they'll be thirsty back there on the trail. They've probably got oxen and mules dyin' left and right by now."

"Do you know where the trail is from here?"

"It crosses a few miles downstream."

I stood, unwilling to let Blue see me on my belly any longer. "Let's go, then."

Full of water, the casks were heavy, and difficult to tie onto the packsaddle, but we managed. We were about to lead Fireball back toward the Santa Fe Trail when a movement down the Cimarron caught my eye. "Someone's there," I said, pointing.

Blue looked, and instantly caught sight of a small line of horses and a mounted man pushing them toward us. I saw an unexpected look of fear enter Blue's eyes for a moment.

"Be damned," he said. "That's Snakehead."

"Who's Snakehead?"

"Bill "Snakehead" Jackson. Whiskey trader."

I wasn't sure what a whiskey trader was, but thought I might learn something by observation; so I kept my mouth shut and watched the stranger approach with his seven gaunt horses.

The man's hat brim rambled around his head like a stained and battered halo, the ridges atop the crown making two peaks like the horns of a devil. He sat his saddle as if he and his buckskin mount had become a centaur. Everything he wore grew fringes, from his leggings, to his sleeves, to his beard—the latter caked with grease into black, dirty, stringy locks. A necklace made a looping frame under the ends of his matted whiskers. The necklace seemed to be made of small black sticks or crooked little cigars strung at intervals along a beaded string. Each greasy string of whiskers branching from his beard seemed to point to one of the black sticks on his necklace.

As the whiskey trader rode directly toward us, Blue Wiggins and I stood waiting silently, one on either side of Fireball. Now I saw a hideous scar that began below the stranger's left eye, ran down his cheek, and parted his beard. He carried a large butcher knife and a revolver under his belt, a smaller blade in a sheath, a double-barreled shotgun tied to the horn of his Mexican saddle, a long rifle in a fringed scabbard across his lap.

He rode nearer, and my horse began to fret. Something waved a warning from Snakehead's bridle. Long, dusty strands of hair, three on each side of the headstall, dangled with every bobbing stride the pony made. The buckskin pony was a fine one, muscled yet lean, but its eyes held less expression than Fireball's blind one.

As Snakehead Jackson rode near enough to speak, I felt as if a dark cave or a brutal storm cloud had enveloped me. I could sense an evil stench, though the wind did not favor me. I realized now that the dusty black strands hanging from Snakehead's bridle were scalp locks. The necklace framing his matted beard was made of blackened human fingers, recognizable only by the fingernails that pointed down. The presence of this man made me feel ill. Even Fireball seemed to fall under some malignant spell, his head hanging low, and his body becoming rigid.

"Howdy," Blue Wiggins said, his voice neither friendly nor hostile.

"Blue," the whiskey trader said, as his horses began to drink. Then his gaze drifted across my face, his eyes meeting mine only for a glancing moment as they swept by me and scanned the horizon beyond.

"This fellow's name is Orn'ry," Blue said.

"Don't look orn'ry," Snakehead replied. Without looking at me again, he asked, "Where'd you get the quiver?"

I spoke quickly, before Blue could answer for me. "We had a fight with some Indians a few days ago. One dropped this."

"You drop him?"

"Nobody even got hurt."

"Quahadi Comanche," Jackson said. "Belongs to a young buck name of Pakawa. Means 'Kills Somethin'.'"

I had to wonder why he had asked me where I had gotten the quiver if he already knew the whole story. "Do you know him?" I asked.

"You shamed him bad fightin' off his tomahawk with your sword. He finds out you're wearin' his weapons, he's gonna be out for you like lightnin'."

"Maybe I'll take them back to him," I said.

Snakehead Jackson stared off into the distance. He made a single lurch that may have been caused by a scoff or a belch. "His band camps down on the Canadian, if you want to try it. Where you goin' with them kegs, Blue?"

"Charles Bent's caravan is behind us. All the holes are dry between here and the Arkansas."

"Two kegs ain't enough for a caravan."

"We left two more empty kegs up the North Fork, along with two dead mules and a dead horse."

Jackson nodded, still looking at the horizon. "Good luck." Without another word, he pushed his loose horses out of the riverbed and rode on in the direction he had been traveling. When he had gone a safe distance, Fireball took a deep breath, releasing the sigh with a warning rattle in his nostrils.

Blue, looking relieved, pointed downstream with a nod, and we began to lead Fireball back toward the trail and the caravan. We walked quite a while before I spoke.

"He didn't offer to help," I said.

"No, he didn't. Not that we'd want him to."

"Where'd he get a name like 'Snakehead'?"

"He puts snake heads in the barrels of whiskey he trades."

"Why?"

"Gives it bite, I guess."

Blue remained silent for a while. He must have been thinking about where to begin. Then he eased into a talkative mood, which came as a relief after two days of dry silence.

"It was before my time on the plains, but I've heard the story. Jackson was a trader working out of Fort William. He took him a Cheyenne squaw. This was back in 'thirty-three.

The Cheyenne and Comanches were at war then. That was
before William talked them into smokin' the peace pipe.
Some Comanche raiders up and stole Snakehead's bride.
Took her down south. He packed some whiskey down there
to ransom her. William never has 'lowed his traders to deal
much in drink, but Snakehead wanted his squaw back. It
was a brave thing, maybe foolish. Story goes he bargained
hard for his wife and almost bought her free. But the whiskey can make an Indian crazier than hell, Orn'ry, and
shootin' started before he could get her ransomed. Snakehead grabbed his Cheyenne squaw and rode. She caught a
bullet, and it killed her, but he got away with her body.

"Been tradin' whiskey to the Indians ever since, especially the Comanches. That's like tradin' raw meat to a grizzly bear. Hell, Comanches like to fight even sober. If they're
gonna be anybody, they've got to fight and kill. Whiskey
makes 'em mad as a hornet every time."

"How many whiskey traders are there out here?"

"A bunch. Most stay clear of Snakehead's range, because
he's partial to it. He works different than all the others."

"How?"

"Most of these whiskey traders bargain first, before the
Indians start drinkin'. Then they leave the whiskey and ride
off with whatever they traded for—robes, ponies, slaves.
But ol' Snakehead will sit right there amongst 'em and trade
'em drink for drink. He's got out of more shit than a tum-
blebug."

"What do you mean about slaves?" I asked, astounded at
the suggestion of slavery among the Indians.

"Oh, the Comanches are always takin' white and Mexican
kids. Women, too. There's money in payin' ransom for captives and sellin' 'em back to their families at a profit."

We trudged ahead for a mile or more, found the Santa Fe
Trail, and turned back to the east. Fireball lumbered along
under the ungainly weight of the water barrels.

"How did he get that necklace?" I asked.

"Same way he got the scar on his face. Snakehead had
him a guard for a while to watch his back while he was

tradin' drink. Big Osage warrior, over six foot. Must have weighed one-ninety, all muscle. Snakehead called him 'Injun Jack.' Well, one night Jack got into the stock and got drunk. Him and Snakehead got into a fight over somethin'. Injun Jack caught Snakehead across the face with a knife or tomahawk, and they took to fightin'. Snakehead killed him. I guess Snakehead was drunk, too. He cut off all of Injun Jack's fingers and made that necklace he wears."

It made me ill to listen to all of this, but I was glad that Bill "Snakehead" Jackson had ridden on. We were listening to the dull slosh of water in the kegs lashed to Fireball, striding long over the parched ground to save our comrades on the trail. I fancied myself a hero for hauling this little bit of precious water back on my horse. I expected a hero's welcome. But, alas, those were the days of expectations lost.

TWELVE

The sun wavered overhead like a red-hot stove lid, and I felt as though walking among the coals in an oven. Cactus spines had penetrated my moccasins in three places, making my feet sore. The long walk from the Cimarron had exhausted me, yet I knew the men in the caravan had to be in worse shape, for I had drunk my fill. Blue Wiggins marched ahead relentlessly, leading Fireball and our two precious kegs of water. To take my mind off the rigors of this trek, I entertained myself with thoughts of my friends greeting me as I came to save them. It was about this time that a distant rumble stopped me in my tracks.

Blue Wiggins stopped beside me, and turned to look west. He began to chuckle.

"What's so funny?" I asked.

"It's gonna rain pitchforks and horny toads."

I looked over my shoulder and saw the storm clouds building far in the west. We continued our march eastward, but the storm seemed to swoop down on us like an eagle. Huge black clouds billowed like wings unfolding, and lightning bolts struck like talons on the land. The wind shifted, bringing the sweet smell of rain, making Fireball toss his head and shift his feet. Blue called a halt and began untying the ropes from the water kegs.

"What are you doing?" I asked.

"I'll be damned if I'm gonna pack forty gallons of water through Noah's flood."

I saw his logic, but still felt cheated. We had gone to no small amount of inconvenience to collect our casks of water. I deserved better than this, I thought. But I was green to the plains, and couldn't think beyond myself in those days. Now I am part of the land, and know that I should have rejoiced in that coming thunderstorm. It would quench the soil and feed the flowing springs.

"Easy," I said to Fireball, helping to steady him as Blue Wiggins and I lowered the kegs to the ground. The wings of the storm had spread around and over us, blocking out the sun. Fireball snorted his warning again in a long rattle that rolled from his nostrils. The smell of rain came stronger on a cool blast from directly overhead. A hailstone the size of a man's fist suddenly struck the ground near us, making Fireball flinch as if some other horse had stomped to warn him. Blue Wiggins pulled his hat down tight. I looked around for cover. Fireball was the only cover I could see, and I wasn't desperate enough to crawl among his stamping hooves.

"Better leave him go," Blue said.

"Pardon?"

"Take the bridle off and leave him go. He'll just get loose and break a rein if you don't. He come back before, didn't he? Anyway, he's a target."

"For whom?"

A lightning bolt struck the open plains less than a mile away.

Blue grinned and shrugged. "The good Lord? The Thunderbird?"

Reluctantly, I pulled the packsaddle and bridle from Fireball. He took off in a head-high lope and disappeared into a wall of rain swinging around to engulf us from the south. Hailstones, smaller than the first one, began to pelt the earth around us, causing me to hunker under my hat brim and flinch with every one that struck me on an unprotected shoulder or knee. I soon realized that flinching accomplished nothing, and simply let the icy missiles pepper me, preferring them to the bolts of instant electricity that struck all around, threatening to skewer me with white-hot heat powerful enough to rip me open like gutted venison.

Soon, however, the hail and lightning passed on to the east with the vanguard of storm clouds. Then the rain mounted. No amount of mathematical calculation could allow me to fathom how so much water could have hung in the sky. It came down like one of our Cimarron River kegs dumped instantly over my head, followed by another, then another, then countless others—not just over me, but over everything that surrounded me, though I could no longer see anything around me. Astounded, I held my hand out at arm's length and watched it all but disappear behind the veil of rain. But I had grown so cold in the chill torrent from above that I had felt compelled to wrap my arms around my chest and tuck my hands under my arms. I shivered uncontrollably. When I looked at Blue Wiggins for reassurance, I found him curled up and hunkered over like me, waiting out the deluge.

At length, the rain slackened. We stood up and watched rivulets twine everywhere around us like snakes. Our feet sank into the softened ground up to our ankles. The sky brightened, and patches of blue could be seen through the clouds to the west. To the east, the distant thunder blasts rumbled like memories.

I felt drenched and humbled. I sat down on one of the kegs we had filled at the Cimarron. A returning hero no

more than half an hour ago, I was now afoot, my mission
no longer even necessary.

Blue sat on the other keg and we watched the purple
tempest shrink away to the east. "I'm hungry," he said at
last. "Let's go get supper."

We trudged east through the mud for two hours before
the first wagon appeared over a rise in the plains. From a
distance, we recognized Charles Bent tending his team of
oxen as they sniffed for graze around his wagon. The next
wagon was barely visible in the distance.

"They must be strung out for miles," Blue said. "When
it gets bad, the only thing to do is let the strong go on ahead
and the weak drag behind. Somebody's got to get to water
if anybody's gonna live."

We slogged the last leg up to the mired wagon as Charles
stood ready to greet us. We walked up to face him and saw
a wry grin lifting one side of his mouth.

"I know I sent you boys for water, but damn . . ."

We waited the rest of the day, and half of the next day
for the rest of the caravan to catch up. As Blue had suggested, the weaker animals had lagged behind, and the
wagons had become separated by miles. Though normally
slower, the oxen had fared better and had moved to the front,
while the mule teams had slipped farther and farther behind.
However, the puddled rainwater renewed the strength of the
animals quickly. Within a day and a half, the men and beasts
were all accounted for and back on the trail to the Cimarron.

That day, we reached the two water barrels Blue Wiggins
and I had left on the trail. Fireball stood beside them, his
one good eye turned up the trail to watch for our approach.
I was so glad to see him that I hugged him, and he seemed
so pleased with our reunion that he virtually thrust his nose
into the bridle.

We camped a day at the Cimarron to let the rainwater recede. Blue Wiggins and I took advantage of the stop to ride

upstream and retrieve the saddles and water barrels we had left behind. Blue had purchased another mount from Tom Boggs to replace the gelding that had died of thirst. We rode bareback on saddle blankets.

We passed the bones of Blue's dead horse first, along with his saddle and the two empty barrels. I was amazed at how quickly the wolves, coyotes, and vultures had stripped the skeleton. He put his saddle on his new horse, and we rode on up the North Fork to find my saddle. But before we reached it, we surprised a herd of about three hundred buffalo that stampeded out of the river basin the moment we appeared to them around a bend. Fireball wanted to give chase, but I held him back. Perhaps if I had had my saddle, I would have tried to kill one, but I was not yet accustomed to riding bareback in those days. That would come later.

"Keep your wits about you," Blue said. "Those buffalo were spooky."

The farther we rode up the North Fork, the more buffalo we encountered. Soon they made a solid mass above the riverbank that rolled on for miles over the rises in the plains. I had to stop on the brink of the riverbank and stare at them. For one of the few times in my life, my ability to enumerate failed me. My brain would not make the usual calculations and estimations. In that writhing mass of hide and horns, I could sense interminable boundaries out of sight and incalculable. Here was something incomprehensible, and it fascinated me.

"How many do reckon there are?" Blue Wiggins asked.

"I don't know," I admitted.

"I reckon there's a million."

"Do you understand what a million of something would look like if you could see it laid out before you?"

"I reckon it would look like that," Blue said, pointing his chin at the great herd.

We took a step over the riverbank, and the animals close enough to define us all bolted, as if in complete terror.

"Check your firin' cap on that pistol," Blue said. "If we

run on to Indians, don't you shoot, you hear? Save that round. They'll try to draw our fire, but don't you let them bluff you. We use our first round, and we're scalped."

"I'll string my bow," I said.

Blue chuckled. "Yeah, they might laugh to death. I've seen you shoot that thing. You just stick to usin' your pistol."

We found my saddle, cinched it onto Fireball, and turned back. It was only mid-morning, as we had made good time with our refreshed horses, and we were on schedule to return to the caravan by mid-afternoon. We stopped to lash the empty barrels onto Fireball's saddle. We tied the packsaddle on behind Blue's cantle and took turns riding his horse. We had drifted back in good time, and were only an hour or so from the Santa Fe Trail and the safety of our caravan.

I was riding Blue's horse, and he was leading Fireball. I saw the Indians first, for I was higher up. "Oh, no," I said. "Blue."

He followed my eyes to the riders across the North Fork of the Cimarron. "Get down, Orn'ry. Maybe they won't see us."

I swung down from the saddle and hoped we could get into the riverbank timber before the braves saw us. I counted five of them at a glance. The war cry that pierced the rush of running water told me we had been discovered.

"You remember what I told you," Blue said.

"I know."

"We'll stand back-to-back." Blue took up his position behind me. "Use your horse for cover and save that shot."

"I understand." My heart raced and my stomach sickened with fear, but my hand felt steady enough and my eyes darted with anticipation of the coming encounter.

The braves came across the river, plunging their mounts into the stream at a gallop. They descended on us quicker than I could have imagined and surrounded us, staying just outside of effective pistol range. Then they began to circle. One rider would attempt to distract us with a feint or a yell, while another rider on the other side of the circle would charge even closer with seemingly foolhardy courage designed to make us spend a precious pistol round.

"Hold your fire, Orn'ry. We're alright. We've got to stand our ground here."

They circled for what seemed hours, playing a deadly game of bluff, coming closer each time, until finally I could look each warrior in the eye. Over the sights of the pistol I dared not use, I saw expressions in their faces. In two of the warriors—one on a painted pony, the other on a fine bay—I saw pure loathing for me and my race. In one rider on a sorrel mount with flaxen mane, I saw a look of joy, as if this business of feint-and-bluff made him laughably happy. In the two youngest riders, one riding a gray and the other a dun, I recognized the same fear that I felt while looking back at them, yet they charged and wheeled and threatened me with recklessness equal to their older comrades.

Then I recognized the young warrior on the dun. We had traded blows hand-to-hand with sword and battle-axe. Even now I wore his quiver and bow case slung across my shoulders. According to the whiskey trader, Snakehead Jackson, his name was Pakawa, or Kills Something.

He charged at me, and though I saw the shaken pride in his eyes, he turned back only when he could see the dark center of my muzzle, flung himself to the side of his mount, and yelled at me under the neck of the pony in Spanish:

"Coward! I will kill you for taking my weapons!"

"I will return your weapons to you," I replied.

Instantly, he wheeled his pony around and stopped. "You have touched them and destroyed their power."

"You should not have attacked me the day I killed the buffalo."

Kills Something circled. "You should not have killed my buffalo."

Blue Wiggins took aim on another circling warrior. "What the hell are you two yammerin' about?" he said.

"That's Pakawa."

"Who?"

"Kills Something."

"What?"

"I'm wearing his weapons."

"Shit!"

With my back pressed against Blue's back, I kept Fireball in front of me most of the time for cover. He pranced nervously at first, as the warriors charged and circled, then seemed to settle down when he sensed this was just a game.

"They won't shoot the horses," Blue said. "That's what they're after. That and our scalps. Use your mount for cover and stand your ground."

At length, the warriors stopped circling, for the exercise only tired their mounts. They stood evenly spaced around us. The two angry warriors chided us in Spanish with words like *"cobarde"* and *"cabron."* The happy warrior laughed at us. The young brave on the gray simply watched and looked toward his friends for courage. Kills Something gestured at me in anger and frustration. He hated, yet respected me.

My arms got tired of holding my pistol and my reins, so I let them fall to my side.

"Don't get too relaxed," Blue said.

"Are they all Comanches?" I asked, surprised to hear my voice come out sounding so calm.

"That one happy buck might be Kiowa."

"What makes you think that?"

"All them metal earrings and tinklers all over his leggin's and bridle. Kiowas like all that shiny metal stuff all over."

My eyes swept from Indian to Indian. "How long is this going to go on?"

"Till dark, unless they get tired of it and leave."

"What happens at dark?"

"They'll likely rush us and kill us, unless somebody comes to help us."

"Then why are you so calm?"

"I don't want to die all tensed up, do you?"

"I don't want to die at all."

"Then stand your ground and stay awake."

"I haven't slept in two days, and I'm not likely to sleep in two more."

Blue Wiggins chuckled, and I could feel his shoulders bouncing against mine. "You're a funny feller, Orn'ry. Now, look out. They're gonna start shootin' arrows. Try to keep a horse in front of you or behind you. They won't shoot a horse."

As Blue predicted, the warriors strung their bows and notched their arrows. I watched every enemy warrior I could keep in front of me, but I knew that one, two, or three of them would be on my blind side at all times. I tried to keep Fireball in front of me and Blue's mount behind for cover, but with the warriors milling constantly about us, Blue and I had to duck and turn all the while, until the ground under us looked as if two bulls had been fighting there. Only three times did a warrior actually loose an arrow, and each time it hissed past my head—once passing between my head and Blue's.

"Don't shoot back," Blue warned. "You spend that round, and we're done. They'll rush us faster than you think."

The game went on, and my exhaustion mounted. The sun moved west in the sky. The riverbank shadows reached and gathered us in. The warriors around us laughed or taunted, but Blue Wiggins and I stood steadfast, our fingers on triggers we dared not use.

"Pakawa," I shouted at last, growing weary of the game.

The Indians halted their deadly mill, perhaps astounded that I knew a name among them.

"You speak my name."

"This is *loco*. What reason do you have to kill me? We should be friends. I have things to trade to you. I have good hickory for making bows, and other things you can use."

"What things?"

"I will bring them. You will see."

"You will bring me your scalp."

"I will bring weapons to replace the ones you dropped. We will start a trade that will benefit us both."

"I want only your scalp for my belt!"

"What are you doin'?" Blue asked.

"Reasoning with him."

"Reason's asshole. He's a Comanche, dammit."

The deathlike chill of evening had begun to seep into our clothes when we heard the shouts and the hoofbeats. From downstream came our salvation. Seven riders, including Charles Bent and Tom Boggs, galloped up the river valley, guns roaring and voices shouting. Wisely, the Indians fled, but not before one of them sank an arrow into Blue Wiggins's new horse. The point sank deep into a hindquarter. Right then and there, we roped and threw that horse to the ground, and pulled out the arrow. Luckily, it was a hunting point and had no barbs.

"Looks like they had you boys hemmed up awhile," Charles Bent said, studying the trodden ground under us.

"We stood our ground," Blue said. "Me and Orn'ry. Back to back." He said it casually, as if merely relieved, but he was proud.

I simply nodded. I felt tired. I thought, tonight, in the protection of the guarded caravan, I might actually sleep.

THIRTEEN

MAY 11, 1845
HEADWATERS OF THE CANADIAN RIVER,
NUEVA MEXICO

I sat near enough to the fire to work by its light, far enough
away to roll into the shadows should Indians attack. We
hadn't encountered any hostiles since our stand on the Cimarron, but I had adopted my own ritualistic survival habits.
Leaning against the spokes of a wagon wheel, a blanket over
my shoulders, I reclined comfortably as I worked on my
weapon.

The ramrod for my single-shot pistol was made of a
wooden dowel capped in brass on one end. I had filed the
end away from the brass cap, making it into a tube. I had
repositioned this tube by moving it farther out onto the end
of the dowel. I had slightly flared the exposed end of the
brass tube so that it would accept and hold a bullet, yet still
fit into the muzzle of the weapon.

Now I practiced my deception. I poured the gunpowder
down the muzzle of my pistol. I dropped the bullet in and
pretended to tamp it down with the ramrod. In reality, of
course, the open brass end on my ramrod seized the bullet
and retrieved it from the pistol barrel when I withdrew the
ramrod. Palming the bullet deftly, I continued the normal
loading process, stuffing paper wadding into the muzzle. Casually, I reversed the ramrod and used the end opposite the
brass tube to pack the wadding in, while simultaneously
securing the bullet from the flared brass tube. Now my pistol
was loaded with powder and wadding, but the bullet was
tucked away in a crease of my palm. Anyone who might

have been watching would assume that the bullet had remained in the gun, for I had practiced the illusion to the point that the entire procedure appeared perfectly routine. I could now hand the pistol to a volunteer, ask him to fire the gun at me, and pretend to catch the bullet in midair, though, of course, I would have the bullet already palmed neatly away in my hand.

I didn't know if I would ever actually employ this trick. My book on legerdemain had warned that it was fraught with myriad dangers ranging from powder burn to death. Nevertheless, I could clutch that bullet in the folds of my palm with such practiced facility that I could shake a man's hand without his feeling the projectile there.

As I practiced this trick, I noticed Charles Bent approaching from across the camp. Quickly, I patched the bullet and rammed it into my pistol, loading the weapon now in earnest. It would require only a live percussion cap to make it ready.

Charles came to the wagon where I sat and crouched next to me, resting one weathered palm on a wheel spoke. "That's a good thing to practice," he said.

"Pardon?" I asked, wondering if he had discovered my illusion.

"Loading your weapon. Could save your scalp if you can shave a few seconds off. Of course, it's different under fire."

"Yes, sir," I said.

"I need you to stand guard tonight. Antone has come down with some cramps and fever. I think he ate something gone bad."

"I'm ready," I said, fixing the percussion cap on my pistol.

"Take the west side of camp. I'll relieve you myself about four so you can sleep."

I looked up at the moon, rising one day shy of full. "I won't sleep tonight," I said. "I can stand guard till dawn."

Charles glanced at the moon. By now he knew of my peculiarities. "That's better yet." He looked in silence over the camp for a few seconds, as if to admire its layout and neatness. "There's going to be a change tomorrow."

"Sir?"

"The Delaware scouted ahead. Snow's melted early in the mountains. We can get a wagon over the pass to Taos." He patted the spoke of the wheel against which I leaned. "This one's bound for the store in Taos, anyway. Most of the loose stock is going to my ranch outside of Taos, too, so I'm going to take the shortcut over the mountains with this wagon and the cavvy, while Blue leads the rest of the caravan 'round the mountains to Santa Fe."

"Yes, sir?"

"Choice is yours. You can go with Blue if you want to see Santa Fe, but I could use another rider with a good one-eyed horse."

"I'll go over the mountains with you."

"Well, think about it overnight. It's a tougher road."

"I've already thought about it, Mr. Bent."

He nodded. "It's cool up there."

He stared across the corralled wagons again. We were camped near the Canadian River, and during the lull in the conversation, I could hear it singing in its bed.

"Canadian's down," he said. "Not much snow last winter. You know how far this river runs?"

"No, sir. I haven't seen a map."

"No mapmaker's ever been down this river. It flows smack into Comanche territory, and then runs all the way to the Arkansas in the Indian Nations. William has sent traders out there before. Even been there himself. Too wild. Damn Comanches. Can't figure 'em."

"The whiskey trader—Snakehead Jackson—he trades there."

Charles snorted. "Snakehead's going to be the guest of honor at a scalp dance some night. Damn whiskey! You stay away from that drink and that trade, Honoré. That's my advice, and I don't give advice often."

"But if they'll trade with Snakehead, why won't they trade with your brother?"

"They don't *have* to trade, they're Comanches. If they

need something, they either make it or steal it."

"Seems like they'd rather trade than steal."

Charles Bent looked right at me for a moment. "You don't understand, kid. They're not like us. They don't have the same rules. William figures the whole Comanche nation couldn't mount more than five thousand warriors even if they could all get together, which they can't. There are different, independent bands. So they've got five thousand warriors, scattered far and wide, with no central leadership, and yet they rule a territory darn near the size of the states back east. Everything from San Antonio to Santa Fe to the Great Bend of the Arkansas. They raid as far north as Fort Laramie and as far south as Chihuahua, Mexico. They ride like . . . well, nobody knows."

I nodded. "I've seen them ride."

"You haven't seen squat yet. They ride where they will, take what they want, do what they please. They don't hoard gold or silver, but they are rich beyond the dreams of European kings and queens. A good trade with the Comanches would mean untold profits in buffalo robes, pelts, and horses. Especially horses. Some say they own as many as six ponies for every warrior, and that's just average. I've heard stories of chiefs who own two or three hundred horses. They steal them from Mexico. Riding stock like that will sell for a tidy premium in Missouri with settlement moving west."

"They must need something we could trade to them."

Charles shook his head. "Need, no. Now, we do have a few little things they want, like iron and steel, tobacco, paint, blankets, beads. The warriors are vain. They like mirrors. You'd think they'd want guns, but most of them prefer their bows and arrows. Not much to base a trade on. On top of all that, they're scary as hell. William's sent traders down there. Of the few that have survived, only John Hatcher is willing to go back."

I listened to the Canadian surging toward Comanche country. "I'd like to try it."

"I'm sure you'd be welcome. They'd probably give you

to the squaws to roast real slow. That's not just talk, kid. Every man among them makes his own rules out there, and some of them are mad enough to torture you to death for two days if they think it'll even the score for something some other white man did to them five hundred miles away. You don't know those people."

"I know one of them by name. Pakawa. Kills Something."

"He probably figures *your* name is *Something.*"

"I know they're frightening," I said. "I almost wet my britches back on the Cimarron. But look at this." I drew an arrow from Kills Something's captured quiver. "No barbarian could produce something like this. This arrow speaks like a violin. This is art. They've got to appreciate something other than iron and steel." I turned the arrow in my hand, admiringly. "I think I can relate to them."

"You can relate to a lance point in your guts. Get it out of your head." He stood abruptly, obviously annoyed at me. "Take the west guard, like I told you, and be ready to ride at dawn."

Charles was right. It was cool up there. Our mule-drawn wagon lurched up a trace too narrow and steep to pass as a road, the jaded beasts grinding hooves against stone and nodding their heads in laborious affirmation as they leaned into the harness. The trace snaked among piñon pines that gave way to ponderosas as we climbed higher, and those grew in size as we continued to ascend. The rare vibrance of the mountains sank into me gradually, filling me by increments with a rapture I had never known.

The cavvy gave me absolutely no trouble, for the beasts had long since grown accustomed to following the sounds of a traveling wagon. Green grass appeared, first in bunches, then in sprawling meadows. I cannot explain the pleasure I felt watching those stupid beasts snatch up mouthfuls of grass as they ambled along with the lone freight wagon.

"Better turn around and look at it," Charles said, riding back from the point.

I turned, not knowing what to expect. Hundreds of feet below, the plains I had crossed sprawled away to the far horizons, deceptively serene from this lofty vantage. It looked so huge that I could not gather it, and it occurred to me that I would have to pace off a mile some time and study the distance so that I could understand such a measure by extrapolation of the known quantity.

"I've heard that you crossed the ocean," Charles said.

"Yes, sir. On a cotton packet."

"How does it compare?"

"With what?"

"Crossing that." He gestured in one sweeping motion across the whole great expanse of carved flatlands before us.

"I slept in a hammock instead of on the ground. I gathered sail instead of stock. I thirsted for wind instead of water, then got more than I wanted. I'd trade a gale in the upper spars for a skirmish with Comanches."

Charles Bent chuckled. "I don't know whether you mean the one is preferable to the other on account of danger or in spite of it."

"I don't either, Mr. Bent. But I know I'll never cross the ocean again."

"You don't know any such thing. You might circle the world before you're done."

"I can't imagine why, sir."

"That's what happens in life. Stuff you can't imagine."

Charles Bent was a wise man. Over the scores of years that have passed since that day, I have thought often about his simple and profound words. How many times have I seen the sun set on some strange scene that I could not have envisioned at sunrise? Your life is the same, yes? What comes next for you? For me? We make our plans as if we enjoy control over this precarious existence to which we cling. Yet chaos is our reality, and we just scarcely manage day by day to keep our affairs from whirling beyond all control. Charles Bent's words would haunt even himself soon enough. Events he could not possibly have imagined would draw him into an inescapable vortex and etch his name ever deeper into the historical annals of the American West.

<hr />

We continued our exhausting trek up the mountain until the mules had almost given out. Charles called a halt in a high pasture surrounded by firs and pines. A brook ran nearby, filled with water so cold that it hurt my mouth to drink it. We made camp. Charles rode a horse up the trail and looked over a ridge to the north. He came back at a lope, drawing rein next to me.

"Let the cavvy drift," he said. "I want you to gather as much firewood as you can get your hands on before dark."

I rode back to the wagon, tied Fireball, and began gathering armloads of pine, sweeping the area around camp in increasingly broad arcs to make the most efficient use of the little daylight I had left. When I carried back my first armload of wood, I saw the Mexican muleteers tacking an old wagon sheet to the underside of the wagon bed so that it would reach the ground. The sheet covered three sides of the wagon and was open to the south. One Mexican was digging a trench around the sheet and using the dirt to weight down the bottom of the canvas.

"Throw that wood here," Charles ordered, pointing to the ground in front of the opening the wagon sheet made to the south. "We'll need a lot more than that."

A French-Canadian trader named Antone gathered wood with me, but he wandered aimlessly about in search of it, unlike me in my deliberate sweeps through the forest. My woodpile was so much bigger than his that I finally just kicked all the wood together to prevent any embarrassment.

By this time, I had gathered that these mountain nights might get somewhat cool, yet the exertion of wood gathering caused me to sweat. The cook had started a fire in front of the opening of our makeshift shelter and was preparing the best feast he could muster under the circumstances.

"I hope you boys have an appetite," he said. "It's going to get cold tonight, and you'll need warm grub in your bellies."

I could not imagine the temperature dropping off to any extreme degree. In fact, the climate was so pleasant that I went about in my shirtsleeves feeling perfectly comfortable.

"You don't have a coat, do you, Honoré?" Charles asked me.

"No, sir, but I'm alright. I can cover up with my saddle blanket."

"Son, you're as green as a branch. Honoré Greenwood, that's your name. There's a damn blue norther coming, Mr. Greenwood. Can't you see the sky?"

I had noticed a dark bank of clouds to the north, but the term "blue norther" meant nothing to me. Charles climbed into the wagon and threw out several blankets and a tattered piece of tarpaulin. He ordered me to take them.

We ate salt pork and fresh venison the Delaware had killed, and even broke into the high-profit supplies of canned sardines and smoked oysters normally reserved for the store at Taos. We gorged ourselves by order of our wagon master.

"By morning everything will be too frozen to eat," he said, "so you boys better stuff your stomachs while you can."

As the last light of day faded, I saw Fireball stroll into the woods. His head hanging low, he backed his rump up to the south side of a large ponderosa pine. If I couldn't believe Charles Bent, I could trust Fireball. It was going to get cold.

After eating, I walked north of the wagon. Stars hung over me and behind me to the south, dusting the sky in a way I had not yet before seen, for I had never climbed to such an altitude in such crisp air. But the storm clouds, now invisible in the dark, had obliterated the constellations to the north. I stood waiting for the blue norther for almost an hour, enjoying the sounds of friendly voices—the only noise in a mysteriously still forest.

Then I began to hear the roar. It came as a distant whisper at first, but grew quickly. I looked overhead. The stars had disappeared. The far side of the mountain seemed to rumble. A mischievous whistle sang over the summit to the north. Then a blast came over the peak, as if from the wing beat of a colossal bird of prey. The forest before me began to shriek, and its roar engulfed me. An icy wall of wind slammed into my face, tearing my hat away. I stood facing it a mere second or two, then turned in terror, already shivering, and ran to the suddenly pitiful shelter of wagon box and canvas.

I dived under the wagon box by the light of a fire that seemed all but blown out. It gave no warmth. I wrapped myself in the blankets Charles had given me. The roar of the storm ridiculed any attempt at conversation, so we simply huddled and shivered and tossed branches onto the fire.

I felt like a human thermometer, my quicksilver plunging cold into the tips of my toes. The first snow came in pellets that rattled the canvas. Then, a silent deluge of heavy frozen flakes began, falling so thick that it threatened our fire. We tossed more wood on. Something nudged my shoulder, and I found a flask of brandy. I took a useless swig, and passed it on.

The cold that had already penetrated my blankets seeped into my very skin. As the snow whitened the ground up to the edges of our fire, the cold ate deeper into my limbs, chilling my very bones. As minutes turned to hours, that same marching chill of death invaded my lungs, my guts, and my very heart. The roar of wind lessened to a howl, and the howl diminished to a moan; but the cold only intensified. Looking back, it may merely have been the muffling quality of the snow that made the wind seem less loud. I didn't think of it at the time, for I had grown too cold to think.

A few hours of trembling can tire a body to the point of exhaustion. I tried to move my limbs to keep myself from shivering; but every time I shifted, I felt the cold touch me in a new place. It was better to remain still and keep the thin, warm layer of air next to my body. Once I crawled out of the shelter to kick some pieces of firewood closer, but I found myself shaking violently by the time I crawled back into my blankets.

At length, the wind died, and our fire, which had crept gradually closer to us as we tossed on wood, seemed to cast some heat on us. We would turn occasionally to let the flames warm our backsides. One of the Mexicans backed so close to the flames that the tail of his coat caught fire. Yet it was so mercilessly cold that he didn't feel the flames until they had burned his coat all the way up to the collar.

We spent the whole next day stranded in the snow. Twice we made wood-gathering forays into the forest, and I was able to check on Fireball, who hadn't moved. We had melted some snow to drink, and I carried a pan full of it to my horse. A thin sheet of ice covered it by the time I got it to him. He wouldn't drink. He just seemed to want me to leave him alone.

Breaking a trail through the waist-deep snow, I went about gathering wood, my feet turning to aching blocks of ice. I came across one of the mules that had pulled the wagon up the mountain the day before. He was standing up, covered in snow except for his rump and withers. His head was low and buried in snow. He had frozen to death standing up in the forest.

The cold relented later that day, but it never rose above freezing. Sitting under our shelter near the fire, the men told stories of blizzards much colder and longer than this one. The snow had quit, though the sky remained cloudy. My toes warmed up enough to hurt like crazy. We chewed on dried meat, and I listened to the stories. They spoke of friends who had lost toes and fingers to frostbite and the horror of amputation. Some had lost a foot. One that Charles knew of lost both feet. Ears, noses, hands. I inched closer to the fire.

"If the clouds break tonight, it'll get colder than last night," Charles said.

"The clouds will break," Don Turo said.

I slept some that afternoon, covered in borrowed blankets, my feet close to the fire and my hands curled next to my chest. I dreamt of amputation. I made three more advances into the pines for firewood before dark. The clouds broke just in time to let us see the sun before it sank over the crest to the west. I could literally feel the temperature drop like a kingfisher plunging into frigid waters.

Indeed, I believe it got colder that night than the night before. I wondered how many more mules would freeze. I vowed that I would not. We kept the fire stoked, and in the absence of wind, it benefited us much more than the previous night. We made a semicircle around the flames. Seemingly of their own accord, our robes and blankets had overlapped around and between us, forming a barrier to the cold, trapping each man's warmth. Still, we shivered violently, but survived. Had we run out of fuel, we would have frozen to death like that mule.

Nothing makes a man yearn for civilization like a blizzard. I had been on the trail almost two months, and the wilderness had lost its allure. I longed for Taos—a town I didn't even know, yet one I assumed would have houses and beds and fireplaces. I could not have foreseen that in that dusty little village on Mexico's northern frontier, I would find the girl who would capture and hold my heart for a lifetime.

FOURTEEN

My first glimpse of her came from a distance, as she was walking across the San Fernandez de Taos plaza. The hem of her skirt swirled seductively above her ankles. Her hips shifted and glided invitingly. A breeze tossed waves of her hair, long and dark. Her skin looked like coffee with lots of cream, and I saw in her face the features of Spanish beauties I had glimpsed occasionally in Paris. Yet no girl had ever looked so beautiful to me. I felt at once a desire, a desperation, a hopefulness and a hopelessness. All this at first glance!

Someone called her name, "Gabriela!" and she pivoted lithely on one foot, caught sight of a friend, and flashed a smile that struck like a sunbeam. This was the moment our wagon entered the plaza behind me, and the clatter of wheels and hooves attracted Gabriela's attention.

According to custom, our entire party had bathed and laundered our clothes outside of town, so I rode in fresh, straddling Fireball, sleek and lean. My pony pranced at the excitement of trail's end, strange people and beasts flaring his nostrils and walling his one eye. Jibber darted ahead of me, eager to tangle with any new rival. My saber swung in its buckskin scabbard. My pistol jutted from my belt. My hat brim flapped at the same gust that had tossed Gabriela's hair. As Fireball pranced sideways to enter the plaza, Gabriela's gaze caught mine.

I thought perhaps I should look away politely, but I could not. Her eyes blazed into mine, marking my soul. The look she gave me was part warning, part invitation, part thrill, part sorrow. Eventually, I would understand, but at that moment I knew only that I must meet her, speak to her, try to make her life one with my own. And I knew, somehow, from that first furtive gaze, that Gabriela wanted the same from me, however impossible.

"You're too late," Charles Bent said. He missed nothing that concerned his men and his business.

"Sir?" I replied as he rode between me and Gabriela, breaking my line of sight with her.

"She's promised to one of the Zavaleta boys. The wedding's been arranged for years."

"I'm not sure whom you mean," I said, somewhat embarrassed.

"Ha!" Charles blurted. He was in a good mood, having arrived safely at Taos after the long haul overland. His wife and children lived near the plaza, I had learned, and he would see them soon. "She's to be married this spring, and there will be no changing her father's mind. Don Bernardo Fortunado Badillo would chase you clean out of Taos if he saw you ogling his daughter that way. Anyhow, there's plenty of other *señoritas* in town, so just forget about Gabriela Badillo."

When Charles moved out of my way, Gabriela had gone, and I felt my heart sinking over what he had said about her. I heard Jibber bark, and located him at the corner of a building. Around that same adobe corner, I glimpsed Gabriela peeking at me. I caught her eye again, briefly. I smiled. She returned the smile, and disappeared.

We continued on to the Bent–St. Vrain store, followed by barefoot Mexican boys and comely women, some with cheeks painted red. Old men stopped to watch us pass. Dogs barked at our mounts and our mule team and business owners stepped from their adobe storefronts to judge our outfit and cargo. A dignified yet slightly disheveled gentleman stepped from the Bent–St. Vrain store and smiled.

"Hey, partner!" he yelled.

"Hello, Ceran," Charles called.

Ceran St. Vrain, his shirt half untucked and his hair and beard sticking out everywhere, strode out to shake hands with Charles Bent after the wagon boss dismounted. Charles ordered the wagon unloaded immediately, so I climbed into the back and began handing goods to the men outside who carried them from the wagon to the store.

"How are things in Santa Fe?" St. Vrain asked.

"I don't know. I came over the mountains with this wagon."

"Didn't it snow?"

"Not bad."

"So, you've avoided customs with this wagon," St. Vrain said in a lower voice, glancing both ways down the street.

"So far. That's why I want to get this thing unloaded. I sent the other wagons to Santa Fe with Blue Wiggins and the boys. Maybe they'll keep the customs agent too busy to worry about this one, but we'd better make up some sort of inventory just in case."

"I'll do it."

"Tell them we got caught in a blizzard and had to eat all the canned foods. That'll help."

"Right," St. Vrain said, eyeing a crate of sardines I had slid to the back of the wagon. He looked right at me. "Who are you?" he demanded.

"My name's Honoré." I offered my hand.

"He's alright, Ceran. Joined in Missouri and served as cavvy boy. Mr. Greenwood, this is our partner, Ceran St. Vrain."

"I'd like to set up a trade with the Comanches," I said boldly, shaking St. Vrain's hand.

He looked at his business partner, Charles Bent. "I thought you said he was alright."

"He's just green. Honoré, unload the wagon and keep your ambitions to yourself." With that, he pulled Ceran St. Vrain aside to continue their business discussion, but my hearing and powers of concentration were such that I caught important parts of the conversation.

St. Vrain said that feelings toward Americans—and all non-Mexicans—had hardened in recent months. Reports of *Americano* troop movements, and attacks by renegade Texans had led to the belief that war between Mexico and the

United States would soon erupt, especially since President
Polk had promised to bring Texas into the Union. Ceran
said he and his family members had received threats. He
had made escape plans for his family and advised Charles
to do the same. To this, Charles gave only a grim nod.

The thought struck me, as I unloaded the wagon and
eavesdropped on my employers, that this was no time or
place for a fugitive French boy to fall in love with a Mexican girl promised to someone else, but not even a genius's
mind can control his heart.

With the unloading accomplished, Charles Bent invited
his employees into the store and paid every man with Mexican silver counted from an iron strongbox. I had taken my
possibles sack containing my Stradivarius from the wagon
and now slung it over my shoulder. As I waited last in line
to take my pay, I began to absorb my first strong impres-
sions of New Mexican architecture. Because it was strange
to me, I found the style of building both charming and fascinating. The room felt cool and smelled slightly musty. The
walls muffled noise and made the interior seem soft. A fireplace bulged from one corner, shaped like a quartered bee-
hive, blackened inside with soot. Above, whole timbers
spanned from wall to wall, layered over with smaller beams
running perpendicular. The place felt secure and substantial,
and it charmed me with mysteries. The very walls around
me possessed the lure of the unknown and, as such, appealed
to me.

As the men got paid, they left the store in long strides.
The muleteers drove the wagon away as Charles handed me
my pay. Ceran St. Vrain asked for my signature in a ledger
book, and I wrote it in fine scroll with a quill pen under the
X's of illiterate bullwhackers and mule skinners witnessed
by Ceran St. Vrain:

Honoré Greenwood

Greenwood was a new alias I had taken on, and one that
would stick with me awhile.

You write with a fine hand, Mr. Greenwood," Ceran said.
"Thank you," I replied.

As Ceran and Charles pored over books and ledgers, I
stepped outside with silver coins jingling in my pocket. I
swept the plaza for a glimpse of Gabriela, but did not really
expect to see her. The other men had left for places unknown to me, so I sat alone on top of a keg. Fireball stood
tied at the hitching rail beside Charles's mount, so I knew
my employer would emerge sooner or later—though perhaps he was my former employer, because I didn't know
whether or not my services were needed any longer.

I watched the plaza of San Fernandez de Taos. Three old
Indian men sat across the open square from me, dressed in
a combination of cotton cloth and deerskin. I assumed they
hailed from the Taos Pueblo, a couple of miles away, which
I had seen from the mountainside as we descended. Charles
had told me that the pueblo was older than anyone knew—
perhaps a thousand years old, he said. He had also pointed
out a Spanish mission church, only a hundred years old,
standing near the pueblo. I wanted to ride to the pueblo and
explore it, but for now I was content with watching the Taos
plaza.

In the shade of some cottonwoods, I noticed a cluster of
five bearded men dressed in various articles of threadbare
store-bought clothing and blackened buckskin leggings or
shirts. One wore a cap of fox fur. The others wore felt hats
or went bareheaded. They sprawled on the ground, a couple
of them on colorful blankets they had spread. Two smoked
pipes, and one passed an earthen jug to another. Scattered
about them, within easy reach, lay an impressive assortment
of weaponry including long rifles, knives, war axes, and
horse pistols. A peal of laughter burst from them as they
held council there in the plaza.

A dark-skinned man in white cotton entered the plaza, a
string of four burros following him, the tail of the leader
tied to the head of the follower all the way down the line.
He wore a large sombrero like the one my friend Don Turo
owned. I saw him glance suspiciously at the mountain men

in the cottonwood shade. He nodded at the three old Indians, and one of them raised a languid hand in return. The Mexican did not seem to notice me, for I was small and plain and still. It made me wonder why Gabriela had noticed me when I entered the plaza. If not for Fireball's prancing, I thought, I might have never caught her eye. She had probably forgotten about me by now, and I would never see her again. Still, I held a vague hope.

Charles Bent stepped out of the store, walked right past me, and then noticed Fireball standing at the hitching rail. He turned, and only now saw me where I sat against the wall on top of a keg. He looked at me and sighed.

"Well, come on," he said. "No need in you getting robbed and killed with all my pay in your pocket."

We mounted and rode but a short distance through crooked streets to the home of Charles Bent. All manner of commotion broke out as servants and children welcomed him home. His wife, Ignacia, wept and clung to him. She was petite and attractive and spoke only Spanish. She held a three-year-old daughter, Teresina, as eight-year-old Alfredo Bent wrestled with his father's leg, growling like a bear.

Tom Boggs was already there, for he was engaged to marry Charles's oldest daughter, who was about my age. "Orn'ry," he said, "this here's my fiancée, Rumalda. Rumalda, this is Orn'ry Greenwood." He looked at me with a devilish grin. "You keep your hands off, now, you hear?"

I could tell that Tom said this only half in jest.

Rumalda was, in reality, Charles's stepdaughter, for he had married a widow. She was shy and pretty, and I liked her right away, but not, of course, as I had fallen for Gabriela Badillo after one glance in the plaza. However, it occurred to me quickly that in a town as small and remote as Taos, everyone would know everyone else. Rumalda would know Gabriela, for we were all about the same age. Perhaps Rumalda could arrange a meeting for me. I decided that I must exercise patience and remain on my best behavior in order to earn the trust and friendship of Rumalda, so that I could at least have a chance to speak to the beautiful Gabriela.

That night, after a huge feast with the Bent family, Charles showed me to the guest quarters—a cozy room with a single tiny window and a corn-husk mattress on the floor covered with a buffalo robe. He gave me a glass of brandy as a nightcap and handed me a burning candle. Jibber followed me into the guest room and curled up on the floor.

"Tomorrow I'll expect you to play some violin tunes for Ignacia and the children," he said.

"I'd be happy to," I replied.

"You're welcome to stay here until you figure out your future plans. You can go to the fort and work for William, if you want, or you can work here a while, then go back to Missouri with me. I'll make at least one more trip this summer."

"I think I'd like to stay in Taos awhile, then go to the fort. Louis Lescot and I had plans to trade with the Indians."

"Very well. As long as you listen to Louis and give up that fool idea of trading with the Comanches. In a few weeks, I'll be arranging for a small party to ride to the fort. I'll make sure you're part of it."

"Thank you," I said. "For everything. I didn't know where I might stay tonight."

"About Tom," Charles said. "He's a good young man, but he's got something of a temper, and he'd just as soon fight a grizzly as back down. Do you see what I mean?"

I nodded my understanding. "He and Rumalda make a strikingly handsome couple."

"You might let him know somehow that even though you're staying under my roof, and even though you're about the same age as Rumalda . . . Well, you get the picture."

"Yes, sir. I'll make sure Tom knows that my interests lie elsewhere."

Now Charles narrowed his eyes. "You think you're still smitten with that Badillo girl, don't you? I suppose you're going to steal her away from her family and her intended fiancé and drag her out onto the plains to trade with the

Comanche, huh? Kid, you've got more crazy ideas than a liquored-up Texan."

I shrugged and blushed, not knowing how to reply. I honestly hadn't thought about taking Gabriela out onto the plains, but Charles had a point. How was I going to live up to all of my fool ambitions if none of them could coexist?

"Get some sleep, and try to dream up some sense. That girl's father is Don Bernardo Fortunado Badillo. He's one of the richest men on the *frontera,* and he's not crazy about outsiders, though he puts up with us. He didn't inherit his fortune, he earned it. He's tough as a rawhide boot. He'll kill any man who tries to undo the marriage he's arranged for his daughter and, by Spanish custom, he has that right. This is not just idle talk, Mr. Greenwood. That girl is forbidden."

I nodded. "I understand."

He smirked and left me in the guest room.

It didn't take me long to lie down on the buffalo robe and the corn-husk mattress. I pulled a woolen blanket over me, for the night had turned cool. This was the first real bed of any kind upon which I had lain since leaving Saint-Cyr. In spite of Charles's advice, I dreamt up no *sense.* In fact, I failed to dream at all. I slept the sleep of ten dead men. I slept more soundly than I had ever slept in my life. I woke up late the next morning, wondering for a moment not only where, but who I was.

FIFTEEN

I did not understand what Charles had in mind when he put me to work at his adobe yard. I knew he intended to build another couple of rooms onto his house in Taos, and needed the adobes. That was part of it. But Charles seemed always to have more than one aim for anything he did.

Perhaps he just wanted to keep me busy and out of the kind of trouble a young loiterer with money in his pocket can get into. With the war mood in the air, I might have indeed wound up dead my first week in New Mexico if Charles hadn't employed me. It did occur to me that Charles was grooming me for a future with the Bent–St. Vrain Company and thought I should know how to build with adobe. Bent's Fort, I had heard many times, was built of adobe.

I began work at the adobe yard my third day in Taos. Because I spoke Spanish, I managed to make some friends among the peasant class workers who toiled with me. Once they found out I was not American, they became less suspicious of me and soon accepted me as a poor wayfarer from a faraway land. Also—and this may sound like far-fetched conjecture, but you must understand the mood of the frontier, where every newcomer attracted attention and raised questions—I believe some of the men with whom I had crossed the plains had concocted stories as to why I never spoke of my past and would not carve my name at Pawnee Rock. This hint of outlawry attached to my arrival seemed to impress the Mexicans with whom I worked, shoulder to shoulder, at the adobe yard. They spoke to me with respect, and seemed careful about every move they made around me.

Meanwhile, I learned to appreciate the fruits of my toil. An adobe brick represents more labor than thought; yet, as an architectural solution, it embodies a genius unto itself. My first job as an adobe builder involved shoveling clay. The clay deposits lay between the town of Taos and the Rio Grande Gorge. The place looked like a dry lake bed and, indeed, collected water during a deluge. When this low spot dried up, clay could be dug there. With a couple of helpers, I would fill a two-wheeled carreta with this clay every morning, using a grubbing hoe and a shovel. Then we would drive the cart behind a yoke of oxen to the adobe yard, a mile away, Jibber wisely trotting in the shade of the cart.

The adobe yard stood near the Taos River, which supplied the water needed for making adobes. The Mexicans had built a large stone vat there, into which I would empty my cart with the help of other laborers. We added water and made the clay into mud. To the mud, we added chopped straw to act as a binder when the clay dried in the brick molds.

Now, all this may sound simple, but the mud had to reach just the right consistency to create a quality adobe brick that would last a thousand years, if properly maintained. In addition, the stalks of straw had to be chopped into lengths that fell into a certain range, the maximum and minimum lengths of straw corresponding to the width and depth of the bricks, with also a sufficient percentage of stalks corresponding to the length of the bricks. And just the right amount of straw had to be added to the mud. Too little straw would result in a lack of binding, causing the adobes to crack apart when dried. Too much straw would make the adobes spongy and rot prone, leading to crumbling.

When the master adobe maker—an old mestizo named Bonificio Ramírez—decided that the right amounts of water and straw had been added to the clay mud, we began scooping the mixture into wooden forms. The forms were notched and pegged together with marvelous craftsmanship by men who had worked lifetimes with their hands. These molds had to be wetted down with water before filling them, so the mud would not stick. Then we would use our very hands to press the mud firmly into the molds, squeezing out air pockets, and packing the mud tightly. Once each form was filled with the mud and straw mixture, we carried it into the sunshine and gently, lovingly overturned the mold and lifted it from the soft mud brick, letting the wooden mold slip away, leaving the young adobe in the rays of the sun that would gradually nurture it to maturity. After a couple of days in the sun, we would turn the bricks and let them continue to bake.

Each brick represented considerable labor of the most menial stripe. In a sense, I felt that I had been reduced from a flamboyant plainsman to a mud-shoveling proletarian, but I knew this was temporary employment, and I had come to appreciate the practicality of adobe in such arid country. I worked hard and walked back to Charles Bent's house every day, crusted with clay and bits of straw.

Every day, Charles's stepdaughter, Rumalda, brought lunches for the workers at the adobe yards, and one day I persuaded her to stay while I ate my tortillas, beans, and peppers. We had exchanged a few words now and then at her father's house, and she had come to trust me. In the rustling shade of the Taos River willows, we talked about the plans to add on to the house for a while, among other bits of idle conversation.

Finally, I eased into the subject of Gabriela. "Do you know the Badillo family?" I asked.

Rumalda flashed a knowing smile at me. "Of course."

I made designs in the dirt with my heel. "The day I arrived in Taos, I met Gabriela Badillo. Well, I didn't meet her, I just saw her, but—"

Rumalda was giggling.

"What's so funny?"

Her smile broke like snow on the mountains and she laughed out loud at the willow leaves. "Gabriela has been asking me about you."

This made my heart leap like an eaglet learning to fly. "About me?"

"She wants to meet you. I told her I would tell you, but I don't want to get into trouble, so now it is up to you. You are to wait near the spring behind her *hacienda* at twilight every night. It may take days, but she will slip outside when she can."

I blushed and hid my face behind my hat brim, but I was as giddy as a schoolboy. Finally, I managed to look up at Rumalda. *"Gracias,"* I said.

She smirked. "Don't take that violin. It is too loud. Take a rose from my mother's garden." Her smile faded and she rolled her eyes. *"Ay, cuidado,"* she warned. Be careful.

A cloud seemed to move over the sun, but it was nothing more than reality darkening my hopeful mood. "She is promised to marry someone, is she not?"

"Yes. Mariano Zavaleta. In less than a month." She must have seen my eyes cloud with sorrow. "Many things can happen," she said with girlish romanticism.

I was only beginning to understand the culture of this foreign land, but I knew that the breaching of an arranged marriage could lead to bloodshed. "I know only that I must meet her."

This made Rumalda color with excitement. "I will go now, and tell her you will wait near the well."

I would steal a rose every evening from Mrs. Bent's garden, and walk to the Taos River to bathe. I would change into a new suit of clothes I had bought on the plaza. Then, with my rose stem concealed up my sleeve, the bud cupped protectively in my palm, I would sneak across town to the Badillo *hacienda,* which stood on high ground above the rest of the adobes in Taos. I would veer from the road and hide away in a cluster of piñon pines and willows near the spring. Jibber would wait obediently at my feet.

The fifth rose proved the charm. It was a fine rose, unblemished and symmetrical. I was studying its design when I sensed Gabriela at the spring. She came with a dipper, as if to get a drink. Her eyes swept the line of trees for me as she crouched to dip the gourd into the clear pool of water.

"Gabriela," I said, speaking low.

Her eyes flashed, finding me instantly as I stepped from the cluster of scrubby piñons. I motioned for Jibber to stay put, and he obeyed. Gabriela glanced back toward her *hacienda* as I approached her.

"Gabriela," I repeated, loving the feel of her name on my tongue. "I am Honoré."

"I know your name," she said, "but who are you? Where have you come from?"

It was the first time I had heard her voice, and it warmed me with its sensuality. "Does it matter?" I asked.

She looked into my eyes. "I don't know."

Our eyes locked for what seemed a long time, but it may have been only a second. Mechanically, time remains constant. But in the chaos of human experience, time fluctuates like a wild tide. With Gabriela, time would first slow to a glacial crawl, then a moment would bolt with meteor speed, and a minute became a blink.

I forgot all the things I had planned to say to her, so I merely repeated her name: "Gabriela."

"Yes?"

Just then a voice boomed from the *hacienda*: "Hija! Gabriela!"

"My father," she said. "Hide!"

She pointed to the ground behind a large boulder near the spring, so I crouched there.

"Hija!"

"I am here, Papa."

"What are you doing out there?"

"Getting a drink of fresh water from the spring."

I saw her brandish her dipper to bolster her story.

"You should send a servant. Is not the moon almost full? What if the Comanches struck?"

"I'm sorry, Papa. I'm coming back."

She pretended to drop her gourd dipper behind the boulder. It landed at my feet. She bent to pick up the dipper, and her hair fell around my face where I crouched. She kissed me quickly and unexpectedly, and I grasped her free hand as she retrieved the dipper with her other hand.

Now the rose came from my palm, the stem from my sleeve. I pressed it into her hand, and heard a gasp, a sigh. I glimpsed at once her disbelief, her desire, and her fearful desperation as she slipped away from me.

And that was all. I remained hidden behind the well until after dark and recited *Romeo and Juliet* quietly to myself.

Good night, good night, parting is such sweet
sorrow,
That I shall say good night till it be morrow.

SIXTEEN

The sun baked mud and straw to adobe. The new addition to Charles's house began to take shape, brick upon brick. I became adept at mortaring with mud and laying each course straight and level. This occupied my mind while I yearned for Gabriela.

Nightly, a rose would vanish from Mrs. Bent's garden, until I could no longer cut them in good conscience. Nightly, I waited near the spring. But Gabriela did not return. I wondered. Having met me, did she loathe me? Had I caused her trouble with the gift of a rose? Had she forgotten about me already?

Finally, a message came through Rumalda. "Gabriela cannot see you again. She said her marriage has been planned for her, and there is nothing she can do. Her father would kill you if you interfered."

"Kill me?" Disbelief was plain in my voice. "Just for seeing her one more time?"

"Trust what she says, Honoré. You are an outsider. You are poor. You make adobes. If you tried to claim her, you would be killed, either by Don Badillo, or by Mariano Zavaleta, or his father or brothers."

"How many times could they possibly kill me?"

"Don't joke. You brought her the rose. That is something. Let it be enough. She smiles when she speaks about it and clutches her hand to her heart. But she knows she cannot see you again. She does not wish to endanger you. I should have known better than to help you. You could end up dead."

I thought about Gabriela smiling and clutching my rose to her breast. "I will be leaving soon," I said. "I will go to

Bent's Fort, then out among the Comanches. I will not cause Gabriela any more trouble then. But I want to see her one more time. Just once more."

"No," she said. "It cannot happen. It would only make things worse."

I tried to persuade Rumalda to help me, but she would not. Finally, I had to content myself with building grief upon sorrow, like the heavy adobe bricks I layered round the new rooms at Charles's house under the apprenticeship of the master *albanil,* Bonifacio.

Somehow, Charles Bent sensed what ailed me. He found me at the stock trough the evening before Tom Boggs and Rumalda were to wed. He leaned against a hitching rail as I used the water from the trough to clean mud from a make-shift wooden trowel. "We've got to get you out of here," he said.

"Why?"

"Because Ignacia wants to save what's left of her flower garden. Anyway, you'd be safer among those blasted Comanches you want to trade with. Don't you think somebody might have seen you and that dog hanging around the springs back of the Badillo *hacienda* every night? Word gets around. Are you hell-bent on getting yourself into a bind?"

"No, sir," I replied, as I washed my hands with water scooped from the trough. "Trouble just seems to follow me around like Jibber, there."

Hearing his name, my dog looked at me and wagged his stump of a tail.

"Well, the boys have come up from Santa Fe for Tom and Rumalda's wedding tomorrow."

"Who's here?" I asked, anxious to see friends again.

"Blue Wiggins, Blackfoot Smith, and some of the other boys. They'll be getting drunk tonight. Tomorrow, after the wedding, I want you to play your fiddle for the fiesta. The next morning, I'm gathering the boys together to ride to the fort, and I want you to go with us."

I picked up my tools and arched the hours of labor from my back. "That's good, I guess. Yes, that's best."

"Glad you see it that way, so I won't have to knock you over the head and drag you there. Enjoy yourself at the wedding and the fiesta tomorrow, because it will be your last day in Taos. We're going back out yonder. Your mud-dauber days are over."

As a foreigner and landless laborer In Taos, I was lower than a peon. The chapel was small, and filled with family members and friends closer to the betrothed than I. I did not get to witness Tom and Rumalda's wedding. I knew Gabriela was inside the chapel, but I did not get to see her. I could only hope that she would be allowed to attend the fiesta after the wedding, and I might catch her eye.

I arrived at the Taos Plaza after sundown for the fiesta. Torches lit the street in front of the Bent–St. Vrain store. Someone pounded a spigot into a keg of local corn liquor known as Taos Lightning. I spotted Blue Wiggins, and we swapped yarns about what we had seen and done since we parted.

"That watch tell time yet?" he asked.

"I haven't gotten around to fixing it. Anyway, I have a clock in my head. I always know the time within a minute or two."

"Let's just see," Blue said, pulling a brand-new gold watch from his vest pocket by a leather fob. "I'll bet you five dollars you can't come within five minutes."

"It's eight twenty-seven," I said.

He frowned at his new timepiece and fished a gold coin from one vest pocket as he tucked the watch and fob into the other. "Go play that damn fiddle," he ordered. "Tom and Rumalda are coming down the street."

I stepped up on the boardwalk in front of the Bent–St. Vrain store and slipped the Stradivarius carefully from my old drawstring bag. I checked the strings, finding it still in tune from Charles's house. I looked over the dirt street and saw that I had already attracted some attention just by pluck-

ing the strings. For a moment, Taos looked peaceful. Don
Turo in his sombrero stood next to Blackfoot John Smith in
a fox-fur cap. An American bullwhacker offered a twist of
tobacco to a Canadian trader. Local citizens of all classes,
from adobe maker to *hacienda* owner, milled among the
outsiders. I could not imagine these people choosing up
sides in an impending war, and hoped it somehow might
not come to pass.

I tucked the violin under my chin and saw my own shadow
lurch across the dirt in the torchlight. This gathering called
for something light and lively, of universal appeal, so I lit
into a Mexican song I had learned from the adobe makers,
called *"Las Margaritas,"* as if I had taken it upon myself
to save the world from war. Smiles broadened, talk rang
with laughter, and eyes danced with mirth as the Stradivarius, the Taos Lightning, and I worked spells on the listeners.
I followed with an American song called "Jerusalem Ridge"
without allowing time for applause, and kept right on playing as new arrivals filtered in from all points of the plaza.

I played tirelessly, alternating folk tunes with symphony
pieces, Scottish hornpipes with Mexican rancheras. As I
played, I watched the crowd, studying reactions. Some of
the listeners seemed barely aware of my presence, as if I
were just another chirping sparrow. Others tapped their toes,
yet offered no further acknowledgment. Some applauded politely at the close of each selection. And a precious few
stood agape, marveling at my talent and training, hanging
on every note.

Finally, I broke long enough to sample a cup of the Taos
Lightning someone had brought to me. Just as the liquid
touched my lips, I saw Gabriela enter the courtyard in the
company of an older woman serving as her chaperone. The
lightning flared in my chest as my heart pounded, and my
gaze met hers. She stopped in her tracks and stared at me.

"Play somethin' else, Orn'ry!" Blue Wiggins blurted.

I tore my eyes away from Gabriela, and glanced at Blue.
"Alright," I replied. "Something for the ladies. "The Rose

of Avenmore." I will play this like a rose I would bring to
a beautiful *señorita.*"

I intended this to be subtle, but it seemed everyone looked
first at me, then at Gabriela. I caught sight of a warning
stare from Charles Bent. Between Charles and Ceran St.
Vrain stood a man who could only have been Gabriela's
father, Don Bernardo Fortunado Badillo, for he pierced me
with a murderous glare. His loud leather and silver concho
outfit strained against his muscular build. Without taking his
eyes from me, he said something out of the side of his
mouth that obviously bothered Charles. The peaceful gathering seemed almost to divide as I watched. The Mexicans
drifted one way, and all the outsiders went the other way. I
suddenly felt that I was about to single-handedly start the
war with Mexico.

But "The Rose of Avenmore" moves like a masterpiece
upon the senses, and it charmed the listeners to the point
that I thought I must have imagined the tension. As I played,
I looked at Gabriela, and found her eyes glistening, her lips
parted slightly and trembling. But when I finished the tune,
she said something terse to her chaperone and, turning away,
left the plaza, stopping only long enough to embrace the
bride before she vanished. Don Badillo nodded his satisfaction that his daughter had passed beyond my sight. My heart
sank, and I wondered if I had offended her in some way. I
tried another sip of the Taos Lightning, and it tasted as bland
and powerless as tepid water.

I played listlessly for another hour, then put my violin
away and stepped down from the boardwalk. I kept looking
the way Gabriela had left, but the street ached for her
shadow.

I tried to take another sip of Taos Lightning, but could
not. Strong drink never appealed to me, anyway. I talked to
Blue Wiggins and Don Turo, but they were getting drunk,
and my mind and heart were elsewhere, though I could carry
on a perfectly good conversation with half my mind. I swept
the plaza constantly with my eyes, hoping for Gabriela's
return. Instead, I caught Rumalda's eye. She made a subtle

motion of her head that I understood. I ambled over to her and tipped my hat to Mrs. Bent. The groom was talking to his new father-in-law.

Rumalda stepped close to me and said, very quietly, "She will meet you tonight at the spring. Later. Be careful."

<hr>

A couple of hours later, I found myself approaching the Badillo *hacienda* in the moonlight. Coming near the spring, I heard Gabriela's voice.

"Here," she said. "I am waiting over here, Honoré."

I saw her in the edge of the pine and willow cover, and went to her. She took me by the hand and led me into the shadows. She had spread a fine Navaho blanket on the ground, and I remember thinking that she was going to have quite a time picking all the pebbles and dead pine needles out of the wool fabric. We sat on the blanket, held hands, and whispered. I remember every word we spoke, of course, but it would be silly to tell you, for it would sound like the ridiculous ramblings of star-crossed lovers to you.

We inched closer together. I felt her warmth. Our cheeks brushed. We kissed. After that, we seemed to become one being, of one mind, one heart, and one desire. We undressed, my hands and hers working together, for our thoughts had melded. Our flesh became one, like our souls, our breath, our heartbeat. Her passion amazed me, almost to the point of fright, but it quickly became my passion, her pleasure became my pleasure, our ecstasy became one.

We lay on the blanket touching each other, saying nothing for a long time. I began to drift into a peaceful trance, but she roused me again, and made me amaze myself with the new lust I had discovered with her. I knew then that she would have to leave me soon, for dawn approached. I knew also that she did not want to leave, nor did I want her to.

She was wise and poetic. She did not say good-bye. She said, "I will be with you. I will love you always."

And I said, "*Si. Te amo*, Gabriela."

What else could I do? I rose, and picked up her blanket for her. I kissed her. She tried to turn away, but I held her. I kissed her again.

Then I let her slip away.

SEVENTEEN

The next day, we rode. We left the squalor of humans and the stench of dogs, and rode. We climbed mountains and stepped fetlock deep into icy alpine streams. I rode silently, lost in a youth's longing for love. I won't belabor you with my pinings anymore, except to say that it did not pass with days, or weeks, or months, or even years. The spell of Gabriela stayed with me through everything else I will relate, so as you listen, assume it. The hold she had on me did not loosen, but what could I do? Run with her to St. Louis, almost 800 miles away? Take her to live among the Indians? A girl raised in a protected *hacienda?* I did the only thing I could do. I left her in Taos and rode for Bent's Fort on the Arkansas.

I rode with Charles Bent, Blue Wiggins, Don Turo, and a Taos Indian scout named Wolf Leg. We followed a well-worn trail back over the mountains, to a camp at Eagle Nest Lake near the place where we had almost frozen to death in the blizzard a couple of months earlier. Now the whole high-country basin lay basking in sunlight, and patches of snow lingered only in the darkest shadows on northern slopes. Eagle Nest Lake lay at the bottom of this gently sloping basin, surrounded by luxuriant grass that was in turn surrounded by walls of timber. The grassy basin opened for a distance of a mile or more all around the lake, affording a wide and beautiful view.

When we rode from the timber and Eagle Nest Lake came

into view, I spied a herd of thirty-three horses grazing near the lake, three mounted men keeping them gathered. One of these men came riding toward us at a graceful canter. I gathered from the smiles on the faces of my companions that this man was a friend. When he rode nearer, he angled toward Charles Bent, and I saw that his right leg consisted of a wooden peg below the knee, fixed into a stirrup modified to accept it. I knew from stories I had been told that this had to be Peg Leg Smith, who had once stolen my pony, Fireball, from Mexico's California. It occurred to me, also, that the herd grazing near Eagle Nest Lake must also have been stolen from California.

The most incredible story about Smith concerned the loss of his leg. While hunting with a party of fur trappers, an Indian had shattered his leg with a rifle ball. In camp, gangrene had begun to set in. None of the mountain men wanted the unenviable task of cutting off his leg, so Smith had shamed them into it by starting the amputation with his own hands and his own knife. Now here was this legend, in the flesh, minus the famous leg.

Like the rest of the men, I rode near enough to hear the talk between Charles and Peg Leg.

". . . like nothin' I ever seen," Peg Leg was saying. "They chased us clean through Apache country. Kilt one of my Indian boys in a runnin' fight up the Gila."

"Who was it that was after you?"

"Seemed like the whole goddamn Mexican army, and about a half the *rancheros* in California. I'd say they finally had just about enough of ol' Peg Leg borrowin' their hoss-flesh." He grinned a tobacco-stained smile and pointed at his *caballada*. "We did get away with a few, though. Say, how you boys feel about bear meat for dinner? We kilt a fat one this mornin'."

We feasted and camped at Eagle Nest Lake under a sky so pristine that I felt I might tangle stars in my hair. The talk was so amusing among these old friends that I didn't even have to play the violin. In those days, the glorious beauty of just a single peaceful night in the mountains was

reward enough for a lifetime of toil and trouble, even to a
young man whose heart lay wounded by the arrow of impossible love. Up there, at night, the air breathes so crisp
and clean that you can almost smell the fire of a shooting
star scorching its way across the belly of the great speckled
sky.

The next day, on the trail, Peg Leg Smith dropped back
along the herd and rode in close to Fireball.

"Blue told me that Tom Boggs said you paid twenty dollars for that horse."

I smirked. "That doesn't speak well for Blue's memory
or Tom's honesty," I replied. "I paid exactly five dollars for
him, but I wouldn't take a hundred now."

"He's one to hold on to. Story is he was once a Comanche
horse. I stole him from a *hacienda* in the California country
owned by a retired Mexican Army officer. This old soldier
claimed he captured that horse in a battle with Comanches
down on the Rio Bravo. That fancy brand's the California
brand," he said, pointing.

"What about all the other brands?"

"I guess that horse had been owned all over northern
Mexico before the Comanches got aholt of him. I take it he
was a second-grade racehorse and got swapped off a bit. If
he'd talk, he'd tell us some tales, sure."

"Do you know what happened to his eye?" I asked.

"Hell, yes, I know what happened to it. It went blind."

I looked at Peg Leg for some sign of a joke, but he
seemed serious. "But do you know how?"

"If I knew how, I'd have told you when you asked the
first time. What difference does it make, anyway? He's ain't
gonna get no less blind now."

I rode on a minute or two without reply. It seemed I had
riled Peg Leg simply by asking him a question he couldn't
answer.

"They say you're on the run for killin' somebody," Peg
Leg mentioned casually. "Who'd you kill?"

This breech of frontier etiquette surprised me, but I

framed an answer. "What difference does it make? He's not going to be any less dead now."

It took a second or two, but then Peg Leg Smith burst into a rasping laughter that caused horses to flinch and men to look over their shoulders. "You're alright, kid. And that Blue Wiggins or Tom Boggs, one of 'em's a liar. Twenty dollars! Hell, I knew you wasn't green enough to pay that for a half-blinded, second-rung racehorse."

"No, sir," I replied.

"They say you want to trade with Comanches."

"Yes, sir."

Peg Leg spat a tremendous stream of brown between us. "Don't call me 'sir,' kid. This ain't the army. Anyway, if somebody's after you for a killin', I don't reckon they'll chase you all the way into Comanche territory. They'll just let the Comanches get even for 'em, 'cause them Comanches are like as not to kill you sure."

"I'll chance it."

He shrugged. "Might as well. Hell, I'll chance California again. What's a man don't take a chance now and then?"

"Bored."

"Damn right."

With that, Peg Leg rode off at a lope down a trail too steep for a lope. We did not see him again until we reached that day's camp. Peg Leg had firewood stacked and waiting, an antelope hanging from the limb of a ponderosa pine. This camp lay in a sloping meadow flanking a cold stream that gushed down from the high country. The meadow afforded easy access to the water, so we didn't have to scramble up or down a steep bank to water our stock or fill our canteens. Yet, we camped away from the stream, on the high side of the sloping meadow, on ground that had obviously felt the heat of campfires in days past.

I am always curious about everything, and wondered why we didn't camp nearer to the stream, where the ground was more level and the water handier. I reasoned that the stream probably rose abruptly in times of heavy rain, and might sweep away our camp outfit, such that it was. I was begin-

ning to analyze and understand this sort of thing, for my
mind worked incessantly. I knew from my plains crossing
how much water could come suddenly from the sky. I imagined gravity pulling this volume of water down a steep
slope, gathering it into stream beds like the one nearby. A
larger watershed, and a steeper slope, along with a more
rocky and therefore less absorbent geological surface, would
only make such a stream rise faster and rage wilder. I took
note of these factors. Someday soon, I would have to start
choosing my own campsites.

"I seen Indian sign at a crossing down below," Peg Leg
said to Charles Bent as we set up our camp. "If I'd have
found the sign before I seen this doe, I'd have let her go,
and we'd have gone hungry. But, I only shot once't and
there was only three riders, to judge by the tracks I seen.
Still, better we gather the cavvy tonight and take turns on
guard."

After the horses had watered, we made a makeshift corral
by stringing all the lassos and rope in camp from tree to
tree. We herded the loose stock into this enclosure. We
made a small fire after dark and cooked enough antelope to
stuff our bellies. I volunteered for the first shift of guard
duty, for the moon was coming full and I would not sleep
anyway. Blue Wiggins grabbed my arm as I prepared to
leave the relative safety of my comrades.

"Orn'ry, don't you shoot anything that moves. Them Indians might not even know exactly where we are; but if you
shoot, they sure will. If you pull your trigger, you better be
killin' somethin' about to kill you."

I took up my post on the far side of the rope corral,
leaning against one of the trees the rope had been lashed to.
Jibber curled up at my side and used my foot as a pillow.
It was odd how a little dog could give me such courage.

About three and a half hours into my shift on guard duty,
as the men lay snoring in camp and the oval moon rose over
the slanting ridge to the east, Jibber suddenly raised his
head. The next instant transformed him from a resting pet
to a snarling beast. He charged into the moonlit opening and

attacked something that seemed to have appeared out of nowhere. A dust cloud caught the moonlight as Jibber's claws
dug in, and a mass of fur whirled to fight off the terrier's
advances. A deep-throated snarl answered Jibber's barks and
made them sound like a sparrow's chirp by comparison. I
saw the long legs, the full tail, the ears and nose of a wolf,
and I shouldered my rifle hoping for a clear shot to save
my dog.

Horses were stomping and stirring behind me, and I heard
my friends among them, having sprung from their bedrolls
to calm them. I kept my sights trained on the canine fight
in the clearing as I felt Blue Wiggins to one side, and heard
the thump of Peg Leg's wooden limb to the other.

"Just a wolf," Blue said. "Don't shoot."

The wolf wheeled and snapped at Jibber, its teeth popping
loudly as it missed the terrier's flesh by a hair.

Peg Leg laughed. "Look at that little bastard fight!"

At that moment, Jibber feinted and jumped clear of the
wolf. I had my finger on the trigger and the shoulder of the
wolf in my sights, and I didn't care what Blue Wiggins said.
I was not going to watch my protector get torn apart by the
snapping teeth of a vicious wolf while I did nothing. I
wished for the silence of my bow and arrows, but knew
Jibber didn't have time for me to fetch them. The powder
flash from the muzzle froze an image of wolf and dog in
my eyes and caused a near wreck in the rope corral behind
me as frightened horses lunged.

"Shit!" Blue said.

My eyesight came back to me and I saw the wolf lying
on the ground, Jibber still snapping and circling.

"You damn near spooked my herd for nothin', kid," Peg
Leg said. "I guess you want to fight Indians, 'cause they'll
damn sure know we're here now."

I said nothing. I rose from my guard post and walked
toward Jibber and the dead wolf. Blue and Peg Leg followed, grumbling about my dog and the Indian attack we
were likely to suffer before dawn. As I got closer, I noticed
that something was strange about that wolf. I saw a couple

of white bones against the ground. Death seemed to have deformed the wolf into some bizarre misshapen beast. Then I saw a human hand on the gleaming moonlit bones, and I stopped dead in my tracks.

"Goddamn!" Blue said, jumping to one side and brandishing his pistol.

"Damn Indian with a wolf skin on," Peg Leg said. "Sneakin' up on the downwind side of camp to steal horses. He figured we wouldn't shoot no wolf."

"Look at them bones," Blue Wiggins said, crouching carefully beside the dead body of the Indian. "Jawbones from a wolf, and he'd snap 'em at that dog. Sounded for all the world like a damn wolf poppin' his teeth, by God."

Peg Leg turned to me. "How'd you know, kid?"

My head and stomach were in a turmoil, for I had killed a complete stranger for no other reason than to protect my dog. Yet, I was about to discover how frighteningly calculating I could become. Though I wanted to cry, and pray forgiveness, and somehow make that stranger under the wolf skin come back to life, I nonetheless recognized an opportunity to bolster my reputation in the minds of my companions.

I swallowed the lump in my throat. "Jibber told me," I said. "He wouldn't go after a real wolf like that."

"Well, you and your dog likely saved us from goin' on afoot. That buck was comin' to steal horses." Peg Leg kicked the wolf costume off the man, revealing a warrior in his prime, except for the fact that he was dead. I saw the sickening glint of moonlight on a black pool of blood, and a horrible gaping hole in the man's side where my bullet had exploded from his body. Beside him lay a bow, strung tight, with an arrow still notched to the bowstring.

"You want the scalp?" Blue said.

I shook my head.

"I'll take it for you. You might want it tomorrow."

"Take it quick," Peg Leg said. "I feel arrows pointin' at me. He might have friends around here."

I turned away and let Blue scalp my kill. I walked past

the horses to the other side of the rope corral. I felt like puking, yet knew I could hold it off. Blue came looking for me after a short while.

"I left that scalp on a stob of one of them trees the rope's tied to. You can take it in the mornin' or leave it there."

"I guess I didn't have to kill him."

"He'd have sure killed you if it wasn't for that dog. He had his bow strung and was sneakin' up on you. Don't think he didn't know you was there. He probably seen you leave camp hours ago and he's been crawling, wolflike, ever since, to get a shot at you. If you didn't have that dog, that buck would be wearin' your scalp right now, and runnin' hell-bent for breakfast with all our horses."

I felt a little less murderous hearing this. "Was he Comanche?"

"Some kind of Apache. Mescalero, I think."

"Are the Comanches at war with the Apaches?"

"On and off. Comanches are generally at war with everybody."

"Then, if I wanted to impress the Comanches, I should keep the scalp?"

Blue shrugged. "Hell, I guess. Who knows what a Comanche thinks? Anyway, the Apaches are gonna be at war with us now. And especially you."

"You think they'll attack us?"

"They will if they can outnumber us or ambush us. We'll try to make Bent's Fort in two days, and that means two days of hard ridin'."

I forced my mind to calculate through the ever-present heartache of Gabriela and the gut-wrenching pangs of guilt over having killed my second man. I found my mind a valuable asset in situations like this. I could set it to thinking about some task, and it would work in spite of what was going on in my heart and guts and soul. In this way, I identified the most advantageous and rational way to progress, in spite of myself.

When we broke camp at dawn, I carried the scalp of the unfortunate Apache warrior tucked into my possibles sack. When the time came for me to ride into Comanche country, I would wear it on my belt. I intended no disrespect to my departed victim. I was simply trying to get the most out of a situation not of my own making.

EIGHTEEN

As Blue had warned, we rode hard. We caught glimpses of Indian riders following, watching, flanking us. That night, north of Raton Pass, I heard myriad wolf and owl calls in the darkness. We posted guards. No attack came.

We rode hard the next day, too. Some of the other mounts became sore-footed, but Fireball-the-Half-Blind plodded on over rocks and cactus as if they didn't exist. Again, we saw and sensed Indians around us. Peg Leg Smith found where they had crossed in front of us at the head of a canyon on the Purgatoire River. Three horses—one of them without a rider.

Down the wild Purgatoire we pressed, hoping to beat darkness to Bent's Fort, using our spurs on our tired ponies. At last, before twilight, we came to the Arkansas breaks, and I caught my first glimpse of Bent's Fort in the distance across the valley. The mere sight of it astounded me. It looked like a castle, spread low and broad across an ample measure of ground, bastions towering at two opposing corners, smoke streaming from multiple chimneys.

"We'd better stretch out," Charles Bent ordered. "Cross before dark and sleep inside the walls."

"Let's do it," Peg Leg agreed. "If they attack, they're most liable to do it when we cross the river."

Blue Wiggins surveyed the rough terrain between us and

the river; then between the river and Bent's Fort. After a hard day of riding, this was going to be the last exhaustive push. This only made Blue chuckle.

Somewhere down there, a pair of Apache warriors waited, anxious to avenge their brother whom I had killed; yet we were going to ride right into their laps. Peg Leg's two men took the time to shift their saddles to fresher mounts, but most of us had been riding our best horses all day, in anticipation of a fight, and chose not to change now. I could have tried one of the stolen Mexican horses, but I trusted Fireball and knew he could swim me across. Even now, he held his head high and trained his one good eye on the fort far across the river. I took only enough time to loop my possibles sack around my neck so it would ride high on my shoulder and keep my Stradivarius out of the river water.

Now Peg Leg grinned, the last ray of sun glinting from his tobacco-browned teeth. He quirted a horse at the back of the cavvy and started the stampede to the river. We cantered downhill over rough ground, whistling the loose stock into a tight bunch. Fireball gathered himself here, stretched himself out there, and chose the ground as well as he could. Dust blew around me, rumbling with the beat of hooves, and I felt my whole body charged at once with emotions ranging from abject fear to rapturous exhilaration.

The abode walls of Bent's Fort sank behind the tops of trees through which we very soon went crashing, jumping our stock over dead limbs and ducking live ones that could unhorse a man with a careless blink. I couldn't see Jibber in the underbrush, but knew he would be somewhere near.

The river came next, and here the men lashed out at the loose horses with vicious curses and leather quirts that whistled the air. We refused to let our animals drink. This was no time to let our cavvy get bogged down with water when the last push to the fort lay across the Arkansas.

Fireball seemed to understand our plan as he bit one of the slower horses on the rump, lay his ears back, and chased others into the current. His legs churned through water and mud until I felt his body lift, and I slipped off to float along

side of him and let him swim. Jibber swam ahead of me,
though I hadn't even seen him jump in. I shifted my possibles sack on my left shoulder to keep it above the water,
and held my single-shot pistol above the surface of the water
in my left hand while I clutched the saddle horn in my right.
The other men likewise attempted to keep their firearms
above the water.

The scream of a horse turned my head, and I saw an
arrow shaft angling from the side of one of the riderless
horses, blood pouring into the muddy water like a tragic
tributary. An instantaneous analysis of trajectory and windage told me from where the arrow had flown on the bank.
As I held my pistol high and turned to look at that place on
the bank, I caught a glimpse of a flying blur and felt a jolt
and a searing pain in my right shoulder blade. I must have
cried out because suddenly I saw the wild eyes of my friends
glaring at me.

"You hold tight, Orn'ry. Hold on, dammit, whatever you
do."

I could crane my neck and see the feathered shaft of the
arrow sticking out of my own back. The horse that had been
hit started floundering. It's head went under once, then
again. At last it gave a pitiful moan and sank.

I did not want to sink like that horse, so I heeded Blue's
advice and held on to my saddle horn with a grip like
shrunken rawhide, despite the pain that weakened me. The
arrow had flown a long way, so it had not hit as hard as a
near shot. My shoulder blade had protected my vitals, but
oh, how it hurt with every lunge Fireball made through the
water. I was tired of holding my pistol up, so I pointed it
behind me through a gap the boys seemed to have opened
for me, and fired a retaliatory blast toward our hidden enemies.

"Get mounted!" Blue swam his horse next to mine and
grabbed my arm. "Get astraddle of that rig, damn it."

My powder spent, I plunged my pistol into the water and
stuck it under my belt. With Blue's help, I slid between
pommel and cantle as I felt Fireball's hooves find the river-

bed. "I can ride," I said, though no one had asked.

"We're out of their range," Peg Leg said. "Let's get to the bank and give 'em a volley."

We whipped our heaving mounts onto the north bank, found dry footing, and turned. Every man with a dry firearm leveled his sights across the river and fired. Only four shots went off, for the crossing had dampened some of our loads.

Blue Wiggins rode to my side and said, "Get aholt of somethin'."

Before I could ask why, he snapped the shaft that protruded from my back. He tried to be careful, but twisted the arrow point just enough to send a lightning bolt of pain all the way down to my boots. I growled in pain.

"Didn't want that wavin' around when we ride through the trees. Might tear you up worse than I just did." Blue handed me the feathered arrow shaft. "Carry that in your teeth. It'll help with the pain."

"William will be coming with help," Charles said. "Let's go."

The men whipped the tired *caballada* of horses through the timber and up the bank. Ducking low-hanging branches, I was grateful that Blue had broken the arrow shaft, for it would have raked against many a branch under which I now rode. Also, biting on the wooden shaft seemed to take away a little of the pain. I was worried about how badly I might be hurt. Because I was drenched from the river crossing, I couldn't tell how much blood I was losing, and my right arm seemed to be going numb. I just wanted to get inside the fort, where someone could take care of me.

We emerged from the timber to find a party of some twenty men riding to our rescue. Silhouetted against the evening sky, this was the wildest, fiercest lot of men I had ever seen—wilder even than the Comanches I had faced on the Cimarron with Blue Wiggins. They bristled with weapons and taunted the wind with fur and buckskin fringe.

"Anybody get hurt?" William Bent asked as the party swarmed around us for our protection.

"One wounded." Charles, pointed at me. "Arrow in the back."

"Come on."

We rode to higher ground and I saw the great square outline of Bent's Fort, looming like a walled city, rising tall and broad from the open plain that stood above the river-bottom timber. As we approached, several men cut Peg Leg's herd of California horses to the west end of the fort where a corral gate opened to take them in. With the broken arrow between my teeth, I rode on toward the east end of the fort with Charles and William Bent, Blue Wiggins, and some of the men from the rescue party.

One of these, I now realized, was my friend, the tailor, Louis Lescot.

"Honoré, that is you, no?" he said, riding in close to me so that he might recognize me in the fading twilight.

I simply nodded and grunted my reply.

We rounded the curved walls of the bastion on the south-east corner of the fort, and I saw a huge span of double gates open on the east wall, torchlight fanning from the portal to guide us in. I rode into Bent's Fort in a rolling lope, an enemy arrow clenched between my teeth. Before I could rein in, someone had taken Fireball's bridle in hand and I was being pulled from my saddle. I heard William shout for a bed, a lantern, bandages, and a sharp knife scalded in boiling water.

I only glanced around the great hollow square in the middle of Bent's Fort, and noticed people on a balcony that went all the way around on the upper floor. Men ushered me through a small door and into a room.

A grizzled man in a stained hat faced me, took the arrow shaft I held between my teeth, and said, "Let go."

I obeyed, and he handed me a cup.

"Drink it all," he said.

I did, and felt the warmth of brandy pour down my throat and into my stomach. Someone unlooped my possibles sack from my neck.

"Open up," the man said, and he shoved the arrow shaft back between my teeth.

They pulled me facedown onto a surprisingly comfortable corn-husk mattress that rested on the floor, and cut open the back of my shirt. After prodding the wound and discussing it for a while, William Bent must have made some sort of sign or gesture for the men to hold me down, for suddenly I felt several big pairs of strong hands on my arms, legs, and head, and I decided I might just as well remain as still as possible rather than fight what felt like a dozen men.

The next few seconds crazed me with searing pain. I heard my teeth cracking the wood of the arrow shaft and saw tears blur my vision. Then I felt the war point come free with a tug. They cauterized my wound with a knife blade heated red-hot. I smelled my own flesh burning and thought of Peg Leg Smith cutting off his own leg through this same stripe of incredible pain. They stood me up, dabbed some kind of balm on my wound, and wrapped it with clean bandages wound around my chest and shoulder and neck.

By now the pain had subsided somewhat, so I spit the arrow shaft out on the ground. "Let me see the war point," I said.

They gave me the iron point and another shot of brandy, wrapped me in a soft blanket, and lay me back down on the bed. They may have put something in that brandy to make me sleep because I lasted only a few seconds after I got horizontal. Perhaps I simply passed out. Before I fell asleep, I heard men celebrating outside, and felt Jibber jump up on the foot of my bed and curl up between my knees.

NINETEEN

I awoke feeling stiff and sore with every breath I took, yet my hunger and thirst made me sit up almost immediately. Jibber sprang from the bed and wagged his stub of a tail. "Hey," I croaked.

The door to my room was open, and sunlight streamed in. I found a glass of water on the packed dirt floor near my bed and, near it, the arrow point that had been carved from my back. I drank the water and refilled the glass from a nearby pitcher. As I drank my second glass, I saw a new buckskin shirt draped across a chair, and thought about Louis Lescot. I rose, groaning in pain as I did so, and donned the shirt, which made my wound flare with pain. I put the iron arrow point in a small pocket the tailor had sewed into the front of the shirt. Then I opened my possibles sack and retrieved the scalp taken three nights before. This I tucked under my belt. The arrow in my back had made it clear that the Apaches who had followed us north had intended all along to kill us—to kill me. That wound taunted me with pain, and gave me the right to wear that grisly trophy.

I stepped into the doorway that faced the protected hollow square of Bent's Fort, and a man passed by—a stranger to me. He was short, weathered, and wiry, aged somewhere between young and old, perhaps slightly past his physical prime, but formidable in experience. I could tell that much with one glance into his eyes.

He stopped. "You hungry?" he asked.

I nodded.

"Sit down, I'll bring you something."

I sat on a bench as the man angled across the plaza,

passed a wooden machine of some sort, and disappeared into another doorway. As I waited, I observed a few plainsmen and mountain men, a Mexican *caballero,* and an Indian woman in deerskin, as they all went about their business inside the fort. I saw a black woman emerge from a doorway and pour a bucket of water onto what looked like a cultivated pepper plant. I heard the ringing of a smithy, the snort of a horse, the crow of a cock, the cry of a hawk.

In a couple of minutes, the man who had greeted me came back across the plaza with a big plate of food including scrambled eggs, tomatoes, onions, slabs of bacon, two boiled potatoes, a tortilla, and a pile of beans. He also carried a large cup of steaming coffee, strong and black.

"Thanks," I said, taking the plate. "My name is Honoré."

"Christopher," he replied. "You sore?"

"Yes, sir."

"You know where you're at?"

"Bent's Fort," I said past a mouthful of eggs. I used the knife and fork he had given me to cut a piece of bacon for Jibber.

"You remember who you rode in with?"

I nodded and swallowed, and figured he must be testing my memory to determine whether or not the wound had caused my mind to fever. "The Bent brothers, Blue Wiggins, Louis Lescot, Peg Leg Smith. Some others I didn't have time to meet." I shoveled more food into my mouth.

He chuckled. "You made quite a picture galloping in here on a one-eyed horse with an arrow between your teeth and that dog running circles around you."

I tossed another bite to Jibber. I looked again at the large wooden contraption in the middle of the plaza. It had a spiral screw shaft with a long handle on it that I could tell was meant for squeezing or compacting something. "What is that thing?" I asked before blowing on the coffee to take a big slurp.

"They use that to press and bale beaver plews and other hides and pelts for shipping back east."

I nodded. "Where is everybody? I expected more people."

"Most everybody's outside. Some went to meet the army. Captain Frémont is coming to make another expedition, so some of the boys rode downstream to meet him. Others are tending the stock or fishin' or huntin' or whatnot. It's cooler out there than it is in this plaza. I've been mending saddles."

With this remark, I assumed that Christopher was the fort's saddle maker and leather worker. I gulped down the mouthful I had taken and said, "Thanks again for the food."

"You're welcome," he said, and took a seat beside me on the bench. He seemed not to mind that Jibber sniffed his boots as he looked out across the plaza of the fort.

"I've read about Frémont," I said, trying to make conversation. "They call him 'The Pathfinder.' "

Christopher looked at me briefly and sort of grunted. "You know who that is?" he asked, pointing toward a man in a sweat-stained felt hat who had been sitting across the plaza all along, sharpening a knife on a whetstone.

"No, sir."

"That's John Hatcher. Captain Frémont's a good man, but John Hatcher has forgotten more paths than the captain's found. I hear tell you want to trade with the Comanches."

I nodded.

"Now, son, that's a crazy idea, if you ask me, and I'd advise you against it at peril of your life. But if you're determined to try, don't try without John Hatcher. He's the only trader this fort ever employed who's made any kind of profit off the Comanche trade."

I looked back across the plaza at John Hatcher, and memorized what I could see of his face and outfit.

About that time, a black man wearing the leather apron of a smith emerged from a dark corner of the plaza, carrying a piece of iron he must have just forged for someone. I was still stuffing food into my mouth, but I looked at my new friend with a quizzical expression.

"Dick Green," he said. "William Bent's manservant. Good farrier. Heck of a blacksmith."

I nodded.

"That Negro woman you saw a while ago—that's his

wife. She cooked you that grub, so you know who to thank. Her name's Charlotte."

"I'll surely thank her," I said.

About that time, I heard a voice like gravel in a pan announce its owner at the open gates on the east wall of the fort. "Goddamn!" the voice said. "I said, goddamn! Where the hell is everybody?"

I paused in consuming my meal to watch a man on foot lead in a string of five pack mules. Another man rode in behind the mules—a rawboned man with long white hair and beard.

"That's Lucas Murray," Christopher said. "The Cheyennes around here heard him blaspheme so much, they thought his name was "Goddamn," so most the men have taken to calling him Goddamn Murray. The Comanche call him Flat Nose. That's Thomas Fitzpatrick with him."

"Broken Hand?"

"The Indians call him that."

I saw another old trader ride in behind Fitzpatrick. "Who's that?"

"Old Gabe."

"Jim Bridger?"

"The same. They've been out trading with the Utes and Cheyenne."

"Goddamn, I said where is everybody?" Murray bellowed across the square.

Christopher stood. "I guess I'll help 'em unload and tally." He took a step or two, then turned back to me. "I took the liberty of doing some work on your saddle. I was fixin' my own up and looked yours over while I had my tools out. Just replaced some strings and leathers and such."

"Let me know what I owe you."

"Nothin', of course. I wouldn't have done the work without your say-so unless I was doin' it free."

"Thanks," I replied. "What was your name again, sir?" I stood and wiped the bacon grease from my hand, hoping this Christopher would tell me his last name.

"Christopher Carson."

I took his hand in mine and said, "Good to meet you," suddenly realizing that I was shaking hands with Kit Carson. I couldn't let go of his hand. "Uh," I said. "Well . . . Good to meet you, Mr. Carson."

He grinned, and gently extricated his hand from my grip by grabbing my wrist with his left hand and pulling away. "Call me 'Kit.' "

I nodded. "I'll help you when I finish my breakfast and get my moccasins on."

"If you're up to it."

I spent the next few hours sorting and counting hides with Kit Carson, Jim Bridger, Thomas Fitzpatrick, and Goddamn Murray. Kit told them the story of my arrival, and they all had to inspect my wound, pulling my shirt up over my shoulder and pulling aside the bandages.

"Goddamn," Murray said.

"Looks pretty clean," Broken Hand said.

"It'll heal," Bridger added. "Don't favor it none. Work it."

"Goddamn," Murray repeated. "You heard him, son. Get back to work."

By observation, I soon figured how much Bent–St. Vrain and Company were paying traders Fitzpatrick and Bridger for each type and grade of pelt they had brought in. I could not help keeping a running tally in my head, for my brain makes such calculations on its own, without any need for effort on my part. When Murray, who was head trader at the fort, finished sorting, stacking, and counting, he looked at his tally sheet and began to add things up.

"Goddamn, let me sit down and figure it," he said, scratching his head.

As he turned into the fort's warehouse to make his calculations, I said, "Seven hundred and twenty dollars."

The four mountain men stopped and stared at me—Carson with amusement, Fitzpatrick with incredulity, Bridger with indifference, and Murray with scorn.

"Bunch of shit." Murray grumbled. "You mean to tell me you figured that all in your head? Goddamn bunch of shit.

Anyway, it can't be a penny over six hundred."

"No offense, Mr. Murray, but it's seven hundred and twenty dollars."

"You don't know shit. I'm guessin' six-fifty, tops."

"Seven-twenty, sir, and I'm not guessing."

"Now, goddamn it, I'm just as smart as you are, you dumb son of a bitch!"

For a moment, the trading house fell silent. Then Broken Hand Fitzpatrick, who was seldom known to even smile, burst into roars of laughter. The other traders soon joined in, and even Murray had to cuss himself and chuckle over what he had said.

Eventually, after sitting down and adding up the tally more than once, Murray simply paid Fitzpatrick and Bridger in American coin without announcing the total, which was, of course, seven hundred and twenty dollars. Bridger just took his pay and walked past me toward the kitchen.

But white-haired Broken Hand Thomas Fitzpatrick looked me in the eye as he jingled his coins in his hand. "Thanks for your help, kid."

"Anytime, Mr. Fitzpatrick."

He shook the coins again, and for a moment I thought he was going to give me one, but he didn't.

Kit said, "Come get a cup of coffee with us."

"Thanks, but I don't drink it. Anyway, I wanted to meet John Hatcher and talk to him about the Comanches."

We stepped out into the plaza, and I saw Hatcher sprawled out asleep on the ground, in the shade of the adobe wall. Fitzpatrick, Murray, and Bridger would normally have walked right past him to get to the kitchen, but instead they went well around him, as if not to disturb him.

"I wouldn't bother John just now," Kit said. "Never pass up a chance to eat or sleep. Tomorrow you might not be able to do either. And don't disturb another man's meal or his nap—unless you aim to save his life. John will wake up soon enough, and you can introduce yourself."

As we walked around Hatcher to get to the kitchen, I felt compelled to get a better look at him without waking him.

As I passed closer to him than the other men, I recognized
him as the man who had ordered me to drink the night
before in preparation for my surgery. John Hatcher lay with
his whetstone still in his left hand, and his knife in the relaxed grasp of his right. He had made a pillow of his dirty,
sweat-stained felt hat. His shirt was patched army wool, his
trousers canvas. I made scarcely a sound as I stepped within
a few feet of him, but I clearly saw his right hand tighten
around the handle of the knife. He snored. I backed away.

I left the men to the coffee and the kitchen, and found
Louis Lescot's buckskin tailor shop on the west side of the
square, upstairs. I sat with him an hour or more, catching
up on events.

"Charles told me that he had to get you out of Taos before
Don Badillo cut your throat," he said, at length. "You should
know better than to trifle with proper Spanish belles. She
must be beautiful, no?"

I smiled, thinking of that lost and fleeting collection of
moments I had spent with Gabriela. *"Oui, très belle,"* I said,
thrilled that someone besides myself would know of my
longing. "You are a fellow Frenchman. You understand."
And I went on, hinting vaguely of the pleasures I had shared
with Gabriela.

Louis nodded knowingly, but at last changed the subject.
He told me of John Charles Frémont's approaching expedition. "The previous two expeditions were exploratory.
There is no doubt of that. It was said that Frémont's task
was to find a path westward, for immigration, or perhaps
even for a railroad route, if you can imagine such a thing
as a locomotive crossing the Great Shining Mountains. But
this expedition—it is different, I fear."

"How?"

"It is three times the size of his previous two. Our Indian
informants claim that his party is well armed and even includes a thunder gun."

"A cannon?"

"Yes, my friend. The war clouds are beginning to gather.
Texas will soon become a state, and now the Americans

have inherited the border troubles between Texas and Mexico. I know you are searching for direction, and you will be tempted to ride with Frémont, The Pathfinder. Remember, if you do so, you will likely end up making war on the Mexican people, and that includes the family of your lover, Gabriela Badillo."

Suddenly, I could see very clearly that Louis was right. All the signs pointed to the oncoming conflict: the tensions toward Americans in Taos. The fact that Peg Leg Smith had been chased out of California for the first time. The gathering of all the great mountain men and frontiersmen here at Bent's Fort. The increasing troubles with Indians, who themselves had smelled war in the air and knew they could raid more successfully if the Americans and Mexicans were made busy fighting each other. And now, the approach of Frémont's troops.

There was going to be war with Mexico. I had no quarrel with Mexico. As yet, I claimed no allegiance to the United States of America. I was merely a fugitive vagabond. I would not ride with Frémont. I would not make war against the nation of the girl I loved. It seemed increasingly likely that the most dangerous place to be—among the Comanches—might turn out to be the safest place in the world for me.

Later that afternoon, Louis and I walked around the fort. I tried to keep my mind off of the throbbing pain in my right shoulder by studying my surroundings. I noticed two bald eagles caged in the lookout tower over the main gate of the fort. When I asked Louis why the Bents kept the eagles there, he explained that the Indians valued the feathers and would trade for them.

"Twenty-four feathers equal the value of a horse," he said, "and the tail feathers grow back as many as three times when they are plucked."

Louis had buckskins to sew, so I walked around outside the fort by myself. Bent's Fort was a marvel of frontier engineering. Having recently spent so many days toiling in the adobe yards, I appreciated how much effort had gone into the making of the scores of thousands of adobes used in its construction. The walls were plastered over, so I couldn't determine exactly what size of adobe brick had been used in the construction. But I knew the dimensions of the typical adobe brick, and I could come up with a reasonable estimate of how many had been required to raise the walls, which were fifteen feet high, and averaged three feet in thickness. Using my facility with measurements and numbers, I quickly took into account the dimensions of the walls.

The fort described a trapezoid 180 feet long, and 135 feet wide along the west wall. The east wall measured 100 feet. Taking height and thickness of the walls into account, and making appropriate additions for the 30-foot-tall bastions at diagonal corners, along with the high adobe walls of the attached corral on the south side of the fort, I did a few simple multiplications in my head and calculated that some 100,000 adobe bricks had been used to erect the imposing edifice, with a margin of error not to exceed 7,355 bricks, depending on the exact size or sizes of the bricks used. Anyway, exactitude is a thing usually not applied to adobes.

To sustain the dirt roof of the fort—and here I will spare you the tedious details of my reckonings—about two hundred huge cottonwood logs had been hauled from the river bottom. Inside the rooms, I had seen the whole timbers running parallel, straight branches on top of them running perpendicular to the timbers, and then a layer of grass on top of the branches. On top of the grass, a thick layer of dirt stood. On top of the heavy layer of dirt, a veneer of packed clay turned all but the heaviest downpours. Louis had told me that a torrential rainfall would eventually seep through the dirt roof in places and drip or trickle into the rooms. But in fair weather, the denizens of the fort could walk about on the rooftops and enjoy the scenery that surrounded the fort.

The design and architecture of the fort suited the climate and environment. The thick adobes and the dirt roof proved poor conductors of changing temperatures and, as such, kept the rooms cool in the summer, warm in the winter. From loopholes cut in the cylindrical towers at the southeast and northwest corners of the fort, men could defend every face of the fort, for the four main walls of the structure intersected the rounded watchtowers at their axes, allowing a total enfilading of the perimeter. Even the livestock were protected by high adobe corral walls, whose tops were lined with cactus plants to discourage breaching.

At Saint-Cyr, I had studied the history of architecture, including the construction of defensive edifices. In some ways, Bent's Fort ranked as one of the great castles of the world, and I could tell that William Bent, who had supervised the construction of the fort for over three years, somehow had been educated in the ways of military architecture. Walking around the building, it was apparent to me that recent repairs and improvements had been accomplished on the walls, gates, and corrals. The talk of war with Mexico, I assumed, had led to these improvements. Bent's Fort would be a natural gathering place for American forces, perched as it was on the north bank of the Arkansas—the border with Mexico. Even now men were being drawn here in anticipation of the oncoming war.

Frémont's expedition did not arrive that day, but other traders and plainsmen continued to wander in, and I got to know them, one by one, sometimes by introducing myself, and sometimes by merely observing. That night, my second at the fort, Lucien Maxwell rode in after dark, having come from the south where I heard he was trying to establish a ranch on a stream called the Rayado. He was a burly man with large flaring nostrils—a physical trait that had led the Indians to name him "Big Nostrils." It seemed that the whole population of the fort came out into the square to greet him.

"Maxwell was once superintendent of the fort," Louis told me as he and I and Blue Wiggins looked on from the balcony above the square, at the door of the tailor shop. "He is Ceran St. Vrain's brother-in-law, for they both married daughters of Judge Carlos Beaubien, in San Fernandez de Taos."

"Who is that man leaning on the fur press?" I asked, locating another new face. "The smiling man with the long hair hanging over his shoulders?"

"His name is Baptiste Charbonneau. He is a half-breed, French and Shoshone. His father was Toussaint Charbonneau, who went west with Lewis and Clark, forty years ago. His mother was Sacagawea, the Shoshone woman who guided the expedition all the way to the Pacific Ocean. Baptiste was born during the expedition, and his mother carried him on her back."

"He doesn't dress like an Indian."

"Baptiste grew up with his mother among the Indians, but then she allowed him to go with an army officer to be educated in St. Louis. There he met Prince Paul of Württemberg, who took him across the ocean for further education for several years. Imagine, having seen Europe, Baptiste wanted to return here, to the plains."

"I ain't never seen Europe," Blue said, "but damned if I'd want to live anywhere else but out here. The thing about Baptiste is that he never rides a horse. But I'll tell you what, Orn'ry, he's the best man afoot from here to Fort Bridger."

Just then, I saw a man enter the light of a lantern, and saw silver earrings gleaming on both sides of his head. "Is that Sol Silver?" I asked, remembering that Blue Wiggins had described such a man to me at Pawnee Rock. "There, under the lantern?"

"None other," Louis replied.

"Who are those two old-timers with John Hatcher?" I asked, for I kept a close watch on the Comanche trader.

"The shorter one's 'Uncle Dick' Wootton," Blue said. "Remember, we seen his name at Pawnee Rock? The tall, lanky one is Old Bill Williams. He's about as crazy as he is redheaded, too. I hear tell he once was a circuit preacher back east."

"Is that Mrs. William Bent standing between William and Charles?"

"Oui, that is Owl Woman, daughter of the great Cheyenne chief, Gray Thunder."

"Who's that talking to them?"

"Robert Fisher. Another trader, Honoré. He came in today with a string of horses he bought from the Jicarilla Apaches. He knows the Comanche and Kiowa as well. They call him 'Fish Man.' "

I burned Fisher's face into my memory. I intended to remember anyone who knew anything of the Comanche. "Does John Hatcher have an Indian name?"

"They all do," Blue said. "The Indians call him 'Freckled Hand.' "

"The only trader I know who claims no Indian name is Ceran's little brother, Marcellin," Louis said. "The Cheyenne just call him by his real name, and they seem to like to say it."

"Maybe it sounds like their word for goose shit or somethin' like that," Blue added. "Don't let nobody tell you an Indian ain't got a sense of humor."

"Is he here? Marcellin St. Vrain?"

"Yeah, that's him with William and Charles's little brother George Bent, leaning on the hitching rail in front of Sol Silver. You ain't gonna remember all these names and faces right off, Orn'ry, but you'll git to know 'em if the Indians or the Mexicans don't git you first."

I didn't bother explaining to Blue that my memory was infallible, and that I already remembered all the traders' names, plus their Indian names, the tribes with whom each traded, and the caliber of firearm each man carried—all this without any particular effort. I just nodded and said, "Let's go down there and listen.

"Louis," Blue Wiggins said, "let's go."

TWENTY

I had found three smooth round rocks, each about the size of a hen's egg. In spare moments, I would go to the room that had been provided for me, and juggle these stones, believing that the exercise provided excellent therapy for my mending shoulder. I was in the room juggling when I heard the cannon fire.

Rushing to the door, I saw several Indian children in the fort running for cover from the noise of the cannon. "Mr. Carson," I yelled, having spotted Kit heading toward the corrals. "Are we under attack?"

"No, Kid." (The men around the fort had taken to calling me "Kid," or "Kid Greenwood," lending me yet another welcome alias.) "Just saluting the army. Frémont's here."

I saddled Fireball and rode behind Kit, Lucien Maxwell, and the Bent brothers to the camp of Captain Frémont's expedition, just downstream. Some other men rode with us, including John Hatcher, the Comanche trader. Frémont's troops had made a hard ride up the Arkansas, and looked almost as tough as the frontiersmen who mingled with them as the two parties came together. As we approached, I saw John Charles Frémont come out of his tent, a mapping compass in his hand. This he tossed back inside, and strode forward with a wry smile on his face. He was lean and handsome, and walked with a proud bearing that bordered on arrogance.

Charles and George got down from their mounts to shake hands with Frémont.

"Are you lost again?" Charles said.

"Never," Frémont replied. He greeted and shook hands

with Kit Carson and Lucien Maxwell, both of whom had accompanied him on previous expeditions.

"Come on up to the fort for the evening," William offered. "Might be the last roof to come between you and the stars for a spell."

"I'll race you there." The Pathfinder grinned.

"William wouldn't have it any other way," Charles said.

William laughed. "Don't reckon I would. I'll sure race you, Captain."

They stood and talked while an army sergeant walked and trotted Frémont's horse around the camp to warm him up. He was a big American horse, long-legged and deep-chested, and stood a full hand taller than William's Spanish pony. Lucien Maxwell volunteered to ride ahead to the gate of the fort and witness the finish. Then William Bent and Charles Frémont mounted, much to the delight of the men. Charles started the contest by standing in front of the horses and dropping his hat from his raised hand as the signal. Frémont's horse shied from the hat on the ground, giving William the better start.

The race covered almost three miles, allowing Frémont time to close the distance on William's fleet Spanish stallion. They entered the fort neck-and-neck, thundered through the gate, and as they entered the plaza they ran over Lucas Murray, who was on his way to the trading room in total ignorance of the coming horse race.

"Goddamn Pathfinder, hell!" he was shouting when I rode up behind the racers on Fireball.

Frémont and William were sitting in their saddles, laughing at him as he dusted himself off.

"The path don't run straight up my ass, goddamn it!"

Lucien Maxwell declared the race a draw, though each rider claimed he had won. Looking back, it hardly seems possible that all those legends of the American frontier could have stood in my presence at once. And yet, there they were, gathered around me, drawn together by an already shrinking wilderness, a secure outpost on the border, the warnings of war with Mexico, and the arrival of The Pathfinder. I seem to recall that I appreciated the cumulative decades of wilderness and frontier experience represented by the men in whose shadows I stood, but I wonder if I really could have then. For my own particular reasons, I found most fascinating a taciturn Indian trader who has been almost forgotten by history. His name was John Hatcher. Freckled Hand. He had traded with Comanches and lived to tell about it.

❧

That night, Dick Green found me shoveling horse manure in the corral. "Mr. Charles wants to see you up in the parlor," the black man ordered.

"Yes, sir," I replied.

He laughed. "You don't have to 'sir' me, boy. Just git on up to the parlor."

I had not yet received an invitation to the parlor, so I hurriedly washed my hands in a horse trough and hustled through a narrow adobe passageway that led me, mazelike, past the armory and into the plaza. I climbed the wooden stairway, taking two steps at each stride, and stepped into the open doorway of the parlor.

Through a cloud of tobacco smoke, I saw Charles Bent and John Charles Frémont engaged in a game of billiards. The mere sight of the billiards table took me by surprise, and I stood agape long enough for Charles to make a shot that apparently ended the game, for Frémont slammed his cue stick down on the table.

"I claim something of an advantage on my own table," Charles allowed.

"Advantages be damned!" Frémont growled. "I like to *win.*"

Charles chuckled, then noticed me standing in the doorway. "Come on in, Kid, and close the door."

Frémont glanced at me as if he hated my guts—I suppose for having had the audacity to have witnessed his shameful defeat. I looked away from him quickly, and swept the smoky, lantern-lit room with my eyes. William Bent sat in the shadows of a corner, hunkered down in his chair with his legs crossed. His younger brother, George, sat with him, and compared to William, George seemed much less burdened by life and the responsibilities of the fort.

Across the billiards table stood John Hatcher, the Comanche trader, his stained felt hat in his hand and his hair slicked straight back behind a pale brow that rarely saw the sun. White-haired Thomas Fitzpatrick leaned on the wall beside him, and I could not help thinking of them as "Freckled Hand" and "Broken Hand."

Frémont's second-in-command, a Lieutenant James William Abert, stood at the bar, his recent West Point education evident in the military bearing he maintained even with a drink of whiskey in his hand. I had met him briefly at Frémont's camp that day, but knew virtually nothing about him, except that this was his first trip beyond the frontier. Considering the gathering in the parlor, I had to wonder why I had been summoned. The stares I felt from the men in the room told me that they were wondering the same thing.

"Young Mr. Greenwood has been in my employ since I last left Missouri," Charles explained. "He has proven himself useful." Then Charles turned and addressed me. "Kid, you're in luck. You wanted to see the Comanche country. Now you're going to see it."

Charles sat down at the bar beside the young lieutenant and motioned to his brother across the room.

William spoke from the corner. "Captain Frémont is sending Lieutenant Abert back to St. Louis by way of the Canadian River to explore the country. He'll go right through the Comanche country. John, I recommended you and Beaver Tom as guides and hunters for the expedition. The army pays good. Kid," he added, looking at me, "you're goin' along for Bent–St. Vrain and Company, if the captain and the lieutenant have no objection."

"Why are you sending *him?*" Captain Frémont inquired.

"For twelve years, I've been trying to establish a reliable trade with the Comanches," William replied. "They are rich in horses they steal from Mexico, and they'll trade 'em cheap. I've tried to set up a camp down there, but the Comanches are crazier than hell. The Texans have got 'em stirred up, and the whiskey traders keep 'em supplied. That's Snakehead Jackson's own domain down there. They're at war with the Pawnees and some of the Apaches, too, and that keeps 'em edgy. What we need, if we're going to establish a regular trade, is a fort on the Big Crossing of the Canadian."

"That doesn't explain why you'd send *him*," Frémont said. "He's just a kid."

"Mr. Greenwood worked in my adobe yards at Taos," Charles explained. "He knows more than you'd think, just to look at him. Hatcher can choose the site for the fort, and the kid can look for materials suitable for making adobes."

Captain Frémont looked me over. "They seem to think quite a lot of you."

I shrugged. "I guess so, sir."

"Can you shoot?"

"Yes, sir. Rifle, pistol, or bow and arrow."

Thomas Fitzpatrick chuckled for some reason.

"Ride?" Fremont said.

"Yes, sir."

"He's got him a one-eyed horse and a bobtailed dog," Charles added. "Plus he speaks Spanish, French, and English. He's not afraid of work, even with an arrow wound in his back. And he doesn't seem to sleep much, most of the time. Not much at all."

Frémont looked at his second in command. "Lieutenant?"

Lieutenant Abert trained his pair of soft, curious eyes on me. "How old are you?"

"Seventeen."

"Where are you from?"

I hesitated. It was obvious that the lieutenant didn't understand the code of the frontier, but I had to frame some sort of answer. "I was a sailor before I came west, sir."

"And your home port?"

Captain Frémont, who did understand the ways of the wilderness, covered for me. "He comes recommended by the Bent brothers, Lieutenant, and that's good enough for me. The question to you is do you have any objections to this civilian accompanying your exploration party as a representative of Bent–St. Vrain and Company?"

Abert looked at me a second or two. He seemed a bit slow compared to the captain. He smiled slightly and lifted his glass. "No objections whatsoever, Captain."

I felt a sudden sensation of excitement surge throughout my body, and I knew I would soon follow my destiny. "When do we start?" I asked.

Charles chuckled. "Whenever the lieutenant says, 'go,' Kid. You just be ready." He turned to Abert. "Lieutenant, Mr. Fitzpatrick will guide you all the way to St. Louis. Mr. Hatcher will accompany you as far as the Big Crossing on the Canadian River. There, he and Mr. Greenwood will leave your expedition and begin making preparations for the construction of the fort."

"I'll lead a party with the trade goods and the building crew to meet you on the Canadian," William said from the dark corner. "Kid, you'd better have dirt, straw, and water aplenty located by that time, because I'm investing a fortune in this work crew, and I want that fort finished in time to recoup my investment with the winter trade."

"What dimensions will the fort be?" I asked. "As big as this one? How many men should it house? Do you want bastions and corrals?"

"That's up to you and John. Mostly, John."

"Good," Frémont said. "Hatcher and Fitzpatrick and this kid will report to Lieutenant Abert in the morning, and begin making arrangements. Now, if you gentlemen will excuse me, I've got to go over some maps with Kit."

Frémont grabbed his hat and left the room, casting a hateful glance at the billiards table—the field of his recent defeat.

When he left, I felt everyone relax. I thought about introducing myself to John Hatcher, but he nudged Thomas Fitzpatrick about that time, and the two of them left. I felt so excited about the upcoming expedition that my stomach began to flutter. Still, I felt somewhat out of place with the three Bent brothers and the lieutenant, so I thought I should also excuse myself. Just then, however, Lieutenant Abert nudged my shoulder.

"Do you play billiards?" he asked.

"I never have."

"Come on, then. Give it a try."

The game of billiards, I soon discovered, serves to illustrate well many of the basic precepts of physical science. When I applied the principles of geometry and Newton's Laws of Motion, combined with my ability to coordinate my keen eyesight with my manual dexterity, I found that I had little trouble defeating Lieutenant Abert in my first game of billiards.

He took it with much more grace than Captain Frémont.

TWENTY-ONE

SEPTEMBER 8, 1845
CANADIAN RIVER, TEXAS PANHANDLE

Twenty-three days after leaving Bent's Fort with a force of thirty-three men, I found myself riding at the head of the column between Lieutenant Abert and John Hatcher, discussing the geology of the Canadian River valley with the lieutenant.

"Look at this patch of ground here," Abert was saying. "Seems to be covered with a coralline formation. Imagine this once being the bottom of an ocean."

"Shall we collect a specimen?" I asked. In addition to making excellent drawings of topographical features along our route, the lieutenant had gathered myriad geological samples ranging from fool's gold to petrified wood. I had found that I enjoyed the company of this educated fellow after so long communing with unschooled men. He was no genius, mind you, but he was intelligent enough. Abert had graduated fifty-fifth in his class of fifty-six at West Point, but he ranked first in drawing. He had an artist's heart, an army officer's discipline, and a mind keen enough to make him an intrepid explorer. He was not as aggressive as Captain Frémont, but his passive, observational nature would keep him and his men out of trouble during his exploratory trek back to St. Louis.

"Let's have a closer look," he said, swinging down from his horse.

I dismounted with Abert and crouched over the outcropping. When he had looked closer, the lieutenant flaked some of the formation away with his knife and said, "Perhaps I was wrong, Mr. Greenwood. The madrepore structure seems to be wanting."

"Judging from the friability and composition," I suggested, "it must be a silicious deposit from an extinct thermal spring."

"Perhaps."

"Look yonder." Hatcher interrupted our geological speculations, in which he held no interest.

I followed Hatcher's eyes to a ridge ahead of us, and saw a lone Indian on a horse.

I mounted quickly, as did the lieutenant. This was the first Indian we had seen since leaving Bent's Fort.

"Can you tell who it might be?" Abert asked.

Hatcher's black eyes peered out from under his old hat brim. "Looks sort of hunkered down, like a Comanche. Hard to tell from this far away."

"Can you signal for him to approach?"

Hatcher spread his arms, showing his open palms. With one hand, he made a respectful invitation for the rider to approach.

The Indian did not move.

"How 'bout if I ride halfway there? He might meet me alone."

"Alright," Abert said. "But only halfway. He might have friends just over the ridge."

Hatcher went forward at a trot, riding a quarter mile before he stopped. He waved another invitation, but the Indian still would not approach. The stranger looked at us for more than a minute, then turned away and disappeared over the ridge.

After that sighting, the men stayed close to the wagon, fearful of a surprise attack by hostiles. Yet, we rode the rest of the day without seeing any sign of Indians, our wagon lumbering and squeaking noisily behind us. Toward evening, we approached a ridge, and I noticed Hatcher studying the sky. He spurred ahead, and I fell in beside him, as did Abert. We loped a short distance then slowed to peer cautiously over the ridge from our saddles.

In the ravine over the ridge, hundreds of buffalo milled—the first we had seen on our journey. Some grazed, some lay chewing their cuds. Here and there pairs of young bulls butted and hooked one another in fierce duels that made dust clouds rise—these having attracted Hatcher's attention.

"We should camp on the river back yonder," Hatcher said. "Up next to the bluff, so's the Indians can't charge through us. I'll sneak around and shoot us some meat."

We made our camp against the bluff as Hatcher had suggested. Abert ordered the wagon driven up next to the bluff so that it would shield our camp from a second side. The river itself ran along the third side of our rectangular camp, creating a secure position with but one opening. As I helped gather wood from a hackberry thicket, I heard Hatcher's shot.

For days we had ridden over the arid tablelands above the valley, for the plains there were flat and more easily traversed by wagon, though we often encountered deep sand. We explored between ravines that branched from the valley, but had to drive the wagon around the heads of most of these. In the evenings, we would leave the treeless plains covered with grass and dotted with cactus patches, descend the Canadian breaks, and find a campsite on the river.

The habitat in the valley differed greatly from that of the plains above. Descending, we would find groves of cottonwood, willow, hackberry, and plum trees. Grapevines twined among many of the trees. Feathers and deep droppings identified places where wild turkeys roosted by the hundreds every night. Coveys of quail burst from undergrowth as did deer of two species—white-tailed and blacktailed. Antelope dotted both the plains and the valley. We had to watch out for rattlesnakes when we dismounted. We were deep into Comanche and Kiowa country, where Apaches and Pawnees also came to make war, and even Cheyenne and Arapaho risked Comanche wrath to hunt the buffalo. Yet, except for the lone rider we had spotted today, we had had no contact with Indians.

"Have you noticed the lack of fruit?" Lieutenant Abert said as I carried an armload of wood to the camp.

"Yes, sir."

"The plums and grapes are all gone here."

"Even the prickly pears have been picked from the cactus." I threw the wood down, satisfied at the musical sound it made.

"I believe there's a large Indian village nearby. Perhaps the buffalo attracted them here. Mr. Hatcher says they make a dish called pemmican with dried fruit and meat."

"Yes, sir," I replied. "Here he comes now."

We walked to the edge of camp to greet our guide and hunter as he dragged a dead buffalo cow behind his sweat-lathered horse. "Kid, take care of my horse and tack. I want to get this butchered before dark."

"Yes, sir," I said, taking the reins. Despite his ill-tempered exterior, John Hatcher had proven himself a good and fair man, and I had no problem taking orders from him. I removed his saddle from his horse, arranged it neatly in the wagon, and walked the horse awhile to cool it down before taking it to drink.

While leading Hatcher's horse to the river, I heard a shriek from downstream—a piteous call of distress from some animal. The cry made me cringe with nebulous dread,

yet filled me with curiosity, so I flung myself bareback onto
Hatcher's horse and rode downstream to investigate.

Several of the soldiers and Lieutenant Abert came looking
for the same piercing alarm, and we found it at the riverbank. The shriek was coming from a frog whose foot had
been caught by a large black snake that was trying to swallow
it. The snake seemed so engrossed in its hunt that it paid no
attention whatever to the men who gathered around it.

"What'll we do, Lieutenant?" one of the soldiers asked.

"Let them be," Abert said, with scientific detachment.
"Let them work it out as if we weren't here."

The riveting distress cry came again from the doomed
frog, when Hatcher pushed his way past me, stepped on the
snake behind its head, drew his knife, and decapitated the
serpent with one sure stroke. Sensing its freedom from the
slack jaws of the snake, the frog sprang between two soldiers and disappeared into the muddy water at the river's
edge. Abert and the men looked at Hatcher with astonishment.

"You call for help, you want everybody to stand around
and watch?" He swished his knife in the river to rinse away
the snake blood, and went back to his butchering as the
headless body of the reptile writhed on the ground.

After watering Hatcher's horse, I went to help him. Thomas Fitzpatrick had gone out scouting, and had now returned to help us butcher the cow. I had seen one buffalo
butchered on the Arkansas, but the old voyagers here used
a different process on this one.

Hatcher had partially skinned the cow by cutting the hide
along the ridge of the spine. He had pulled the skin away
just far enough to get at the long muscles that ran on either
side of the ridge of the spinal column. I had heard this cut
of meat called the "back strap," but Hatcher and Fitzpatrick
called it the "fleece."

After taking the fleece, they broke off the longer spinous
processes of the anterior dorsal vertebrae. These bony spines
that extended upward from each vertebra were all of a foot

and a half long, and created the hump of the buffalo. The mountain men called them "hump ribs." They provided good eating when roasted over a fire. After taking the hump ribs, Hatcher cut the tongue out of the cow, then gutted the beast to take the tenderloin along the spine inside the body cavity. He left the rest of the carcass on the ground. Dusk had fallen when he and Fitzpatrick and I carried the meat back into the protection of the camp.

"Will we butcher the rest tomorrow?" I asked.

Hatcher looked at me briefly. "What for? We want more meat, we'll kill another."

"There's plenty more meat on that one," I suggested.

"Why eat anything but the choice cuts?" Hatcher said.

"Anyway, it's dark," Fitzpatrick added, "and you don't want to be making a fire with Indians about."

"You want to spend all day tomorrow makin' meat over a smoky fire, you go ahead," Hatcher said. "Me, I'm movin' on."

I let the matter go, but the waste of meat defied logic to me. True, the valley abounded with game, but with hundreds of pounds of fresh meat lying on the ground, why not put the soldiers to work slicing and drying it over the fire? Not that it would have made any difference in the long run, for even with my ability to recognize and predict social, economic, and geographic trends, at that moment I could never have foreseen the near-extinction of the American bison within my own lifetime. That tragedy would come later, and in it, I would play my shameful role.

We passed the night quietly, and I had managed to sleep over three hours when a wolf howled and woke me. The howl of the wolf had come from the side of the camp opposite the buffalo carcass. I also noticed that the cry came from a point that was downwind of neither the camp nor the carcass. Then I heard an owl hoot, and became suspicious that Indians, not animals, were making the noises.

John Hatcher must have suspected the same thing. In the light of a quarter moon, I saw him rise from his bedroll, take up his rifle, and sit on a water barrel near the door of

Lieutenant Abert's tent. I remained still, but my pistol was near me, and my ears tracked every sound from the hushed passage of the river to the breeze stirring the tops of cottonwoods. I lay awake until dawn, but no attack came.

We were just cooking breakfast and watering stock when Fitzpatrick said in a low voice, "Indians, boys." I looked and saw eighteen warriors riding down the breaks into the river bottom. They came directly toward our camp.

"What do you want to do, Lieutenant?" Hatcher asked.

Abert scratched at the stubble on his chin for a moment, then said, "I suppose we should invite them to breakfast."

Hatcher walked beyond the army wagon and made the invitation with a wave of his hand. He made other gestures, as well, but his back was turned and I couldn't see them. I assumed he had signified food.

"You men gather the mules and horses near the wagon," Abert ordered. "Stay together and do not make a move without my order to do so."

The soldiers obeyed, opening the way for the Indians to ride into camp. As they approached, each warrior looked with disfavor at the partially butchered carcass of the buffalo on the ground. Hatcher led them, his back turned to them in a show of trust, though he knew we would be watching his back for him.

"Mr. Fitzpatrick?" Abert said quietly, the question obvious in his tone of voice.

"Kiowas," Broken Hand replied. "No paint. Like as not, they'll stay friendly if we do. Looks like they know John."

I scanned the riders as they approached, and noticed characteristics most held in common. They wore their hair long, braided in the back. The braids fell over the shoulders of some, and I saw a couple adorned with silver disks. Each rider had wrapped a blanket around one leg, then around his waist, then around his other leg. This, I reasoned, must help the rider stay seated on his horse, for none used a saddle. Several of the warriors wore moccasins with fringe on them long enough to reach the ground. This alone told me that these men preferred to ride rather than walk, for walking in those moccasins would equate to a white man's strolling about with his boot laces untied and dragging on the ground. Hatcher led them to the edge of camp, where they dismounted. Their ponies were well trained, for they did not require tying.

"Tell them they are welcome to come to our camp in peace," Abert said. "Ask them if they'd like to join us for breakfast."

"I don't speak their language good, but I know the signs," Hatcher said. "Have the kid talk to them in Spanish while I make the signs; then we won't have no mistakes."

"Mr. Greenwood," the lieutenant ordered.

I made the welcome and the invitation for breakfast in Spanish as Hatcher made the signs, and we began a discourse with our guests, who were really our hosts, for we were camped on their soil.

"This warrior is called Teh-toot-sah," Hatcher said. "Means Little Bluff. We've traded before, and he can be trusted. He's not a chief, but he's what they call a Great Warrior, which is probably about like a colonel to us."

When I looked at the man Hatcher was introducing, I found him smiling at me, though not looking at me directly eye to eye. I recognized him as the happy warrior who had helped the Comanches surround me and Blue Wiggins on the Cimarron. I could not help cracking a slight smile myself. I knew he recognized me. I was still wearing Kills Something's weapons, and my own saber, but had added the Apache scalp to my ornaments.

Jibber growled, and I nudged him with my foot to quiet him.

As the cook and some of the soldiers began cooking all the meat we had in camp, along with some cornmeal cakes and cured bacon, Little Bluff told why they had come to our camp.

"Yesterday I was hunting," he told me, speaking excellent Spanish accompanied by signs he made with his hands. "I found the trail of your wagon. I thought you were *Tejanos*. Last night, I crept close to your camp. You will find my tracks there, between the tent and the wagon. A wolf cried, and an owl answered, and I think Freckled Hand's heart told him his enemies had made these sounds, for he rose from his bed. I saw him. He sat near the tent with his gun. I did not recognize him, for the night was dark. I strung my bow and notched an arrow. I aimed at Freckled Hand, thinking he was an enemy *Tejano,* for he had come to my country to frighten away the buffalo. I drew my bow. Then my heart told me not to kill this man. My heart told me this man was a friend. So I put my arrow away and made a stack of rocks behind your wagon, so you would know I had come near and spared your lives, as a friend."

"There is a pile of rocks over yonder," Fitzpatrick said. "I saw it at dawn, but figured one of our boys made it."

"Lieutenant, just so's there's no mistakes," Hatcher added, "you ought to have the kid tell 'em that you're American and not Texan."

"But the Texans *will* be Americans soon, Mr. Hatcher."

"Not to a Kiowa or a Comanche. A Texan is a devil to them, and you don't want to be mistaken for one."

"Mr. Greenwood, tell them we are from America. Tell them we come here in peace. Tell them we are not Texans, but the Texans now are part of America, and must do as our president says. Tell them there will be no more trouble with the Texans."

I translated all that into Spanish, while Hatcher made signs that burned themselves into my memory.

With a curious smile, Little Bluff asked, "Why do you come here?"

"Tell him we come to see the beauty of his country and make a lasting peace with his people," Abert ordered.

I translated this, but the Kiowa pointed at me and said, "No, why do *you* come here?"

I told him that I was neither *Americano* nor *Tejano,* that I had come for my own reasons, and that I wished to establish a mutually beneficial trade with the Kiowa and the Comanches."

"Care to let us in on your foreign policy?" Abert said.

I explained what had been said, and the lieutenant suggested I make my private business arrangements on my own time. By now, the smell of food was in the air, so we offered breakfast, which the Kiowas devoured, and coffee sweetened with sugar, which they seemed to relish as a rare treat. Abert made each warrior a gift of tobacco, and this pleased the whole party immensely.

I had a chance to talk to Little Bluff while he smoked a cigarette that John Hatcher had rolled for him. I told him that I had come from the big fort of William Bent, and that I would build a similar fort near the Bent trading houses, which John Hatcher said could not lie more than three days downstream. Little Bluff simply laughed at this idea; but then, he seemed to find almost everything laughable.

"We have seen very few Indians along this river," I said. "Where are all the people?"

Again the Kiowa laughed. "Do you see my friend, Fur Man, over there, leaning against the wheel of your wagon? He was camping at Bent's Fort when your party got ready to leave. William Bent came to him and sent him ahead of your party to tell us you were coming. Fur Man decided to play a trick on the Comanches. He told them that instead of Americans or traders, a big war party of Texans was coming down the river to kill everybody. The Comanches moved their women and children away from the river, and now my friends and I are killing plenty of buffalo because there is nobody else around here." He took a deep drag on the cigarette, and his laughter came out in a cloud of smoke.

"Will this make the Comanches angry?"

"They like a joke. They will make a revenge joke on Fur Man- one day. Maybe they will tell him to go kill some buffalo over the next hill, and he will find Pawnees instead, and they will kill him."

Even Fur Man laughed at this suggestion.

When the laughter died, Little Bluff glanced at the scalp on my belt and said, "You have won something."

I told him how I had killed the Apache, mistaking him for a wolf, and how the dead man's friends had retaliated during the crossing of the Arkansas. To give my story more credence, I produced the arrowhead that had been removed from my shoulder blade.

I reasoned that if the Kiowas indeed appreciated humor, they might also enjoy some of my sleight of hand. "Little Bluff," I asked, holding the war point in my hand, "have you ever seen a magic arrow point?"

"Magic?" he asked, the curious smile again appearing on his face.

With a flourish of my hands, I palmed the point and revealed the backs of my hands. Another flourish, and I shifted the point to a backhand palm, and showed my empty hands to the Kiowas. A twist of my wrist, and the point was back in my hand. It seemed as though someone had sent a charge of electricity through the Indians. One stood all the way up, in amazement and consternation. A few gasped in disbelief. The smile vanished from Little Bluff's face, and his mouth hung open wide for a moment.

"Easy with that business, Kid," Hatcher warned. "They'll expect you to have power you can't live up to."

This made me nervous, but the smile soon returned to Little Bluff's face, and he laughed his loudest yet. Then he stood up and began speaking the only English he knew, stomping about the camp white-man style, saying, "Howdy! Howdy! Shit! Goddamn, howdy, shit! Yes, yes! No, no!"

The Kiowas and the soldiers burst into simultaneous laughter, and the camp suddenly seemed peopled by the best of old friends. One of the Kiowas clipped some black hair from his horse's tail and held this above his eyes to caricature the bushy eyebrows of a white man. As his friends howled, he walked about the Indians, touching bows, arrows, and quivers; picking up lances to study them as a fascinated white man would.

Right in the middle of the frivolity, Jibber began growling in a rumble that seemed too deep to come from his diminutive throat. The camp quickly fell quiet. I followed my guardian's piercing glare and, just as he burst into paroxysms of barking, I located the rider entering the far side of the river to cross to our camp.

Snakehead Jackson rode his buckskin into the current, leading three mules, each laden with a pair of wooden kegs. The water was not deep enough to swim, but his pony balked twice, apparently dubious of the footing in waters that sometimes held quicksand bogs that could mire a mount. Snakehead let the pony choose its own crossing and came over just downstream of our camp. He made his string of mules, tied head-to-tail, stop belly-deep and rode around them, splashing water on the barrels until they were well soaked.

"Do you know him?" Abert asked.

"Yep," John Hatcher said.

"Well?"

Hatcher seemed annoyed and refused to reply, so I said, "His name's Snakehead Jackson. He's a whiskey trader."

"What's he doing?" Abert asked.

Thomas Fitzpatrick answered. "Soakin' his kegs. Swells the wood. Keeps 'em tight."

"Whiskey tight," Hatcher added.

When Snakehead came out of the river, I got a closer look at his kegs. Four were of rude make, used and reused, with rusty barrel hoops binding them, like the casks from which I had tasted lightning in San Fernandez de Taos. The packsaddle on the lead mule canted noticeably to the right side, giving the impression that the right-hand keg on that mule was full, the left one empty. The two kegs on the last mule looked comparatively new and bore the brands of a St. Louis distillery that made a low grade of rotgut for the frontier trade.

Snakehead rode right into the camp, uninvited, soaked from the chest down. "John," he said. "Tom."

Our two guides nodded a greeting, and Hatcher said, "Bill."

"Where the hell is all the Indians?"

"These Kiowas are it," Hatcher said. "The Comanches have scattered."

"I'm Lieutenant J. W. Abert of the United States Army," the West Pointer announced.

Snakehead smiled. "Pleased to meet you, Cousin."

"You're in my camp. Please state your business."

"Nun-ya," Snakehead replied.

"Beg your pardon?" Abert said.

"My business is *nun-ya* business." A devious smile appeared in the middle of Snakehead's beard.

Abert's youthful face darkened. "It *is* my business. You're standing in a U.S. Army camp."

"This is Texas, Cousin."

"Texas is soon to be a state."

"I don't give a damn. Anyway, the Indians hold this ground. Line on a map don't mean a goddamn thing."

"Do you have whiskey in those kegs?"

"I do."

"What do you intend doing with it?"

"Trade it, Cousin."

Abert glanced at his guides. "Why do you insist on referring to me as your cousin?"

"Because you're a little son of my Uncle Sam." Snakehead glared, then broke into laughter which nobody joined.

"It's against the law to supply the Indians with whiskey."

"Ain't against *their* law, and their law is what decides whether or not you live or die here. Now, that's a pretty powerful law."

"For all practical purposes, you are on United States soil, Mr. Jackson, and here it is illegal to trade whiskey to Indians."

"I'll trade 'em any goddamn thing they want, Cousin, includin' your scalp, if the profit warrants."

Abert remained unflappable. "You won't find that trade profitable. I've already forged a friendship with this band."

Snakehead snorted. "Sober."

I saw Abert's chest swell, like a boy about to pick a fight. His eyes flashed, but he held his temper and spoke deliberately. "You will not trade any whiskey in my camp," he said.

I heard a bit of shuffling behind me, and knew some of the soldiers were easing toward their stacked rifles, or shifting positions to use their pistols if the lieutenant gave the order to arrest the whiskey trader.

"Never intended to," Snakehead replied. "Your camp don't suit me. I choose my own camps."

The conversation seemed mired, but then Snakehead's horse began tossing his head. Snakehead only smiled. He did not seem to be giving the horse any kind of signal, but could have been squeezing with his knees. The buckskin continued to wave its head, then began to paw with one foot. The Kiowas seemed agitated for the first time. Still, Snakehead sat his saddle as the horse shook his head, then ramped and pawed the air. When his hooves landed back on the ground, the whiskey trader loosed a yell—half scream, half growl—that echoed across the canyon and fired every man there with boiling blood.

"*Aguardiente!*" he shouted, in an almost musical tone. "*Hoy, malos cabrones! Aguardiente, borrachos!*" And he whirled his mount to ride away, tugging on the halter rope of the lead mule as he trotted his whole outfit out of the army camp.

The Indians moved almost in unison toward their horses. They mounted with marvelous agility—some swinging astride their mounts, some literally vaulting. Each loosed a yell that rivaled Snakehead's example, and they thundered away in pursuit. Only Little Bluff remained behind long enough to offer some sort of departing gesture, and that was only a mock white man's shrug.

"What did he say?" Abert asked me.

"He said, 'Firewater,' " I answered. "Then he said, 'Listen, you bad goats! Firewater, you drunken ones!' "

John Hatcher chuckled. "That's awful fancy, Kid. What he said was more like 'Whiskey, you drunk bastards. Some other warrior humps your wife and you don't do a goddamn thing about it, so come and get your whiskey!' "

"I didn't know you understood Spanish, Mr. Hatcher," I said.

"Just the rank words, Kid."

Abert grunted, then seemed to shake off the entire confrontation. "Sergeant," he said to his second in command, "break this camp and hitch the wagon."

⋯⋯⋯⋯

We made our new camp some dozen miles downstream, near a line of creek-side timber. The sun stood two fists above the top of the riverbank when he unhitched the wagon. The calls of bobwhite quail whistled in the underbrush, and a red-tailed hawk overhead seemed to be listening and looking for them. I was hanging harnesses on the wagon when John Hatcher came to me.

"Follow me, Kid."

I went with Hatcher to Lieutenant Abert's tent where he was sitting outside, writing in his journal.

"Lieutenant," the guide said, "we need to have the boys drag up some timbers. Build a kraal around the camp so the Indians can't charge through."

Abert looked up from his pen and paper. He nodded. "Build a what?"

"A *kraal*." When Hatcher said "corral" it came out in one syllable, sounding like *"kraal."* Apparently, the lieutenant was so green to the west that he had never heard of a corral. He stopped to write something down, and I assumed it was this word. He questioned Mr. Hatcher about the construction of the *kraal,* and Hatcher told him to have the men fell trees and make a circle of the timbers, the wagon to be included in the circle. The timbers should be overlapped, end on end, three courses high. Then, the timbers should be interlaced with brush to make a secure enclosure.

"From now on," the guide said, "as long as you're in Comanche country, you ought to make a *kraal* at every camp. I don't care how much work it takes. Even after me and the kid quit the party at the Big Crossing tomorrow, you ought to build your *kraal* of a evenin', every evenin'."

"As you say," the lieutenant responded.

"Now, while the men build the *kraal*, me and the kid are gonna scout ahead a piece, with your permission, sir."

"Granted." The lieutenant looked at the sky, and closed his journal. He got up and began issuing orders to the soldiers as Hatcher and I mounted our horses and rode downstream.

"What are we scouting for, Mr. Hatcher?" I asked as a covey of quail exploded in front of Fireball, prompting the hawk above us to fold his wings, and dive. The raptor plummeted and struck an unfortunate hen with its talons, driving her to the ground, where it killed her.

Hatcher watched all this without expression or comment. "Scout's ass," he said. "I know where we're at. The Big Crossing is just three or four miles on ahead. I want you to see the whiskey camp. You're of a mind to trade with Indians, you need to see 'em drunk. Snakehead'll be there at The Crossing. His camp will lay right where we're gonna build our adobe fort for Bent and St. Vrain."

We swam the river to the north bank. The cool water perked our horses up, so we struck an easy canter for a couple of miles as shadows lengthened in the wooded valley. Deer scattered ahead of us at every bend, their tails waving like white flags of surrender. From one patch of brambles, a black bear raised up on its hind legs, took a look at us with frightened eyes, and crashed away into a thicket as if we had ridden right out of bruin hell.

The trail here was a good one, wide enough for two or three riders abreast. It ran down the valley about a half mile from the river, generally halfway between the water and the flat plains above the breaks. It was well marked and beaten deep, and I could tell it was often used by Indians. We slowed to a walk and continued at this pace for another mile before we smelled the smoke and heard the beating of a drum.

"Git down," Hatcher said. "We'll creep up afoot."

I tied Fireball, and followed Hatcher along the trail into a creek bottom. I could feel the ruts of lodge poles under my moccasins. The sun had rounded the horizon by the time we crept up the opposite side of the creek, and I saw the orange flicker of a fire through the underbrush. A tribal chant accompanied the drumbeat now, with several voices wailing at several pitches, making a kind of music I had never before heard—a kind that stirred my soul with its chaos.

As Hatcher and I snuck to a place where we could get a clear view, the timber and brush began to open. A broad prairie fanned ahead, the seedy heads of grasses waving like ripples on a tawny lake. The horses and mules grazed in this prairie, and beyond them, I could see the timber line of another creek; then, farther on, bluffs rising against the slate sky. The drumming, the singing, the dancing grass, the horses, the smoke. I felt intoxicated. A windflaw roared somewhere in a treetop. I had been here before. This was the place of my restless dreams at Saint-Cyr. I had crouched in this very place in some past vision. This was The Crossing on the wild river. My calling. This was the place. This soil was mine. Every whiff of sap and dung and nectar on the wind belonged to me.

A cold shaft of air crept up from the creek bottom and touched us with clammy hands as we parted the bushes to get an unobstructed view of the whiskey camp. Five of the Kiowas, including Little Bluff, sat in a circle around the drum, each man beating it with a stick as if he meant to pulverize it. Several other Kiowas danced in a circle, each facing inward, shuffling his feet, stooping slightly over and tossing his braids till they writhed like snakes.

Snakehead was standing, watching, one foot on a whiskey barrel as he leaned forward on his knee. All six barrels were on the ground, near the three packsaddles and Snakehead's riding saddle.

Suddenly the song ended with one great drum beat, and the Kiowas erupted in a war yell as Snakehead took his foot down from the keg and joined in the maniacal screaming. He pointed to the drum, and Little Bluff started the rhythm again. Snakehead picked up an empty barrel whose top had been taken out, and placed it before the Kiowas. Stepping up to the fire, he poured some gunpowder from his powder flask into his palm. This he tossed into the fire, creating a flare and cloud of white smoke that lifted and vanished. The Kiowas shrieked.

Now Snakehead went back to the open cask and poured a large measure of black powder in through the opening.

"What's he doing?" I whispered to Hatcher.

"Mixin' up his own special brew."

"With black powder in it?"

"That ain't the half of it. Watch."

From a buckskin pouch he wore over one shoulder, Snakehead produced some object too small for me to identify. He offered it to several of the warriors, but each refused. Finally, Snakehead tossed the object in his mouth and chewed it.

"What was that?"

"Dried pepper," Hatcher said. "That thing will scald a blister on a rawhide boot."

Snakehead produced another pepper and shamed a young Kiowa brave into eating it as he had. The young buck tossed it proudly into his mouth, chewed for a few seconds, then spit the pepper out. But it was too late. He began hopping as his friends howled with laughter, and finally found a canteen made from a buffalo bladder, and poured the water into his burning mouth.

Snakehead laughed and threw a handful of peppers down on a barrel top. He drew his knife with a theatrical flourish and began chopping the peppers in time with the drum beat. He hacked meticulously at the peppers for a long time, then began scraping the pieces up with his knife blade and letting them fall into the open keg.

Now he waved his hand at Little Bluff, and the drum beat ceased abruptly. The Indians waited quietly, watching Snakehead, even the young warrior who had eaten the pepper and was still swishing water in his mouth. Snakehead stooped and picked up a cloth sack that lay near his saddle. The moment he lifted the sack, the muffled-yet-unmistakable warning of a rattlesnake sang across the prairie and I could see the viper writhing inside the sack.

Snakehead upended the sack and let the snake plop on the ground, the buzzing sound coming clearer now. Instantly, he stepped on the snake behind its head, then grabbed it and picked it up as if it were a harmless pet. For a while, he taunted the Indians with the fatal fangs of the reptile, and each man backed away fearfully. Then Snakehead carried the reptile to the fire, held it over the flames, and laughed at the way it lashed about crazily in his grasp.

"What's he doing that for?" I asked, sickened at the senseless torture of the snake.

" 'Cause he's mean," Hatcher whispered back, no emotion in his voice.

Snakehead tortured the diamondback until his own hand must have been roasting from the heat. Then he pinned the rattler's head down on a barrel top, drew his knife, and slowly decapitated the serpent. The still-writhing body he threw into the fire, where a couple of braves poked at it with sticks to keep it from rolling out of the coals. He speared the severed head with his knife point, brandished it to the sky, and then tapped the blade on the rim of the barrel to add the snake head to his recipe. For the first time, I understood the whiskey trader's wicked nickname.

Now Snakehead ordered the drum beat to resume, and pried the stopper from a barrel of St. Louis red-eye. He lifted the keg and began pouring the amber liquid into the open vessel, filling it a third of the way. He opened a cask of Taos Lightning next, and filled the open vessel, adding to the rotgut, the black powder, the ground peppers, and the snake head. This was the whiskey trader's own brew.

Snakehead Jackson waved his greasy fist at the drummers and the beat ceased. He produced a gourd dipper, and suddenly the braves scrambled to form a line before the whiskey barrel, shoving each other for a favorable position. Snakehead dipped the gourd into his concoction and handed it to the first warrior, Little Bluff, who drank. Little Bluff took the entire dipperful in one gulp, then stepped aside, shaking his head as he handed back the dipper. When he had swallowed and taken a breath or two, Little Bluff released a squall made edgy as a flint arrow point by the whiskey.

"First drink's on the house," Hatcher whispered.

Twilight had descended on my crossing in the wilderness, where the evil Jackson tortured animals and corrupted Indians. I watched by the light of the Indian fire as each warrior took his first drink, then went to find some article to trade for the second.

In this round of bartering, Snakehead accepted knives, pistols, and a fancy Spanish bridle one of the braves had acquired in a raid. He refused lances, bows, and arrows. After the second round, the Indians milled about in confusion for a while, sang, chanted, and engaged in a few wrestling matches.

The next warrior who tried to buy a drink had to give up his musket for one dipper of the brew. The man who followed him offered a flask of gunpowder, but Snakehead refused the bargain until the man added a fine buffalo robe to the deal. By this time, some of the Kiowas had already taken three or four shots of whiskey, and some began to show signs of intoxication. One of them tripped and fell into the fire, the flames igniting his braids. Too drunk to do anything but scramble out of the fire on hands and knees, his friends laughed and kicked dirt at him in a mock attempt to put out the blaze, although one warrior actually crouched and blew on the smoldering braids, trying to keep the fire going. Finally, Little Bluff kicked the young warrior onto his back and stomped the flames out of his hair, while the young man began to howl from the pain of the burns.

Snakehead's pile of loot began to mount, and he stood fearlessly in the midst of the chaos he had created. He was taking rifles and robes now. Then one of the warriors brought up a pony he had gone to the prairie to fetch. Snakehead accepted this animal in trade for a shot of whiskey, half of which the warrior spilled down his chin and chest.

About this time, the young warrior who had burned his mouth on the pepper left the fireside and wandered away from the camp. As he staggered directly toward me, I watched him. He seemed to wanderer casually, but then he suddenly flung himself to the ground. In a drunken mockery of Kiowa stealth, he attempted to sneak through the grass, circling wide, coming around behind Snakehead. I soon understood his aim, for he was crawling up to the mound of merchandise Snakehead had acquired, in an attempt to steal something back for another drink.

Snakehead sealed a trade for a fine Mexican-made rawhide reata just as the young buck reached the pile of goods, took hold of a rifle, and attempted to retreat. Turning, Snakehead caught him red-handed and retaliated instantly, advancing on the drunken warrior with the coil of rawhide in his hand. He beat the Kiowa viciously with the heavy reata, finally knocking him down. The Kiowa staggered to his feet, and reached for a knife he had already traded. Now Snakehead picked up the rifle the Indian had dropped, turned the butt to the young warrior, and smashed it mercilessly into his mouth and nose, sprawling the drunken thief unconscious across the grass.

One of the older warriors made a complaint, and Snakehead turned on him, begging for a fight. The warrior advanced, but the whiskey trader clubbed him to the ground. Now Snakehead laughed and shouted a war cry through the air. He dipped the gourd and took his own shot of whiskey, his beard glistening with the rotgut he let dribble from his mouth. He offered a round of free drinks, and the Kiowas stepped over their unconscious friends for another shot.

Someone lugged a fancy Spanish saddle to the pile for trade. The others began swapping their ponies brought in from the prairie.

"You seen enough?" Hatcher asked in his hoarse whisper.

"Yes, sir," I replied. "I would just as soon we left now." My stomach felt twisted and ill. I had found the place of my calling, but found it defiled beyond my ability to anticipate.

TWENTY-TWO

On the morning of September 15, 1845, I bid adieu to Lieutenant James William Abert. I would stay on the Canadian River with John Hatcher and build a fort. Abert would explore the Canadian to its junction with the Arkansas, then ride successfully back to St. Louis. He would complete his military career without particular incident. He would serve in the Mexican War and in the Civil War until a fall from his horse at the Battle of Shenandoah would force his retirement as a colonel. He would make a comfortable living as a mercantile trader and college professor, and die at the ripe old age of seventy-six.

Though he followed his instructions to explore the Canadian River and completed his mission without losing a single man, his expedition really did not seem to count for much. The army would not pass this way again for years. Before and after Abert's exploration, the country was known much better by civilian traders, such as Hatcher, Fitzpatrick, and me. The land would be conquered and settled by the traders, the buffalo hunters, and the cattlemen, not the army. Abert's fleeting track upon the ground would be forgotten. It seems to me that the only reason for his journey in the vast scheme of the universe was to provide the vehicle that would carry me to my destiny. For this, I will be eternally grateful to James William Abert, my friend.

"Mr. Hatcher," the lieutenant said as we prepared to part company with the expedition, "you have comported yourself as a gentleman at every turn of our journey. I thank you for your service to your nation. I shall mention you with favor in my report."

Hatcher nodded and shook the officer's hand. "About my pay," he said.

"I will send it back to Bent's Fort in the care of your friend, Mr. Fitzpatrick."

"That'll do, sir. Now, listen. The Comanches will find you before you leave their range. Don't let the boys stray ten rods from the party, or they'll be lanced by Comanches in sight of their friends." He shook Abert's hand, then shook Fitzpatrick's, saying, "Tom."

"John," Fitzpatrick said in return. "Mind the roots of your hair, old hoss."

Chuckling, Hatcher turned to his mount.

All this time, I had been tying a single adobe mold and a sharpshooter shovel firmly onto my saddle so that the implements wouldn't bounce about when I struck a canter. I made the last knot around the old adobe mold and approached the lieutenant. "About your report," I said quietly. "No need to make much mention of me."

"I agree," Abert replied. "I shall simply note that a mysterious Mr. Greenwood will leave this expedition with Mr. Hatcher today, and cross the Canadian River to fulfill his destiny."

I smiled. "Don't forget to build your *kraal* tonight," I said, impersonating Hatcher's frontier dialect.

He laughed. "By all means. Godspeed."

We shook hands.

I mounted Fireball, whistled Jibber out from under the shade of the wagon, and struck a canter to catch up with Hatcher, who was already halfway to the river. Our trail, an ancient one, led down the right bank of White Deer Creek, whose name that day I had yet to learn. The mouth of White Deer Creek opened wide into the valley of the Canadian. Here we rode between a bluff sixty feet high on our right, and the marshy creek bottom on our left. The trail under us was plenty wide enough for ponies dragging travoises made of tepee lodge poles.

Entering the flood plain of the river, Fireball found the footing solid—more so than in other places we had crossed on this river. His legs sank only to the pasterns in sand, then found solid soil or bedrock below, creating a natural ford at this place. In time I would come to understand that this was the easiest place to cross the Canadian within a hundred miles either way up or down the river. No steep banks had to be ascended or descended on either side of the stream, and no quicksand bogs mired the beasts of burden who made the crossing. The crossing was an ancient one for humans and wildlife alike.

We rode our horses belly deep across the Canadian and started up the gentle slope on the north bank. Here we stopped, and looked back. Up a ravine, on the south side of the river, we saw Lieutenant Abert's party pass around the head of the draw. The lieutenant himself waved at us, then disappeared.

"You ever get him figured?" Hatcher said.

"I guess. What's to figure?"

"What's to figure? Kid, it ain't every day a couple of Indian traders get a army escort. Somebody ain't tellin' us somethin'."

"Like what?"

"Hell if I know. Maybe we just think we're here to build a fort for Bent and St. Vrain. Maybe we're really buildin' it for the damn army."

This prospect hadn't occurred to me, and left me speechless.

"You ain't in on it, are you?" Hatcher said.

"Me? I just thought we—I mean, you and Mr. Fitzpatrick—were here to guide the expedition."

"Guide, hell. Any fool can follow a river. The damn army's up to somethin'."

"But what?"

He shrugged. "Maybe they told William to build the fort and they'd buy it. I hope not. Even if Captain Frémont and Lieutenant Abert mean well, next thing you know, they'll get orders to Jackass, Mexico, and some Colonel Shithead will come in here and just take the fort. Ain't a army ever mustered that had a conscience."

"Well, I'm not in on it, if that's the case," I said. "Really, I'm not."

He looked at me and grinned. "I believe you, Kid. You don't know what the hell you're doin' here, do you?"

"Not yet," I admitted.

We rode on and soon came to a trail that I recognized as the one we had ridden the night before to spy on the whiskey camp. We stepped upon our own tracks, and entered the creek bottom where we had concealed ourselves only hours ago.

"This here's Bent's Creek," Hatcher said. "William was the first white man to camp here, far as I know. Not countin' Spaniards, anyway."

When we rode out of Bent's Creek we stopped to look at what was left of the Kiowa camp. The fire had long since burned out. All the horses were gone, along with Snakehead and his loot. A couple of the Kiowas were sitting up, holding their heads in their hands. Others lay in states of insensible sleep in the shade or sun. An enemy could have walked among them, slaughtered them, and taken their scalps without struggle.

"Let's just leave them be a spell and look around," Hatcher said.

We rode up the right bank of Bent's Creek a short distance until we came to a burned place on the ground where a few blackened stones remained in a rectangular pattern.

"This was the Bent–St. Vrain trading house I built a couple of years ago," Hatcher said. "Built it myself with hackberry logs. Some cedar and oak where I could find 'em straight and long enough."

"What happened to it?" I asked.

Hatcher looked at me as if I was stupid. "It burnt, boy. Can't you tell?"

"Yes, sir. I meant to ask who burned it."

"Then why didn't you?"

I waited for an explanation, but none came.

"Who burned it?"

"Comanches."

"Were you here?"

"If I was here then, I wouldn't be here now." Hatcher leaned forward on his pommel. "Last time I left this place, it was still standin'. A Mexican fellow who'd come down with me from Bent's Fort decided he'd live here at the trading house year round by hisself. As a kid, he'd been captured out of old Mexico and raised by Comanches. He spoke their lingo and all, so he thought he could get away with it. I tried to talk him out of it. The Kiowas tell that some Comanche warrior lost a brother in a fight with Mexicans, so in revenge, he come and kilt the nearest Mexican he could find. Burnt him out of the tradin' house and shot him full of arrows."

We left the ashes and rode a short distance up the creek. I could hear the faint trickle of water in its bed. The view of the creek bed opened upstream, and I could see that Bent's Creek issued from a box canyon above us.

"Does the creek run with good water all the time?" I asked.

"There's a good spring three miles up keeps it runnin' even in a dry spell, near as I can tell. I never stayed here more than a couple of months in the winter. Afraid I'd wear out my welcome with the Comanches. But the Kiowas have always held that there's sweet water here every moon."

We turned away from Bent's Creek here and rode across the broad prairie that extended northward like a rough-edged rectangle about two square miles in extent. Tall grasses of at least nine different varieties covered this prairie, each identifiable by distinctive seed clusters and other features. I knew at a glance that enough grass stood here to provide straw for the making of thousands of adobe bricks. I had already located a ready supply of water. Now all I need find was clay that would make mud of the proper density and viscosity for the production of adobes.

Fireball grabbed a mouthful of grass as he walked, so I jiggled the bit in his mouth to tell him this was no time to eat. He obediently refrained from taking a second bite. Jibber could not be seen down in the tall grass, but I could see the seed tassels of the grasses quiver above him wherever he went. Suddenly his speed doubled, and I realized that he had jumped a rabbit down in the grass, and now scampered in pursuit, springing into the air every few yards in his attempt to see his prey above the tall grass. He made such a comical spectacle vaulting wide-eyed into view that even Hatcher laughed.

"That damn little ol' dog's a pretty good one," he said.

I didn't want Jibber straying too far, so I whistled once, and he abandoned the chase immediately and came plowing back through the lake of tall grass to rejoin the horses. We rode now over a high roll in the prairie. It reminded me of a buffalo hump, standing twenty feet above the natural pasture, covered with the same dense thatch of grass. Coming over this high roll, we enjoyed a splendid view of the prairie.

"There's good springs here and there all around this prairie," Hatcher said as we rode. "These bluffs all around give some shelter from the blizzards. There's game here to hunt all the time. Black bear, deer, antelope, turkey. Rabbits and squirrels galore. Winter brings ducks, geese, and cranes. Buffalo drift through from time to time. A man who can handle a smoke pole can keep hisself fed."

"But you can't live off of meat alone," I said. "What about scurvy?"

"You can trade with the Indians for their cakes and pemmican and stuff. And there's plenty of fruit in season. Mustang grapes, wild Mexican plums. A bee tree or two will git you enough honey to fill a deerskin."

We came to a place in the middle of the prairie where two springs issued from the flat ground and snaked away toward the creek to the east.

"What is the name of that creek?" I asked.

"It ain't got no name."

"Maybe we should call it 'Hatcher Creek.' "

"Like hell. I don't care what you call it; just don't name it for me."

Beyond the nameless creek to the east, a pair of bluffs

rose abruptly, eighty to a hundred feet in height. To the north, the ravine of the creek jagged into the flatlands that stood above this valley. To the west, a broad hillock rose a hundred feet above us. To the south stood the high roll in the prairie.

"This might make a good place for the fort," I boldly suggested. "Here, between these two springs."

Hatcher shook his head. "Too far from timber. You want to haul wood that far every other day?"

"Bent's Fort is farther from timber than this," I argued.

"Bent's Fort pays a full-time woodchopper. Get it through your head, Kid. This ain't gonna be no Bent's Fort. It won't be a quarter the size. It might hold ten men at the most during the winter trading season. Like as not, nobody will stay here all year round. Who'd be fool enough?"

"*I'd* stay here."

"You ain't met no Comanches yet."

"But I have. On the Cimarron, with Blue Wiggins."

"I heard about that. You two got lucky."

"I'm not afraid of them."

"Then you'll die a fearless man. Now, listen. It's my say-so where the fort is built, and I say it goes back where the burnt cabin was. Timber's handy there, and so is water."

"Why don't we recommend to William the building of a permanent fort to stand right here? You can see how easily the surrounding field could be defended—just like at Bent's Fort. Twenty men could operate it as a smaller version of Bent's Fort. We could call it 'Fort Hatcher.' "

John Hatcher spit between his horse and mine. "Kid, you can call it 'Fort Greenwood,' for all I care, but it ain't goin' here. Don't think you can butter me up callin' it after me. I don't give a hoot in hell. All I want is a safe place to trade for a couple of months where I can roll out my cotton without losin' my scalp in my sleep. If I'm gonna git scalped, I'd just as soon see it comin' wide awake."

I made no further argument for the site of my own choosing, but something about this level field between the two springs appealed to my intellect, my common sense, my formal education, my scant frontier training, my appreciation for natural beauty, and my very guts and soul. Someday, I knew, I would build something here. For now, I would have to follow Hatcher's orders.

"I'm going to check that creek bed for signs of clay deposits," I announced.

"I'll ride with you. Watch your back for you."

We walked our ponies lazily the half mile to the nameless creek. Reaching its bed, I turned downstream and began studying the soil formations along the cutbank. Hatcher kept his eyes trained on the surrounding bluffs and hills while I searched for clay. After searching no more than twenty minutes, I found a broad deposit of dark reddish-brown clay painting a deep horizontal streak along the cutbank. It lay just under the surface, two to three feet deep, and forty yards wide. Depending on how far it extended away from the creek, it might provide enough clay for half of the fort I had in mind to build. Riding another quarter mile down the creek, I found another such deposit, then another, and I knew I would have enough clay, straw, and water to build an adobe structure of ample proportions. I waved to Mr. Hatcher, and he rode down into the creek bed where I showed him what I had found.

"The most efficient thing would be to haul the loose clay and straw near the construction site and use the water from Bent's Creek to make the adobes."

"Alright."

"But we won't have a wagon or cart to haul the dirt until William and the adobe makers get here."

"We'll kill us a buffler or two," Hatcher said. "Make sleds out of the flint hides."

I nodded. "Well, I'd better get to work."

I dismounted and untied the sharpshooter shovel from the back of my saddle, then dug up enough clay to fill both of my saddlebags. This cargo I carried back to Bent's Creek, and the burned-out remains of Hatcher's cabin. By this time, the Kiowas had begun to stir. Some of them had already left on foot for the village upstream. Little Bluff came to speak to me before he took the trail. He seemed to be still nursing a fierce hangover yet he maintained his ever-present smile.

"My woman is going to be angry," he said. "I have traded away my rifle and my pony. I do not even have my best robe anymore, and the winter is coming." He turned his face to the sky and laughed.

"Then why do you laugh?" I asked.

"Because I feel much better than I did this morning when the sun burned down in my face and my head felt like it had an arrow sticking through it."

I dumped the dirt out of my saddlebags and untied the adobe mold from the saddle strings. "Why do you drink the whiskey if it makes your head hurt?"

"The good things in life number like this," the Kiowa said. "Whiskey." He held up a finger. "Guns." He extended the second finger. "Tobacco, horses, and women." With his five fingers representing his five favorite things, Little Bluff offered his hand for me to shake.

"I agree with horses and women." As I shook Little Bluff's hand, I caught a brief glint of remorse in his blood-shot eyes before he turned away for the long walk home.

"What was all that about?" Hatcher asked. I translated what had been said, and the old trader replied, "Hell, he traded his horses and guns for whiskey and would have traded his wife, too, about moonrise last night."

I nodded, and felt a sad foreboding sensation creep through me, spoiling the sense of hope this place in the valley gave me. But the sadness passed as I went to gather grasses.

By sundown, I had gathered nine varieties of prairie grasses. I tied each type into a bundle that resembled a small shock of wheat. I made a tenth bundle of all the grasses combined. By this time of year, the grass had begun to dry naturally, and I knew that a full day in the sun would finish drying out the shocks completely.

The next day, while the grasses dried, I hauled more clay in my saddlebags until I had enough to make ten adobes.

As I checked on my little bundles of grass, Hatcher's curiosity finally got the better of him. "What the hell?" he asked.

"I intend to make an experimental brick from each type of grass to determine which provides the best binder. The last brick will be made from a combination of all the grasses."

Hatcher grunted and turned toward the skinned carcass of a doe he had killed that morning and left hanging in a tree. "I'm gonna make meat," he said.

While Hatcher built a fire, I used the sharpshooter to dig a small hole near Bent's Creek. With the dirt from my saddlebags and the water from the creek, I mixed mud in the hole I had dug. To the first batch of mud, I added the first type of grass, chopped with my knife into appropriate lengths of straw. Meanwhile, Hatcher suspended several smoking spits over his fire with green branches held at the ends with forked sticks driven into the ground and bolstered with stones around their bases. He began draping cuts of venison over the spits about the time I got the first batch of mud and straw mixed to perfection.

I moistened my adobe mold with creek water to keep the mud from sticking to the wood, then filled the wooden mold with the mixture of mud and straw. After I had pressed the mud into the mold and packed it well, pressing out all the air pockets, I carried the mold out onto a bare spot of ground that would feel sunlight all day long. Gingerly, I turned my brick mold over and let the soft brick of mud and straw slip slowly from the mold. So perfect was the viscosity of the adobe that it retained the integrity of its original dimensions even after slipping free of the mold. I had learned my craft well from the old *adobero*, Bonifacio.

Now Hatcher had a hind quarter butchered and ready for the spit, and I went back to my pit to mix the second batch of mud. By the time I slipped the fourth brick from the mold, Hatcher appeared over my shoulder.

"You better mark each one," he suggested.

"What do you mean?"

"Each adobe has a different kind of grass in it, right?"

"Yes, sir."

"Then lay a stalk of that kind of grass on top of the brick that's got it in it. That way you'll know which brick come from which kind of grass."

"I'll remember. I've got a good memory."

"Comanches kill you tomorrow, how am I supposed to know which kind of grass you used in which brick?"

I think Mr. Hatcher meant mostly to remind me that my life forever tiptoed on the brink of peril here at this wilderness crossing, but I appreciated his logic, anyway. Also, it was a bit of a compliment to think that he would really carry out the experiment I had begun, were the Comanches to succeed in snuffing out my young life.

By the next day, Hatcher had most of his venison cured, and I went to turn the adobes, which had set up nicely. I set each brick on edge now so it could continue to bake in the sun. I had just turned the last brick when I heard Hatcher give a whistle. Jibber growled about the same time, and I quickly located five riders coming from The Crossing, their horses still dripping from the fording. A glance told me they were Mexican, for their sombreros with the high pointed crowns gave them away.

Hatcher and I met at the site of his burned cabin. "Comancheros," he said. "Like as not, I'll know a couple of 'em."

This was the first time I had heard the word, Comanchero. Because of my understanding of linguistics, and my knowledge of Spanish, I knew it meant one who traded with Comanches. I would hear the term many times in years to come. In those days, the term "Comanchero" carried no real stigma. In later years, the Comancheros were considered responsible for supplying renegade Comanches with guns and ammunition. Still later, after all the Comanches were chased onto reservations, many of the Comancheros turned to cattle rustling and other nefarious activities, and the infamy of the handle grew. But in 1845, a Comanchero was just another Indian trader from Mexico.

Sure enough, the leader of the Mexican trading party recognized John Hatcher and greeted him warmly. His name was Mauricio Anzaldua, and he hailed from San Fernandez de Taos, New Mexico, whose name made my heart throb with pain.

"Seen any Comanches, Mauricio?"

"Not a single one," the Comanchero replied in a passable English tinged with a Mexican accent. "Only some Kiowas. Mostly women at a village up the river. They didn't have much to trade, but said their men would come back with horses to swap."

"Snakehead already got their horses."

Mauricio frowned. "So he is back."

Hatcher nodded.

"You are going to build something," Mauricio said, glancing at my adobes drying in the sun.

"Si, señor," I answered. *"Un presidio para Señores Bent y St. Vrain."*

"I wish you luck," the Comanchero said, refusing to speak Spanish with me. "You are going to need it. I don't think the Comanches will let you stay in this place. You should only come and go, as we do."

"William wants to give it one last chance here," Hatcher said. "If it don't work this time, you'll have the Comanche trade all to yourself."

"Nonsense. You know you will always come back here, John Hatcher. The trade is rich and getting richer. A war is coming. Everyone will need horses, and no one has more horses than the Comanches. Fort or no fort, you are going to keep trading with the Comanches until they scalp you."

"There's worse things than scalpin'," Hatcher said. "I don't intend on sittin' still for any of it."

Mauricio laughed loudly, then turned his eyes to me. "There was talk about you after you left Taos."

"Me?" I said, surprised that the man even knew who I was.

"Yes. It was a good time for you to leave when you did. Your tracks, and the dog's, were found at the spring near the Badillo *hacienda*. Don Bernardo Badillo wanted to follow you to Bent's Fort and kill you in a duel, but Gabriela insisted that she didn't even know you, though her tracks mingled with yours."

My face must have flushed even through my sunburned flesh. "Did she marry Mariano Zavaleta?" I asked.

"The night before we left Taos. Twenty-two days ago. The wedding was the biggest I have ever seen."

Every morsel of hope and purpose I owned bled out of my pores at that very moment. I remember turning to walk rudely away from the Comancheros, and I remember Hatcher asking "What's wrong with him?"

I remember hearing Mauricio answer, "He is French."

I walked northward and passed my adobe bricks, lined up there like sleeping soldiers. I walked out into the prairie and just stood there among the nodding heads of the stalks of grass. I don't know how long I stood there. My usual facility for tracking time escaped me.

Eventually, I started to hear things. Things I can neither explain nor describe to this day. That place was trying to talk to me. I heard the ground attempt to speak to me in a voice and a language I could not understand. That place was trying to heal me, console me. There are such voices in the earth. Perhaps you must be desperate to hear them, but they exist. Though I felt my heart breaking on that day, I knew I would survive. The very ground upon which I stood would support and lift me. I had found the place I would forever call home. The place I would protect and defend. The place that would drink my blood and nourish my dreams. The place that one day would devour my flesh to sustain its own existence. The place that would make me Plenty Man.

TWENTY-THREE

The Mexicans went the way of the Kiowas, and the Crossing on the Canadian became a place of exquisite quietude. John Hatcher and I each killed a buffalo and made enough meat to last the two of us a month or more. I broke the adobes I had made to determine which grass binder had produced the toughest brick. Luckily, it turned out that the one with the combination of grasses was as resilient, or more so, than any other brick. This meant the workers, when they came, could mow prairie grasses at random, the mixed straw producing a fine binder for the mud.

I made myself busy locating trees long and straight enough to serve as roofing timbers for the living quarters inside the fort I would build. Otherwise, I scouted the area, hunted, explored, and let the solitude of The Crossing soothe my broken heart. But The Crossing was an ancient place of gatherings, and it never remained quiet for very long. If you will allow it, I will tell you what happened the day the Comanches came.

I walked out of camp with my rifle that morning to explore a ravine down the river. I left Fireball and Jibber behind in hopes of sneaking within range of a deer. As I crossed the open prairie between Bent's Creek and Adobe Creek, which I had named, and listened to my moccasins shush through the grasses, the first glint of sunrise stained the treetops above my head with an ocher hue. A mere breath of wind carried the songs of mourning doves and the distant chatter of a kingfisher at the river. Then I heard and felt a rumble like that of thunder, and saw a swarm of riders, seven strong, streaming from the timber of Adobe Creek ahead of me. I turned back once, but knew I would be overtaken if I tried to run to camp on foot.

Jibber had watched me leave, and now began barking from camp. I had barely enough time to yell before the Indians were upon me, and I yelled the only thing that came to mind in my moment of terror: "Mr. Hatcher!"

I cocked my rifle and my pistol. I held the pistol in my left hand and rested the barrel of the rifle across my left forearm, giving me two angles of fire. If they shot and wounded me, I figured I could fire the rifle ball and save the pistol round to the bloody end. Yes, I would fire the rifle first so I could then drop it and draw my saber with my right hand. I would make them kill me quickly. The old voyagers had hammered home the atrocities of torture.

Nothing exists in the whole world of horrors more terrifying than a mounted band of attacking Comanches. They lack the decorum to advance politely like a drilled battalion of soldiers. Each moves like the nightmarish progeny of an impossible mating between horse and man—a beast with four legs, two heads, two arms. Together, they close with pack-hunter harmony. The dust and thunder and yelping havoc they spawn in their descent on their prey can cause virtual paralysis in the most courageous of men.

I thought about Jed Smith. This was how he had died. Surrounded by Comanches and shot.

They seemed to bring their own wind with them, for it tossed my hair in my face as they closed tight around me. I tried my best to blink away the dust and scowl at them in defiance. I kept my guns moving so they would not see me tremble. Perhaps justice would catch up to me after all. I would die here for my crimes in Paris. I would die lonely and brokenhearted. I was ready, almost eager for the execution of my sentence.

Having surrounded me, one warrior lowered the honed metal tip of his lance so it would point at me, and I recognized him.

"Matalgo." I called Kills Something's name in Spanish. "I have brought your weapons back to you."

"Bueno," he said. "I will let the old women torture you with my arrows you have defiled."

"I have come here with Freckled Hand. We come to trade."

"You come to die."

He urged his pony forward, encroaching on me with the razor edge of his lance, held underhanded. I covered him with the rifle muzzle, and came damn close to pulling the trigger. A yell from Hatcher saved Kills Something. Perhaps it saved us all. With unaccountable valor, Freckled Hand charged into the middle of the Comanche surround on his horse to join me. He turned his mount, taking up a back-to-back defensive with me. I was the frog in the snake's mouth, and I had yelled for help.

The Comanches seemed to have been unprepared for this act of bravery, and had let Hatcher, whom they knew well, into their circle to join me. Hatcher said something to them in their tongue, and a brief conversation flew between Kills Something, Hatcher, and a couple of the other warriors.

Kills Something addressed me now in Spanish. "You have come to pay for taking my weapons. What will you pay?"

"Much tobacco and gunpowder," I said, remembering what Little Bluff had ranked among the good things in the world. "A good pony, a blanket, a limb for making a bow, and one other thing."

With a haughty glare aimed over my forehead, Kills Something glowered down from his pony. "What thing?"

"I am going to let you shoot me one time." I held up my pistol. "With this gun."

For a long moment, Kills Something and the rest of the Comanches stared.

"What the hell did you say now?" Hatcher asked over his shoulder. He spoke Comanche and English, but had somehow avoided learning much Spanish, except for the cuss words.

"I told him I would let him shoot me for taking his weapons."

"I reckon he already thought that up on his own."

"I know what I'm doing, Mr. Hatcher."

"If you knew what you was doin', you wouldn't be surrounded by Comanches."

About this time, Kills Something waved his lance in the air to silence our conversation. "The gun is no good," he said to me in Spanish. "It is a trick."

"I'll prove that it is good," I said. Quickly, I threw my hat on the ground in front of me and aimed the pistol at it. Before anyone could complain, I pulled the trigger, blasting a bullet hole in the crown, and peppering the felt with powder. Ponies lurched, but the riders had complete control of their mounts. The shot, still echoing now through the canyon, seemed to sap some of the fight out of the Comanches.

I cradled my cocked rifle in the crook of my elbow as I reached for my powder flask. "I will load it now, so you can shoot me. You agree that this is payment for taking your weapons."

Kills Something seemed confused and wary of me now. His uncertainty mounted, but he watched closely as I loaded the pistol. I worked methodically, pouring the powder so that the Comanches could clearly see it entering the muzzle. Next, I produced a pistol ball from my pouch. I tossed this bullet to Kills Something, and he caught it.

"Mark it with your knife," I suggested.

Kills Something narrowed his eyes, but drew his knife and marked a cross on the lead ball, then tossed the bullet back to me. I caught it, and made sure it remained in full view of the Comanches so they would suspect nothing. Now I made a grand production of dropping the lead ball down the pistol barrel. Drawing my ramrod from the brass loops under the pistol barrel, I tapped the ball tightly against the powder in the barrel—or seemed to.

I had practiced this illusion dozens of times since reading it in my magician's book of tricks. But I had never actually performed the trick before, and now my life depended on it. It was with indescribable relief that I withdrew the ramrod from the barrel and felt the pistol ball pressed into the hollow of my palm as I secured a bit of buckskin from my pouch to use as wadding to secure the bullet the Indians thought was still in the gun. If that ramrod had failed to extract the bullet, I think I would have died of fright before Kills Something could have shot me.

Using the opposite end of the ramrod, I shoved the wadding down the barrel, completing the false charge. I found a percussion cap in my pouch, fixed it under the hammer, and held the pistol out, butt-first, to Kills Something. The same hand that offered the pistol palmed the marked bullet.

Kills Something was no fool. His suspicion showed in his eyes, yet he knew this was a challenge he could not refuse. I can still imagine the confrontation from his perspective. *I can kill this white boy now with my lance,* he is thinking, *yet when I do, Freckled Hand will kill one of my friends before the rest of us can slay him. They will say my power has gone bad if one of my friends dies, even though we will have taken two white scalps. Anyway, the season to trade has come, and we need metal and powder from Freckled Hand. I will play this game with this white boy's pistol. I will see what kind of medicine he makes.*

Then Kills Something spoke in Comanche, and the Indians lowered their weapons. They broke the circle surrounding us and lined up on either side of Kills Something. Kills Something came forward on his mount, took the pistol from my hand, and backed his horse into the line of Indians once more.

Hatcher moved his horse aside and lowered his rifle. "Kid," he said, "I can't help you now. You done talked yourself into a bind."

Looking down the muzzle of a gun—even one you have loaded yourself with a blank charge—makes you feel less than delighted. Kills Something stood only half a dozen paces away. I could see his eyes line up behind the irons. He was aiming at my face. Would the powder blast blind me from this distance? What if Kills Something was a magician, too? Had I watched closely enough? Had he dropped something down the barrel? The book had warned against this.

Suddenly Kills Something changed his mind about where he would shoot me. He lowered his line of fire to my chest. The powder flash and the sound of the blast staggered me, merely out of abject dread, and left me engulfed in white smoke. As the cloud cleared, I gathered the presence of mind to clutch my breast as if I had been shot, and indeed I thought I had for a moment, for my heart was pounding pangs of agony through my chest. But I knew I had survived, unblinded, when I saw the looks of astonishment on the faces of the Indians.

Now for the finale. I opened my fist to reveal the marked bullet cradled in my palm. I took a few halting steps toward Kill Something, and glanced at Hatcher long enough to witness a rare expression of disbelief on his bearded and weathered visage. Kills Something leaned forward far enough to see the cross marked on the bullet. I could feel the uneasiness course through the whole party of Indians. Sensing and assuming the fear of their riders, their mounts began to toss their heads and stamp their hooves. I offered the bullet to Kills Something for his closer investigation. He took it, looked at it, then threw it down on the ground. His pony wheeled and made a marvelous leap, and he led a thundering retreat of the whole Comanche band.

"You got 'em spooked," Hatcher said. "Don't know as I like a spooky Comanche all that much."

"I didn't mean to scare them. I only wanted to impress them."

"You did that, alright. I hope that wasn't your best trick, though, 'cause they're likely to expect more."

"That was my best trick," I admitted.

"Humph," he grunted. "How the hell did you do that, anyway?"

"I have medicine," I claimed.

Hatcher laughed—a rare expression. "Kid, all you got is gall. Maybe that's enough. Maybe it ain't."

Later that day, Kills Something returned to our camp alone.
I would one day understand, from the Comanche point of
view, how much faith in his own spirit powers this action
represented. He had to show me that he did not fear my
bulletproof medicine. Yet this time he came with a new
respect for me.

I first saw him standing on the high roll in the grassy
prairie. I don't know how long he had been watching me,
for I was busy making preparations for the building of my
fort. I was making a sled from the raw hides of the two
buffalo Hatcher and I had killed. I would use the sled for
transporting soil from the clay diggings to the brick-making
site. The diggings were located on Adobe Creek, but I had
decided to establish the brick yards on Bent's Creek. I reasoned that loose clay would be easier to transport than finished adobe bricks.

I had staked one buffalo hide in the sun to dry. Before it
stiffened completely into what Hatcher called a "flint hide,"
I pulled the stakes up and used them to prop up the perimeter of the hide so it would finish drying with its edges
curled up, and therefore hold a load of clay more efficiently.

I had laboriously cut the second buffalo hide into a single
strip, three fingers wide, by starting at the edge and spiraling
inward. This produced a strap almost fifty yards long. I tied
one end of this to a tree. I tied the other end to a green
limb, which I used to twist the strap into a cord. I made just
over a thousand twists with this handle. After the twisted
hide had dried for one day, I doubled it and began twisting
it again to produce a length of rawhide cordage that was
crude, yet strong as a steel cable. I was in the process of
this second twisting when I happened to look up to see Kills
Something on the high roll in the open prairie. Jibber was
sleeping in the shade, and Hatcher had gone on a scouting
expedition upstream.

Fixing my twisting lever in the fork of a tree, I raised my

hand to the Comanche. He returned the gesture. I waved him into camp, and he came at a walk on his horse—a fine paint, small but well muscled and sleek. Arriving downwind at the edge of camp, he dismounted, dropping the rawhide reins that looped tightly around the lower jaw of his pony. He left his shield attached to a pad saddle made of bearskin with the fur still on. He carried neither lance nor firearm. He wore a new quiver full of arrows on his back, with an attached bow case. The unstrung bow was in the case. He wore a knife in a beaded buckskin scabbard, but it had a loop over the hilt.

"I have come for the things you promised," he said in Spanish.

I nodded. "Your weapons are tied to my saddle."

"Burn them after I am gone. I do not want them anymore. I have new weapons. I want the tobacco, the gunpowder, the pony, the blanket, and the hickory limb."

"You have a new bow already. What will you do with the hickory?"

"Trade it for ponies."

I nodded, then went to my saddle, and took one twist of tobacco from my saddlebags.

"You said much tobacco," Kills Something reminded me.

I took a second, then my third and last twist from the saddle pocket. Luckily, this satisfied Kills Something, for it was all I had brought with me from Bent's Fort. "You must wait until William Bent arrives with the trade wagons for the blanket, the powder, the hickory limb, and the pony. I do not expect you to take this pony." I motioned toward Fireball. "He has only one good eye."

To my surprise, I saw Kills Something smile slightly. "I would not feed that pony to a dog."

I returned the smile as I handed the tobacco to Kills Something.

"Are you American?" he asked.

"No."

"*Tejano?*" His eyes narrowed.

"No."

"You are with the Mexicans."

"No. I am not with anyone."

"You are French?"

"I was once, but no longer. I am a nation alone. I had to leave the old country across the ocean."

"Across the Big Water?"

"Yes."

"I have heard stories about it. How big is it?" Kills Something swept the grass aside with his foot and sat on the stalks he had flattened with a graceful, almost balletic motion.

I, too, sat on the grass, some six feet from the Comanche. "I rode a boat that moved day and night as fast as a horse can trot. The crossing took seventy-seven days."

Kills Something stared westward for a moment or two, trying to gather the extent of my claim. "There is not that much water anywhere."

"I have seen it. I have crossed it. I traveled two moons without seeing land."

"You circled in the middle. The land was hidden by mist."

I shook my head. "We followed the sun and the stars, going south and west all the while."

He sat silently for a while, and seemed to be listening to the wind. With this Comanche, I did not feel awkward sitting in silence, and he apparently felt in no rush to talk. Finally he asked, "What is your name? What kind of medicine do you possess?"

"I have no name. I came here to find my medicine, and my name."

He nodded, as if this made good sense to him. "How did you know to come here?"

"I dreamed of it, long ago, over the Big Water."

"It is a powerful place. If your heart is good, you will find strong medicine here. If not, you will die poorly and suffer forever in the Shadow Land."

I thought about the hallucinations I sometimes had before I fell asleep—the horrible dreams that played before my open eyes against the backdrop of reality when I could neither move nor cry out. "I believe I have seen this Shadow

Land and its beasts in visions. I do not want to suffer there."

Kills Something nodded. "When William Bent comes, will he bring the red cloth, the beads, and the presents for the women?"

"Yes," I answered, hoping I was right.

"Good." He rose. "When the wagons get here, I will come back for the things you owe me. Then we will trade for more things. I have plenty of horses and mules from Mexico. You will see."

"Good," I said, rising to my feet.

"When you get ready to find your medicine, tell me. I will show you the good place to seek your vision."

With that parting, Kills Something turned and walked toward his pony. He mounted and rode away at a leisurely walk without so much as another glance over his shoulder. Yet, somehow, I knew I had passed the first obstacle standing between me and my career as an Indian trader.

TWENTY-FOUR

The report cracked through the October air like a small-bore pistol shot. I paused with my hands on the shovel, my breath the only thing I could hear for a moment. Then the sound came again, a sharp snap up the ravine to the north. Standing in the makeshift sled harness, Fireball lifted his head and craned his neck to look northward with his good eye. Then came the words muffled by two miles of prairie air: "Goddamn, haw! I said get over, goddamn! Haw!"

I knew the crack had been a whip; the voice that of Lucas "Goddamn" Murray; the object of his scorn a team of recalcitrant mules. My heartbeat quickened with joyous expectation. Finally, the wagons had arrived. Had the adobe makers come, as William had promised? Would my fort begin to take shape?

Fireball began to paw the ground. He let loose a long singing call to the mules he had seen or heard or smelled. I admit that I was anxious to see my friends. Perhaps that anxiety led to the haste which brought about the calamity. Mainly, I was just ignorant. Ignorance afflicts even the most intelligent and educated minds. The world offers so much to learn—how could one mind possibly learn it all? I thought I knew horses by this time—particularly my own. I know now that a soul can live among horses his whole life and not know them through and through.

Hatcher had warned me about the sled. "Careful," he had said that morning. "That saddle pony may not take to draggin' somethin' like that behind him." With that bit of advice, he had taken his axe into the creek bottom to harvest timbers suitable for roofing the fort.

While Hatcher chopped, I had worked with Fireball for two hours, letting him gradually become accustomed to the sled. He did not like it at all at first. The sled raised quite a hellish din hissing over the grass, the stiff rawhide rumbling almost like thunder as it dragged over the occasional rock or tree limb. At first I just dragged it past and around Fireball, as he stood tied to a stake I had driven in the ground. To him, it must have looked like the shadow of everything evil on the earth moving across the ground, for he rattled his nostrils and tugged at the end of his stake rope. I dragged the sled around him for a good hour, until he had accepted that it would not harm him. Then I tied the thing onto him.

"Put a slipknot on it," Hatcher had warned, having returned to camp, ostensibly to file a keener edge on his axe. "He's liable to bolt."

Hatcher was right. The first time Fireball caught a glimpse of that sled moving behind him, he took off like a racehorse from the starting line, and I barely had time to release the sled with the slipknot Hatcher had advised. After about an hour of this, however, Fireball accepted that the sled would not overtake and devour him, and he even allowed me to ride on the sled behind him with a pair of long reins directing him. In this way, I had driven him to the deposits on Adobe Creek, where I had spent just over three hours shoveling clay onto the sled. One thousand and eighty-five shovels full, by my unerring count. Two tons of clay, plus or minus one hundred pounds or so.

Now the trade wagons had arrived from Bent's Fort, and Murray's blasphemies were echoing across the prairie. I could not wait to drive Fireball back to Bent's Creek with my load of clay and show my friends all that Hatcher and I had accomplished toward preparing the site for the fort.

I jumped aboard the loaded sled, standing just in front of the pile of dirt. I picked up the long reins and shook them, clucking my tongue at Fireball. Obediently, he stepped into the makeshift harness I had fixed about his neck and shoulders. The twisted rawhide ropes strained and stretched, and I lashed Fireball's rump impatiently with the end of a rein. Once the sled began to move, it sprang forward on the natural elasticity of the rawhide lines.

The fact did not dawn on me that it would feel appreciably different to my beast of burden, even though it now carried two tons of clay. I was satisfied that I had adequately broken my horse to the sled, yet I myself could hear that the conveyance sounded different, creating a fiercer growl as it scraped hard over the virgin prairie. Already excited by the arrival of the wagons, Fireball must have thought the sled an entirely new monster, for he leaped forward in an attempt to escape, but of course only succeeded in making the sled pursue him with still more noise.

At the first unexpected leap, the sled jerked forward under me, and I fell backward. In his sudden attempt to flee, Fireball kicked and stepped over the right rein with his right hind leg. Feeling the rein inside his thigh on his blind side, he must have imagined the monster groping with a deadly tentacle. Poor Fireball the Half-Blind blew up like a powder keg and took off in headlong flight toward the only chance he thought he had for salvation—the wagon train.

In an instant, I felt the ground speeding under me through
the rawhide sled as I attempted to gather reins and check
my horse. I remember saying, "Whoa! whoa!" in a ridiculous attempt to reason with my panic-stricken horse. The
buffalo hide found a ridge in the prairie, threw me in the
air, and tossed ten shovels of clay onto the breeze. This
horrid cloud only made Fireball run faster, and bounced me
around on the sled like a buffalo chip. I felt one of the reins
tangle around my leg and suddenly had visions of getting
dragged to death. I pulled at the rein on Fireball's blind side,
hoping to turn his good eye away from the sled, but I had
no leverage, no purchase. I was bouncing around in a great
pile of dirt I had labored three hours to create as the prairie
hissed and roared under me.

Another rough spot in the prairie tossed me clean off of
the sled. I felt the ground battering me and knew I had to
turn loose. I released the rein and slid to a stop as I felt the
leather scorch a rope burn across my neck and ear that I can
still feel to this day when I think about it. I looked up to
see my horse, the bouncing sled, and the cloud of clay hurtling toward three mule-drawn wagons.

The mules went berserk. Goddamn Murray's sobriquet
echoed incessantly through the canyon. One wagon team
plunged into Adobe Creek, snapping an axle and throwing
half the mules down, which at least stopped the team. Another team charged into the timber of Bent's Creek, the two
lead mules taking opposite sides of a sapling as big as a
man's leg and snapping it off like a twig, about the same
time that it shattered the wagon tongue.

By this time, Hatcher was mounted and closing on Fireball, who was running with the third crazed mule team, being driven by Murray. Hatcher managed to close on
Fireball's blind side, wrap a long rein around his saddle
horn, and bring my exhausted gelding to a standstill. Murray
succeeded in circling the mules on the prairie until they ran
out of steam, but not before half the trade goods had
bounced out of the wagon.

I stood and watched all this with helpless fascination and

humiliating mortification. Now I ran to the wagon in Adobe Creek, and found William Bent along with Bonifacio Ramirez and some of his Mexican adobe workers cutting harness loose to free the downed mules.

"Is everybody alright?" I asked.

William scowled and pierced me with a glare. "Shit, no we ain't alright. We're madder than hell!"

"I'm going to look after the other wagon!" I said. I sprinted to Bent's Creek, passing Goddamn Murray as he cussed me soundly with every allusion in the unwritten book of profanities. I arrived winded, and found Ceran St. Vrain and Blue Wiggins, along with three laborers untangling their mule team.

"Orn'ry, I don't know whether to shoot you or your damn horse or both!" Blue said.

About this time, Fireball, having been freed from the harness by Hatcher, came trotting up to me as if nothing much had happened.

Hatcher rode up to Blue's wagon, saw that men and beasts had all survived, and began laughing. He laughed so hard that he had to get off of his horse and lay on the ground. I really think Hatcher needed that laugh. He remained in a swell mood for days afterward.

By some miracle of chance, neither mule nor horse nor man had been seriously maimed. My own rope burn was perhaps the most painful of our injuries, and it served me right, for Hatcher had tried to warn me about the sled. I should have left the slipknot tied on the harness so that I could have released Fireball.

Lucas "Goddamn" Murray perhaps summed the whole affair up best. "Goddamn!" he shouted. "Goddamn you, goddamn it!"

Anyway, by that night we were all laughing about it, and the next day the nine adobe makers from Charles's brickyard in Taos began hauling clay, mixing mud with straw, and forming adobes. My fort was about to rise from the very earth, grass, and timber of The Crossing on the Canadian.

TWENTY-FIVE

A change came over me at The Crossing. I began to grow. I got taller, seemingly by the day. My clothes became snug as I built muscle and bulk. Coarse whiskers took root about my mouth and jaw. I ate ravenously—mostly meat of the buffalo, the deer, and the antelope, but also buffalo bone marrow, brains, wild turkey, sourdough biscuits, canned peaches, wild plums, and the so-called pear-apples from the prickly-pear cactus.

And sleep. I had never known sleep so sound. After working from sunup to sundown with the adobes and the timbers, a belly full of hot food would make me virtually drowsy. I could sometimes enjoy as many as five hours of sleep a night—except, of course, during the full moon, when I didn't sleep at all.

On October 21, after two weeks of adobe making, I personally placed the first sunbaked brick at the southwest corner of the fort. From that moment, the edifice took shape with remarkable rapidity, for the nine adobe workers were skilled masons. Though none could read nor write, each could lay a wall string-straight simply by eyeballing it.

We made the walls three feet thick at the bottom, tapering to 18 inches at the top, reaching 12 feet in height. We made only one entrance gate, facing the open prairie to the east. Inside the hollow square, 60 by 60 feet, we built the adobe walls of eight rooms along the north and west walls. Since William intended the fort mainly for winter use, he decided to place the rooms along the north and west walls, where they would absorb the most sunlight and benefit from the stored warmth even into the night.

To roof these eight rooms, we started with oak and hackberry rafters, pitched ever so slightly to drain toward holes in the main fort walls where the water could drain out. These would also double as loopholes for firing out at attackers. At right angles across the timber rafters, we placed stout green limbs which we lashed into place with rawhide. Over these, we layered brush, then an ample thickness of prairie grass. On top of the grass, we dumped tons and tons of dirt.

The fort was large enough to house twoscore men. Two hundred horses could be driven inside and protected in case of attack, though we planned to keep the stock in a corral outside most of the time. We dug a well in the southeast corner, striking sweet water at a depth of only eight feet. At the southeast and northwest corners, we built platforms that extended beyond the adobe walls and would allow defenders to enfilade all four walls of the fort. Bulwarks of straight timbers, lashed vertically together with rawhide would protect the guards stationed here from arrows or bullets. We referred to these simple wooden platforms as "watchtowers."

We could stand on the roof of the living quarters inside the north and west walls, and defend those two walls of the fort. The perimeter walls extended chest-high to me over the dirt roofs, and made a fine set of breastworks. Around the inside of the south and east walls, we built a wooden walkway on poles, accessible by ladders. The walkway would allow us to defend the east and south walls of the fort, and connected with the southeast watchtower. It was wide enough to allow two men to pass.

William had hauled a small brass cannon from Bent's Fort, and this we placed just outside the gate, where it could be fired or hastily brought inside.

"It's shapin' up to make a right fine fort," William said, the day we hung the thick timber gates on huge iron hinges set six feet deep into the adobe walls. "What'll we call it?"

"I wanted to call it 'Fort Hatcher,' but Mr. Hatcher won't have it," I said.

"No, John don't lend his name out easy. Can't name it for you—you're just a kid. Anyway, we're not sure what your real name is, are we? 'Fort Greenwood' don't have much of a ring to it."

I was honored that William would even think of naming the fort for me. "Why don't we just call it 'Fort Adobe'?" I suggested.

William nodded. "Good enough. No need to hang a man's name on it. Hell, it might curse the poor bastard it's named for."

"Goddamn, look at the ducks!" Murray shouted, coming around the corner of the fort. He paced a V-shaped flock with an imaginary shotgun. "I'll bet you your ass there's a blue norther comin'. Better chop wood, boys."

As Murray predicted, a great blue cloud loomed that afternoon, and swept down on the new fort with rain, sleet, and temperatures that plummeted forty degrees in a single hour. The dirt roof of our quarters leaked some, but William assured me that this was to be expected, since the dirt hadn't yet settled. We simply gathered the leaks in homemade rawhide buckets, which we dumped outside as they filled. This storm washed away some of the fresh mud and straw the workers had plastered on the adobe bricks that day; but when the sky cleared the next day, we quickly repaired the damages and continued applying the mud. The cool, dry air behind the norther helped set the plaster quickly.

I helped apply much of the plaster myself, scooping up the mud and straw mixture with my bare hand, and smoothing it onto the walls. Once we had gone all the way around the fort at ground level, we built ladders of green limbs notched and lashed together with rawhide so we could plaster the upper reaches of the wall. The plaster stuck better if the adobes were moistened, so I had to lug a bucket of water and a bucket of mud up and down my ladder all day long in my apprenticeship as a mud plasterer.

Working with these men—shoveling dirt with Blue Wiggins, felling trees with John Hatcher, laying adobes with Bonifacio Martinez, building ladders with Ceran St. Vrain—this combined effort of a dozen men plus two—gave me a peculiar feeling I had never before experienced. For the first

time, I was part of the creation of something. I played an
integral role in a plan I saw coming to fruition before my
eyes. I could rush to help a man raise a timber to the top
of an adobe wall, and feel waves of unexplainable things
course through me as we muscled the beam into place as
neither of us could have alone. At the time, I thought it was
a feeling of gratitude for this work and these friends, or
pride in job done well. I know now that what I learned to
feel at Fort Adobe, for the first time, was pure love of life.
I had purpose. I was living in a glorious time of freedom
and opportunity. I lived with men who made their own rules
and lived by their own code, harsh but fair. I was one of
them. I belonged. I could not have chosen a better fate. Only
my love for Gabriela could have tempted me away from this
place and this purpose. In this, I began to sense an intelligence behind the vast fabric of destiny. I could not have
possessed both the girl and the life I loved, so my fate had
chosen one for me. Yes, my heart ached. But in some unexplainable, ironic way, that pain was part of my joy.

We worked hard into the winter. On February 22, 1846,
Jibber and I walked out to the high grassy roll in the prairie,
about a half mile north of the fort. I stood facing the icy
north wind for a moment to prepare myself for what I was
about to see. I turned up the red collar of my blanket coat,
then faced around to look at the trading post. The construction of Fort Adobe now completed, I beheld the *presidio* for
the first time from this advantageous elevation.

Tapering slightly inward as they rose, the fort's walls
glowed golden in the sunlight like new buckskin. The
wooden gate stood open on the left wall, the cannon muzzle
on guard like the head of a coiled snake. The earthen ram-
parts rose almost as high as the stark, leafless branches of
the trees beyond. The wooden watchtowers perched on two
opposing corners gave a jaunty air to the otherwise imposing
bulwarks.

The sight made my chest swell with pride, and my eyes blur with the mist of endeavors well done. It was a veritable castle. Perhaps smaller than Bent's Fort, but a castle nonetheless. I remembered what Kills Something had said. If my heart was good, my medicine would be strong. This I must remember. I had not come here with my castle walls to conquer, I had come to trade. I was a free merchant. My mentor was William Bent, who held peace among the nations with skill matched by few men in history. My fort had risen from the prairie. Then, as now, I considered that fort mine more than anyone else's. Whether it should succeed or fail depended on me. I knew this even if no one else did.

Goddamn Murray had brought my violin with him from Bent's Fort, but I had refused to play it these four months, until the construction of the fort was finished. Now it was time to play, for the fort had come to be, and George Washington's birthday had provided the Americans with an excuse to feast and celebrate. I didn't exactly consider myself an American in those days, but I saw no harm in celebrating Washington's birthday with the men from the states.

Blue Wiggins, John Hatcher, and Goddamn Murray had gone hunting and had killed a great number of turkeys and ducks, four deer, two buffalo, and an antelope. This was more fresh meat than we could consume; but now that the fort was finished, we would have plenty of time to make meat. For now, the meat hung on poles inside the fort walls, perfectly preserved by temperatures that had scarcely risen above freezing in three days.

I saw a great column of smoke rising from the fort, and knew the men had struck a spark to the bonfire inside the walls. I smiled. I was going to play plenty of music today. Though I had refused to touch my bow to my strings, I had sat up many hours while others slept, going through entire symphonies with my right hand to toughen my fingers. I knew I could play all day and night if I had to. One of the Mexicans had brought a guitar, and John Hatcher claimed to have been one of the best spoon players in Kentucky in his youth. All the men were eager to celebrate the completion of Fort Adobe.

Just as I prepared to stroll back to the fort to start the celebration, I heard Jibber growl, and saw him thrust his nose into the wind. Turning on my heel, I looked north and saw a long, thin column of riders twining into the valley from the north.

Already rapt by the sight of my fort to the south, I now stood transfixed by this image of an Indian village on the move. There were horses of many colors, some encumbered by travoises loaded with all manner of cargo. An equal number of horses carried warriors equipped with lances and bows. Then, on the very canyon rim, behind the main body of the band, I saw a gathering of loose horses appear. They stretched fully a mile as they came to the edge to peer down into the canyon. By ones and twos, these loose ponies began to test the footing that would take them into the windbreaks of the valley, with its protected ravines and timbered creek beds. They poured into the Canadian Breaks like a living cascade of horseflesh.

My heart began to beat furiously. I watched the warriors swarm protectively around the women and children in the serpentine file that held to the trail. These riders dashed everywhere—up, down, and across impossible grades, over boulders, under branches. The herd of loose stock continued to pour down into the sheltered valley, two hundred, three hundred, four hundred strong and more. The clatter of hooves, the snorts of stallions, and the whinnies of colts swelled beyond the farthest canyon rim and echoed back in a hellish gnash of noises.

I heard a whistle behind me, turned toward the fort, and saw men lining the bulwarks. One, whom I recognized as John Hatcher, waved for my return. With Jibber at my heels, I trotted toward Fort Adobe. Reaching the base of the wall while the Indians were still a mile away, I looked up at Hatcher, who had his elbows propped on the rampart to steady the brass telescope through which he peered.

"Who are they, Mr. Hatcher?" I asked.

"Kotsoteka Comanches. Shaved Head's band."

"Is that good?"

He lowered the telescope and looked down at me. "It's payday, Mr. Greenwood."

I ran into the fort through the open gates, and climbed the ladder that led to the wooden walkway running around the inside perimeter, allowing defense of every face and corner of the presidio. Standing between William Bent and Blue Wiggins, I watched the descent of the Indians into the valley. In clusters, they spread out in the prairie, some taking their travoises to the banks of Adobe Creek, others riding around the grassy hump to the timber of Bent's Creek.

Arriving at their chosen campsites, the women leapt from their mounts and began untying the long poles of the travoises. These long, slender pine branches became lodge poles for the tepees. I asked for the telescope, and trained it on one lodge. Two women working together lashed the slender ends of four lodge poles together and raised them to form a four-legged frame. After spacing the four legs properly, they began to lay other poles at regular intervals against the first four, until twenty poles described the shape of a circle on the ground, and a cone that rose high above the grass. The cone leaned a bit to the west, and I thought this was an oversight at first, until I saw the surrounding lodges set slightly off center in the same way.

Once the frame of poles had been erected, one woman staked it fast to the ground by a line that dangled from the top of the four original poles. Now, as I watched through the telescope, the women began unfolding, and dragging into place a lodge cover made of well-tanned buffalo hide, painted with shapes and crude but strikingly beautiful images. They fixed the base of the cover around the lower reaches of the poles first, fixing it in the east with pegs as a mother would button the front of her child's coat. Now, to my surprise and delight, one woman stood on another's shoulder inside the cone of lodge poles to fix the upper part of the tepee cover in place. A third, then a fourth woman appeared from a neighboring lodge to help. With the cover tied in place on the frame, two final poles were jammed into pockets of the bannerlike wind flaps, and the women went on to the next lodge to help their neighbors, in turn, set up house.

By the time the last travois had entered the prairie, the leading families had already erected several lodges, as the process averaged about eighteen minutes by my calculations. The Indian camp began to take shape in this way, as a band of twenty-two armed warriors rode boldly up to the gate of the fort.

William Bent and John Hatcher had prepared well upon first sighting of the Indians. This was a friendly band, as Hatcher had suggested, but a strong defensive posture had to be maintained.

"For all we know, a bunch of Texan cutthroats might have attacked them yesterday," Bent had said. "Keep your guard up, boys, until we're sure they ain't mad at us palefaces in general."

Now, scrambling down from the ladder, Bent shouted at two Mexicans guarding the gate: "Pull the cannon in, boys. Leave the gates open, but keep 'em ready to close."

Bent, St. Vrain, and Hatcher walked outside to greet the Comanches, and I went with them. Bent scowled at me, but did not order me back inside. The riders thundered up to the gate and drew up abreast in a broad line facing the three of us. We were vulnerable to attack, but we knew the guns of our friends stood ready behind the high parapets of the fort. My eyes swept the line of riders, and I recognized Kills Something three ponies away from the obvious chief of the band, Shaved Head.

Recognizable by his name alone, Shaved Head was the only warrior there with one side of his head completely shaved, though the other side grew long locks in the typical Comanche fashion. Hatcher had told me that some of the Comanches even wove horsehair or human hair into their own head of hair to increase its length. Shaved Head seemed to have done this on the unshaven side of his head, for the locks reached his waist, streaming over his shoulder and down his back.

Hatcher exchanged a few words with Shaved Head in Comanche, then translated: "They come to see the big lodge. Says they got plenty horses to trade."

William nodded. "Tell them they can enter six at a time, and we will give them meat and presents to take to their women. Tell them we'll have a feast tonight, then commence tradin' tomorrow."

Hatcher made the translation, Shaved Head nodded, and the Comanches all dismounted. The six warriors in the middle, Kills Something included, handed their reins to their compatriots, and followed the four of us white men into Fort Adobe. Hatcher gestured here and there as he spoke in the halting, guttural tongue of the Comanches. Kills Something angled toward me, looking with disfavor at the bonfire in the middle of the fort.

"Why do white men make a fire so large and hot that they cannot get near it?" he asked me in Spanish.

My mind raced for an answer, then found it. "Because they have never taken the time to watch a tree grow."

He nodded and seemed to appreciate my response. "Come to my lodge, and I will show you a proper fire. You can bring the pony, the blanket, the hickory limb, and the powder you owe me." The young warrior said something to Shaved Head, and the chief looked at me suddenly, hawklike.

"You gonna let 'em take another shot at you?" Hatcher said.

"Not if I can help it."

Shaved Head approached me cautiously. He made gestures and said something in Comanche.

"Wants you to open your shirt up, so he can see where the young buck shot you," Hatcher said.

I pulled open my coat, unbuttoned my shirt, and bared my chest to the cold wind. Shaved Head looked closely, then spoke curiously to Kills Something. The younger Comanche pointed to the spot over my heart where he had aimed. Shaved Head muttered his disbelief, but another young warrior who had been there that day came to Kill Something's defense. Shaved Head backed away, looking me over from hat to moccasins. Finally, he grunted as if impressed, and went on with his tour of the fort.

All day, the Comanches came into the fort, six by six. The men came first, then the women who had finished their housekeeping chores. Some of the warriors came back for a second look with their wives, and maybe an older child or two. All the men were given tobacco; but when one warrior returned later with his wife, he refused a second gift of tobacco, even though it was offered. The women received beads or ribbons and as much meat as they wanted to carve from the carcasses hung in the fort.

In return, some of the women brought gifts of pemmican, stuffed sausagelike into cleaned buffalo guts. I tried some, and asked Kills Something, who had returned with a friend named Mexican Horse, how the pemmican was made.

"By women," he replied.

"Yes, but how?"

"Meat dried and pounded." He smacked his fist against his palm. "Mix with berries, plums, and much tallow from the buffalo. Maybe some pine nuts, walnuts, or pecans. Stuffed in a gut." Here, he jammed his fist through a circle made by the fingers of his other hand.

I hadn't seen a pine tree since crossing the Raton Mountains with Lieutenant Abert. I hadn't seen a pecan tree since St. Louis. "With whom do you trade for the nuts?" I asked.

He looked at me curiously. "Trade for nuts?" he repeated, as if in ridicule. "If our women want walnuts or pecans, we move the village south and get them. If we want pine nuts, we ride west."

"How far?"

"I have enough ponies to ride until next winter."

"How many ponies do you own?"

"I have only four times ten," he replied. "Some Pawnees stole many of my ponies, but soon I will get more."

"How many ponies does Shaved Head own?"

"Our chief owns three times one hundred."

If Kills Something was an average warrior, which I suspected he was, and he owned forty ponies, and Shaved Head's band included some fifty warriors, as Hatcher had estimated, I calculated that the band should include some two thousand horses. "Where are all these ponies?" I asked. "I counted only five hundred in the valley."

"We bring these ponies to the valley to trade. We keep our finest horses above, on the plains. The young warriors guard them all day."

"Do you guard the ponies?"

Kills Something seemed insulted. "I am like you. I have taken scalps and counted coup. I no longer guard ponies, I take them from our enemies."

Just then, Blue Wiggins shouted down from the southeast watchtower: "Mr. Bent! There's more Indians comin'!"

John Hatcher left his post at the door of one of the adobe rooms, where he had been handing out trinkets to Comanche women. "Kid, get the Indians out of here," he shouted to me as he took up his long rifle and headed for the ladder that led to the walkway.

I motioned toward the gates to Kills Something and Mexican Horse. "Let's go see who's arriving," I said. I led them outside and, glancing over my shoulder, saw that the other two warriors in the fort were following, their wives in tow. I passed William at his place in the gateway where he had been greeting the Comanches and making sure no more than six of them at a time entered Fort Adobe.

"Keep them outside, Mr. Greenwood," he ordered.

"Yes, sir."

Hatcher was looking though his telescope from the walkway. "Looks like Little Bluff's Kiowas comin' up from the ford," he shouted.

"Well, this is turnin' into one hell of a rendezvous," William said. "Mr. Greenwood, I want you to see that a fire gets built forty paces outside the gate. We're gonna have one hell of a feast, with Indian dancin' and fiddle playin'. Keep the gates bolted and guarded. No more Indians allowed in until we commence tradin' tomorrow."

"Alright," I said.

"Would it break your jaw to say 'sir'?"

"No, sir," I replied. I excused myself to Kills Something and Mexican Horse, and found three of the Mexican adobe workers. I asked them if they would help me stack the wood for the fire, and they agreed in their own unexcited way.

The arrangements for the feast and Indian dance had just about been completed when Blue Wiggins raised another shout from the catwalk. "I'll be damned," he yelled. "Mr. Bent, there's somebody comin' from the north. I believe it's Sol!"

I looked north, and saw Sol Silver loping a sorrel mount between the lines of lodges that flanked the two creeks. He scattered the herd of Indian trade ponies as he came through. The evening sun was shining through the bare branches of the treetops now and painting Sol with gray and orange streaks that passed over him like the shadows of wings. Behind him, the peaks of the tepees rose, each issuing a stream of wood smoke to the wind.

"I ain't never seen the likes of Indians!" he shouted as he pulled rein at Fort Adobe. "I've never been so glad to see a fort in all my life!" He touched the silver ring in his left ear, as if it had granted him luck.

Little Bluff had broken away from the main body of his band and was now closing on the fort. "Shit!" he shouted, as he galloped nearer. "Howdy, howdy, shit, goddamn!"

" 'Goddamn' is right!" Murray yelled. "Sol, you still at war with Kiowas?"

"Only with Yellow Wolf's band. Is that them?"

"No, that's Little Bluff's people."

"I always got on fine with Little Bluff. He's a funny son of a bitch." Sol swung down from the saddle, looking grateful to have his feet on the ground for a change. The sorrel heaved clouds of vapor into the cold evening air.

Little Bluff came galloping up to the fort, a huge smile on his face. "Howdy!" he said.

In English, Spanish, Comanche, and Kiowa, the plans

were hastily made for feasting, playing, and dancing after dark. All parties were to withdraw to their respective camps until then. Sol Silver's arrival had raised the curiosity of all the men in Fort Adobe. We had been on the Canadian River five months or more, and were hungry for news from the outside world.

Sol shook hands with everyone, clasping my palm in his as he came through the gate. "Kid," he said, his eyes rolling around to inspect the interior of the fort. He spotted the fire and gravitated toward it like a moth. He opened his coat to let the warmth of the flames creep in. William sent the Mexican cook to serve up some stew and tortillas we had failed to finish at midday, and Goddamn Murray produced a flask of hard liquor which he offered to the grateful rider.

"Been cold as a well digger's ass," Sol said. "So many Indians I've had to travel mostly at night and lay up at day. War parties prowlin' everywhere out there."

"How many days out of Bent's Fort are you?" William asked.

"Would you believe eleven? And hardly no sleep at all. Livin' on cold pemmican and coffee. Been scared to let a fire burn longer than that. Started with two extra ponies. Wore them plumb out."

"Maxwell still in charge of the fort?" William asked.

"Yes, sir. Everything's fine there. Soldiers comin' and goin' all winter."

"More soldiers?"

"Yes, sir. And more on the way. Maxwell asked somebody to volunteer the ride and bring the news. I'd had my fill of soldiers, so here I am."

"What news?" William asked.

"Well, sir. You're standing on American soil. Texas joined the Union two days after Christmas as the twenty-eighth state."

"Well, I'll be goddamn!" said Murray. "We ride to the wildest, most Indian-infested country in the wilderness, and it turns out we're back in the goddamn States." The white men around the fire burst into laughter—Lucas Murray,

Blue Wiggins, John Hatcher, and even William Bent and me—but the Mexican adobe makers only peered with dark eyes out from under the brims of their sombreros, their moods clouded by the arrival of Mexican Sol Silver.

Though Sol was full-blood Mexican, and looked it, he had been raised a Comanche Indian captive. He had been traded by the Comanches to a Kiowa chief named Yellow Wolf, who had treated him little better than a slave. Sol had escaped and gone to live with the Osage, then had led the Osage in a raid on Yellow Wolf's band and had taken the satisfaction of personally killing Yellow Wolf with an Osage lance. Yellow Wolf's Kiowas had been hunting him since, though he had remained friendly with most other Indians.

After taking revenge on Yellow Wolf, Sol had ridden to Bent's Fort, where he learned to speak mountaineer's English and became an Indian trader—one of the few who knew the Comanche-Kiowa range. The Mexicans at Bent's Fort, and in Taos and Santa Fe, always regarded Sol with suspicion, for though he looked Mexican, he dressed more like an American trader, and spoke English much better than Spanish. Perhaps more than any man at Fort Adobe, Sol Silver found himself at the center of the Mexican-American conflict that had trickled down the Canadian River to muddy the middle ground we all shared.

"What's the attitude in Santa Fe and Taos?" William asked.

"Cautious. President Polk wants to treat with Mexico, but the soldiers have moved down to the Rio Grande in Texas."

"What the hell is there to treat about?" Blue asked.

"The border," Ceran St. Vrain explained, and everyone knew he spoke with authority, having lived in Taos for some twenty years. "Texas claims the Rio Grande as its border all the way past Santa Fe, and into the mountains. Polk and the Congress bought that claim. The Mexicans claim the Nueces River is the boundary. That makes everything between the Rio Grande and the Nueces no-man's-land."

"I've seen that miserable country when I was with the

Comanches," Sol said. "Hell if I can figure why it's worth fightin' over."

"The land between the Rio Grande and Nueces is not what the fight is about," Ceran said. "It's the land *east* of the Rio Grande far upstream. Far north of the headwaters of the trifling Nueces. This includes Albuquerque, Santa Fe, and San Fernandez de Taos. Ridiculous as it sounds, the Texans have claimed since 1836 that they own this land and those cities. Now the United States has assumed those same claims."

The traders and laborers shuffled their feet around the fire, to a man agitated by the prospect of hostilities. I wondered how much of this the Indians had absorbed. The Comanches hated Texans. If Texas had joined the Union, did that mean the Comanches would hate Americans, too, or would they continue to think of Texans and Americans as two different nations?

"Where's Charles?" William asked, inquiring after his brother.

"Back at Taos," Sol said. "If anybody's got the sense to keep war from bustin' out there, it's Charles."

"I hope so," William said. "Well, if a war is comin', the army is bound to send troops west along the Arkansas. Probably General Kearny's dragoons. I'd better strike the Santa Fe Trail north of here and turn east to meet him. If he's got any sense, he'll wait another month."

"I'll ride with you," Blue Wiggins said, "but I wouldn't count on the army havin' much sense."

"Alright, you can ride with me," William replied. "I'd be obliged. The rest of you boys had better head back to Bent's Fort with the horses as soon as the tradin's done here."

William didn't have to explain how valuable the horses would be to the U.S. Army if border negotiations broke down, and the war with Mexico commenced. The Mexican laborers looking across the fire at me must have found themselves in an awkward position. They had built a trading post that would soon result in a large herd of horses bought cheap by the traders. These horses were likely to end up carrying

American soldiers into battle against their own families in Taos.

"We can wrap up all the tradin' in two days," Murray said. "Then we'd better all vamoose before the goddamn Comanches figure out a war's a-comin'."

"I'm staying," I announced.

Every man looked right at me and the fire crackled a vicious warning.

"You're *what*?" William Bent said.

"I'm staying at Fort Adobe. I'll take care of it until more trade wagons come from Bent's Fort."

"Are you out of your goddamn mind?"

"Nobody's stayin'," William said.

"I am," I said. "If I have to camp in the woods or stay with the Comanches, I'm staying here."

"Why the hell would you want to do a goddamn fool thing like that?"

"The Indians burned Mr. Hatcher's cabin last year. Maybe they can't burn Fort Adobe, but they can burn the gates and the rafters. If I stay, maybe I can keep them from destroying what we've built."

"The kid's right, William."

The eyes of the traders turned to John Hatcher, who spoke now in my behalf.

"Let some whiskey trader come around, and they'll make a wreck of this place. "I'd just as soon stay a while and trade into summer myself. There's plenty of horses yet to be had."

"I'll stay, too," Sol Silver added. "I'll take a Comanche over a soldier any day."

"You're all goddamn crazy."

"I advise you all to return to Bent's Fort," William said, "but you're grown men, so you can make up your own minds. "Anybody who's leavin' better be ready to ride the day after tomorrow, at dawn."

I tuned up my fiddle and held a recital by the fire outside the gates of Fort Adobe. The Comanches and Kiowas stared at me as if they had never before heard music. When I finished, they smiled, and copied the Americans by clapping their hands together.

William made a brief speech about George Washington, the great white grandfather, whose birthday we celebrated today. The Americans responded with more applause, but I noticed that the Mexicans left their hands in their coat pockets.

Indians and traders brought food to the feasting grounds: roasted hump of buffalo, tenderloin of deer, Mexican tortillas, Indian cakes made of seeds and tallow, pemmican, buffalo bone marrow, and enough coffee to wash it all down. The evening passed happily, until a couple of the Mexican adobe makers got into the Taos Lightning, or perhaps some tequila they had smuggled with them. When Sol Silver went back into the fort, himself for another shot of whiskey, the two troublemakers followed him.

I happened to be following behind the two drunken adobe makers, merely taking my Stradivarius back to the safety of the fort. I could tell the two men were drunk by the way they walked, and that alone made me nervous. Even in my inexperience as a trader, I sensed that a drunk man among all these Indians was likely to make some silly mistake and spawn a massacre. Hatcher was guarding the gate.

"I think those two are drunk," I said.

"I *know* they are. I ain't lettin' 'em back out. You and Sol go take care of your business, and come on back out, but those two Mexicans are stayin' inside if I have to knock 'em over the head."

I nodded and went in through the gate Hatcher opened for me. As soon as I stepped inside, I saw Sol squared off against the two drunk men. He was trying to reason with them, but one of them pulled a knife and lunged at him. I saw Sol dodge the knife, but then the other man came after him as well.

Outside, the Indians had commenced a drum beat and a chant that covered the sound of the scuffle. I pushed the gate open and said, "Trouble," to Hatcher, loud enough for him to hear. I lay my violin on the ground, ran to help Sol, and looked over my shoulder to see that Hatcher was following.

The two drunk Mexicans didn't know I had seen the whole thing, and I was able to run quietly up behind them in my moccasins and hit one of them with a forearm smash between his shoulder blades, knocking him to the ground. The other turned on me with his knife, but Sol grabbed his arms about the time Hatcher arrived and thumped the Mexican soundly on the head with his rifle barrel. The man dropped his knife and slumped in Sol's grasp. The other drunk was getting to his feet when Hatcher's rifle barrel split his scalp and sent him rolling backward.

"What was that all about?" Hatcher asked.

Sol kicked the knife across the ground. "Aw, they just wanted to gut a *Yanqui* lover."

"Let's drag 'em in this room and tie 'em up," Hatcher suggested. "Go put that fiddle away, Kid, and get your rifle. You can guard 'em."

I did as I was told, but I didn't like the idea of missing my first Indian dance, watching unconscious prisoners inside my own fort. When I got to the makeshift jail, Sol Silver and John Hatcher had the two men tied hand and foot.

"They give you any trouble, knock 'em on the head again," Hatcher ordered. He left to resume his post at the gate.

Sol Silver took a swig of whiskey, then offered the bottle to me. I took the bottle and pretended to take a shot, merely wetting my lips with the drink.

"You ever seen a Comanche dance?" Sol asked.

"No, sir."

He smiled. "Go ahead and watch from the walkway. I'll guard your prisoners awhile."

Somehow I knew instinctively that Sol would not harm the prisoners, even though they had attacked him. I trotted to the ladder that ascended to the walkway, and Sol sat on the ground outside the room that had become our temporary jail. This turned out to be quite advantageous. Here, from the high walls of Fort Adobe, I could gather in a broad view of the Indian dance. The Kiowas and Comanche warriors had formed two circles—one for each tribe—and were shuffling together with an energy that made the two circles turn like living wheels that consumed all the powers of the sky and earth. All the while, the chant and tempo of the drummers rose in pitch and intensity, until the best singers were wailing as they beat their drums in perfect time.

Under the light of the quarter moon, the ponies grazed in the prairie, the tips of the hide lodges glowed with firelit smoke trails, the coyotes answered the Indian song from the far canyon bluffs, and the river sang its silent song to me. I was at once enamored and frightened by this wilderness, this danger, this chaotic turmoil among nations.

Looking down on the celebration, I noticed the Mexican adobe workers huddled together, scowling and talking among themselves. Then I saw William Bent and Ceran St. Vrain standing aside, conversing in private—hatless Ceran with his hair and beard standing out crazily, and William with his buckskin fringe shaking at his sleeve as he gestured to punctuate some point.

It suddenly became all too clear. Ceran and William had met in private with Captain Frémont. Frémont had come from Washington, perhaps carrying secret dispatches, but certainly carrying intelligence from President Polk himself. They had sent me and John Hatcher with an army expedition to build this fort, with the blessing of the U.S. Army. William and Ceran knew more than they let on.

We would trade with the Comanches for horses. This would only encourage the Comanches to raid Mexico for more horses—in effect, making the Comanche nation an ally to the United States in the coming war with Mexico.

Then what? If the war went well for the Americans, Mexican troops would be pushed out of New Mexico, and Fort Adobe might be used by the American army in a campaign to pacify the Indians. If the Mexicans somehow surprised the Americans with a campaign that pushed north into

Texas, Fort Adobe could be used as part of a line of defense
between New Mexico and Missouri.

I was not just a free merchant. This was not just a trading
post upon whose walls I now stood. Some genius. I was a
pawn.

TWENTY-SIX

"You're the one they tried to knife," William said to Sol
Silver. "What do you reckon ought to be done with 'em?"

The two Mexicans stood in a low beam of blood red
sunlight that had vaulted the canyon rim to the east, and
now flooded through the open gates of Fort Adobe. Their
bloody heads hung low this morning, their spirits sapped.

"I'll give them the choice," Sol replied, his voice flat and
his eyes angry. "Either they can fight me fair, one at a
time"—he nodded at me to translate this into Spanish—"or
we can settle it the Indian way."

Shaved Head, Kills Something, and Little Bluff looked
on with interest. Somehow, they had sensed the trouble in
the fort last night and had made inquiries. William had allowed them to enter the gates to watch the white man's
justice.

"What is the Indian way?" one of the prisoners asked
through me.

"Only one way to find that out," Sol said. He drew his
knife and stepped forward to cut the ropes that bound the
hands of the prisoners. "Fight me, or settle it like an Indian
would settle it."

"Make up your mind," William said.

The two men whispered to each other for a moment.

"Make up your mind, or I'll decide for you!" William said.

"The Indian way!" one of the Mexicans blurted, his voice croaking. The other nodded, looking fearfully at Sol's knife.

Sol scowled. He pointed his knife blade at one of the men. "You owe me a horse," he said. Then he turned to the other man, who had pulled a knife on him the night before and said, "You owe me three horses."

"Well," William said, "you gonna pay up or not?"

The two men looked confused, but nodded, relief flooding their bloody faces.

"Now listen!" William said, his voice rising so everyone inside the walls would hear. "The next man who gets drunk and causes trouble in my fort will be tied to a post and whipped until he is unconscious. We need every able-bodied man here to work together, and I won't tolerate any foolishness beyond a fair fistfight."

He paused to let me translate into Spanish, and to let his anger settle.

"We come here to trade," he continued. "Let armies and governments make war if they will. We can't stop 'em. The Mexicans say this is Mexican soil. The Texans say it's Texas. Congress says it's America now. But we know this country is the land of the Comanche and the Kiowa. The damn war does not mean squat to us here. We come in peace. We come to trade. That's all."

"Hey, *jefe*," said Bonifacio, the leader of the adobe crew. "You said only last night that you are going to guide General Kearney across the plains to Bent's Fort. Tell the truth. Will you lead the attack on San Fernandez de Taos? On Santa- Fe?" This was a bold demand, but these men were worried about their families.

"What would you have me do, Bonifacio? Sit back and leave 'em to their own devices, or rein 'em in as best I can? How many times have you men seen me ride out to meet a war party and try to find a way around a fight? This is no different, except this war party is American—that's all. Hell, they think I'm some kind of king out here. They think I'm the law. You all know I'm just a trader. You know I'm as much Mexican as I am American, and you know I'm more Cheyenne than anything. My children are half Cheyenne. Hell, my mother-in-law is full-blood!"

Sol Silver chuckled, and a few of the men followed suit, lightening the tension inside the walls.

"Yes, by God, I'll ride with Kearny or whoever else they send, and I'll do my damnedest to stop any killin' they might have on their minds. My brother's got a Mexican wife in Taos, don't he? You think I want harm to come to my own kin? My own nieces and nephews? Well, do you, Bonifacio?"

The adobe boss peered at William for a moment or two. "No, *jefe.*"

"Alright. Then let's get our tradin' done, so I can go meet that war party. Maybe I can stop some of their nonsense."

After this speech, I had to wonder what had caused my suspicions the night before as I looked down from the fort walls. Perhaps William was privy to secret information; but, if so, I could think of no one I would rather have on the inside. I respected and trusted him. He would do his best to keep things as peaceable as possible. But I was still a pawn.

William now went to shake hands with Little Bluff, Shaved Head, and Kills Something. The trading commenced with these three men. William negotiated with Little Bluff, John Hatcher with Shaved Head, and I with Kills Something.

"Now I will have the blanket, the wood for the bow, and the pinto pony."

"*Bueno,*" I said, and led Kills Something first to the stack of blankets the wagons had hauled from Bent's Fort. Most of the woolen blankets were black or dark blue, but Kills Something found a yellow one.

"The color of the Trickster's eyes," he said.

"The Trickster?"

"Coyote. An ancestor of the *Noomah.*"

"*Noomah?*"

"Comanche. The name we call ourselves. Coyote is a

great-grandfather from the days when the animals spoke and walked like two-leggeds."

I nodded, committing all he said to memory. "If that is the blanket you want, now you can choose the wood for your bow."

We strolled across the grounds of Fort Adobe to the stack of hickory limbs Louis Lescot and I had harvested months before at Council Grove. Kills Something picked one up, smelled it, and frowned.

"Mubitai," he grumbled.

"What does that mean?"

"This wood. This is not the best kind for making bows."

"What is the best?"

"Etoo-hoo-upi. The Texans call it horse-apple."

Hatcher had told me about the tree called the horse-apple. He said it was also called *bois d'arc*, which I knew was French for bow wood. Hatcher pronounced it "bow-dark," as in "I wish we had some *bow-dark* posts to build this here *kraal*."

"I don't have any *etoo-hoo-upi*," I said to Kills Something. "This *mubitai* is all I have."

He seemed stunned that I had learned the Comanche words so quickly. "You will give me four pieces of this poor *mubitai*, so that I can trade for one good piece of *etoo-hoo-upi*."

I shook my head. "I have brought this wood a long way. I will give you two pieces."

"Three."

"Done. Now, about the pony."

"I want a fine pinto pony."

"I do not have any ponies yet, but when the trading is finished, I will have many."

"Come," Kills Something said, motioning for me to follow him. He went to the pole ladder that ascended to the walkway. I went up after him, and from the top of the fort wall, we were able to look out over the herd of trade horses. "Do you see the pinto stallion with his head down? Straight between here and the third lodge."

"The black and white?"

"Yes. That is the one I want."

Just then the pony took a step to reach new grass, and I saw him lurch on a front foot. "He is lame," I said.

"That pony belongs to Shaved Head. He was a fast pony. He has a cracked hoof, and now Shaved Head no longer wants him. Our chief has so many ponies, when one gets hurt, he just rides another."

"Why do you want a pony with a cracked hoof?"

"The spirits tell me I have the medicine to mend that hoof and make the pony fast again."

"How?"

"When you get that pony and give it to me, you will see."

I looked down into the fort and saw John Hatcher still bargaining with Shaved Head. Quickly, I descended the ladder and motioned Hatcher aside as Shaved Head unfolded blankets to find one he wanted.

"Shaved Head has a black-and-white paint stallion with a cracked front hoof on the off side."

"Yeah?"

"I need that pony."

Hatcher shrugged. "Alright, I'll git him for you."

"What will it cost me?"

"A pony with a cracked hoof? One of them hickory limbs will do."

"Done," I said. "You can choose any limb you like."

"You settlin' with Kills Something?"

"Finally."

"'Bout time. You been a Indian trader goin' on seven moons now, and you ain't made a profit yet."

"Like you said, Mr. Hatcher. It's payday."

He smiled. "That's a fact, Kid."

I told Kills Something he would have the pinto pony, and he nodded, looking well pleased with himself.

Just then, I turned and caught William's eye as he motioned for me. He and Little Bluff both seemed annoyed, so I walked over to them to see if I could help.

"Kid, my Kiowa ain't worth a damn, and I don't use my

Spanish near as much as my Cheyenne and French. Tell
Little Bluff that I'll purchase any white captives he's got in
his camp. I'll give two ponies—or the equivalent—for each
one."

My astonishment must have showed in my face.

"Well, go on and tell him," he said.

I made the translation in Spanish. Little Bluff replied,
saying he would spread the word, but that he doubted the
owner of the one white captive in his camp would part with
her for two ponies.

"So he's got a woman or a girl. Tell him I'll bargain, but
three ponies is as high as I'll go."

I made the offer in Spanish, but felt mighty peculiar deal-
ing for humans with horseflesh. After helping William trade
with Little Bluff, I asked him how he knew a white captive
was being held in Little Bluff's camp.

"Just a gut feelin'," he replied. "Anyway, I always ask,
just in case."

"What will be done with her if you get her back?"

"She'll be returned to her people, if possible."

"Will her family pay you back for the ransom?"

"Most times they'll double and triple it if you let 'em,
but I've never taken a penny in profit for captives. Just don't
seem right to me."

"I imagine whoever she is, she'll be glad to go home."

"Maybe not."

"Sir?"

"Would you be glad to be sent home about now?"

"No, sir."

"You never know with these ransom cases, Kid. Maybe
she's a grown woman, and she's been defiled. Hell, raped,
is what it is. Maybe she can't face her people because of
that. Captured women have been known to hang theirself,
or stab theirself. Others just go Indian. A little girl, on the
other hand—that depends. Maybe she's been given to a
mean squaw that whups up on her and makes her carry
wood and water. Or, maybe she's replaced a child some
mother lost, and she's been coddled and loved on. You

never know. Now, boys, sometimes they can't wait to get home, and sometimes they'd just as soon ride and hunt and run around half naked. Sometimes the Indians won't sell their captives for all the horses in Mexico, and sometimes the captives refuse to go back home, even given the choice."

"I didn't know this would be part of our trade."

"Well, it is, so get used to it. Every case is different. Don't worry about it. You'll know what to do."

I nodded and wondered what else I didn't know. "But . . ." I said. I was thinking of Nicole. I was thinking that I had killed a man—Segarelli—for having raped her. How could I live among people who raped captive women?

"Well, what?" William demanded.

"The rape. It's not right. Any man ought to be punished."

"You're not among Christians now. A Comanche sees it different. He takes a woman from his enemies, and he makes her good with his seed. That's the way he looks at it. If she survives all that, maybe she's tough enough to be a Comanche squaw."

"It's still not right."

"Not by everything we've ever been taught in Bible school, hell, no, it ain't right. But this ain't the land of Bible school. This is Comanche land, paid for in Comanche blood. Any white woman who steps onto it—even one foot over the edge—is part of an enemy army. They run the risk of capture, torture, and rape. So do their daughters. Hell, they ought to know better, or their menfolk ought to know better than to drag 'em out here."

"But why not punish the rapist? Make an example out of him?"

"You're not listenin', Kid. To them, it ain't a bad thing. It's their duty. They take this woman—she may be white, she may be Mexican, she may be Apache or Pawnee—they rape her, and that makes her good with their seed. That's the way they say it. They make her good. You can't turn back a thousand years of Indian logic by punishing one Comanche rapist inside the borders of his own country."

William spoke these words as harshly as he had ever said

anything to me, and I knew he was warning me to set my Christian sensibilities aside on this matter.

When Shaved Head, Little Bluff, and Kills Something finished their trading, they left the fort and spread the news in the village that business had commenced. The warriors now came into the fort six at a time to make deals. The Kiowas proved much more accepting of the hickory bow wood. Depending on how hard I bargained, I could get one, two, or even three horses in trade for one solid branch of hickory. When my stack of hickory was about half gone, Hatcher walked over and shook his head.

"What do you aim to trade when that's all gone?"

"I'll be finished. This is all I've got."

"That's no good, Kid. Trade for somethin' other than horses for a while. Get you some buffalo robes or moccasins or parfleches. Find out what one fellow wants to get rid of— maybe a lodge pole. The next buck you deal with might need him a lodge pole, and you can trade up. Don't run clean out of trade goods before the hand's played."

I took Hatcher's advice on this and began to accumulate a variety of goods. Toward the end of the day, my hickory wood was gone, but I still had lodge poles, robes, and rawhide "parfleche" bags for future trading. I had also settled with Kills Something, presenting him with the lame pinto he had wanted. The trading ended at dusk, and the men began loading the wagons for the return trip. The wagons would depart at dawn, leaving me, Hatcher, and Silver to take care of Fort Adobe.

My career as an Indian trader had finally begun. I was off to an encouraging start. You must know how I felt. What have you accomplished that pleases you when you think about it? Have you built something? Raised a happy child? Harvested a large red tomato? Cleaned up a mess? If you have done anything of the kind, you must know something of the way I felt, filled with the rapture that comes with success. But The Crossing on the Canadian drew all kinds of characters in those days, not all of whom respected peace and free commerce. Some could not have cared less whether I failed or succeeded in the Indian trade.

TWENTY-SEVEN

Kills Something spread the coals from the Indian fire across a patch of ground about the size of a saddle blanket. He had been leading the lame pinto around and around the fire for some time, and had stopped to spread the coals while I held the lead rope, tied around the pinto's neck.

"Now you will see," he said. He took the lead rope from me and walked right through the coals he had spread, his thick bison-hide moccasins protecting his feet. To my surprise, the pinto stepped right into the coals behind Kills Something with never a flinch of pain. Kills Something doubled back and brought the stallion through the coals again— and again and again until the smell of scorched hooves hung in the air. Jibber stood downwind, his nose in the air and his nostrils quivering at this strange odor.

Next, we led the pinto to Adobe Creek, where Kills Something had a patch of rawhide soaking in the water. Jibber hunted along the creek bank as Kills Something picked up the injured hoof. The pony stood obediently on his three sound feet as Kills Something checked the hoof crack to make sure no pebbles or other debris were lodged in it.

"Look," I said. "I brought something." I reached into a new buckskin possibles sack I had gotten in trade and produced a pair of hoof trimmers that Hatcher had insisted I carry with me.

Kills Something looked at the tool, then back at the hoof. He felt the thin edges of the hoof where it had cracked and begun to curl up. Without looking at me, he held out his hand for the trimmers. Like a giant pair of pliers with clippers on the business end, the trimmers bit off the ragged ends of the hoof that had grown long where the pony had been favoring his sore foot. Now Kills Something tossed the trimmers aside and used his knife to detail the trimming, leaving the hoof shorter around the crack so the pony's weight would fall on more solid portions of the hoof.

Kills Something put the hoof down and let the pinto stand on it. He went to the creek and scooped three handfuls of water into his mouth, but I could tell that he didn't drink. Holding the water in his mouth, he picked up a circular patch of rawhide and a long rawhide strip he had been soaking in the creek.

The Comanche farrier lifted the hoof again, and used the water in his mouth to clean and flush out the crack in the hoof, preparing it to heal. I thought it was ingeniously simple for him to squirt that water out of his mouth, into the crack, to rinse out any dirt that might have collected there. Now he wrapped the wet rawhide circle around the bottom of the hoof, and began securing it with a rawhide strip that he wound around and around the hoof many times. He took care not to wrap the strip above the hoof, as the rawhide would shrink and tighten, cutting off blood circulation in the ankle if wrapped too high.

Having wrapped the hoof, we tied the pinto short to a tree where he would stand until the rawhide dried and shrank, pulling the hoof crack together.

"How long will he wear that moccasin?" I asked.

"Until it falls off."

"Then what?"

"I will make another moccasin, then another. When four moons have passed, the hoof will be healed. Then I will ride this pinto, and you will see how fast he runs. I will win many races and get many horses."

"Why do you want so many horses?"

He looked at me as if he could not believe I did not know. "To get a good wife. I saw a girl in Peta Nocona's band. She is the one I want."

"How many horses do you need?"

"Many. She is pretty. Her father will want fifty or more."

For some reason—I suppose because I had lost my own chance at love—I wanted Kills Something to win that girl he wanted. "While the hoof heals," I said, "you can still win horses."

"How?"

"You can borrow my pony."

Kills Something burst into such roars of laughter that the pinto tossed his head, and Jibber came up from the water's edge to investigate.

"He runs fast," I insisted.

My Comanche friend had to crouch on the ground and hold his stomach.

"I'll show you. I'll race him. Find someone who wants to race from this creek to the other, then back again. Fireball will win."

"Fireball?"

Kills Something sat on the ground and laughed for three minutes. Then he got up, found a warrior who wanted to race, and watched me win by three lengths on my half-blind pony, taking possession of my opponent's mount as my prize.

"I will ride and race your pony," Kills Something said to me after the race. "Half the ponies I win, I will give to you. When the pinto's hoof has healed, I will not need your horse anymore."

❦

Over the next four months, Kills Something won twenty ponies on Fireball—ten for each of us. Fireball lost only one race, to a fleet sorrel mare stolen recently from the Texas settlements. More importantly, Kills Something began using Fireball to exercise the pinto. As its hoof became sound, Kills Something would spend several hours each day riding Fireball and leading the pinto. This proved to be good exercise for both horses, yet kept the weight of a rider off the pinto as his hoof mended. As he had promised, Kills

Something kept a rawhide shoe on the pinto through four moons. Only then did he mount the pinto.

My Comanche friend was right. That pinto could sure run. Ordinarily as docile as an old pet, a rider would convert him into a volcanic beast whose tossing head and churning legs sent mane and tail streaming with speed. By this time, the crack in his hoof had been held together long enough to grow out completely, being trimmed off and replaced with a new, sound hoof. Kills Something's confidence in the treatment was complete. He believed in his medicine. After taking off the last rawhide pony-moccasin, he never gave the healed hoof so much as a suspect glance.

During these months, Kills Something began teaching me how to ride like a Comanche. He showed me how to fashion the arm sling that was woven into the horse's mane and looped under its neck. An accomplished Comanche rider could thrust his arm into this loop while leaving one heel over the back of his mount and, in this way, cling to either side of his pony, effectively using the pony as a shield.

The first time I tried this stunt, in spite of my inborn gifts of coordination and athleticism, I groped Fireball's left flank awkwardly until I fell off at a mere walk. Half the Comanche village roared with laughter at my attempt. Then Kills Something demonstrated again. He mounted the fleet pinto, carrying lance, shield, bow, and arrow. At a gallop, he threw himself to the left side of his mount, as I had failed to do at a walk. Then he righted himself again, but let his momentum carry him to the right flank of the pony as he drew an arrow from his quiver. Clinging now to the off side, shield strapped to a forearm, and lance cradled in an elbow, he somehow notched an arrow, drew the bow, and sent the arrow slamming into a rotten log we had been using for a target. The village erupted in falsetto cries of "Yee-yee-yee!"

Undaunted, I redoubled my efforts, practiced, and by the end of the day could hang on to Fireball's flank at a trot for a short while.

"You gone Indian?" Hatcher asked me when I rode back to the fort at dusk.

"No, sir. I don't think so. Just learning how to ride."

"You're talkin' a right smart Comanche nowadays, I've heard. You sure you don't aim to just go plumb Indian?"

"You speak Comanche," I reminded him. "Why don't you ride like them, or shoot a bow, or learn some of their other ways?"

"I've always been skeered as hell of 'em."

"Then why do you come out here to trade with them, Mr. Hatcher?"

He spit a brown stream of tobacco on the ground, pulled at his beard, and glanced at the Comanche village through the open gate of the fort. "I always liked things I'm skeered of."

I nodded. "Me, too."

I had work to do around the fort, but I am a marvel of efficiency and don't need much sleep; so I could get my chores done in half the time the others took, leaving plenty of spare hours to practice riding and shooting my bow with Kills Something. Next, I learned to pick up a wounded man by reaching down from my mount and pulling him over my lap. This took several weeks of training.

Kills Something started me by picking up a canteen on the ground. "I learned this when I was five winters old," he boasted. By the end of that day, I could swoop low, snag that canteen, and lift it at a gallop, for I had become quite a rider. The next day, Kills Something replaced the canteen with a parfleche bag stuffed full of old blankets. After a couple of days, he removed half the blankets and replaced them with rocks, making the bag heavier. A few days later, he filled the whole bag with rocks.

"Can you lift that yourself?" I asked.

He replied with a demonstration, galloping an arrow shot away and returning at full gallop. Somehow, at the last possible instant, he swung low, holding the pinto's mane, grabbed the parfleche without slowing down, though I feared it would rip his arm off, and hauled it up over his lap. The first time I tried this, at a trot, Fireball got so frustrated with my dragging the cumbersome bag under his feet that he stopped short, throwing me to the ground.

Amid the laughter of all who had seen, Kills Something said, "We will ride together, one to each side. Only the best warriors can pick up a wounded or dead man alone."

"I will learn," I replied, with more than a slight growl of determination in my voice.

With Kills Something's help, I began to advance. In a week, I could pick up the heavy parfleche by myself, though I had to slow down almost to a standstill to do it. Next, Kills Something began recruiting boys to play dead. We practiced on them, and my Comanche mentor chose a slightly larger volunteer every day. We would warm up by riding to either side of the prone Comanche boy, who always remained perfectly still in spite of the hooves that thundered almost upon him. Kills Something would grab one arm, and I the other. We would lift the boy and throw him across my lap, or Kills Something's.

That was only an exercise. The real feat was picking up the volunteer single-handedly. One day, I volunteered to play dead, and Kills Something lifted me from the ground as an eagle would pluck a fawn from the ground. He used any method necessary, even grabbing a handful of my hair, just as he clung to the pinto's mane with his other hand. Then we switched places, and I succeeded in completing the rescue maneuver with Kills Something playing possum, though I had to slow to a walk to lift him, then resume the gallop.

This was only the beginning of my training. We ran all manner of races between Adobe Creek and Bent's Creek. Races where we had to jump some objects and duck others. Races where we had to leap over a pole, then stop within two strides or tumble off a ten-foot bluff over the creek, then turn, leap the pole again, and race back to the beginning. Our races trained both horse and rider for all manner of heroics.

In one race, a dozen or more riders would start from a

line, a single tree our goal. The first to touch the tree won; so as we neared at top speed, the warriors would commence a mad scramble for position, pushing and pulling each other relentlessly. Riders were often bloodied and trampled in this contest, but he who whined had to endure endless ridicule.

Through these months—or moons, as I had begun to think of them, especially since my own clock revolved so slavishly around the lunar cycles—Kills Something began to rise in the estimation of his people aboard the pinto stallion. He had amassed quite a herd of ponies by this time, and rode them all, but he lavished a disproportionately large amount of attention on the pinto, even staking the stallion near his lodge at night, and adorning his mane and tale with feathers and ribbons.

I began to see the power of the horse to these people with whom I traded goods and ideas. The Comanches were not numerous; this much I knew. From talking to the traders and the Comanches themselves about the various bands and villages roving about the plains, and their respective numbers relative to Shaved Head's band, I was able to confirm the entire Comanche population at no more than twenty thousand. Yet they held the best hunting grounds on the continent. Their country sprawled hundreds of miles in every direction around Fort Adobe. To hold and defend this vast empire, they had to ride. I mean, *ride*. Though they used rather than worshiped the horse, they did possess a reverence for the beauty and power of the beast.

No one thought as highly of any horse as Kills Something thought of the pinto. By Comanche standards, Shaved Head was getting old. He was pushing forty. The people in his band had begun to look toward the younger warriors for a new leader. With the power and speed of the pinto under him, Kills Something looked forever more like the heir to the big lodge.

One evening, after exercising the pinto, I was helping Kills Something rub the pony down with dried grass. As we meticulously rubbed away the dirt where it had clung to sweat, making the stallion's coat gleam, Kills Something

worked his way around the hind end of the pony to join me
on the off side.

"I will tell you this," he said. "Maybe you are a white
man. That is true. Anyway, you are my friend, and that is
good. But I love this pony with my whole heart."

TWENTY-EIGHT

Do you ever dream of snakes? I do. The dream is always a
warning. That has proven invariably true. I will tell you how
I first learned this.

One night, at Fort Adobe, as the dark of the moon drew
me into the deathlike clutches of irretrievable slumber, it
happened. I had been sleeping for over twenty-four hours.
My friends had grown accustomed to my peculiarities and
knew not to try to wake me when I finally fell into such a
trance. Well, I was sleeping hard, but then I woke up halfway between dusk and dawn—the darkest, loneliest hour—
the middle of a new-moon night.

As I lay there on my back, my eyes suddenly flew open
like shudders. Jibber lay between my feet, sleeping. A
strange odor filled the room. It was pitch-dark, but somehow
I could see. All was quiet. Not even the crickets sang. Then
I heard a noise. It sounded like something being dragged
ever so slowly across the ground. In a moment I realized
what it was. It was the belly of a snake making its way
slowly across the dirt floor toward me.

I tried to move, but could not. I tried to speak or whistle
to Jibber, but I could not even draw breath. My heart began
to beat so furiously that it pained me, and then I saw the
head of the viper appear at the foot of my buffalo-robe mattress. My lungs ached for want of the air I could not breathe.
I hoped beyond hope that Jibber would wake and save me,

but the snake—a giant diamondback—crawled right over Jibber, his evil, lifeless eyes piercing mine. I could feel the horrible undulations of its belly scales as the rattler crawled up my crotch and stomach. Though I could not breathe, I could somehow smell the foul breath of the snake. I attempted all manner of heroics to muster the strength to move, or cry out, but I was at once as rigid as a statue and as limp as a corpse.

The tail of the snake left the floor as his head reached my chest, and here the snake quickly gathered himself into a coil, never releasing me from his penetrating glare. Lifting his head high above my chest, he hissed, and set his rattlers to buzzing, the hellish sound of which still makes the skin crawl all over my scalp.

Now, horror of horrors, more snakes came. They slithered in through the door, emerged from under the mattress, dropped from the brushy ceiling, and burrowed out of the very walls. They joined their leader until I thought their weight would crush me. I knew that if I did not wake myself, this nightmare would kill me, for my heart and lungs verged on explosion. The first snake drew his head back to strike at my face, and my whole body became a shuddering mass of fear. Down came the awful head. The mouth gaped, and two fangs glinted as they swung downward and forward, coming like arrows to pierce the eyes I could not even blink closed. The moment those fangs stabbed painfully into my tortured orbs, they jolted me from my trance and well-nigh electrocuted me with exploding energy. An involuntary shriek tore past my throat and my body lifted a full foot off the mattress.

When I opened my eyes again, the snakes were gone. Jibber was darting everywhere in confusion. My lungs ached as I sucked in ragged gasps, and my heart felt like a Comanche drum beating the inside of my chest. I blinked and knew I was really awake this time. I saw Sol Silver peer briefly into my room, but the men knew by now of my occasional nightmares, and Sol didn't bother long. Jibber came to me, sniffed around the mattress, and licked my ear a couple of times to let me know all was well. I found the strength to lift a hand and stroke his head. At length, he curled up again between my feet, and I drifted into the blackest, emptiest void of exhaustion I had ever known.

When I woke—a day and a half later—I could still feel the pricks of the fangs in my eyeballs. Finding a trade mirror in which to look, I saw the most horribly bloodshot pair of eyes I had ever seen looking back at me.

"Maybe you should see a medicine man," Sol Silver said. "Something about you ain't right. Anything makes you scream like that in your sleep can kill you—I don't care if it *is* just a dream."

I nodded. "I feel as used up as an old man."

"Tell you what," Sol said. "You ought to have old Burnt Belly come make medicine over you. He was struck by lighting when he was young. He knows a thing or two."

"I've never heard of him."

"He drifts from band to band. Last I heard, he was camping with the Honey Eaters. We'll put the word out, and he'll be here with the next new moon."

"Thank you," I said. I knew Sol was right. Another dream like that would kill me for sure.

Anyway, the day after I woke, I was feeling much better. I was watching Kills Something win a race with the pinto over three other riders when Sol Silver whistled from the fort. Turning, I saw Sol pointing north from the walkway. I looked and noticed a rider ambling down into the Canadian Breaks. The distance was still over a mile, but the two mules—each carrying two kegs—identified their leader. Snakehead Jackson was slithering into the valley.

A cry of joy rose from the Kiowa camp. Within seconds, Kiowa warriors were mounted and riding north to escort Snakehead to their collection of tepees on Bent's Creek. Why they took such joy in his arrival was a confusion and a mystery to me. They had to know he would take everything they owned in trade for vile drink and leave them sick and poverty-stricken. Yet they rode to greet him as if he were a brother.

Snakehead himself came riding merrily into the Kiowa camp singing his hoarse jingle: *"Aguardiente! Hoy, bravo cabron! Aguardiente!"*

The Comanche camp differed. A few of the warriors drifted cautiously toward the whiskey trader, but none rode out to welcome him as had the Kiowas. I saw old Shaved Head and some of the gray-haired elders beseeching the younger warriors to stay in camp, but I could see the curiosity on some of the young Comanche faces.

Kills Something cantered up to me, having won the race over his rivals. He was leading a black pony he had taken as a prize from one of the riders. "Are you thirsty?" he asked in Comanche.

"Not for firewater," I replied.

"They say the firewater makes spirits talk to you."

"It makes you vomit. It is evil. I dreamed of snakes last night."

I saw Kills Something's eyes flare, as if he respected my dream powers. "I heard you scream all the way to my lodge."

"Have you ever heard of a medicine man named Burnt Belly?"

"A rider has already left to find him."

Sol Silver whistled again and waved me back to Fort Adobe. Kills Something went back to his people, and I rode to the fort on Fireball, with Jibber circling. John Hatcher was saddling his favorite horse at the gate.

"Let's drag in a mess of firewood," he said. "Then we'll round up the best horses and run them inside the walls."

Sol and I obeyed, and within half an hour we had collected our finest mounts, and gathered enough wood to burn for days.

"Make a fire just inside the gate and keep some water on to boil," Hatcher said. "As many kettles as we've got, boilin' all the time."

"What for?" I asked.

"Just do it."

As we carried out his orders, John Hatcher closed the

gate, and positioned the cannon just inside it, loaded and
ready to fire. He tied an iron pothook to the end of a rope,
and tied the other end of the rope to the walkway so the
pothook would dangle just inside the gate, near the cannon.
I had an idea what the hook might be used for, and it filled
me with dread of the coming night.

Hatcher began to pace the walkway with his rifle in his
arms, his knife and pistol conspicuously jutting from his belt.
I filled our kettles with water from the well in the corner of
the fort, and hung them over the fire to heat. The penned
horses watched me with curiosity from the opposite corner
of the fort. Finally, Sol and I joined Hatcher on the walkway, all three of us bristling with all the weaponry we
owned. We watched the Kiowas dancing around Snakehead,
singing and howling gleefully.

"Do you expect they'll try to take the fort?" I asked.

"Don't know what to expect of a drunk Indian."

"Maybe we should go out and talk to Snakehead."

"You'd git further talkin' to one of his rattlesnakes."

Sol nudged me on the shoulder and chuckled. "Just watch,
Kid. You're gonna see a show like you've never seen in
your life."

"I've seen it before," I said.

"That was only a few Kiowa bucks," Hatcher said.
"There's Comanches and squaws here this time."

What happened that day—and into the night—is something horrible to relate, but I will tell it.

The whiskey trader went through his ritual snake torture
and killing, and mixed his putrid blend of whiskey, black
powder, dried peppers, and severed snake heads. Then the
trading and drinking began. The young men got drunk. Then
drunker. Snakehead's pile of loot began to mount. Some of
the Kiowas tried to ride and fell off. A few lucky ones
staggered into the woods and passed out. The rest kept
drinking and began fighting. Two bucks squared off with
knives, the rest of the rabble urging them to fight. One dis-
emboweled the other—a friend of his. The wounded man
lay among his own guts without help from anyone. The

drinkers traded away horses, blankets, weapons, lodges. One warrior crazed with drink traded his daughter to Snakehead, who took her into a lodge and surely must have raped her as the Kiowas howled outside as if they approved.

I had to watch all of this. Hatcher would not let me go down to the Kiowa camp, for he knew I would have been murdered for trying to stop the debauchery. And it was only beginning. As dusk fell, a few young Comanche bucks appeared by the Kiowa firelight.

"You boys go down and build a big fire in the middle of the fort," Hatcher said. "We'll keep our backs to it and we can see if they try to climb the walls. Make sure them kettles is still full of water over the little fire."

Sol and I followed orders and returned to the walkway. By this time, the young Comanches had gotten drunk and were fighting with one another and with the Kiowas. Two combatants wrestled right through the fire, screaming as their flesh burned, but their friends only tried to kick them back into the fire. Even some of the Kiowa women were getting drunk now. One was staggering around with a lance, trying to stick anybody in her path. A drunken Comanche knocked her down, took her lance, and tried to rape her, but she squalled and fought, and other drunks joined the melee until everyone in the Kiowa firelight looked bloody and crazed.

Through all of this, Snakehead continued trading, occasionally knocking some drunken Indian on the head with his gun barrel as a warning to others. How he had survived this chaos time after time mystified me. I began to wish and hope that I would see an arrow appear in his back, though I realized that some other whiskey trader would take his place if the Indians killed him. The inhumanity demoralized me until I wanted to vomit.

About two hours after dark, the frenzy in the Kiowa camp seemed to take a new twist. Warriors began huddling, talking, chanting, screaming war cries, and looking all too often toward the three of us on the walkway. When one buck led a yelping, staggering charge toward the horses, the others followed. It took them a while to get mounted, but eventually they came weaving toward the fort on horseback. There were both Kiowas and Comanches among the drunken attackers.

"Sol, go down and keep the water boilin'. Be ready to hook a kettle on that pothook when I holler."

"Alright," Sol said.

"Kid, you stand up here with me. Watch my back and I'll watch yours."

"Yes, sir," I said.

"Let's not kill any of 'em if we can help it," Hatcher warned.

As Sol went down the ladder, I glanced toward the Kiowa camp and saw Snakehead sitting on a keg of whiskey, one leg crossed over the other, his arms folded across his chest. He was watching the attack on the fort as if he were sitting in some theater, taking in a play.

"Mr. Hatcher," I said.

"What?"

"I'm a good shot. I can see in the dark like an owl."

"So?"

"I can hit Snakehead from here."

"So can I, but I reckon he's thought of that. We can fight off these few drunks, but if Snakehead sees us drawin' a bead on him, he'll rally the whole lot. Then it will get close around here."

"We ought not to let whiskey traders around our fort."

"If we was to run him off, he'd just trade up the river a ways. Then we'd have to watch over our shoulder, because Snakehead would just as soon shoot us in the back as chop a head off a rattler."

"Maybe somebody ought to shoot him in the back."

"I've thought of that myself. Well, that would make me about as low as him, and then some other whiskey trader would come around, anyway. It ain't good this way, Kid, and it ain't pretty to watch; but it's better here, where we can keep an eye on everything."

I could feel the same anger and hatred coming on as

caused me to murder the rapist, Segarelli, as he lay drunk in his bed. I had sworn never again to resort to such vengeance, but Snakehead tested my resolve.

The drunken attackers rode up to the walls of the fort, screamed defiance at us, and then milled in confusion. A couple shot the adobe walls with arrows. One loosed a pistol ball over our heads.

"It'll take 'em a while to figure out what to do," Hatcher said.

One young Comanche began attempting to throw a rope over the wooden parapet on the northeast corner. He was so drunk that he almost fell off his horse every time he tossed the rope. Finally, he managed to snag the corner with his loop. This concerned me. Not that I felt in immediate peril. But if a drunken Indian could lasso the parapets, then a sober attacker might enjoy much better luck at breaching the walls this way. Even amid the chaos, I began thinking of how the parapets could be modified to prevent this.

As the Indian tried to climb the rope he had fixed around a corner of the parapet, I walked to the corner, drew my saber, and cut the rope with one well-placed stroke. The warrior fell about eight feet and lay on the ground.

The drunks howled, circled and loosed a few more rounds at us. Hatcher stood on guard at one corner, I on the other. I glanced down into the fort and saw Sol rolling a cigarette. I looked toward Snakehead in time to see him stroll over to the wounded Kiowa who had been gutted in the knife fight. The whiskey trader made sure he was not being watched, then cut the Kiowa's throat with a quick and vicious stroke of his knife. Then he went back to his whiskey barrel to watch the rest of the ineffectual attack on the fort.

It was my friend, Little Bluff, who figured out what to do even in his drunkenness. He rode recklessly back to the Kiowa camp and fetched a glowing ember from the fire. Some other drunks gathered grass and sticks and began piling the fuel against the wooden gates of Fort Adobe. I felt as if they were preparing to burn my very flesh. It angered me to the point that my own ire surprised me. Little Bluff's drunkenness did not excuse what he was about to do. He was going to fire the gates of Fort Adobe. *My fort*.

"Boilin' water!" Hatcher shouted down to Sol Silver.

Sol hooked a pot on the hook tied to the rope that dangled from the walkway. Hatcher hauled it up, grasped the edge of the pot with his kerchief to protect his hand, and poured the boiling water down on Little Bluff as the Kiowa attempted to light the kindling piled against the gate. Little Bluff squalled like the panthers whose chilling cries sometimes echoed through the canyon. He scrambled away as his own friends laughed at him, and eventually found enough sense to stagger to Bent's Creek and throw himself in the cool water.

No other Kiowas attempted to burn the gates. Their resolve fell apart completely, and those still sober enough wandered back to the whiskey trader's fire. Snakehead set up shop again, finding a few more young Comanches wandering over from Adobe Creek. The Kiowas continued to drink, brawl, and trade their earthly goods. For a drink, some offered their wives, and even their daughters.

Sol Silver and John Hatcher caught some sleep, leaving me on guard. I watched through the telescope and, with my naked eyes, though the heinous spectacle made me feel ill. Toward dawn, Snakehead took a young girl whose father had traded her for a cup of the putrid brew. Snakehead dragged her into a lodge. She fought until he struck her in the face with his fist. I know he raped her inside that lodge.

For the same crime, I had murdered Segarelli in Paris, and I wanted to kill Snakehead Jackson now, though he was sober and would likely have killed me instead. I could not understand how Hatcher and Silver could sleep through the howling madness outside the fort. I swore I would find a way to end it, to spare the Indians from this self-destructive path of drunkenness. A way to thwart the abominable Snakehead.

Within an hour, however, I would understand very well how and why Sol Silver and John Hatcher had chosen to

rest before dawn. They were more experienced than I. I
could not have foreseen what would happen next. As bad
as things looked in the Kiowa camp just now, the gates of
hell had scarcely swung ajar.

TWENTY-NINE

An Indian sees no dishonor in ambush. As a panther might
lay for a deer, or a snake for a prairie dog, an Indian will
secrete himself so expertly along a trail that his victim might
never know whence came the fatal shot. For this reason, I
chose not to attempt killing Bill Snakehead Jackson from
the walls of Fort Adobe.

I knew that if I drew a bead on Snakehead, and somehow
failed, that he would put a bounty on my head. My scalp
might sell for no more than a cup of rotgut whiskey, but
some buck thirsty for the mood-twisting effects of *aguardiente* would lay a trap for me. I might last a week, or I
might last a year, but it would be a year of nightmares. I
chose not to look upon Snakehead over my rifle irons.

Snakehead knew I hated him. After he came out of the
tepee in which he had raped the Kiowa girl, he remained
cautious. As he packed his spoils on his mules, he would
glance my way often enough to know whether or not my
sights might be trained on him. Using lodge poles he had
taken in trade, he made travoises for his mules. He heaped
robes and other booty on the travoises, snugging it all down
with ropes. Having thus packed in less than half an hour,
he then mounted his horse and led his mules northward,
keeping one eye on me.

Only after he thought himself beyond my range did he
turn his back completely. Now I knew I could kill him. Had
I not sworn an oath against murder, I would have sent a ball

through his back at that moment, for I could hit a target half again as far away as the average marksman's range. But I would not suffer the same regrets that had haunted me after my cowardly murder of Segarelli. If I was going to kill Snakehead Jackson, it would be in a fair fight, face to face. A duel. He would see it coming. But, frankly, I did not have the courage for that yet. I was afraid of him.

When the whiskey trader vanished behind a bend in the timber, I sighed a breath of remorse and relief. Perhaps, I thought, the basin prairie here at the Crossing on the Canadian would heal, shed the filthy aftermath of Snakehead's sojourn, and once again gleam and glow and smell of good musky things. Exhausted by my all-night vigil, I bowed my head forward on the adobe battlement I had built and defended, the felt crown of my hat against the sunbaked bricks. I looked at my boots and thought about what I must do next. Go down to the Kiowa camp and tend the wounded brawlers, the ill-treated innocents.

Then—suddenly—all my plans for the day changed. I heard a distant collection of almost musical thumps, like the deadened strings of a harp quickly strummed. Before I could draw a breath, I knew that a volley of arrows had flown from enemy bows. I dropped to the walkway so quickly that I came right out of my hat. I heard at least two arrows hiss over the parapet and a third made a popping sound as it tore through my felt crown.

"Mr. Hatcher!" I yelled.

Sol Silver and John Hatcher were on their feet with their guns in their hands before my hat fell among the horses with a new hole in it. I scrambled a few feet over so that I would emerge in a new spot from the behind the battlements, and rose above the wall long enough to get a look at the enemy. In this half second's glance, I saw one wave of Apache foot warriors storming toward the Kiowa camp as another assaulted the fort. I saw arrows speeding my way, and ducked as the first enemy gunshot erupted.

"Apaches!" I shouted. Adobe dust sprayed around me, and splinters flew from the northeast parapet.

Hatcher was halfway up the ladder to the walkway. I rose again, shouldering my rifle as I stood. In an instant, I found the lead warrior advancing on the Kiowa camp. Though the range was great, the shot rushed, and the target moving, I saw the warrior on the ground the moment the powder smoke cleared.

I dropped to reload behind the adobe parapet as Hatcher fired the second shot. From this point, I cannot tell it as it happened, for everything occurred at once. I piece it together now mostly by memory of the sounds; for while I couldn't watch it all at once, I couldn't help but hear all the ghastly noises that intertwined to form one hellish din of battle. The gunshots, hoofbeats, and war whoops. The fearful cries of men, women, and children. The barking of dogs and the screaming of horses. I can only list what happened here so that you, having once taken it all in, piece by piece, can then rethink it all at once.

Now the Apaches stormed into the Kiowa camp on foot, despite the two leaders Hatcher and I had shot. They killed warriors too drunk to rise, dragged away inebriated women, slew those who tried to fight, carried away screaming children.

And now Apache horsemen stormed the gate of my fort, though Sol Silver wounded their leader in this charge with a rifle ball through the middle of his guts. This wounded man tossed a blazing torch to the warrior nearest him, who succeeded in reaching the wooden gates, where the drunken Comanches and Kiowas had already piled wood the night before.

"Take the other corner, Sol!" Hatcher shouted as he manned the northeast parapet. From these two points, the two men could fire upon all four walls of the fort. "Kid, you fire the cannon, if it comes to that."

And now Apache warriors breached the west walls of the fort by climbing poles they had brought for the purpose. Before Sol could reach his post, three had come over. He shot one almost point-blank as he ran along the catwalk. I shot the second with my rifle, bowling the Apache back over the wall where he fell twelve feet to his death. But the third Apache succeeded in landing on the roof of our kitchen and dropped quickly to the ground inside the fort.

"Get him, Kid!" Sol shouted as he ran along the walkway, fighting off attackers with the butt of his rifle as arrows sped all around him in bee-line blurs.

I lay my spent rifle down on the promenade, strung my bow, and notched an arrow from my quiver. But the Apache warrior inside the fort was wily and snuck in among the horses, using them as shields as he made his way to the gates.

"The gates are fired!" Hatcher shouted. "Fight, boys, the Comanches are mounted and comin' to help!"

Now Jibber entered the fight, dancing and dodging around the Apache invader with barks and growls until the horses shied, giving me a clear shot at the enemy. My arrow hit him squarely in the middle as he ran from my right to my left, toward the gates. It was a good shot, yet he did not fall. He ran on, breaking off the arrow shaft where it protruded. The horses circled again, stirring dust and covering the wounded warrior.

I swung down into the fort. Through the dust and between the horses, I could see the wounded Apache struggling with the heavy beam that barred the gate as Jibber nipped his ankles valiantly. I spotted Fireball among the horses and whistled to catch his attention. I ran right at him; and though the other horses bolted in every direction, Fireball stood firm, for I had trained him to stand even when I ran right at him.

I sprang upon Fireball without saddle or bridle, but he knew how to follow cues from my legs and feet. Tangling my left hand in his mane, I urged him forward, drawing my saber as I charged the gate.

The Apache, already wounded by my arrow, heard me coming. He kicked at Jibber, turned, and drew his toma-hawk, a shiny one gotten in a swap from some Indian trader like me. He continued to lift the heavy beam with his left shoulder as his tomahawk expertly warded off the first downward thrust of my saber. My second attempt caught him in the throat, cutting his jugular. He screamed his death cry as his own blood covered his body. But in a last dying burst of strength, he succeeded in lifting the beam away from the iron cradles that held it. The beam hit the ground about the same time as his body.

"Jibber!" I shouted. "Circle the cavvy."

At this familiar command, Jibber charged the herd and drove the horses into the far corner of the fort, holding them with barks and growls as he dodged their kicking hooves.

Now the gate swung open slightly, the smoke from the fire outside streaming in like a black snake that climbed the wall. Too late to replace the beam, I knew I had seconds to act before the Apaches outside realized that their brother had died opening the gate for them.

I sheathed my saber as I wheeled Fireball and swooped low with my right hand to grab a smoldering branch from the edge of last night's fire. Sol Silver and John Hatcher were busy firing, reloading, and defending the walls. Their shots had proven true enough to keep the Apaches moving, and many had retreated to the timber. Nonetheless, Hatcher and Silver were vastly outnumbered, and each time they rose to fire, a dozen Apaches peppered the timber of the parapets with arrows and bullets.

Now a mischievous breeze blew the gate ajar, and I heard the Apache war cry rise. About twenty of them stormed the open gate as the wood smoke curled around the hand-hewn planks. Fireball and I stood at our post beside the cannon. The touchhole was full of black powder, the barrel loaded with scrap iron, rocks, and horseshoe nails. Rifle balls and arrows sang around me as the Apaches fired blindly through the smoke that covered the now-open gateway.

When the first attacker appeared through the veil of smoke, I lowered my burning brand to the black powder in the touchhole. The Apache saw me, and his eyes grew wide. He tried to turn, but by then his fellows had come up behind him and the main charge in the breech ignited. The cannon lurched and Fireball reared, but I held on. The concussion inside the adobe walls deafened me. It drove Jibber into the kitchen with his tail between his legs and stampeded the horses toward the only daylight they could see: the open gates. The animals poured outside, some leaping over the very cannon that had spooked them, and carrying Fireball and me outside with them.

Horseflesh rammed into me on all sides as we leapt two stunned or dead or wounded Apaches at the gate. The cannon had completely surprised and demoralized the attackers, who were now in retreat. Once outside the fort walls, I gathered that the Comanches had come to the aid of the Kiowa camp first, driven away the Apache attackers, and only now were riding to help us defend our trading post against a common enemy.

The prairie between the creeks had turned into a chaotic swirl of riders. Some of the Apaches had grown bold enough to attack the Comanche camp, though most had felt satisfied with slaughtering the drunken Kiowas. Now Comanche horsemen darted everywhere, attempting to recover captured women or children or horses, and driving away the Apaches, most of whom were now mounted and fleeing. Even on the slopes of the Canadian Breaks, far to the north, I could see riders scrambling.

Then, on a bluff overlooking the valley, I saw Snakehead. He was just sitting there on his horse, watching the battle that he had brought in his wake. Perhaps he had known the Apaches were coming. Perhaps he had even invited them.

"Kid!" Hatcher shouted. "Git back in the fort. Bar the gate."

My ears were still ringing from the cannon blast, but I heard Hatcher. I started to obey his order, but just then I heard a scream that would curdle anybody's blood, except maybe Snakehead's. To the northeast, across the big hump in the middle of the prairie, I saw an Apache warrior riding away from the Comanche camp with a captured girl. Somehow he had dodged Comanche lances and arrows and had ridden away with his prize. A quick glance told me I was the closest chance she had for salvation.

"Git in here, Kid!"

I heard Mr. Hatcher quite clearly, but even louder I heard the echo of his words from upstream, the day he killed the snake that had caught the frog. "You call for help, you want everybody to stand around and watch?"

I dug my heels into Fireball's ribs and slapped his rump with the flat blade of my saber, launching him like a cannon shot. A full gallop on a fleet steed always makes a rider's blood rise, but hurdling headlong, Indian-style, without saddle or bridle, into a hand-to-hand fight, can raise your hair and bring skin to a crawl. As I rode, I felt something building inside my chest until it grew too large to contain and erupted as a maniacal squall—a war whoop. Now Fireball miraculously gathered newfound velocity and closed on the Apache captor.

I began to think in a whirl. I could not use my saber for fear of striking the girl, so I sheathed it. I would have to wrestle the Apache from his horse. In this madness, the enemy warrior saw me coming only two seconds before I closed on his left. Using the natural momentum of Fireball's gallop, I rose, placing my left knee over Fireball's withers. With the next rise in my mount's gait, I leapt from his back, pushing away and flying from one horse to the next. Fireball had come to fight, and he rammed the enemy horse with teeth bared as I slammed into the Apache, butted his cheek with my forehead, and wrapped my arms around him.

The Apache, the Comanche girl, and I all hit the ground together. The landing took the wind out of all of us; but in our desperation, we all rolled and scrambled to our feet. I did not realize it just yet, for the dust had not cleared, but my rescue of the girl had thrust me into the center of the battle as Comanche riders came to carry the girl away to safety, and Apache raiders came to aid the warrior I had unhorsed.

An Indian would rather die than abandon a brother or sister. To turn his back on his own is to subject himself to a lifetime of scorn from his own people. Even his own family. For this reason, the violence of the entire skirmish now imploded on me. I drew my saber as my eyes locked onto the Apache's. He glanced at the scalp I wore on my belt, yanked a knife from a scabbard and ran at me, his ragged war cry tearing up from his chest and through his throat.

I saw this Apache's leg explode, and knew Hatcher had fired a shot to protect me. My attacker fell, but hoofbeats rumbled behind me. I felt horsemen everywhere. The nearest came at me with a lance. I pivoted to parry the blow, but a bullet struck my saber blade at this moment—a bullet that might otherwise have torn my chest open—and drove the tip of my weapon against my head, above the left eye, where I still wear the scar.

The blow staggered me, but knocked me just out of the way of the Apache lance. I landed on my back. Dazed, I glanced around. I saw an Apache warrior dragging the man Hatcher had wounded onto his horse. I saw my friend Kills Something much more effectively swinging the girl I had rescued onto the pinto's rump. I saw Fireball storm blindly through the whole fracas. I could hear Jibber barking somewhere in the distance.

Then I saw the Apache lance thrusting again at me and thought I had better get to my feet and fight. I struck the lance aside with my hilt. It cut my right shoulder and pinned my buckskins to the ground, but I writhed so violently that I tore my sleeve away from it. I rolled and came to my feet under a horse that kicked, at me, but missed. Gunshots erupted, and I felt the bullets pulling at my clothing like children trying to get my attention. And they got my attention, by God. A horse bumped me toward an Apache rider who took a swing at me with a war axe. I ducked it and countered with a thrust of my saber that stuck the warrior between the ribs, but only deep enough to provide him with a battle scar to flaunt around camp.

I found myself surrounded by four Apaches, all trying to stick me or chop me up with sharp things, and suddenly the training of my victim, the late Segarelli, remembered itself to every muscle I possessed and every morsel of composure I could muster. With precise defensive strokes, pointed advances, and blind backhanded sweeps, I carved out a perimeter no enemy cared to cross, and held it with my last particle of energy.

Now a moment of stunned silence fell among the Apaches, and all the violence and fear and glory and defiance that had crashed in on me seemed to explode against itself, as if I had dashed away the entire struggle with a single stroke of my saber. Riders scattered everywhere, fragmenting the battle into running skirmishes. I watched it fade from me as my heart pounded and my lungs ached for air. My saber felt as if it weighed fifty pounds as I forced it into its scabbard. Pulling my bow over my shoulder, I checked the bowstring and found it sound in spite of the fall I had taken. I notched an arrow, but found no target at which to shoot.

Stunned by the ferocity of the Comanche counterattack, the Apaches had tossed aside all their Kiowa captives and fled. But they got away with several horses and scalps, and the wailing was just now beginning to rise from the Kiowa camp.

I found myself standing alone in the open prairie. I had no idea where Fireball had gotten off to, but I saw Jibber running toward me from the fort. Pricks of pain began to remind me of my flesh wounds. Blood ran down my sleeve and dripped from the fingers hooked now around my bowstring.

After a while, I walked to the fort, Jibber wagging his tail at my heels, as if we had just had the time of our lives. Hatcher was throwing buckets of water on the smoldering gates when I dragged myself up. Only one dead Apache lay at the gate, and I reasoned that the other attackers wounded by the cannon must have crawled away or gotten picked up by warrior friends.

Kills Something came cantering over to the fort. "Who will take the scalp?" he said in Comanche.

Hatcher jutted his chin at me as he answered Kills Something in the same tongue. "He made the kill."

Kills Something looked at me briefly, then turned back to Hatcher. "That was my sister he saved."

This surprised me, for Kills Something had never spoken of siblings. Now he laughed, and spoke the only words of English I ever heard him utter:

"Him little, but him *plenty man.*"

That, in case you have wondered, is how I acquired my Indian name. I am Plenty Man.

THIRTY

I had two Apache scalps on my belt now and knew I had become a deeply hated enemy of that tribe. The Kiowas decided that The Crossing on the Canadian had gone bad, and they began to make preparations to move. The Kiowa women would pack their things awhile, then throw themselves on the ground and wail, then slash their arms and breasts with knives, then go back to packing.

The Comanches had not lost a single warrior and, in fact, had saved the day, so the mood in their camp was much more pleasant, though they, too, made preparations to depart. I gathered that the only real reason the Comanches had for moving on was the fact that their numerous horses had just about depleted the grazing around Fort Adobe.

As Hatcher and I worked on repairing the burned gate of Fort Adobe, Little Bluff came dragging over to our trading post. He had spent the entire battle unconscious in the timber, and had awakened to the wailing of his camp's women.

"We are going away," he said to me in Spanish. "My people are all sad and angry."

I looked straight at him, suddenly feeling angry, myself. "The whiskey is bad. You should not drink it anymore."

To my consternation, Little Bluff brushed the idea away

with an arrogant gesture. "The whiskey is not bad. The Apaches are bad. The whites are bad."

"Snakehead is white."

"He is good. He brings the firewater."

"He brings your enemies to slaughter you while you are all drunk."

"Easy, Kid," Hatcher said. I knew he couldn't understand much of what I was saying because I was speaking Spanish, but he understood my tone. "Don't try to force your thinkin' on a Kiowa."

"The whiskey gives me visions," Little Bluff said. "My visions say to raid the whites now. They are taking my country."

I could not argue with this, so I turned away from Little Bluff and went back to working on the gate. Later that afternoon, Kills Something herded twenty horses to the fort and asked me to open the gate. When I consented, he herded the horses into the fort.

"These are not our horses," I said.

"I give them to you for saving my sister," he said in the Comanche tongue.

"I helped your sister because I am a friend of the Comanche."

"I have plenty of horses," Kills Something said, seemingly insulted.

"You owe me nothing," I said.

"Just take the horses, Kid," Hatcher said to me in English, coming up behind me.

Gathering that I had come close to making some kind of diplomatic blunder, I said quickly, "They are fine horses, and I am happy to own them."

Kills Something looked down on me with a haughty grin. "My sister has no husband. Half as many horses will make a fine present to her family, father-of-my-nephews-not-born."

Shocked, I looked quickly at Hatcher.

He grimaced. "You're on your own with that one, son." He turned away hastily and left me to deal with Kills Something with only my poor, scattered wits to help me.

"My friend . . ." I said. "I . . . I . . . I do not know even know your sister's name."

I meant this as an argument that I could not possibly have feelings for a girl I didn't know, but Kills Something took it as a sign of interest.

"She is called 'Hidden Water,' for she was born at a camp where the water hides in a deep cave. You will like her. She will be good."

"But . . ." I stammered. "I do not know what to say."

Kills Something laughed heartily above the distant wailing of Kiowa women. "You will know." His beautiful pinto mount turned and loped away gracefully.

Sol Silver, who had heard the whole conversation, shut the gates to the fort and said, "You ain't gonna go Indian on us, are you, Greenwood?"

"No," I replied. And I sincerely meant it at the time.

❦

The next day, the Comanche band began to move south at dawn, passing right by the gates of the fort on the way to The Crossing. Hatcher, Silver, and I stood on the walkway and waved at the departing Indians. Shaved Head came to wish us blessings of the spirits, and we wished him and his people the same.

Then Kills Something doubled back from the head of the band, and I watched him ride in among the women and children. He singled out his sister, and ordered her with fierce and insistent gestures and words to ride along the right flank of the band, so she would pass directly under my gaze.

Thus I got my first good look at Kills Something's sister, Hidden Water. You must understand those times. A beautiful young woman in Indian attire could fetch the fascination of a young man raised in a city. Growing up, I had scarcely ever seen a woman's bare ankle. Hidden Water's leg was visible to me all the way up above her knee as she rode a fine cream-colored mare with a red blanket. And it was quite a graceful leg, lean and shapely. Her hips moved with the gait of the mare. The fringe of a beautiful deerskin blouse played all about her waist and arms. Delicate breasts lifted her bodice. She wore her hair longer than most Comanche women, and it brushed her shoulders in a shining black curtain.

Then she looked up at me. Her chin was narrow, her jaw straight and broad. Her cheeks strong and colored subtly with red paint. Her Comanche eyes were black, strong, and piercing. She smiled, then looked away. Then she looked at me again and made a gesture that meant, "Thank you."

Were I not still in love with Gabriela, I would have ridden south with the Comanches that very day. Even heartbroken, I felt a certain measure of desire for young Hidden Water, the Comanche beauty whom I had saved from enemies, and whom I knew I could have for the price of a few horses. It was maddeningly confusing. I stood and watched her ride away in all her pure and exotic perfection.

"There goes a damn good reason to turn Comanche," Sol Silver said.

"Don't prod him," Hatcher warned.

After Shaved Head's band disappeared, I stood on the walkway for quite a while. I loved my fort and my little piece of the valley here at The Crossing. But I felt a curious compulsion to just saddle a horse and ride somewhere. I was lost in a maelstrom of confusion and conflicting impulses. I longed for the lost love in Taos I knew I could never have. I desperately wanted a chance I knew I should not take with Hidden Water. I missed the society of cities and towns, but cherished the solitude of my outpost, and the exotic lures of a Comanche camp. I hated Snakehead, feared my fascination for battle. I knew that I only thought I understood the Indians.

John Hatcher sensed what I was going through. "Sol!" he shouted. "Kid Greenwood's been too long afield. Time we take him back to New Mexico a spell."

Sol raised a yell that was a half Mexican *grito*, half Comanche war whoop. "There is war fixin' to bust loose there, *amigos!* Let's take our horses to Bent's Fort and sell 'em to the army. Then we'll go conquer New Mexico with General Kearny!"

The Apaches had gotten away with Fireball after the battle at Fort Adobe, but he returned two days later. He was gaunt and tired from miles of running, but sound. We were packing our mules when he came splashing across Bent's Creek.

"Well, I'll be goddamned," Sol Silver said.

"You will be if you keep talkin' like that," Hatcher replied.

Fireball ran right up to me, looked at me with his one good eye, and rolled a rattling sigh from his nostrils, succinctly summing up the entire unpleasant experience. There wasn't much graze left around the fort for him to replenish himself on, so I hurried myself along with the packing chores so we could ride north and find some grass up on the plains.

We left the gates open and abandoned Fort Adobe that day. It wasn't easy. I did not care to leave the fruits of my labor to the elements, or to our enemies.

"The Indians might set fire to whatever will burn, Kid, but they don't have it in 'em to tear down that much adobe. It'll be here when we get back, and we'll bring a crew to rebuild whatever's tore down."

This relieved my worries. We were coming back. That was the important thing. Hatcher knew I loved that fort. I looked at Jibber, and he began skipping all around the mounts. He could sense from the activity that a great journey was at hand. Fireball fell in with the herd as we eased north. We had almost two hundred horses we had taken in trade from the Kiowas and Comanches since William Bent left us, along with twenty buffalo robes, two deerskins full of honey, and fifty pounds of dried buffalo meat. We would travel slowly enough to let the horses graze on the way to the Santa Fe Trail. There, we would hopefully encounter a trade caravan or soldiers who would lend protection against any Indians feeling hostile.

I was happy to be once again in the saddle and on the move. I worried a little about my fort, but even more about what was going on in New Mexico. Was there really going to be war? How would Gabriela fare? Would the conflict draw me in? Everything had become uncertain. But such is one's fate when one has the temerity to wake up in the morning.

THIRTY-ONE

When we struck the Santa Fe Trail, we found the obvious signs that a large body of mounted troops had preceded us, accompanied by at least ten thousand cattle, hundreds of horses, half a dozen cannon, and a thousand wagons. Hatcher rode along the edges of the trail the soldiers had left, to look for individual tracks by which to read the signs. The ground seemed to speak to Hatcher, for he could see back in time through marks left in dirt.

"The grass ain't quite reared back up yet where the hooves mashed it down. I'd say they're six days ahead of us. Big horses. American horses, by God. We'll find a campground in a couple of miles. These horses were tired. Steppin' short, draggin' their feet. Look there—one stumbled."

Before three miles had passed, we found an abandoned camp, just as Hatcher had predicted.

"How many of 'em you reckon there were, Kid Greenwood?"

I had already counted 142 campfires with a sweep of my eyes. I could imagine 10 or 12 men to each fire, so I made 11 the average. Multiplying 11 by 142, I came up with the figure 1,562. I did all this without trying, for my brain is always making such calculations whether I want it to or not. Not wanting to sound like some smart mouth by quoting such an exact number, I said, "Between fifteen and sixteen hundred, I guess."

Hatcher nodded. "Closer to seventeen, I'd say. Remember, for every fire, there's at least one soldier on picket duty."

I nodded. Even a genius sometimes misses the obvious.

"Well, there ain't but three of us," Sol Silver added. "I'd just as soon we found some timber to make our camp in. This is a naked place for three fools to camp. I know a good stand of trees about eight miles from here, and three miles south of the trail."

"That'll do," Hatcher said. "We'll build us a *kraal.*"

For the rest of the ride to Bent's Fort, we made camps in secluded places, and always went through the tiresome task of dragging up fallen timbers to stack as defensive enclosures. Hatcher was always exhaustively careful on the trail, and lived long because of it. We also took turns standing guard all night.

We overtook the troops without seeing hostile Indians. It seemed the large body of soldiers had frightened them away to other camps. We did encounter large gatherings of friendly Cheyennes, Arapahos, and Utes who had gone into camp near the soldiers. The army had established its camp a few miles downstream of Bent's Fort, and here we also found some four hundred merchant wagons whose owners were afraid to drive into Santa Fe. The numbers of soldiers and merchants stunned the Indians. They would walk or ride to the camps of the white men, and just stare all day. I recognized a Cheyenne named Big Bear Sleep, who spoke English pretty well, and asked him what he thought about the camps of the whites.

He was squatting in the shade of his pony looking out over the wagons. "They make a big tribe when they all come together," he said.

I started to tell Big Bear Sleep that there were many, many more white people in the world, but I didn't want him to think me a liar. Besides, it wasn't the Indian way to spout off like a know-it-all.

We rode on to Bent's Fort and herded our horses into the corral without loss of a single animal. Before the day was out, we would have them all sold to the army, but first we enjoyed a grand back-slapping reunion with our friends. Louis Lescot embraced me in the French way and asked all about the adobe fort I had built. Blue Wiggins roared with laughter at the way I had tied my long hair back and suggested I might as well stick an eagle feather in it if I was going to turn Indian. All the old voyagers were there, from Broken Hand Fitzpatrick to Uncle Dick Wootton to William Guerrier, who called himself "Old Bill Gary."

"Where's Kit?" I asked Louis.

"Still in California with Frémont. That is where the war is more likely to be bloody."

"How about Charles?"

"Charles is in Taos, at peril of his very life, trying to protect the company interests at the store on the plaza. If the locals side with the Mexican army in Taos, Charles will not have a chance."

"Do the Mexicans have as many troops in New Mexico as Kearny has here?"

"Who knows?"

"Has war actually been declared?" I asked.

"You bet it has," said Blue. "Two months ago, in May. There were battles on the Rio Grande in Texas. Now it's war to the end."

After giving us a couple of hours to converse with our friends, William summoned John Hatcher and me into the parlor. He asked us how the fort had fared, and Hatcher gave him a cursory account of the Apache raid as if it amounted to little more than a footnote in his violent and storied career. William paid us for the horses and robes we had brought in, and for our shares in the herd he had brought back months earlier. My share amounted to quite a weighty purse of American gold and Mexican silver. I was anxious to go down to the store inside the fort and spend some of it, but William asked me to stay after Hatcher had left.

"I've been made a colonel by General Kearny," he said bluntly. "I'm to form a small scouting party. The army is calling it a 'spy guard,' but I figure it's just a party of forward scouts. I want you to be in it."

"Why?" I asked.

"You talk Mexican. You've proven to be a pretty good hand."

"What will we do?"

"Hell if I know. Ride ahead of the army and git shot, more than likely."

I shook the pouch of gold and silver coins, enjoying the metallic chink they made. "Alright," I said. I was thinking of Gabriela. If I joined the Spy Guard, I could see that I would have a certain amount of liberty to move about the country unmolested—at least, by the American army. In that way, I could warn Gabriela if it looked like harm would come her way. "When are we going out?"

"Dawn. That's not much time to rest."

"I don't rest much, anyway."

"That's what I know. Be ready before daylight."

"Yes, sir."

As William had promised, we left the next day, August 2, 1846. General Kearny and his 1,700 troops took some time filing past Bent's Fort. Atop the fort, dozens of Mexican and Indian women lined up to watch the parade. The Spy Guard crossed the Arkansas first and rode ahead into unknown perils.

In the seven-man Spy Guard with me were Blue Wiggins, Louis Lescot, Sol Silver, Goddamn Murray, some fellow named Frank Blair and, of course, William Bent. As it turned out, we didn't do much, other than ride ahead of Kearny's column and scout the ground. On a couple of occasions, we detained small parties of Mexican civilians on burros and marched them into Kearny's camp for questioning. The first time we brought in five unarmed Mexicans riding on the rumps of their donkeys, which they guided by tapping them on their necks with sticks, Broken Hand Fitzpatrick almost hurt himself laughing at us, and he seldom laughed at all.

"Here's your goddamn terrible Mexican enemies!" Murray shouted at the regular American troops who had gathered to see the prisoners.

We gathered from our prisoners and from informants who voluntarily came in that the Mexican army, under General Armijo, had fortified Apache Canyon—the gateway to Santa Fe. A couple of days later, I volunteered to ride ahead with some Pueblo scouts. The Pueblos and I found that the Mexican army had abandoned the canyon and fled south. The gateway to Santa Fe was open.

On the evening of August 18, the Spy Guard led Kearny's army into Santa Fe without having fired a shot. This was my first visit to Santa Fe, and I found it squat and dusty, not nearly as appealing as San Fernandez de Taos. As the American flag went up over the ancient adobe Palace of the Governors, I sought out Colonel William Bent.

"Sir, I'd like to volunteer to ride ahead to Taos and scout things out there."

William Bent looked at me harshly, then softened his glare. He sighed, looked up at the flag, spit on the ground, and rubbed his own spit into the dirt with the toe of his boot. "Get something to eat first. I'm going to write a letter to my brother for you to carry with you."

I ate, and saddled a fresh horse, leaving Fireball with Blue Wiggins.

William came to me with the letter.

"Travel at night and lay up during the day. The moon's good right now. Light enough to ride, dark enough to hide. Be careful where you camp, like Hatcher and Silver showed you. Don't start no fires, Kid, not even for coffee. You don't know what kind of cutthroats might be on the prowl with this war in the air. Eat dried meat and hardtack, and get to

Taos quick as you can. Go straight to Charles. He'll tell you what to do next."

I stood there in silence for a few seconds to make sure he was finished.

"Well?" he said.

"I don't even drink coffee, Colonel Bent. I'll be just fine."

He grinned, gave me the letter, and shook my hand. I rode out of Santa Fe on the well-worn road to Taos. I had never ridden this road before, but it was unmistakable, pinched as it was between the Rio Grande and the Sangre de Cristo Mountains.

Anyway, you see quite clearly that I became a spy in the Mexican War because I was in love with a girl whom I could not possess, but whom I nevertheless intended to watch over as if she belonged to me.

THIRTY-TWO

I had been carrying dispatches in and out of Taos for the army and the Bent brothers for seventeen days when I finally got a glimpse of Gabriela. It was the time of morning when the sun rose high enough over the Sangre de Cristos to bathe Taos Plaza with the day's first hint of warmth. I rode Fireball into the plaza, as I had the first time I entered this old town, and saw Gabriela in almost precisely the place she had stood when first I saw her and simultaneously fell in love with her.

I wore my saber and quiver, just as before. I rode my one-eyed horse, followed by my bobtailed dog, just as before. Gabriela wore a red *rebozo* that, like her hair, played on the breeze, just as before. Yet many things had changed. My hair was longer, my buckskins and my face more weathered. And Gabriela was even more beautiful, more shapely, more elegant. And now she carried a child in her arms.

When she saw me, she stopped and gasped, then gave me a wonderful smile that melted away quickly. Her eyes seared into my heart like lightning bolts. Boldly, I went out of my way to ride past her.

"*Hola,* Gabriela."

"Hello, *amor,*" she replied.

This amazed me, that she would refer to me so affectionately, and it sent my insides into a whirlwind, from my brain to my stomach.

"My God, you are beautiful," I said.

She was about to respond when a woman stepped out of a nearby store and saw us talking. Gabriela shifted the sleeping child in her arms, and pointed across the plaza, as if she were giving me directions or something. "We cannot talk here," she said. "I will get a message to you."

I looked in the direction she had pointed—toward the Bent and St. Vrain Co. Store—tipped my hat, and rode away around a stomach full of butterflies.

Three days later, at the home of Charles Bent, Charles's stepdaughter Rumalda Boggs, came for a visit with her husband, Tom Boggs. We sat around the parlor and talked; then I played a few violin tunes at Charles's request.

After my fourth selection, Tom Boggs applauded and stood up. "That's good, Orn'ry. Now let's walk down to the plaza and see what's going on. The air feels pretty fine tonight."

I agreed, put my violin away, and grabbed my coat of gray wool, for the September nights had turned chilly in the high country. We went outside, looked both ways for trouble, then turned toward the plaza.

"I hear you joined the Spy Guard," Tom said.

I shrugged. "I'm a glorified courier."

He chuckled. "Me, too. They've got me carrying mail and military dispatches across the plains to St. Louis. I thought I had rid some till this war started."

"They've only got me making short runs to Santa Fe, or wherever General Kearny is camped."

"Where's Kearny now?"

"He was at the Zuni Pueblo last I saw him, but he's probably back in Santa Fe by now."

"Well, I know you're careful out there on the trail," Tom said, pausing to light a crooked little Mexican cigar with a match he struck on the adobe wall. "I just wonder why you're so all-fired foolish when you're here in town."

"Beg you pardon?" I said.

Tom put his matches away in his pocket, and from the same pocket drew a sealed envelope. He handed it to me. "Put that away till you're alone."

"Orders?" I said.

He began to chuckle. "Hell, no, that's a letter from Gabriela Zavaleta. If her husband knew I just handed it to you, he might have both of us hunted down and gutted alive. I don't even want to think about what her father would do to us."

"Gabriela?" I said.

"You don't have to play dumb with me, Orn'ry, Rumalda tells me everything."

I concealed the letter in my coat pocket, anxious to be alone so I could read it. "Thanks," I said.

"Don't push your luck, Orn'ry. This town is fixin' to explode with war fever as it is. Some of Santa Anna's old loyalists are embarrassed as hell that Kearny waltzed into New Mexico without a fight and conquered 'em. They're itchin' to kill a *gringo* or two. A white man fool enough to dally with somebody else's *señora* right now might light the fuse on the whole miserable town."

"I hadn't thought of it that way," I admitted.

He chuckled. "I know damn good and well what you're thinkin' about. You need to get out of this town and get your mind on another girl."

I could see that he was right, and I felt very selfish for even having the gall to walk the streets of Taos at that moment. "I only came here to protect her if the war broke out."

"Well, the war's all but over here, unless some fool stirs something up. I'd advise you not to be that fool."

I nodded, and we arrived at the plaza.

"Somebody saw you and Gabriela talking over there in the street one day," Tom said, pointing to the place where I had spoken to Gabriela. "It's a small town. You can't get away with a fart here that somebody doesn't smell."

I nodded seriously; then Tom elbowed me into laughter with him.

"Can't get away with a fart," he repeated. "Well, we've seen the plaza. Let's go back to Charles's house."

I agreed, and we returned the way we had come. Tom asked me about my experiences at Fort Adobe. We stood in the street outside of Charles's house for some time while he listened to my tales and smoked his cigar.

"I hope I get the chance to see your fort someday," he said, and I was honored that he called it *my* fort.

"I guess I ought to get back there as soon as possible," I replied. "It's a long way from the temptations of Taos."

"I'd say you belong there." He dropped the butt of his cigar and ground it into the dirt with his toe. "Are you coming back inside to play that fiddle some more?"

"It's late. I'll just turn in. Charles loaned me some books. It's been a while since I had reading material."

"I know what you aim to read, Orn'ry. Good night."

I went down to the next door and entered the small adobe house I had rented. It opened onto the street, and also had a back door facing the creek. It shared a wall with Charles's house, so I was always near at hand when a message had to be carried to William, or to General Kearny. In the dark, I found my flint and the little metal tube crammed with twisted cotton. I had learned how to make fire this way by watching the Mexicans in Taos light their smokes. I pulled a little cotton from the tube, held it between the fingers of my cupped hand, and struck the flint under the tuft of cotton. The spark from the flint ignited the cotton, which burned long enough for me to light my candle. Pulling up a chair, I opened the envelope from Gabriela, and read her words.

The brief note tantalized me with desire. It started, *"Mi*

Amor . . . My love . . . I must see you. Rumalda will tell you
when and where."

<hr />

Two days later, while I was sorting a new shipment of goods
at the Bent and St. Vrain store on the plaza, Rumalda
brought her father and I some lunch. While we were eating,
a customer came to purchase coffee, and Rumalda and I
were left alone briefly.

"Tonight," she whispered. "I will bring Gabriela to your
house. We will come in the back door."

Before I could ask any questions, Charles was calling for
me to fetch a sack of coffee beans from the back of the
store. When I came back with the coffee, Rumalda was already gone.

That very afternoon, a young Mexican gentleman came
to the store. He wore spurs with rowels the size of double
eagles, flared leather riding pants with a matching jacket,
and a sombrero resplendent with gold embroidery. I heard
his horse pawing the ground outside.

"Well, good afternoon, Mariano," said Charles.

From this greeting, I knew that the young man had to be
Mariano Zavaleta, the husband of the woman with whom I
was in love.

"Honoré, have you met *Señor* Zavaleta?"

I thought Charles quite devious to introduce me to Mariano in this way at the time, but later appreciated what he
was trying to do.

Mariano looked right at me, smiled with one side of his
mouth, came to attention as if he were a *capitán* in the army,
and thrust his hand out toward me.

I shook his hand and said, "Honoré Greenwood," quite
dryly. "Pleasure to meet you."

"The pleasure is mine," he said in perfect English, laced
with a heavy Mexican accent. "I welcome you to San Fernandez de Taos."

"Mariano is the owner of the Zavaleta Grant," Charles

said, "but he is best known for being married to the most beautiful woman in New Mexico."

Mariano swelled up like a poisoned pup, pride beaming from his eyes.

"I remember hearing something about the wedding, last time I was here," I said.

"So, you are not so new to San Fernandez," Mariano said.

I was somewhat amused that Mariano didn't even know who I was. "I used to work in the adobe yards." I thought this comment might cause Mariano to look down on me as a peon, but he only nodded, as if in approval.

"How long do you intend to stay?"

"Honoré is one of the best traders we have out on the plains," Charles said. "He speaks Comanche. Trades with them in a fort William and I had him build. He won't be around town long."

"A pity," Mariano said. "Even so, you must promise to pay a visit to my *hacienda* before you leave Taos for the plains."

"Oh, I don't know," I said. I could tell Mariano did not possess the faintest clue that I loved his wife, or that I was going to meet her secretly this very night. Worse yet, I couldn't help but like him.

Mariano feigned insult. "My friend, do you brush off my hospitality so easily?"

"What Honoré means," Charles interjected, "is that he is a very important link between me and William—and between Taos and the army. He is my chief courier and must remain constantly at the ready for a hard ride."

Now Mariano looked at me with a touch more respect. "All the more reason that he should visit my *hacienda* as an honored guest. More to the point, I know that I can speak freely in the presence of Señor Greenwood, no?"

Charles glanced toward the front door of the store. "Absolutely."

"Good." Mariano's friendly conversational tone shifted in that one word to a much more serious mood. "There has been much talk around town, Carlos. I have heard that General Kearny plans to make you the governor of *Nuevo Mexico*."

"That hasn't been decided yet, but the general has suggested it. He believes New Mexico will remain quiet, and he wants to take his troops on to California."

This was the first I had heard of Charles's becoming governor, but I suspected I had carried the dispatches that made the arrangements.

Mariano nodded. "You are the obvious choice for governor. You have the full support of those of us who have been friendly to the Americans from the start. However, you should be aware that there are still plenty of Santa Anna's old loyalists around."

"I thought most of them retreated with Governor Armijo."

"There are still enough here to cause trouble. Mostly drunks and thieves. And, Carlos, I heard something . . ." He glanced at me, as if unsure whether or not he should continue in my presence.

"Go ahead. Mr. Greenwood is most loyal."

Mariano smiled at me briefly, as if to welcome me into the world of intrigue. "I employ a couple of Taos Indian men in my stables. Young men, maybe nineteen or twenty. This morning, I woke early, slipped out of bed while Gabriela was sleeping . . ."

(This made me cringe with envy.)

". . . and went out to the stables to take an early ride into the mountains to check on the flocks. As I entered the stables, I heard a voice strange to me, so I stole ahead quietly. I saw a lantern light in the saddle room, where the voices were coming from. I slipped into an empty stall and looked carefully into the saddle room. I saw a man talking to my two Pueblo stable boys. I recognized him as a local cutthroat named Guadalupe Juarez."

Charles nodded. "I know the man."

"And he knows you. As I listened, I gathered that they were conspiring to rebel against the Americans. They said, in particular, that the new governor would have to be murdered. Juarez said he hoped the new governor would be

Charles Bent, so that he could kill you personally. They were drinking tequila, or maybe some of that Taos Lighting, so perhaps it was just a drunken boast."

"Perhaps not," Charles said. "Lupe Juarez has threatened me before. Never to my face, but his threats always find their way to me. I don't know what I ever did to him, but he hates my guts. Maybe just because I'm American."

"I wanted to confront him," Mariano said. "The man had no business on my *hacienda* in the first place. But then I thought I had better keep quiet until we found out how many cutthroats might be involved. Juarez talked about a great many men ready to fight, and the Pueblos said they could muster one hundred or more braves. I was furious that they were using my stables to conspire against my friends, but I thought it better to let them think they had not been discovered."

"I'm glad you did. Now we have the advantage over them," Charles said.

"What will you do?"

"As soon as I'm made governor, I'll have Lupe Juarez arrested based on your testimony. He'll get a fair trial, and the courts can decide what to do with him."

"I will gladly testify."

"With your permission, I'll also arrest your Pueblo stable boys as conspirators. They probably aren't guilty of much, but they can give us a lot of information on who else is involved."

"I grant you that permission, of course."

Charles patted Mariano on the shoulder. "We'll get to the bottom of this, *amigo*. I thank God you are on the side of peace and the law."

"And democracy," Mariano said. "Always."

"Especially democracy," Charles agreed.

"Now, I had better purchase something. I think I am being followed. Even if not, this little village has many eyes."

"You've probably just saved my life, Mariano. I don't think you need to purchase anything. But take something

from the store to make it look like you came here simply
to trade."

"Perhaps something for Gabriela." He looked around the
store.

At this point, I excused myself. I did not intend to let
Charles maneuver me into helping Mariano find a gift for
his wife. I walked out of the store, Jibber falling in behind
me, and strode aimlessly through the streets of Taos. I found
myself at the Bent stables, where Fireball stood and feasted
on oats and hay and rested between courier runs.

I brushed Fireball awhile, and meticulously straightened
tangles in his mane and tail. He seemed to appreciate the
attention. After grooming my mount, I fetched a sheet of
paper I kept in the stables, and with a quill pen and some
ink, made a few additions to the map of northern New Mexico that I had begun to draw strictly for my own entertainment and from my own observations. I have always
possessed my own mental compass and an unerring ability
to judge distances. These attributes allowed me to chart,
quite accurately, the roads and trails upon which I had ridden from Bent's Fort, to Taos, to Santa Fe, and to various
pueblos. I managed to occupy a couple of hours sketching
and mapping, but my mind was really on Gabriela, and my
meeting with her tonight.

Logic told me I should leave Taos. I loved Gabriela. I did
not wish to bring any scandal down around her graceful
shoulders. I vowed, in fact, that I would leave as soon as
possible to prevent any embarrassment or shame to her. My
heart yearned to beat next to hers, yet I knew enough about
honor to realize that I had to distance myself in spite of my
desires—desires that reached limits not even I could measure. I would leave Taos just as soon as the army moved
on and I was no longer needed as a courier. I would go back
to the plains. To my fort at The Crossing. I would prove
my love for Gabriela with this act of self-sacrifice. I would
explain all of this to her tonight.

The hour finally came. I was lying on my pallet in my adobe room, reading a book of poetry by Alfred Lord Tennyson. I turned to the poem *Ulysses*:

> Much have I seen and known—cities of men,
> And manners, climates, councils, governments,
> Myself not least, but honored of them all—
> And drunk delight of battle with my peers,
> Far on the ringing plains of windy Troy.
> I am part of all that I have met;
> Yet all experience is an arch wherethrough
> Gleams that untraveled world . . .

I have the ability to detach my emotional mind from my intellectual mind; so, while my brain absorbed the printed text my eyes scanned, yet my heart could not help anticipating Gabriela's arrival.

Would she really come? Had something gone wrong? Why wasn't she here yet? What would she say when she got here? How should I behave? Should I touch her? Hold her? Kiss her?

The tapping came so lightly that I thought it might be a gust of wind rattling the door. Still, I sprang up and lifted the hammered iron latch bolted to the pine planks. Carefully, I peered outside, and found Gabriela there, cradling a bundle of blankets in her arms.

I had not thought about her bringing her child, yet realized that she must have had no choice.

Rumalda stood behind her, and all but pushed her into my room. "Hurry," she said. "We do not have long."

Gabriela entered my adobe room and stood staring at me. My Lord, she looked beautiful in the candlelight, and I felt enthralled merely to be alone with her. The moment became everything in life to me, and I knew a fleeting sense of complete contentment.

"I am supposed to be trying on a dress in Rumalda's room," she said. "I cannot stay long without arousing suspicion."

"There's no back door to Charles's house. How did you get out?"

"Through the window." She glanced at my pallet on the floor, raised the bundled child in her arms and said, "May I?"

"Of course," I replied, and I stepped aside so she could lay her sleeping child on the mattress.

When she rose, she turned and came straight to me. I did not resist her embrace. I felt her breath against my neck and wrapped my arms around her tightly. She squeezed me back with a strength I had forgotten she possessed. When we eased apart, I lowered my face to hers and she did not resist my kiss.

"My God!" she said. "Only you can do that."

"If only I could—"

"Quiet, amor. It is beyond us both. If things could be different . . . You must know that I love you."

"And you must remember that I love you, Gabriela. Even when I am gone. You are always in my heart." I felt the lilt and timbre of Tennyson's poetry coming out in my speech.

She sighed and fell against me. "There is not much time," she said. "I have to tell you something. Something difficult. But wonderful, Honoré."

"Just to hear you say my name is wonderful enough."

She shook her head. "Listen. My child was born less than nine months after my wedding day. There is a chance he is your son, Honoré."

I stood transfixed in absolute shock. I looked toward the bundle of blankets on the bed. "Good heavens," was the only thing I could think of to say. The import of her revelation dropped on me like a wagonload of adobe bricks.

Gabriela knelt, and pulled the corners of the blankets back ever so gingerly. She revealed a studious little face, brow gathered as if in perfect concentration of some grand dream. The baby boy looked very much like Gabriela. He was too beautiful to be my son. I knelt over him, smelled the sweet, musky baby smell that rose from him, and touched my lips to his cheek so lightly that he did not even stir. Then I fell back on my heels and smiled in tremulous fascination.

Gabriela knelt beside me and cupped her warm palm on my shoulder. She leaned against me with a wonderful familiarity and seemed to fit every contour of my anatomy she touched. "Perhaps I should not have told you," she said. "I have mentioned this to no one else. Not even Rumalda. Everyone is sure he is Mariano's child. Especially Mariano."

"I met your husband today."

"I know. My God, he came home and spoke of you. I almost died of panic. He said he had invited you to the *hacienda,* and that I should tell the servants to expect your visit."

"To hear him speak of you made me so jealous that I thought I would explode. Yet . . . I found him very likable. God, it was strange."

She turned to face me, and pulled her own steaming body all around mine and touched my face with her palm. "Listen, amor. He is a good man. He will make a fine father. But he does not look at me the way you do. He does not touch me like you. He can never make me feel the way you moved me that night. That is only for you and me."

From outside, Rumalda rapped on the door, and I knew my time with Gabriela was almost over. I did not want to let her go. I wanted to pull her into my bed and gaze into her eyes and kiss her and whisper poetry to her all night. It was all I could do to engage the rational side of my brain and make the moment easier for the woman I loved.

I picked up the child and rose to my feet. I walked to the door and handed the infant to his mother. "What is his name?"

"Julio."

Rumalda was rattling the door.

"I love you, Gabriela. I know you have to go."

"Te amo, amor. This is not the last time I will see you."

"I have to leave. For you. For Julio."

She nodded. "Before you leave, I will see you again. Rumalda will tell you when."

I kissed her lips and wrapped my hand around the back

of her neck, tangling my fingers momentarily in her hair. Then I pulled my lips away from hers and opened the door. I passed her and Julio to Rumalda, who spirited them hastily away. They went around a corner to crawl back into Rumalda's window, and I shut the door.

I collapsed on my pallet, and felt the warmth of the place where the child—perhaps my son—had lain sleeping. I stared at the candle flame as I spoke to myself aloud, saying, "If that is my son . . . this changes things. . . ."

Genius that I am!

THIRTY-THREE

Imagine my torment. I know that in your life you have felt injustice, a lack of control over your circumstances. You have felt the wrongs of your own society heaped upon you. My lot was the same as yours. Gabriela's arranged marriage to a man she could not refuse, according to the customs and edicts of her upbringing, now kept me away not only from her, but possibly from my own flesh and blood in the form of a beautiful child. Yes, it seemed Mariano Zavaleta was a good enough man, but think of how my own son could benefit from me and only me. I was a bloody genius, for God's sake. I knew a thing or two.

Then, again, perhaps he was not my son at all, and I should have known better than to fall for a woman promised to someone else.

For many days, I brooded over the unfairness of it all, my only joy coming in the courier runs I would make between Taos and Bent's Fort, Taos and Santa Fe. By this time, General Kearny had publicly proclaimed Charles Bent provisional governor of New Mexico, and marched his troops to California. The general actually tried to persuade me to go with him, but I was more interested in my adobe fort on the Canadian River than I was in carrying someone else's war to the Pacific Ocean. Charles spent most of his time in Santa Fe now, taking care of territorial business. I was his only link with his private enterprise in Taos and Bent's Fort, and I helped keep things running as smoothly as possible in his absence. Just before Christmas, the plot that Gabriela's husband had helped infiltrate was exposed. Three of the conspirators were arrested, though two others got away.

Duty kept Charles away from his family on Christmas Day, 1846, but I rode down to Santa Fe through ice and snow, carrying a few Yuletide trinkets for the Bent family. Charles thanked me and asked me to walk with him from the Palace of the Governors, across Santa Fe Plaza, to the Bent and St. Vrain Store. He said he wanted to gather some smoked oysters, blackstrap molasses, some caviar, jars of jelly, and some cigars for a celebration he had planned for the next day in the palace. After collecting the goods, he made a small fire in the fireplace and pulled up a couple of chairs so we could roast our shins at the hearth. He gave me a cigar and a snifter of brandy—not because I wanted them, but because he did.

"Let's sit here for a while," he said. "It's quiet."

I sat beside the governor, holding my cigar and brandy, and staring into the fire. I said nothing. A young man whose heart is lost to impossible love does not make brilliant conversation.

"Honoré, what do you expect to do with yourself now that the general has ridden west?"

I sighed as big as a horse. "I want to go back to Fort Adobe and reestablish the Comanche trade for the winter."

Charles stroked his chin in a very gubernatorial manner and considered my proposal for a few seconds. "What does William say?"

"He wants me to go. He's going himself, in February. He says the trade for horses is only going to increase after the war opens up California to immigrants."

"I was thinking of asking you to serve as my aide, but you would probably be less of a danger to New Mexico out there on the Canadian." He grinned at me a little. I always wondered exactly how much Charles knew.

I smiled back. "Yes, sir." I pretended to sip the brandy, though I didn't care much for liquor. I did enjoy the smell. I had no intention of lighting the cigar at all.

"What's it like out there on the Canadian?" he asked.

I looked at Charles and caught a glimmer of something forlorn in his eyes. Here was a voyager of the old trails now pressed into service in an international struggle beyond his control. I knew that when spring came, he would be dreaming of throwing a caravan on the Santa Fe Trail. That was not going to happen for Charles this year. He had risen to the rank of governor, and fate had other things in store for him.

I whistled a few notes from *The Marriage of Figaro* and watched images in the flames. "It's a place where things come together," I said.

"What do you mean?"

"There are two breaks in the canyon, one to either side. Two tributaries that afford an easy ascent. The Crossing. Men and buffalo migrate there without a signpost or trail marker. They just come. The breaks gather rainwater, and the water gathers timber. The timber gathers game. You should see the tracks, Charles. Everywhere, like hieroglyphics for the hunters to decipher. And the grass. It tickles your palms. Tickles your horse's belly."

Charles had been lighting his cigar very methodically all this time, using a brand from the fire, and now paused to watch the smoke rise. He took a sip of brandy and asked a question I never would have predicted: "What does it *sound* like there?"

I looked at the firelight through my brandy, appreciating the fine amber hue of the drink, and smiled with one side of my mouth. "The panther screams. The crane flutes. The swan trumpets. The turkey gobbles. It's loud when the storm breaks or Indians attack. But on a still day, when not even the leaves rustle, I swear you can hear the worms below the sod. You can hear a pony snort a mile away. No, three miles away. It can get that quiet there."

"What does William think about it?"

"He calls it a right strong fort."

"Not the fort, the *place.*"

"You and William look at things differently. You see the larger picture, Charles. The commerce, the international intrigue. But William sees a picture that is . . . Well, that is larger yet. One painted a thousand generations ago. He can see the plains before the horse came. I swear he can. He knows what it was like, somehow. He sees The Crossing in those terms. He knows it is a powerful place."

"My brother's gone Indian."

"No." I shook my head and held the cigar before my eyes. I did not intend to smoke it, but I admired the way some hand had rolled it, smooth, solid, and tight. "He moves among the Indians with an ease I wish I possessed, but he has not gone Indian and knows he can't, as sure as I know I can't. William remembers where he came from. He's more interested in all of these political maneuverings than he lets on. He grills me pretty thoroughly about what's going on down here when I go to the fort."

Charles smiled. "I miss my brother lately. We started all this together. It was more than one man could have taken on, so we divvied up the chores. I handled the Santa Fe trade, and he took the Indian trade at Bent's Fort. He loves that fort. And the Indians. He took to them, and they to him like old kinfolk or something. William Bent has prevented more bloodshed than all the diplomats in American history. The tribes are at peace because of his influence. People don't realize that."

"And you?"

Charles dipped the butt of his cigar into his brandy and enjoyed a pull of both. "I fell in love with Ignacia and New Mexico. If not for those damn Texans, we could have avoided this war and enjoyed a lively trade." Smoke was trailing out of his mouth as he shrugged. "Maybe not. I understand less of this international diplomacy than you think, Honoré. I don't really care whose flag flies over the Palace of the Governors. I only want to keep the peace here. We have avoided shedding the blood of New Mexicans so far in this war, and I intend to do everything in my power to keep it that way."

"Now that you've got Guadalupe Juarez and the other conspirators in jail, maybe the peace will hold."

"I hope so. Thank God the soldiers took Juarez and the others without too much trouble. But Archuleta and Ortiz are still at large. There could be other schemers out there, as well. I suspect my old enemy, Padre Martinez, but can't pin anything on him."

"What will happen to those who got caught?"

"They'll get a fair trial. Could be the courts will look on their plot as an act of war. If so, they could be pardoned and allowed to go south to Mexico or take the oath of allegiance to the United States. Then again, they could be proven guilty of treason and hanged as spies. It's a distasteful business, Honoré. I'd rather be cussing mules on the trail."

"I'd rather be ducking arrows at Fort Adobe."

Charles chuckled, threw back the last of his brandy, and clenched his cigar in his teeth. "You're lucky. You're going where you want to go. I have to stay here and be a governor. Beware of political aspirations, my friend. Avoid them like prairie-dog holes."

We stood, gathered our Christmas goods, and started back to the Palace of the Governors. This was the last private conversation I would ever have with Charles Bent, a great leader and a fine gentleman.

THIRTY-FOUR

Charles Bent and Kit Carson were brothers-in-law. Their wives were sisters. Charles's wife was born Ignacia Jaramillo. Her younger sister, Josefa Jaramillo, married Kit. Both were fine ladies born of a leading Taos family. I had known Mrs. Bent ever since Charles first brought me to Taos, but after the war with Mexico began, I became just as well acquainted with Mrs. Carson.

Josefa Carson would seek me out after my courier rides to ask whether I had heard any news of her husband. I occasionally caught wind of what Kit was up to in California from General Kearny or Governor Bent, and I would pass these morsels of information along to Josefa. Once, I had the honor of carrying an actual letter from Kit to his wife. The letter was given to me by Governor Bent. I went to the Carson home in Taos that day to deliver the letter. From the moment I handed it to her, she would treat me always as if I were her own brother, for she wasn't much older than me.

Because they were sisters, and both their American husbands were away, Mrs. Carson and Mrs. Bent spent much time together in Taos while I was there, and often asked me to run errands for them, which I always did cheerfully. In return, they doted on me, treating me with such motherly and sisterly kindness that I felt like an adopted member of their family. Rumalda Boggs and I also knew a close friendship, of course. I was still in my teens, and the affection these three women lavished on me made a great difference in my life. My own mother, who never knew what became of me, had never treated me with such love. I would have given my life for any of these women. As it turned out, I almost did.

In January 1847, I rode to Bent's Fort with dispatches from Charles to William. Charles was to ride from Santa Fe to Taos about the middle of the month to visit his family, and I was to meet him back there on or about the twentieth to deliver correspondences from William.

I rode all night on the last leg of my journey, arriving at San Fernandez de Taos before dawn. I was cold and tired and, for once, ready to sleep. I hadn't slept in two days, which wasn't altogether unusual for me, but the moon was waning, and I knew I might begin to fall victim to one of my strange trances if I didn't get some rest.

As I rode into town, I heard a commotion unusual for the predawn hour. Voices shouted near the town jail. The sounds of the voices made Jibber growl, and he had good instincts for trouble, so I rode cautiously toward the jail to investigate. From the moment I peered around the corner to see the jail, things happened so quickly that I could do nothing but watch in horror. The town prefect, Cornelio Vigil, was standing at the door of the Taos jail, shouting at a mob of drunken Pueblo Indians. The sheriff, Steve Lee, stood by his side, looking much more nervous than Vigil. Later, I would find out that Sheriff Lee, who was an American appointee, had jailed three Pueblo Indians suspected of theft the day before. Now the Pueblo mob, incited by some Mexican malcontents and further influenced by liquor, had marched to the jail to demand the release of the prisoners. Many of the drunks in the crowd were Pueblo braves whom Guadalupe Juarez had recruited to overthrow the provisional American government before he, himself, had been jailed in Santa Fe as a conspirator.

I remember the scene perfectly. The moment I peeked around the corner, the mob was closing in on the jail like a pack of wolves moving in on a kill. Sheriff Steve Lee looked as though he had been awakened, for his shirttail was hanging out, and he was hatless, with his hair mussed like a bird's nest. He held aloft a lantern that made him squint.

The appointed prefect of Taos, a respected Mexican named Cornelio Vigil, seemed defiant and completely unafraid of the drunken Pueblos. Over their threatening taunts, I heard him shout in Spanish at the Pueblo mob, "Now, you bunch of thieves and drunken scoundrels had better get back to your pueblo before I whip every one of you! You are not going to get *anyone* out of this jail tonight!"

This act of bravery might have stopped a reasonable crowd, but the Pueblos were drunk beyond reason. The silent standoff that followed Vigil's shouts lasted only a moment and ended when a war whoop rose from the middle of the mob. Then the entire body of drunken Indians surged forward, knife blades and metal arrow points glinting in the lantern light.

"No! Alto!" I yelled, but my voice was lost under the battle cries.

Poor Vigil didn't have a prayer against so many attackers. He went down almost immediately, and the Pueblos hacked at his body as if he were a rattlesnake, literally chopping and cutting him into small pieces. I never heard him cry out, but the screaming of the Indians was so loud. I could see Vigil's blood dripping from blades that rose only to strike again.

Steve Lee fought his way aside by swinging the lantern he held. A knife slashed his arm and he dropped the lantern. In a most gymnastic maneuver, he managed to grab an overhead beam and scramble onto the roof of the jail, though he caught two arrows in his back doing so.

All this happened in no more than fifteen seconds, and I was powerless to do anything about it. But when Lee climbed the jailhouse, I spurred Fireball into the street so that I could ride around the side of the jail, and perhaps carry the sheriff away from the mob, should he be able to jump from the roof. As I rode around the mob, Jibber actually attacked a couple of the Pueblo Indians, biting their heels and then retreating before they could strike at him. I hadn't gotten halfway around the jailhouse before I heard

Sheriff Lee screaming. Then I saw Indians on the roof, and knew that Lee would suffer the same fate as Vigil.

A war whoop rose from the bloodletting, and the mob somehow grew in number. They broke into the jail and released the prisoners. It seemed the Mexican malcontents who had incited the riot had been watching from their hiding places, but now joined the mob, and goaded it on to more killing.

"Kill all the Americans!" someone shouted. "Kill Carlos Bent!"

With this, the mob moved as one, like a flock of blackbirds, toward Charles's house. I couldn't see the murderers because I was around the side of the jail, but I heard them run down the dirt street. I whistled for Jibber and rode Fireball down an alley, through a ditch, and around a row of adobe hovels, trying to get to the back of the Bents' home before the murderers reached the front. I came to a low mud wall, which I made Fireball jump, then galloped into a grove of trees where I sometimes left my horse tied. I jumped off him and commanded Jibber to stay, then ran down a narrow footpath that wound between the adobes.

I rushed across the Bents' small private courtyard and reached my own back door about the time the mob attacked the front door of Charles's house. My first thought was to climb into the back window of the Bent home, but the murderers were surrounding the place now and would shoot me if I tried, so I ducked unseen into my own room and listened, trying to figure out what to do.

I heard Charles's muffled voice shout, "Now, now, if there's a problem, we will deal with it peaceably."

After that, I heard only bowstrings and battle cries. I looked at the adobe wall between my room and the Bents' house. I knew which room stood on the other side of that wall. Charles's and Ignacia's bedroom. I knew how thick the wall was. I knew it was made of adobe. I knew from what I had seen at the jail that all the Bents were in the worst peril.

I picked up my iron fireplace poker, and began flailing

madly at the sunbaked bricks. The sharp point of the poker sent spray after spray of dirt into my room, and made headway through the wall quicker than I expected. I paused once for an extra breath, and to judge the sound of the mob, then heard someone chipping away at the opposite side of the wall. Someone in the Bent home had heard my efforts to get to them, and was helping from that side. Encouraged, I tunneled away with new vigor.

In another minute, my fireplace poker went all the way through. The moment it did, I heard Mrs. Bent scream, "Carlos!" with such terror that I knew the mob must have broken in. A brass candlestick jabbed through at me, and I recognized Rumalda widening the hole from her side of the wall. I heard shots fire, more screaming, drunken howls. Quickly, we knocked a few adobes out of the wall. I didn't think the hole was big enough to crawl through, but Rumalda came through anyway, her eyes crazed with fear.

Behind her came ten-year-old Alfredo Bent, then four-year-old Teresina Bent. Josefa Carson came through next, followed by Ignacia Bent.

"Carlos!" she yelled. "Come!"

Now, Charles's bloody head came through the hole. A gash in his cheek gushed blood—a wound I knew had been made by an arrow he had pulled out of his face. As he crawled through, I grabbed him and dragged him into my room with Rumalda's help. He held his stomach with bloody fingers, and I knew he had been badly wounded. He tried to rise, but fell, pulling Rumalda down on the floor with him. She cradled him there. Through the escape hole, I heard a wooden door splinter, a windowpane shatter, more bloodthirsty screams.

I stooped over to pick Charles up, and I heard him whisper, "Get them out, Kid." My eyes locked with his, and I knew it was an order.

I grabbed Rumalda and forcibly lifted her from the floor. I started grabbing blankets and tossed them at Rumalda, her mother, and her aunt. "Wear these like Pueblo women!" I ordered. "One around your shoulders, and one over your head." I drew my bow from its case to complete the deception that we were Indians.

The shouting voices in Charles's house came closer to the hole we had broken in the wall. I cracked the back door and peeked out. To my amazement, I found that the Indians who had been guarding the rear of the Bent house had disappeared. In the chaos, they must have run around to the front when they heard the war cries of those who had broken in.

"Follow me," I said. "Everyone. Mrs. Bent, get your husband on his feet."

I heard shouts and screaming through the hole in the wall and realized that the mob had discovered the escape route. Footsteps thumped on the dirt roof, raining dust down from the ceiling. I flung my back door open and pulled Rumalda out behind me. Glancing back, I saw Charles rising with his wife's help, and knew I must lead the escape now, or we might all be killed.

I stepped out, keeping close to the wall of my house, and skirting the courtyard. I looked back to see Josefa Carson trailing Rumalda, and assumed the rest of the party would follow. Suddenly, a Pueblo warrior dropped in front of me. I think he was as surprised to see me as I was to see him, for he had jumped blindly from the roof. Ululating war cries seemed to come from everywhere. My blade was not in position to strike, but my hilt was, so I slammed it into the warrior's nose, knocking him unconscious. I jumped over the Pueblo and led Rumalda around a corner. Josefa followed, but there was no one behind her.

"Where are the others?"

"Ignacia turned back," Josefa said, her voice shaking.

I heard screams that would raise the hair of the dead, and looked back around the corner to see what had gone wrong. Through the open door of my room, by the light of a torch someone had carried through the hole in the wall, I saw a wild-eyed Pueblo warrior lifting Charles from the floor by the hair of his head. In a gruesome scene that will forever haunt me, I saw the warrior in my room scalp Charles, using his tight bowstring to make the cut in the Pueblo way, and then pulling the scalp away from Charles's head. I heard Ignacia Bent's horrified scream above the crazed battle cries. More warriors dropped from the roof and ran around the corners of the house, trapping Charles and his wife and children inside. The scalp came free and Charles, still living, tried to rise again, but arrows appeared in his body from all angles, and he collapsed in merciful death.

"Fools!" someone shouted in Spanish from inside the room. "You have killed our hostage!"

"We have the woman and the children!" someone replied.

"Keep them in this room! No more killing!"

Now I turned away, wanting badly to avenge Charles, yet knowing I was hopelessly outnumbered. And I had Rumalda Boggs and Josefa Carson to consider.

"Come on," I ordered, and they followed wordlessly. We stole out through the ally and wended our way to the grove where Fireball and Jibber waited. The three of us could not ride one horse, so we hid among the trees for a moment to catch our wind and make our plan.

"Where can we go?" I asked. "Who will take you in?"

"My brother, Pablo," Josefa said.

I shook my head. "They may go there, too. They're killing anyone friendly to the new government, Mexican or American. I saw them kill Vigil at the jail, along with Sheriff Lee. Pablo is Charles's brother-in-law. They may try to get to him."

"Then we must warn him," Josefa said.

"I will. After you two are hidden. Who will take you in?"

"Gabriela," Rumalda said, her voice quavering.

It was so obvious, I wondered why I hadn't thought of it myself. It was true that Gabriela's husband had been friendly to the Americans, and had even uncovered the plot to overthrow the provisional government; but few of the Mexicans knew that. It had been kept a secret for Mariano's protection. His *hacienda* was just outside of Taos, away from the scenes of conflict, and well fortified.

"We will walk," I said. "If we run, we will only draw

attention. We will stay in the shadows, and make it to the Zavaleta *hacienda*."

It seemed that the Indians and Mexican malcontents had taken over the village, and all the peaceable Mexican residents had wisely bolted their doors. On the way through town, we passed several small groups of Pueblo men running here and there, but no one bothered us. A warrior in one bunch raised a bloody knife and yelled a war cry at me. I wanted to kill him. I felt the lust for blood, and understood the Indian way of revenge. But this warrior was not alone, so I raised my bow and answered his war cry. I was very convincing. I was ready for war. The image of Charles being scalped stuck with me like a barbed arrow point that would never come free.

When we got to the Zavaleta *hacienda,* I marched straight up to the door that faced town, and pounded on the rough pine planks. I pounded again and again until I heard Mariano's voice inside.

"Who is out there?" he demanded.

"Honoré Greenwood," I answered. "With two friends."

The bolt rattled and a pistol barrel came into view, followed by a candle flame. Rumalda burst into tears, and Mariano opened the door wide. I ushered the women inside and shut the door behind me.

"What the devil?" Mariano said.

"Charles has been murdered by a mob. The Pueblos and a bunch of drunks have taken over the town."

"Good God!" he said.

I saw Gabriela step around the corner in her nightclothes, and I wanted to run to her. "I have to go back and try to get Ignacia out," I said.

"And Pablo," Josefa reminded.

"Yes." I reached for the door. "I'll warn Pablo."

"Wait!" Gabriela said. She moved toward the pitiful gathering at the door and took Rumalda in her arms, but she looked at me. "Why do you have to go?"

"I'll make it. I look Indian enough."

"Take this," Mariano said, handing me his revolver. "I have others."

"Oh, God, be careful!" Gabriela said.

﹡

I knew I had been ridiculously lucky to have gotten the two women out of the Bent house. When I went back, I found the place completely surrounded, so I knew the mob must have left Ignacia and her children alive, and were now guarding them, holding Charles's wife and two youngest children as hostages. I decided not to inflame the situation by trying to sneak in.

Instead, I mounted Fireball and rode to Pablo Jaramillo's house. To my great horror and grief, I found two bodies outside Pablo's barn. It was light now, and I could see a bloody trail where the two young men had been dragged out of the barn, in which they must have tried to hide. There was enough left of their faces to recognize Pablo Jaramillo and his friend, Narciso Beaubien, both friendly to the Americans. Narciso was the son of an appointed judge.

They had been lanced, hacked, stabbed, scalped, and mutilated. The ground around them seemed stained with more blood than two human bodies could have held. Again, I was too late. Again, I had failed. I had failed to save Charles. I had failed to save his brother-in-law, Pablo, and his friend Narciso.

Even Jibber seemed shocked at the horror of the scene at Pablo's barn. He would sniff at the bloody corpses, then jump back, as if dodging a snake. As much as this scene of murder disturbed me, I could only think of the disagreeable task before me. I would have to return to the Zavaleta *hacienda* to tell Josefa and Rumalda that Pablo had also been killed.

As I was standing there, holding the reins of my horse, looking down on the brutally mangled corpses, I heard a gruff voice behind:

"Turn around."

Slowly and carefully I turned. Charlie Autobee stood there dressed in blackened buckskins and a blanket coat, his long rifle covering me. He squinted. "Kid?" he said.

I nodded. I hadn't seen Autobee for over a year, but had met him at Bent's Fort. He was a Bent and St. Vrain trader and a renowned frontiersman in his day. I was grateful that he recognized me.

"I thought you was an Indian," he said, as if to apologize.

"They got Charles."

"I know."

"And Vigil and Lee."

He nodded. "And that young fellow, the district attorney."

"Leal?"

"That's him."

"What are we going to do?" I asked.

"We'll gather what's left of Pablo and Narciso in blankets and send somebody to bury them. Then I'm gonna ride to Bent's Fort and tell William. I suggest you get a fresh horse and ride to Santa Fe to bring Colonel Price and the army."

<hr/>

I borrowed a good horse from Mariano. I didn't get to see Gabriela, who was consoling Rumalda and Josefa. Mariano said he would take on the task of telling them about Pablo. Then, he said, he would use whatever influence he had to get Ignacia and her children—and Charles's body—out of that house or, at least, get them some food. They were still surrounded by a mob that was sobering up and thinning out.

I rode as hard as I dared to alert the army in Santa Fe, arriving the day after Charles's murder. I intended to ride back with Colonel Price and help clear Taos of the renegades, but Colonel Price had other plans for me. He sent me on to Albuquerque to carry a message to Major Edmonson.

I have no recollection of what happened to me after I handed the dispatch to Major Edmonson. One of my wretched trances overtook me. I hadn't slept in four days.

Later, a couple of soldiers told me that I had left the major's quarters and strolled casually away from the army camp with my dog at my heels.

I woke up in a warm bed to the smell of tortillas. I opened my eyes and saw an old man and an old woman eating. Jibber lay beside my bed. When I stirred, the old folks greeted me with smiles, fed me, and told me what had happened. I had walked up to their door, knocked, and offered to pay for a place to lie down and die.

"To die?" I asked.

"That is exactly what you told me," the old man insisted. He claimed that I had handed him all the money in my pocket, which was probably more than he had ever held at once.

"You can have the money back," he said. "I only spent a little for something to eat."

"No, you keep it," I said. "How long have I been asleep?"

He chuckled. "Four days. That little dog growled at me every time I came to see if you were dead."

I was three miles from Albuquerque, in a goatherd's adobe home near the Rio Grande. I had to walk back to the army camp, borrow a horse, and ride back to Santa Fe. There, I retrieved Mariano's horse from the army and rode back toward San Fernandez de Taos. Much had happened since I had fallen into my long sleep.

A Taos Lightning distillery outside of San Fernandez, called Turley's Mill, had been surrounded and attacked by the Taos mob. Mr. Turley and several of his friends were routed and killed; only two escaped.

Ignacia Bent and her children had finally been released from their house, and Charles's body recovered by friendly Mexican neighbors, thanks to Mariano's influence. Ignacia and her children rejoined Josefa and Rumalda.

Renegade Mexicans and Pueblo Indians roamed everywhere. Colonel Price had defeated a party of the revolutionaries between Santa Fe and Taos, with Captain Ceran St. Vrain leading a company of Santa Fe volunteers. I caught up to the army at the site of this battle, the village of Canada.

Colonel Price immediately sent me riding to the village of
Mora, over the mountains, with dispatches for a Captain
Hendley. Price had heard that revolutionaries in Mora had
killed some Missouri traders and some soldiers. I left Jibber
with the mess cook and rode.

By the time I got to Mora, Captain Hendley was dead,
but his troops had routed the revolutionaries from the village
in a house-to-house fight. A Captain Morin sent me back
over the mountains with more dispatches for Colonel Price.
Three times while acting as courier, I was chased and fired
at by Mexican renegades. But the army always gave couriers
the fastest horses, so I was able to outrun all those who tried
to catch and kill me.

The army kept me riding for days over the snowy passes
and down the ice-crusted roads and trails. I would hand a
dispatch to Colonel Price, and he would look at me as if he
could not believe I had survived. Then he would write another message to another subordinate and send me freezing
on my way.

While I had continued to deliver military correspondences, Colonel Price attacked the Taos Pueblo, demolish-
ing parts of it with cannon fire. The soldiers and a few
mountain men stormed the old Spanish church where some
of the renegade murderers had forted up. They routed the
murderers, killed many Pueblos, and took the rest prisoner.
Several of them were later tried and hanged for the atrocities
committed that night in Taos.

William Bent and a strong force of mountain men came
south from Bent's Fort, also seeking revenge for Charles's
death, but their work had already been done by the time
they arrived. After all the fighting was over and the revolt
crushed, I saw William and spoke to him, telling him how
his brother had died. He just stared at me as he listened. His
face usually looked as expressionless as an Indian's, but
now his eyes went hollow as empty kegs. In time, William
would recover somewhat from his grief, but he was never
really the same after Charles's murder.

After I told him about Charles, I said, "I'm going back

to Fort Adobe, William. I can't stay here. I'm going to resume the Comanche trade."

"Alright," he said. "I reckon I'll be along there myself
before too long. I'll bring a couple of wagons of stuff. You
tell the Comanches I'm comin'."

I agreed. Before I left him, I turned and said, "I had a
good, long talk with Charles at Christmas. I ought to tell
you one thing he said."

"What?"

"He said, 'I miss my brother.' "

William only nodded. I went away before he could see
me burst into tears.

At the Zavaleta *hacienda,* I found a moment alone with
Gabriela. I was returning the horse Mariano had loaned to
me. Gabriela must have seen me ride up, for she met me in
the stables. As I switched my saddle to Fireball, who was
now rested and ready to ride, Gabriela stole quietly up behind me and wrapped her arms around my waist and pressed
the side of her face between my shoulder blades.

I stopped what I was doing and took her hands in mine.
It felt so good that for a moment I could not understand
why I should ever have to leave her embrace.

"Where is Mariano?" I asked.

"He rode to see Colonel Price."

I turned and looked into the glistening eyes of Gabriela.
"I don't want to go, but—"

She placed her fingers on my lips. "You do not have
explain it. I know it all very well."

I tried not to kiss her—a woman married to man whom
I now considered a friend—but my face brushed hers, and
I turned my lips to meet hers. Tearing myself away from
Gabriela took ten times the courage of anything I ever did.

I turned and cinched my saddle as she watched me. When
I mounted, I knew she saw in my face what I saw in hers,
and we exchanged no unnecessary words. She came next to

me and placed her warm little hands on my thigh. I stooped low and kissed her one last time, the soft warmth of her lips moving me to utter madness.

"I love you," I said. "God bless you." For a brief instant, I hoped beyond all rational thought for a Divine Spirit and a guardian angel who would watch over the woman I loved, and her son, who might be mine.

A tear ran down her cheek. *"Vaya con Dios, mi amor."*

As I rode away, Jibber darted all around Fireball's hooves, his tail wagging with the pure joy of just going somewhere. I could not share his lightheartedness. Sorrow was tearing my heart into pieces as I rode. I stopped once to look back. Gabriela and I waved at the same time. Then I turned away. I saw only one hope for any kind of tranquillity. The Crossing. I was going straightaway to Fort Adobe.

THIRTY-FIVE

I took the trail over the Sangre de Cristos, in spite of the danger of snow in the high country. I camped curled in a buffalo robe with Jibber. I got safely over to the east face of the range and made for the headwaters of the Canadian. I stopped at the spot Charles Bent had showed me the first time we crossed over the range with the Bent and St. Vrain wagon—the place that afforded the striking view of the plains we had crossed on my first trip across them. I am not ashamed to say that I sat on my horse and wept, remembering how Charles had so subtly taken me under his wing. I cried so long that Jibber lay down in the sun and took a nap.

I felt a little better after this, and wondered why. I was beginning to get religion. How could a spirit like that of

Charles Bent just be snuffed out at death? He wasn't gone. I could feel him in this place. But that was just a memory, wasn't it? Or was there something else? I wanted to believe so. Perhaps science could not define it. Perhaps not even a genius could explain it. Perhaps there was a loftier intelligence. It all began to make some sort of nebulous sense.

I had read that the great genius of all geniuses, Leonardo da Vinci, had professed atheism all his life until he was an elderly man. Then, one day in his old age, he chanced to look out upon the Mediterranean as the surf came in. He saw patterns in the waves, and in the life that lived at the edges of water and land. Birds, crabs, bugs, waves, winds, clouds, sun . . . They were working in synchronized order beyond the ability of any to coordinate. A lifelong student of nature, Leonardo admitted finally that there was a higher intelligence.

I felt the same realization here, on the east face of the Sangre de Cristos, looking down on the sealike plains.

When the wildfire ravages the prairie, it burns back the chaparral brush, allowing the grass to flourish, benefiting the herds of buffalo, which in turn feed the mountain lion, the wolf, the coyote. The vultures pick the bones. Rodents gnaw the skeleton to dust, attracting the snake which, in turn, feeds the chaparral bird, which hides in the brush still left standing at the edge of the burn.

Then the rains come, and the chaparral advances once more, choking out the grass. These same rains trickle toward the sea, yet evaporate along the way, flying spiritlike back into the very air whence they came, only to fall again as snow, sleet, hail, or rain that perchance may fall upon a wildfire somewhere and quench it.

And so on, around and around, the cycle of rain and drought coupling with the cycle of predator and prey in such a way that each makes the other turn in balance with all the other wheels in the Great Mystery that move and shape and kill and give birth out of death. All this I felt, as if getting glimpses of some great machine through a fog.

A tear fell from my cheek and landed on the ground. This

tear was for Gabriela. I wondered what difference it would make—a single tear. Perhaps a far more significant impact than I could ever fathom. Although a genius, I was still a mere mortal. My genius revealed to me only how much I would never learn. Perhaps, in some great cycle beyond my comprehension, I represented no more than a single tear falling on a mountainside. And yet, perhaps that one tear could set in motion the genesis of something larger than the mountain itself. I decided to find out simply by riding down the mountainside and carrying on with my life.

<hr />

I wore a new pair of boots and Spanish spurs given to me by Colonel Price. As I rode through the leafless scrub oak that grew stirrup high, the rowels of my new spurs would spin against the brush and whir, singing a song that I felt vibrating in my new boots. Strangely enough, I found some joy in this simple song of whirling rowels. That speck of joy gave me a glimpse of hope that I might someday feel happy again.

I had ridden no farther than two miles from that place when I heard a gunshot. I reined Fireball in and listened to the dying echoes. A second shot came, giving me a better bearing on the origin of the reports. The third shot came like the third note in a waltz, in perfect time, and it gave me a good idea of the distance.

From these three shots, I deduced several things. All three blasts had come from the same weapon, for they sounded identical. The sharp crack indicated something of smaller caliber than a mountainman's musket—perhaps a Colt revolver. The shooter was between one and two miles north of me, around the shoulder of the mountain, in the next ravine. And, most importantly, he was in desperate trouble. Three shots in rapid cadence spelled the distress signal of the frontier. There was no reason for a man to shoot three times at anything, unless being attacked, by enemies or grizzlies, in which case the shots would probably come in a

more erratic rhythm. A true frontiersman tried not to shoot
at all most of the time. He saved ammunition and stayed
quiet so as not to attract hostiles. Three shots in perfect time
represented the prelude to the desperation waltz. The code
dictated that I ride immediately toward the shots to investigate and lend aid.

The way was strewn with boulders and deadfalls, steep
ascents and descents, but Fireball picked his way around the
obstacles within fifteen minutes. I knew I was in the vicinity
of the gunfire I had heard. I stopped to listen and heard a
creek running with melting snow. The temperature was almost fifty—warm for February, but still invigoratingly crisp.
I listened, hoping to hear a voice or some noise that would
draw me closer to whomever it was that needed help.

A sudden, unexpected shot made Jibber and Fireball
flinch. Two more shots came in succession, as before. Now
I knew someone really needed help. The reports had come
from the stream bed, no more than two hundred yards away.

I dismounted and made my dog stay with my horse. Taking in hand my new Colt revolver, this also given to me by
Colonel Price, I moved stealthily up the stream bed. I
wanted to help, but did not intend to stumble blindly into a
trap. It had occurred to me that my enemies, the Apaches,
had perhaps fired the shots to lure me into an ambush. This
would have amounted to a heroic and victorious jest in the
minds of the Indians.

I stayed as far from the stream as I could because I didn't
want the noise of rushing water to cover any sound that I
might need to hear to save my hide, or someone else's.
Coming around a bend in the stream bed, I heard a thrashing
sound down in the water, and the groans of a human voice.

I peeked through a cleft in a gigantic boulder and saw the
man in trouble. Though his back was turned, I knew him at
first glance. Snakehead Jackson's horse had slipped crossing
the stream, and had fallen in such a way that he could not
get back up. Snakehead's leg was pinned under his horse,
and he was under frigid water up to his chest. He knew the

cold would kill him if he did not get out, and had resorted to the distress shots.

Nearby stood a mule, laden with two oaken kegs. Snakehead had a stick in his hand, five feet long, and was attempting to tangle it in the mule's lead rope, hoping, I presumed, to pull the mule near enough to tie onto the horse and then pull the horse to its feet. He was having little luck snagging the lead rope, however, and seemed about out of energy.

I ducked behind the boulder. My first inclination was walk away and let the corruptor die slowly in the cold water. Then he would hardly be a threat to the Indians around Fort Adobe, I reasoned. A pang of guilt shot into my stomach for thinking of abandoning a dying man—even one such as Snakehead. I remembered my cowardly murder of Segarelli. And I remembered the words of John Hatcher: "You call for help, you want everybody to stand around and watch?"

Another cowardly thought struck me. What if I abandoned Snakehead to die, and he somehow got himself out of this fix and survived? What if he found my tracks and trailed me? He would kill me for having left him to die.

"Don't shoot," I shouted. "I'm coming to help you."

The battle-scared face turned toward me, emotionless even in this desperate plight. The eyes pierced me like poisoned arrows.

"Come ahead, Kid," he said, recognizing me. "I'm about done in."

I caught the mule and cut the diamond hitch free of the two kegs of whiskey. Falling to the ground, they rolled into the stream. I tied one end of the long rope around the mule's neck with a bowline knot so it wouldn't tighten, and tied the other end to the headstall of the horse in the stream. Angling the mule in such a way that he could pull the horse up from the freezing creek, I swatted his rear and gave the horse some weight to pull against with his neck. He came up with a lurch, leaving Snakehead in the stream.

I grabbed Snakehead's wet buckskins and dragged him out of the water. "Is your leg broken?" I asked.

"I didn't hear it crack or feel it break. Can't feel either leg now." His voice came out in a shudder from the cold he had endured for at least twenty minutes. He began pulling off his wet buckskins, though he was shivering almost too badly to manage. I pulled off my blanket coat and threw it down beside him so he could cover himself when he got his buckskins off. Then I began scrambling around for kindling to start a fire that might just save the only man in the world for whom I felt nothing but hatred.

In two minutes, I had a fire blazing, and I dragged Snakehead nearer to it. He had a bedroll tied on behind his saddle, but it was wet, so I ran to Fireball, and rode him back to the fire. I untied my own blankets and used them to cover the whiskey trader. He was shivering uncontrollably now. I stoked the fire to a higher blaze, then turned to look at Snakehead's horse. One leg was skinned up, and he stood with his head hanging just inches from the ground; but he looked as if he might survive.

I kept the fire blazing, and gradually Snakehead began to warm up. It took almost an hour, and most of that time he was shivering too badly to talk. Finally, he began to move his legs, then went so far as to turn himself around so he could warm his other side.

I gave him some jerked meat and found some coffee wrapped in his outfit; so I put some on to boil, using a little kettle he carried with him. When I gave him the coffee in a tin cup, he said, "Obliged."

He drank the cup and seemed greatly restored by its warmth.

"Good thing for that horse you come along," he said. "Where you headed?"

"Fort Adobe."

"Is that what you call it?"

I didn't answer.

"How come you didn't just leave me to die?"

I knew by this statement that Snakehead sensed my hatred for him. "Wouldn't be right."

He chuckled. "I ain't thought much about what-all's right for a long time."

"Did you ever?"

He shrugged. "Used to. When I first come west to trap and trade. Oh, I'd kill a man quick as a bolt of lighting, but I avoided it."

I rolled a rock near the fire and sat on it. I was sweating from the exercise of building the fire, and the sweat had chilled me; so the fire felt good. "What changed you?"

"A woman. I was an honest trader back in 'thirty-three. Had me a pretty Cheyenne squaw. Comanche raiders got her while I was off tradin' for the Bent brothers, and carried her south to the Canadian River country. Raped her, of course. Beat her some. You'd expect as much.

"I knew I'd have to ransom her back, so I packed some whiskey south and found them goddamn Comanches where your fort sits now, on The Crossing of the Canadian. I had her bought free with that whiskey; but when they brought her out, and I saw how cut and beat up she was, I got mad, and them Comanches, all liquored up, thought it was funny. I got her mounted on my horse behind me; but before I rode out, I just had to shoot one of them bastards, so I did.

"Well, we had a runnin' fight then, lasted about six miles. My squaw got shot in the back. I killed two or three of them bucks, and they finally give up and went back for the rest of the whiskey. I got my squaw off the horse, but she didn't last ten minutes."

"Wouldn't you say you've avenged her enough by now?"

"Yeah, but now I'm just doin' it because I want to. I like seein' drunk Indians kill each other." He got up, wrapped in blankets, and hung his buckskins on a pine branch to dry by the heat of the fire. He turned back to the fire and stood almost over it.

"Whose fingers are those on that necklace you wear?" I asked, for I could see the horrible thing where the blanket opened under his beard.

"I called him 'Injun Jack.' He called hisself somethin' in Osage that I never could speak."

"He was Osage?"

"Was. He was about mean as me, I guess. He was so damn mean, even the Osage wouldn't have nothin' to do with him. They run him off after he kilt some other buck over a squaw or a horse or somethin'. He took up with me as a guard. He'd watch my back while I traded whiskey. Well, one night, ol' Jack, he started drinkin' some of my whiskey. He got drunk and wild and picked a fight with me." Snakehead pointed to the scar that started under his eye and ran into his beard. "He give me this. I killed him fair and honest. I was just as drunk as him. This life of the whiskey trade is hard, Kid."

"*Everybody's* life is hard."

He chuckled without smiling. "Well, I tell you one thing. I owe you. You could have shot me in the back, but you saved my hide. You got a favor comin' from ol' Snakehead."

"Stay away from Fort Adobe."

"Well, I can't do that. That's where my whiskey trade started. I've got to come around there and drunk up some Comanches and Kiowas every now and then. But some other favor you want, you ask."

"I can't imagine what else you could do for me."

"Well, you just remember, Kid. You track me down when you need somethin'."

I stood up. "I'll need my coat. Looks like you're going to be alright."

He tossed me the coat without looking at me. "Remember what I said. Maybe my soul ain't worth a damn, but I pay my debts. You might need me someday."

I left Snakehead Jackson staring into the fire that had saved his life.

THIRTY-SIX

Seventeen days later, I forded the Canadian at The Crossing, and rode into the prairie bottoms where Fort Adobe stood. At first glance, it looked sound; then I saw that the wooden gates and the parapets had been burned. I saw a few lodgepole clusters rising near the timber of Bent's Creek, and knew Indians were camped nearby.

When I came into better view of the Indian village, a dog barked, and within seconds six young Comanche warriors were riding right at me. The lead warrior came with his bow drawn, and I thought I would be killed, for I didn't know these Comanches. This was not Shaved Head's band. I began making hand signs and speaking Comanche as if my life depended on it, which it probably did. Jibber wisely stayed quiet and stood almost under Fireball's belly for protection.

"I am Plenty Man," I said in Comanche. "I come to trade. William Bent will come soon with wagons. We will have blankets to trade, and iron for making arrow points. Also, knives, coffee, tobacco, and things for the women."

The warriors decided to take me to their chief and let him decide what should be done with me. His name was Bloody Cloud, and he didn't think too much of me.

"When will William Bent come?" he asked.

"One moon."

"If William Bent arrives in ten sleeps, we will trade. After ten sleeps, we will kill you."

I said nothing in reply, for I was scared speechless; but at least I had ten days to think of a way out if William didn't arrive by then.

Bloody Cloud's Comanches followed me to the fort.

When I entered the adobe walls and saw that the Indians had fired everything combustible, I got angry. I got off Fireball and began stomping around and kicking charred timbers. When one of the Comanches started to laugh at me, I got even angrier. I had put a lot of work into my fort, and did not appreciate viewing its desecration to the tune of Indian laughter.

So, with a flourish like that of a Spanish *torero*, I whipped off my coat and flailed it overhead in the face of the pony ridden by the laughing Comanche. The pony wheeled and bolted for the open gates with its rider barely hanging on to the side of his mount. The rest of the warriors thought this was hilarious, and followed the spooked pony to taunt the rider.

Left alone, I began stacking charred timbers to burn. I would clean up the rubble in the fort first, then start making repairs as best as I could. Having provided them with some entertainment, Bloody Cloud's Comanches seemed willing to let me go about my business unmolested, so I worked like a beaver, and succeeded in stacking and burning what was left of the ruined timbers in one day. While these burned, I went to the woods along Bent's Creek and found the hollow log where Hatcher and I had stashed some tools, including an axe, which I would use to chop new timbers for the burned-out roof of the rooms inside the fort, the new walkway, and the gates.

At dusk, I was chopping the first of these timbers, when a Comanche warrior rode out to investigate. He had charged me earlier today with his bow drawn.

"You cut down too many trees," he said.

I scowled at him. "I must replace the ones that burned."

"The Pawnees burned your fort. I have seen their sign on the trail."

"What sign?"

He didn't answer. He watched me chop until I paused to catch my breath, then said, "Whose scalps are those on your belt?"

"Some Apaches I had to kill."

"We have the same enemy."

"That makes us allies."

"When the Apaches attack."

"And when we trade. I did not come here looking for enemies. I came here to trade."

"We came here to hunt. Burnt Belly had a vision that told us to come."

I stopped short, leaving the axe blade stuck in the tree I was chopping. I remembered my friend, Kills Something, telling me about this medicine man, Burnt Belly. I remembered Sol Silver telling me he could help me with my strange dreams and erratic sleep patterns. "Is Burnt Belly here?"

"Yes. He wants to see you."

When?" I asked.

"In the morning, when Father Sun touches the tips of Burnt Belly's lodge poles."

I nodded, then made the hand sign signaling that I understood. "What is your name?" I asked the warrior.

"Fears-the-Ground," he said.

"I will see Burnt Belly in the morning. Which lodge is his?"

"The one that stands farthest to the east."

❦

I tried to sleep that night, but couldn't. The coming of the full moon had afflicted me with my usual insomnia. An hour before dawn, I walked to the eastern edge of the Comanche village and waited for the first rays of sun to strike the tips of Burnt Belly's lodge poles. Then I walked to the door of his lodge and said, "I am Plenty Man."

I stood there long enough for the sunlight to creep down the lodge poles and bathe the wind flaps in orange. Finally, a voice said, "Come inside." These words came like a breath of wind and seemed to emanate from the prairie behind me. Confused by this, I nonetheless pulled aside the bear hide covering the entrance to the tepee and stepped in.

The dark lodge smelled of sage smoke and brain-tanned hides, tallow, and roasted bones. A tiny flicker of fire licked occasionally from a neat pile of embers surrounded by a pearl necklace of new white rocks. My sight soon adjusted to the low light, and I found Burnt Belly sitting on a couch made of fine, soft buffalo robes, piled two hands high. He sat there wearing only a breechcloth revealing his belly, which was indeed burnt. The lightning scar started at his shoulder and angled across and down in a horrible slash that ended at the opposite thigh. It looked glossy, like moist biscuit dough—a great, permanent welt. Iron gray hair hung over his shoulders and framed a weathered face.

My eyes drifted upward until they locked onto his, and at this instant I felt myself in the presence of some new and wondrous force, accompanied by a danger of equal power.

"I have traveled far," he said, and the words seemed to come from the smoke hole of the tepee, as though Burnt Belly could throw his voice. Perhaps he could. In later years, I met many excellent ventriloquists and illusionists among the Indians.

"I have traveled far also," I replied.

"They say you make things vanish."

"Nothing ever really vanishes," I said, not wanting Burnt Belly to develop expectations of me that I could not live up to. "The eye does not always see the truth."

"You are honest."

"Not always."

He laughed, and as he did, his voice seemed to swirl around the lodge, and then flow into his mouth, instead of out of it. "They say you fear your dreams."

"Yes. I see dreams with my eyes open, before I sleep. I cannot move. Animals come to attack me. Snakes and bears and mountain lions."

"Those are visions, not dreams. Evil spirits are trying to get into you. You are wise to fear them. They can kill you."

"What should I do?"

He shifted slightly on his couch of robes. "Do you dream of whirlwinds?"

"Sometimes."

"Do you fly in your dreams? Like an eagle?"

"Yes. But, then I fall."

"You make music."

"Yes."

"I have heard it from a long way away. It is beautiful. You have power, Plenty Man. The evil spirits are trying to get it."

"I just want the bad visions to stop. I want to sleep in peace."

"Sometimes sleep comes over you at strange times."

"Yes. When the moon is dark, I fall into trances."

"And when the moon is bright?"

"I do not sleep at all."

Burnt Belly rose from his couch and took three steps, stooping then to pick up a painted parfleche bag. He looked lean, spry and healthy, in spite of his gray hair and sagging skin. He emptied the parfleche bag onto the buffalo-hide couch, revealing medicine bundles of various sizes—buckskin pouches tied up with thongs, each marked with the feather of a different bird. He began sorting through these bundles, seemingly at random.

"Before the Thunderbird struck me," he said, "I was just like any other man. No better, no worse. Then the lightning got me. In the time the lightning takes to flash, I saw too many things to tell about in a lifetime. Now, I see things far away. I hear things, too. Like your music. I see things that have not yet happened, but will happen. Like you, I count things without thinking. I remember everything. And I feel the power in things. Good power. Evil power. I can touch a plant, and I will know how to use it to heal or kill. You must trust that I want to heal you. I could easily poison you."

"Why would you want to kill me?"

"I do not."

"Why would you want to heal me?"

He stopped shuffling his bundles and looked over his shoulder at me. "If the evil powers get you"—he looked away—"you would do bad things." He let his hand pass over the medicine bundles he had spread about on the robes. "Ah-hey," he said, letting his hand hover over one bundle in particular.

"What is that?"

He picked up the bundle. "Dogbane root. When you need to sleep, chew it. It will help."

He picked up the bundle of dogbane root and held it toward me. I stepped forward and held out my hand. Just before he placed it in my hand, Burnt Belly flicked his wrist, and the bundle was gone. He turned his hand both ways, neither of which revealed the bundle. Then he flicked his wrist again, and the bundle reappeared. I have thought about it for years. I have no idea how the old shaman palmed that bundle on the back of his hand. He was the best sleight-of-hand magician I ever saw. He smiled when he produced the bundle again, and then placed it in my hand.

Returning to his bundles, he let his hand pass over them again, until he picked up another one. "This is the root of the moccasin flower," he said. "For those times when you feel the evil visions coming." Soak the roots, then boil them. Drink the broth. It will calm you and make you dream in peace."

I took the bundle of moccasin-flower roots.

"When you feel the trances coming on, use this." He picked up yet another bundle.

"What is it?"

"Fir needles. I use them myself. After the Thunderbird burned me, I would take great walks in my sleep. People told me that I would stop and talk to them about strange things as I went on my way. I would wake up walking, a long way from camp. The fir needles help."

"How do I use them?" I asked, taking the bundle.

"Moisten them and put them on a very hot stone. Breathe the smoke. It will keep you from fainting, or falling into one of your walking trances. This will also make you safe from lightning." He smiled. "I use it all the time."

"Will these things cure me?"

"There is no cure. These things will help. But you will grow careless, and forget to make the broth of moccasin-flower root, and the evil visions will torment you. You will get too busy to chew the dogbane root, and you will go too long without sleep, then fall into a trance because you forgot to make the smudge of fir needles. You will be very diligent about it for a while, but then you will grow careless."

"I can not always tell, before it happens, when one of these things is going to afflict me."

"I can tell, but I have better things to do than to follow you around and tell you when you are going to fall into a trance. Learn to feel it coming. Most of the time, you will know."

"I will do my best." I held the bundles in my hand. "How can I pay you for giving me these things?"

"Did you bring the thing that makes music?"

"Yes."

"I would like to hear it. Also, I must have a pony, a red blanket, some coffee, some tobacco, and a rainbow shell for my sits-beside-me wife."

"When the wagons come, I will get these things for you. I will go to get the music maker now."

"Wait. There is more. I must have one of the scalps you wear. Either one. It doesn't matter. Also, a new metal knife, some beads for my second wife, a horn full of gunpowder, a looking glass, and a small flask of whiskey."

"You drink whiskey?"

"I hold it in my mouth, then spit it on the fire. It makes the flames leap."

"Is that all?"

"For now."

I stared at him in a moment of doubt, wondering if I had just been taken by a charlatan. Even so, the price he asked was not very great. I smiled and told him I was going to get my violin.

As I stepped out of the tepee, I felt refreshed and filled with hope. Many times over the years I have thought about that first meeting with Burnt Belly. The strange thing is that, even though my memory is perfect, I can never recall his voice. It was as if we weren't really talking aloud, but communicated by the power of thought alone. Looking back on it, I believe he really did have knowledge of plants and their healing properties, for his remedies worked when I took the time to use them. But I can't say whether Burnt Belly learned these things from some other healer, or actually had the powers instilled in him by the jolt from the lightning bolt. Either way, I believe he took full advantage of his skills as a herbalist, and became a wealthy man because of it. Wealthy, that is, by Indian standards. When he died, years later, he had four happy wives, and a herd of five hundred horses.

I am old and alone and own a mule and a lame gelding. And I call myself a genius? The hundreds of thousand of dollars I have in various banks under various names mean less to me than a stick of firewood would have meant to Burnt Belly. His genius was all tied up in wisdom.

THIRTY-SEVEN

Five sleeps after my meeting with Burnt Belly, William Bent arrived at Fort Adobe with four wagons full of trade goods. With him came his younger brother, George Bent, and his son-in-law, Tom Boggs. Also John Hatcher, Blue Wiggins, Sol Silver, Goddamn Murray, Bonifacio Ramirez and four Mexican laborers skilled in carpentry and adobe work.

"I'm glad you came when you did," I said to William. "Bloody Cloud said he would have me killed if you didn't show up in a few more days with the trade goods."

"I figured you'd be here with your ass in a bind, so we whipped up the teams and came on," William said. The time

on the trail seemed to have cured some of his grief over
Charles. I felt glad to see him at our fort.

I already had some timbers cut and stacked, so the men
went right to work. Within a week, we had made all the
repairs on Fort Adobe, and prepared to trade with the Comanches, who had spent the time rounding up horses from
various ranges. They now had several hundred nearby to
trade, in addition to some buffalo robes and three captives
to be ransomed.

Because I had become acquainted with Bloody Cloud,
Fears-the-Ground, and Burnt Belly, William chose me to
negotiate for the purchase of the captives. They were Mexican children—two boys half-starved to death, and one girl.
I bought the two boys from Bloody Cloud, whose raiding
party had captured them near Ysleta, on the Rio Grande.
For these two boys, I paid two blankets, a flask of black
powder, a piece of hoop iron, and a hand axe. They were
glad to get away from Bloody Cloud.

The captured girl belonged to Fears-the-Ground. She
seemed to have been well cared for. The whole time I was
negotiating her ransom price, Fears-the-Ground never got
off his horse. It dawned on me that I had never seen him
with his own feet on the ground, and I began to understand
his name, his personality, and his horsemanship.

He let the girl go for a handful of bullets, a fine Mexican
rawhide reata, an eagle feather, and three lodge poles I had
earned in another trade.

We managed to ransom the captives, but the trading that
followed did not exactly go smoothly. Bloody Cloud's people seemed much more belligerent than Shaved Head's Comanches, and made constant threats, forever stringing their
bows and strutting about defiantly when they didn't like the
terms of some deal.

For this reason, William began allowing only three warriors inside the fort at a time. This gave us more control
over the trade, but only angered the Comanches. Sometimes,
while we were trading inside, a warrior outside would lob
an arrow over the walls, into the fort. They could shoot their

arrows straight up, to a great height, after which they would come speeding straight down into the fort. I learned at all times to listen for the thump of bowstrings. When an arrow stabbed the ground in the middle of a trade, the three Indians inside would laugh, though it might just as easily have struck one of them. William said it was the war with Mexico that had all the Indians stirred up.

In the third week of trading, Mauricio Anzualda showed up with his Comanchero band. He stayed only a day or two, and we paid him to take the three ransomed Mexican captives back to Taos. In talking with him, I found out that all was quiet in Taos, which eased my worries over Gabriela.

Though the trading continued amidst the tension, we had a good time inside the fort. Our camaraderie went a long way toward mending my grief over the loss of Charles. I played the violin and, between songs, William and the other old voyagers would tell hair-raising stories of their experiences with wild horses, hostile Indians, buffalo stampedes, and fierce grizzlies.

With the coming of the Comanche Grass Moon, Bloody Cloud's people decided to move on. Burnt Belly came to me the day they left and gave me some more fir needles and moccasin flower roots.

"Use these well," he said. "You cannot do good things if you are walking around in your sleep. Do not let the evil powers kill you, or capture your soul. I have seen two paths for you. One is good. The other is very bad."

"I will take the good path," I promised. "I have stepped onto the bad one before, and do not like the way it makes my heart feel."

"It is not easy. If you need help, find me. You will know how."

With that, Burnt Belly joined Bloody Cloud's band as it moved south to cross the Canadian River. Only three days later, a far-wandering band of Jicarilla Apaches came to trade. William insisted on keeping me hidden in the fort the whole time they were there because of my problems with the Mescalero Apaches. But they stayed only about a week, for they were deep in Comanche country and did not wish to get overwhelmed by enemies.

After these Apaches left, Little Bluff's Kiowas came to trade, followed soon by Shaved Head's Comanches. Kills Something actually seemed glad to see me.

"Hidden Water still has no husband," he advised. "My father refuses offers of fifty horses for her. You could have her, Plenty Man."

I saw her across the camp, and my whole body stirred. No, I was not in love with her the way I was with Gabriela. But what was I supposed to do? I could not spend my whole life longing for another man's wife. Still, I resisted taking a Comanche bride. Perhaps I just didn't want the responsibility of having a wife.

Among these Comanche and Kiowa bands were two Mexican captives, and a white boy from Texas. I ransomed all three for tobacco, knives, coffee, blankets, and a Mexican saddle. My reputation as a ransom negotiator began to increase. I had mixed emotions about it. In one way, I felt that I only encouraged the trade in captured children by paying their ransoms. But on the other hand, I imagined the anguish the families of these children must have felt, and hoped I could ease it. The fact that I had more-or-less been abandoned by my own parents—sentenced to Saint-Cyr—stirred my empathy for these innocent captives who must have pined for their homes and families.

So the trade in captives, horses, and merchandise continued as the season of frost passed and the green grass came on. We left Fort Adobe, taking hundreds of horses back to Bent's Fort for our trouble. I said good-bye to Kills Something and told him I was not yet ready to marry Hidden Water.

"Someone else will get her," he warned.

"So be it. She is not the only woman in the world."

"She is the only one who will make you father of my nephews-to-be," he insisted.

In spite of Kills Something's arguments, I left her with a glance and a smile, and helped push our herd of horses north to the Santa Fe Trail. Some of these horses were sold in New Mexico, some in Missouri, and some far to the north at Fort Laramie to immigrants who braved the trails to the Oregon country.

I stayed around Bent's Fort the summer of 1847, making myself useful, speaking French with Charles Autobee and Louis Lescot, learning to speak Cheyenne and Arapaho, practicing my riding and shooting skills, and risking occasional flirtations with Indian maidens.

That summer, William Bent's Cheyenne wife, Owl Woman, died in childbirth, which added to his grief. In the Indian way, he took Owl Woman's sister, Yellow Woman as his new wife. Then, tragically, William's young brother, George, died of a sudden illness while at the fort. William's life had become a string of sorrows, and I could only pray that it would stop, though I still didn't put much stock in prayer in those days.

When fall came, I rode back to Fort Adobe with William, Sol Silver, and John Hatcher. We had to make more repairs, for the Indians had burned down part of the walkway, and had chopped up one of the gates to use as firewood. A new band of Comanches came under Chief Peta Nocona. Here I saw the famous white captive Cynthia Anne Parker, who was now about eighteen years old, and was married to the chief. Peta Nocona was agreeable enough to trade with, but some of his younger warriors constantly showed fight prompting William to let them into the fort only two at a time.

They didn't stay long. We acquired over two hundred horses and mules from them. John Hatcher and I stayed at our fort while the rest of the men herded the horses back to Bent's Fort. No Indians came to trade for two moons, but John Hatcher and I spent an enjoyable hunting season killing buffalo, deer, and antelope. We didn't see another human being besides each other for sixty-seven days.

In early February 1848, Kit Carson came to Fort Adobe with Lucien Maxwell, Blackfoot John Smith, Robert Fisher, Goddamn Murray, Bonifacio Ramirez, and his nephew, Jesus. This was only the second time I had ever been around Kit, but he remembered me well, and he had heard how I managed to help his wife escape the mob at Taos.

"I heard you and John built a good fort," Kit said. "This is better than I expected."

"The Indians have been troublesome," John Hatcher replied.

"Well, you would be, too, John." Kit turned to me. "Kid, I want to thank you for getting my wife and Mrs. Bent out of that house in Taos. And Rumalda, too, of course."

"I wish I could have helped Charles," I said, the horror of that night coming back to haunt me. I could still visualize perfectly the sight of Charles being dragged about by the hair as the drunken Pueblo yanked at his scalp.

"You did what you could, and more than most men would have been able to do. My wife speaks so highly of you, I feel like we've adopted you."

"Your wife is a fine woman, and brave."

"Well, it was too bad about Charles, but there's only so much you can do against a mob of drunks. It's a miracle you got Josefa out. I'm beholden to you, Kid. If you ever need help, track me down."

Some Kiowas and Comanches came to trade, and we acquired over two hundred horses from them, in addition to some robes and other goods. Soon after they left, however, a band of Jicarilla Apaches attacked, killing Jesus as he was gathering horses. They hacked him up horribly and carried his scalp away for a dance. They got away with all the stock except for Fireball and two mules that I happened to be grooming inside the fort walls when the attack came.

"There's no sense in staying here any longer," Kit commented as we buried what was left of Jesus. "Nobody knows we're in a fix."

"I can ride to Bent's Fort for help," I said.

"No, the Indians are too stirred up. Like as not, you'd never make it. Best we stick together and walk back. We can load some things on the mules, but we'll have to bury the rest of the trade goods and the robes to keep the Indians from stealing it all."

So we dug a deep pit in the timber and buried all our merchandise. We covered it over and tried to make it look natural. Then we began walking back to Bent's Fort. The first few days, my feet were sore, then I got accustomed to hiking. I could have ridden Fireball, but I had chosen to use him as a packhorse so we could carry more goods back to Bent's.

Kit was extremely careful on the trail, which was one reason he had survived so many years in the wilderness. He thought nothing of calling a halt while he climbed a tree or a high point of land and watched the country for two or three hours, looking for trouble. At night, he allowed only the smallest of cook fires for coffee and beans. Then he would make us move a mile away from the ashes of the fire to sleep. He always assigned guards to watch the camp at night.

In spite of Kit's cautious ways, twenty-three Kiowas cut our trail on the eleventh day, tracked us down, and decided to attack us. All the Indians were stirred up on the Southern Plains that year because of the war, soldiers riding everywhere, and the increase in immigration on the westward trails. This was a band of Kiowas none of us knew, and they determined to take our stock and peel our scalps.

"Circle the animals," Kit ordered when it became apparent that the Kiowas were out for blood and war honors. "Don't everybody fire at once, or we're done. Maxwell, you and Murray fire the first round. Blackfoot and Fisher will fire the second volley. Me and Bonifacio and the Kid will fire last."

"Goddamn, don't just fire," Murray said. "Take aim. We've got to kill one or two of the goddamn bastards to get their attention."

When the Kiowas charged, Lucien Maxwell shot a horse out from under one of them in the first volley, but the rest scattered, circled, and continued to make random advances. Blackfoot John Smith mortally wounded a warrior with his shot, while old Robert Fisher unhorsed another. This only seemed to enrage the rest of the Kiowas. They were incredibly brave. They charged right at us with war whoops and shields dancing.

I took careful aim, and when Kit said, "Fire!" I killed a warrior with a shot through the heart. Kit killed the warrior beside the one I had sent over the divide. By this time, Maxwell and Murray had reloaded. The Kiowas were easy targets as they struggled to drag away their dead. Maxwell wounded another, and the Kiowas wisely withdrew.

Though we won the fight, I was mighty worried. I had already made myself an enemy of the Apaches, and didn't care to get crosswise with any Kiowas. Oddly, though, the Kiowas never seemed to know that it was me involved in that fight. I was beginning to learn how not to draw attention to myself. Had I been mounted on Fireball, dashing around with my saber and bow and rifle, they would have remembered me and hunted me to this day. But I was afoot—a small, insignificant voyager in plain buckskins. I never bragged about my role in that skirmish on the plains, and no Indian ever sought vengeance at my expense.

When we got to Bent's Fort, days later, footsore and exhausted, we found Marcellin St. Vrain packing for a hasty ride back to Missouri with a six-man escort. Marcellin, the youngest of the St. Vrain brothers, was thirty-three years old and had been trading with the Indians since he was twenty-one.

"What's your hurry?" Kit asked him, with a good-natured nudge. "You're not very sociable to ride out just after we've walked all this way to see you."

Marcellin didn't even crack a grin. "I've got to go back to Missouri, Kit. I won't last a week here."

"What happened?"

"You know how the Cheyenne boys are always challenging me to wrestling matches. Well, they pitted Bull Man against me yesterday. They figured he could beat me. They had big wagers on the match. It got rough, as usual. I twisted him over the wrong way, and broke his neck. Killed him, Kit."

"Damn," Kit said.

"Goddamn," Murray added.

"He's got brothers and uncles galore. I'm done for if I stay."

"Well, git, then," Kit said. "The States ain't so bad. At least you'll be alive."

So Marcellin St. Vrain snuck out after dark with his volunteer escort. He left two Cheyenne wives behind, and never came back to the plains. The peaceful relations around Bent's Fort, and especially out at Fort Adobe, seemed to have deteriorated into an unending series of skirmishes and squabbles which, in turn, kept leading to revenge attacks and killings.

I spoke with William about it the night Marcellin left for Missouri.

"Yeah, it just gets harder all the time," he said with a huge sigh. "The trade has all but dried up anyway. I'm thinking of selling out, Kid."

"Selling the fort?"

"Yep."

"But the way things are, who would buy it?"

"The army."

I nodded, and remembered what John Hatcher had told me three years before. "What about Fort Adobe?"

"Maybe that, too. What do you think?"

"Don't sell it yet—that's what I think. Don't sell either fort. I don't believe the army can keep peace among the Indians the way you have. From the sound of things, Mexico is almost whipped now. When the war's over, the Indians will calm down, and we can trade with them again."

William laced his gnarled fingers together and propped his chin on them. "Maybe you're right. And there is one other thing you probably haven't heard about. One other reason to keep the forts open."

"What's that?"

"They found gold in California."

I considered this for a mere second or two. "How does that affect us?"

William chortled. "I mean, they *really* found some gold, Mr. Greenwood. For a while, it was just a wild rumor, but now the news is coming from folks we can believe. They found it at Sutter's Mill, first. Now it's turning up everywhere. The native Californios who know the lay of the land are digging up nuggets as big as ten and twelve ounces. Fifty ounces a day. Fifty pounds of gold in a week. All shallow diggings. When that kind of news reaches the States—and it already has—the rush west is gonna beat all you ever saw."

"They'll need horses," I said.

"Hundreds. Thousands of horses. But, Kid, all them gold hunters on the trails are going to scatter game and stir the Indians up something fierce. The Comanche horse trade may be too dangerous to handle."

"I can do it," I boasted. "I've got them convinced that I am neither American, nor Mexican, nor Texan. They don't see me as a revenge target for every little scrap that occurs somewhere else."

"I can't go back there with you for a while. With Charles gone, I've got to oversee the caravans as well as the Indian trade. But I'll send Uncle Dick Wootton and a dozen men with you. If you can't get us some horses, at least you'll stand a chance of fighting your way out."

THIRTY-EIGHT

The war ended that summer of 1848, and the Treaty of Guadalupe Hidalgo ceded New Mexico and California to the United States, including the territory that would become known as Arizona. But I considered all that land poor compensation for the loss of a great man like Charles Bent.

Before Uncle Dick Wootton and I left for Fort Adobe, the rush to California had already begun, though it started as a trickle—mostly Missourians who knew the Santa Fe Trail and figured they could get all the way to the diggings.

Uncle Dick Wootton had a wry sense of humor, but didn't put up with one bit of nonsense. He was one of the most industrious, competitive, capitalistic frontiersmen I ever knew. In later years, he would acquire a deed to Raton Pass, and establish a toll road over it. He knew the country, and he knew how to turn the landscape to his financial advantage.

The day we rode into Fort Adobe, fourteen men strong, we found a small band of Kiowas and Kiowa Apaches encamped on Adobe Creek. Upon sighting us, they immediately mounted, gave a war cry and charged at us.

"Hold your fire!" Uncle Dick ordered as the Indians circled us at a gallop, staying just outside of easy rifle range. "Don't let 'em bluff you into a fight. Just git them wagons into the fort!"

We managed to get two wagons loaded with trade goods through the burned-out gates of the post without firing a shot, but the Indians seemed anxious to fight. They outnumbered us two-to-one. By shouting at them in Spanish from the walkway, I managed to convince them that I was an independent trader not associated with any army or government of Mexico, Texas, or America, and that I was friends with Kiowas like Little Bluff, and Comanches like Kills Something, Shaved Head, Bloody Cloud, and Fears-the-Ground. When I told them I would bring each man a gift of tobacco if they would let me parley with them at their camp, they invited me to do just that.

Uncle Dick and the others begged me not to go, but I went, insisting on going alone. I took enough tobacco for all twenty-eight Indians in the camp. I met the leader of the party, whose name was Loud Water. I gave him his tobacco first, but when I did, I pulled a sleight-of-hand trick that made the tobacco vanish just as his palm tried to close around it. I then produced the twist of tobacco from one of his braids.

This little bit of legerdemain won the respect of the Kiowas, and I assured them that we would enjoy a brisk commerce if they had any horses, mules, or buffalo robes they wanted to get rid of in exchange for more tobacco, beads, knives, tomahawks, kettles, blankets, and other such trade goods.

The Kiowas still proved so aggressive that Uncle Dick would let them inside the fort only two at a time. They left after three days of trading, and promised to spread the word that we had arrived to other bands of Kiowas and Comanches.

Eight days later, a war party of Comanches showed up, forty warriors strong, led by my friend, Kills Something. From a distance, they shouted insults at us and threw dirt in the air as a taunt. They stayed out of range of our guns, but vowed to attack us at dawn.

That night, I slipped out of the fort, asking no man's permission, and snuck into the Comanche camp. I walked right into the light of a small campfire over which the warriors were roasting meat suspended on sticks shoved in the ground.

"*Aho,*" I said loudly, scattering warriors everywhere. It was great and dangerous fun, for every man grabbed a weapon. Kills Something recognized me and started laughing, and the rest of the warriors joined in.

"Why do you want to attack your friends at dawn?" I asked. "We have come here to trade for horses, not to make war with our allies."

Again, Kills Something began laughing. Finally, he explained to me what had happened. The Kiowa, Loud Water, had happened upon their village and informed them that a large party of Texan Indian haters had taken over Fort Adobe and had come to wage war on Comanches and take over the buffalo ranges. This was just a jest, of course, but could have precipitated a battle.

"Come to the fort at dawn and begin the trading," I told

Kills Something. "I will meet you outside the gate."

I didn't tell Uncle Dick or the other traders that I had parleyed with the Indians. So, in the morning, when I walked out to meet Kills Something and brought him into the fort with two other warriors, the men thought I had some kind of magical powers over the Indians. I just let them think what they wanted.

Kills Something made some good trades with us, then rode with two friends to fetch the main camp of Shaved Head's band. After he was gone, the rest of the Indians, whom I did not know as well, got aggressive and tried to start fights with the traders, who themselves had short fuses. Uncle Dick started allowing the Comanches inside the fort only two at a time, which slowed down trading.

When Shaved Head and the main band arrived, things settled down and trading improved. We started collecting a good herd of horses.

While all this was going on, Kills Something came to me and said, "My father said he would take fifteen ponies for Hidden Water, but only for you at that price."

"Why me?" I asked.

"She wants to be your wife. She said she will wait a little while, but you had better hurry, my friend. She will take another husband if you don't give my father the ponies."

"I am not sure."

"Stop thinking like a white man," he advised. "You can have another wife later, if you want to. If you don't like her, give her back to my father, or sell her to another man."

"Why would I want a wife? That is trouble."

"Come," he said.

We rode to the opposite edge of Shaved Head's camp, where the women were busy dressing buffalo hides staked down on the ground. Kills Something found Hidden Water and told me to take a good look at her as she scraped meat from the hide with two friends, all of them laughing about some joke. She was quite a fetching sight. The most beautiful Indian girl I had ever seen, as a matter of fact. I started letting my loins outthink my brain.

"She will make a good wife for you, and I will show you how to live the best way," he promised.

"I will think about it," I said.

The day we finished trading with Shaved Head's band, Bloody Cloud's people showed up, and trading again accelerated. But Bloody Cloud's warriors had been harassed by some Texas Rangers, and two warriors had been wounded. They were angry and vengeful.

One day, a warrior pulled a knife on Blue Wiggins inside the fort and took a slash at him. Sol Silver and Uncle Dick jumped on the warrior and clubbed him on the head. The other warrior inside the fort squalled a war cry and strung his bow, so John Hatcher picked up a billet of firewood and knocked him on the head as well. We closed the gates and poured water on the faces of the Comanches until they came back to consciousness, then threw them outside.

I went straight to Bloody Cloud's camp, against all advice of the men in the fort, and found my acquaintance, Fears-the-Ground. He was in his lodge with his young wife and baby son. I convinced him that we wanted a peaceful trade and had nothing to do whatsoever with Texas Rangers.

"The men who trade out of Bent's Fort do not like *Tejanos,*" I insisted. "We should be friends and have a good time trading."

By this time, the two warriors who had been knocked on the head had stirred up some other young hotheads, and were urging the chief, Bloody Cloud, to attack the fort and take scalps. I talked Fears-the-Ground into urging peace. We went together to Bloody Cloud's lodge to argue against fighting.

"We are not *Tejanos,*" I insisted. "We come from the north and west, not the south and east. If Texas Rangers come to your camp here and try to attack, I will help you fight them."

This was a bold statement for me to make, and I hoped no rangers would ride this far north to test it. But I had decided that I would take the side of the Comanches if the rangers attacked them. I had promised to help red men fight off white men, and was thinking of taking a Comanche wife, even against my better judgment. Was I beginning to go Indian?

Bloody Cloud calmed his warriors, and trade resumed, but Uncle Dick had grown so cautious that he would not let Indians into the fort at all. He cut a small window in the wooden gates of Fort Adobe and traded through that. This slowed things down to a crawl. To some extent, I was able to expedite things by making my own trades outside the fort wall, for I was getting along fine with the Comanches. However, generally, things went slowly.

When the trading ended, Bloody Cloud and Shaved Head took their camps away, leaving behind all the horses they had traded. A couple of weeks later, Little Bluff and his band of Kiowas arrived, and traded us out of our remaining goods. They had with them a white boy, no more than eight years old, whom I ransomed back for a trade mirror, a knife, a twist of tobacco, and a pouch full of beads. The boy would not answer us when we asked him questions in English. He seemed not to understand.

Little Bluff said he had bought the boy from some Comanches who had been down into the Texas settlements. In the fort, I gave the boy some food, and I tried speaking to him in Spanish and French, but he did not respond to these, either. On a whim, I asked him in German where he was from:

"Wo ist deine Haus?"

The boy looked at me in astonishment and began to cry. After a while, he told me in German that he had been caught by the Indians with his brother and sister outside of the German settlement called Fredericksburg, Texas. They were playing in a creek near their family's farm when the Comanches found them. The Comanches had taken all three children to different bands, then traded this boy, whose name was Hans, to the Kiowas.

"What will happen to me now?" he asked me in German.

"We will take you somewhere safe for a while. Then we will take you back to your mother, but it will take a while to get there. Don't worry. We will take good care of you."

By the next day, Hans and Jibber had become great friends. It also became apparent that the Indians had taught little Hans a thing or two about horses, for he could ride like a Comanche. Since the Indians had moved on, I let him ride Fireball around the fort and got him to show off some of the feats of horsemanship he had mastered.

I saw this boy some thirty years later, when he was a grown man who had reassimilated into white culture. He still kept several horses and could ride like no other man in his community. Even the young cowboys marveled at his riding.

This business of ransoming captured children disturbed me.

I hated the thought of children being wrenched violently from their mothers and fathers. Yet, to chastise the Indians for this practice was useless, for they, too, had experienced the loss of children at the hands of the Americans, Texans, Spaniards, and Mexicans. What were they to do about it? They fought and killed, just as they were hunted and slaughtered. And they captured the children of their enemies. Sometimes to adopt. Sometimes to ransom. And sometimes, rarely, though I am loath to think about it to this day, to torture or kill.

Do not think for a second that Comanches did not love children or respect life. They did. So much so, in fact, that you must ask yourself what it would take to make such a people steal or even murder the child of an enemy. Perhaps the loss of everything would drive a person to such a heinous extreme. Everything. The loss of family. The loss of country. The loss of livelihood. The loss of dignity and self-worth. European settlement brought exactly this kind of loss to the Indians—gradually, increasingly, irrevocably. That they did not murder and rape and kill more is to their credit, for they themselves suffered murders, rapes, slaughters, ravages of disease, and other indignities too numerous to mention.

Ask yourself how violent the Comanches were during the

Indian wars. Read your history books. Such accounts represent, by and large, the wartime propaganda of white men. The Indians had no written language. They published no history books. Had they been able to record the atrocities committed against them, we might all benefit from the opposite view of the Indian wars. As a people, they were no more perfect or good than any other race. Neither were they any less worthy or more cruel than the hordes of soldiers and settlers who defeated them.

I was beginning to see all of this at Fort Adobe, back in 1848. When presented with a captured child in the Indian trade, all I could do was try to ransom that child for return to family and home. Some of these children had become so attached to their adoptive people that they did not want to return, and would run and hide from white traders. Some of the Indians had grown to love their young adopted children so much that they would not accept a fortune in ransom. A Comanche who possessed immeasurable wealth in land and buffalo had little use for a white man's fortune, anyway.

I did what I could. I reunited many captured children with their parents and, in later years, would become renowned as a ransom negotiator. Sometimes I failed, and the captive children died among the Indians. Some of them died on the reservations, and some live there yet. Each case was different and, as I would soon learn, some presented particular difficulties.

Hans was one of the lucky ones. He survived both his capture and his return to white civilization. He even enjoyed a measure of notoriety because he had spent part of his life as a wild Comanche. But his lost brother and sister were never heard from again.

Three days after I ransomed Hans from Little Bluff's band of Kiowas, Uncle Dick Wootton decided to round up the horses we had acquired and throw them onto the long trail to Bent's Fort. John Hatcher, Sol Silver, and I elected to stay at Fort Adobe until the next trading party could arrive. These months were among the wildest and freest of my life. I hunted, rode, and learned from the land and my companions, and contemplated my existence.

Then William Bent arrived in February 1849 to take charge of Fort Adobe, and things changed. It wasn't William's fault. He always did his best and more. Things just changed, as things always do. The end began for my fort. Many other things ended, and many other things began. But now I am talking in generalities, and that will get tiresome for you soon enough. Allow me to gather my thoughts, and I will tell you what happened in 1849 at a place called Fort Adobe to a young Indian trader known as Plenty Man.

THIRTY-NINE

Comanches do not eat fish. As a matter of fact, they observe a strict taboo against it. Accordingly, I refrained from catching and cooking fish while Comanches were around, lest they should think of me as a heathen. But one day in the spring of 1849, I noticed a great many perch darting around a clear pool up Bent's Creek, and decided to engage in a little angling. I had grown tired of a constant diet of buffalo, deer, antelope, and turkey, and the thought of fish pan-fried in lard was making my stomach rumble like a Comanche Thunderbird.

Goddamn Murray had brought some fishhooks to Fort Adobe. I bought one from him, made a line of braided horsehair, tied one end to a willow branch, baited my hook with worms I had dug, and commenced to build a pretty attractive stringer of perch.

For a while, I forgot about everything save the sparkling water, the flashing lunges of the fish, and the desperate tugs of my quarry at the other end of the line. I was thus engaged when I heard someone speak behind me.

"They said I'd find you here."

I whirled, feeling foolish for having let someone sneak up on me. Kit would never have been this careless, I told myself. I squinted into the sunlight and recognized Don Bernardo Fortunado Badillo standing at the brink of the creek bank. Jibber had awakened from his nap with a growl, but I silenced him by snapping my fingers once. I had a revolver under my belt, but Don Badillo didn't have a weapon trained on me, so I made myself relax.

"A fish trap is more efficient," Don Badillo said.

"Not for a single day of fishing," I replied. "I've already caught a dozen perch. Had I built a trap, I would only now be getting to the water." My mind was whirling, trying to figure out why he had traveled all the way here from Taos—this man who had once threatened to kill me. Gabriela's father.

Of course, I had thought daily of Gabriela, and knew somehow she remembered me as well. We had not seen each other in over two years, and dared not even send letters through Rumalda. I had resolved myself to the sad fact that I would never have her. Now Don Badillo was looking down on me from the creek bank, and I simply did not know what to think.

"I see your logic," he said. "If you are going to catch fish only today." He was being rather more polite than I might have expected.

"Have you come to carry through on your threat against my life?" I asked.

He chuckled and climbed down the creek bank to join me, uninvited. "Señor Greenwood . . . That was a few years ago now. I misunderstood your intentions. A father feels very protective toward his daughters. You understand."

He stopped several feet away from me and took off his sombrero. In his eyes, I saw heaps of worry. Under his eyes, dark circles of fatigue, like baggage he was weary of carrying.

"Then why have you come here?"

"I need your help. They said you were my best chance."

"For what could you possibly need my help?"

His eyes met mine, and I saw sincere desperation. "Gabriela's child has been carried away by Indians."

I dropped my fishing pole and felt a thunderclap of panic engulf me. "Is Gabriela alright?"

"She is fine. Worried almost to death, but fine. But my grandson . . . The Indians have him."

I wanted to do something immediately. "We'll walk to the fort," I said. "You can tell me what happened." I gathered my stringer of fish and picked up my homemade pole. Jibber jumped up, and we climbed out of the creek bed.

"Gabriela was playing with little Julio outside of the *hacienda*. I always warned her when she was a little girl. I was afraid the Indians would come. Sometimes they come right to the edge of town. I told her a hundred times."

"Just tell me what happened," I said.

"The Indians rushed upon her from the arroyo. One grabbed her, and the other grabbed Julio. He is only three years old. He didn't know what was happening. Gabriela said he started laughing as the Indian carried him away. He thought it was a game. The other Indian picked her up, and she screamed. The Indian struck her, but she got a hand free and struck him back and kept screaming. Mariano was not far away. He came running with his gun. Gabriela said the Indian tried to get her onto his horse, but she clawed at him like a wildcat. The Indian threw her down and drew his knife, but Mariano came charging into the arroyo, shooting. The Indian mounted and rode away. Mariano fired until his bullets were all gone, then rushed Gabriela to safety."

"Did he kill any of the Indians?"

"Unfortunately, they all got away."

I stopped and looked Don Badillo in the eye. "Actually, that's very fortunate. If an Indian had been killed or wounded, they might have taken revenge on the child."

We started walking again, the smell of fish surrounding me as the unlucky perch flapped against my buckskin leggings. I no longer had an appetite for fish—certainly, not for beheading and gutting them. I wished I had thrown them all back into the creek. "What happened then?"

"Mariano saddled a horse and followed the Indians. He took a Pueblo servant to read the trail, but the man was afraid and went slowly. Over the mountains, they found an abandoned camp. After that, the trail split up into three different trails. Mariano didn't know which one to follow, and anyway, his horse went lame from heavy riding. He never caught up to any Indians. The savages rode too hard."

We were almost to the fort now. William was watching us from the walkway. "Do you know what tribe the Indians were?"

"Comanche."

"Are you sure?"

"Yes. The Pueblo servant said they were Comanche. I asked him how he knew. He said he could tell by the way they marked their trail. They gathered stalks of grass into a bundle, still growing from the ground, and made a crude knot in the top of the bundle. He said this was a Comanche sign."

"It is," I said. "That's fortunate. I'm on good terms with the Comanches."

We stopped in front of the gates, and Don Badillo grabbed my arm. "Can you get my grandson back?"

"You know I'll do everything I can. The ransom may be high. You should realize that the Indians may want things that are illegal to trade. Perhaps guns. Maybe even whiskey."

"I don't care. I will pay, whatever the cost. I would give my own scalp if I could."

"We'll try to accomplish this without getting anyone scalped."

"How soon can you leave?"

"No longer than it takes to pack some food and saddle my horse."

"I will saddle your horse for you."

"Very well."

I walked into Fort Adobe, handed my stringer of fish to Blue Wiggins, and went to my quarters to gather my weapons and roll my blankets. Twenty minutes later, I mounted Fireball as William stood by the gate.

"I'll find him first," I said to William. "Then I'll negotiate and send for the goods. Once I find the child, I don't think I should leave the Indians who have got him, so I'll send an Indian rider to collect the ransom."

"Where are you going to start looking?" William asked.

"I'm going to catch up with Shaved Head's band, or Bloody Cloud's—whichever I can catch first. I'll hire Kills Something or Fears-the-Ground to guide me."

"That's a hell of a plan, Mr. Greenwood. Don't you think it would be better to send a whole party?"

"No, sir. That would only stir them up."

"I'll ride with you," Blue offered.

"No, thanks, Blue. I speak Comanche. I'll get along better on my own."

I shook my reins and nudged Fireball with my knees. We stepped outside of my fort.

"*Vaya con Dios,*" Don Badillo said—the same words his daughter had last spoken to me.

"Don't forget to build yourself a *kraal* of an evenin'," John Hatcher advised.

I waved my appreciation and began a long trot toward The Crossing, with Jibber bounding gleefully through the grass.

FORTY

Both bands had taken the same trail to the south and west after crossing the Canadian River. I could plainly see the trail in the daylight because the spring grasses leaned where the travois had dragged over them. I felt lucky to have started when I did. I knew that in a couple of days, the grass would recover and stand straight again, and the signs would be harder to read.

I rode until darkness prevented my seeing the trail. Then I unsaddled Fireball, ate some jerky, and sipped some water. I used my saddle for a pillow and slept for an hour, with Jibber curled at my feet. When I woke, I watched the stars and worried about the future. I did not fear for my own safety among the Comanches. They had accepted me. But I feared the Apaches and hoped I wouldn't run into any in this wild, wide-open country that was strange to me. Mostly, I feared running out of water. I had almost thirsted to death that time before, with Blue Wiggins. I had only two canteens with me.

I felt some apprehension for Julio. I hoped he would be safe among the Indians. Mostly, I worried that something might go wrong during the ransom, and I might fail to bring him home to Gabriela, as I had failed to rescue Charles Bent from the drunken mob. I watched the moon rise with gratitude. It gave me enough light to follow the Comanche trail, so I saddled Fireball as Jibber scouted around the perimeter of our dry camp.

"Would that I were like you, Jibber," I said, "and did not feel compelled to count every last minute of sleep." Then we pressed on all night long.

The next morning, we entered the mouth of Palo Duro Canyon. I had heard of this great canyon. John Hatcher was the only white man I knew who had seen it.

I followed a well-beaten trail through the canyon, wary of Apache ambush at every turn. The trail led me up one of the branches of Palo Duro, and ascended the steep face of the canyon wall. Fireball was winded by the time he reached the top, so I stopped, dismounted, and loosened his cinch so he could breathe easier. I observed the country for twenty minutes. Kit would have watched for a couple of hours, but I was anxious to catch up to the Indians.

The rim of the canyon afforded a wonderful view for someone with eyes as keen as mine. To the east, the plains rolled away, looking like a piece of paper that had been crumpled, then somewhat smoothed out with the palm of one's hand. In that direction, below and away, I could see herds of buffalo up to ten miles distant. But the high plains that stretched away to the west of the Caprock looked as flat as a perfect sheet of parchment laying level on a table.

For a while, the trail led south of Palo Duro, where the Caprock Escarpment began. The Caprock was one continuous cliff that generally faced east, but meandered in sawtooth jags, creating canyons as it trailed away out of sight to the south. The Comanches who had told me about it claimed it extended ten sleeps from north to south, but ten sleeps for a war party measured farther than ten sleeps for a moving village with women and children, so I couldn't determine the exact distance, but reckoned it somewhere between 400 and 900 miles.

After a couple of hours of riding at a jog, the Comanche trail turned abruptly to the west. I did not want to leave the Caprock, for it afforded such a perfect landmark, but I had to follow the trail and venture alone out onto that ocean of grass called the *Llano Estacado*. I had filled my canteens down in Palo Duro Canyon, but did not know where I might find water again.

I rode into the evening, and found the remnants of a camp where the Indians had stayed a few days. There was a break in the flat landscape, where a slight trough cut away to the northeast. I wondered at this choice of campsite at first, for I found no water down in the shallow depression. Certainly they could not have stayed here longer than one day without water.

Looking around, however, I found where many hoofprints and foot trails led to a certain place up above the head of the shallow ravine. Here I found a natural hole in the ground, no bigger around than the open top of a hogshead barrel. Finding a pebble nearby, I tossed it in. I listened to a couple of seconds of silence, then heard the pebble plunk into water.

Right then, I sat down and drank the last from my first canteen. Using my rope, I then lowered the canteen down the hole and let it fill up with water. I found the water cool and pleasant to taste. I wondered if this was the cave that had given its name to Kills Something's beautiful sister, Hidden Water. I made myself drink until I thought I would bust, then unrolled the piece of tarpaulin I used to keep my blankets dry. I gouged a small hole in the ground with the hilt of my saber and lay the tarpaulin inside it, making a bowl. This I filled with water, hoping Fireball would drink. He stood over the water for half an hour, then finally decided to taste it. I kept refilling it as he drank, and I was grateful that he took three canteens. Jibber drank after Fireball, and we rode on to the west, following the trail. I stopped again to rest between sunset and moonrise.

Before I could sleep, I saw a terrible vision of a mountain lion creeping up on me, growling. He crept for hours, and seemed to get closer and closer, yet never quite reached me. At last, I slept for a couple of hours, but woke up feeling exhausted, and hoped Burnt Belly would have fir needles and roots of dogbane and moccasin flower when I caught up to him.

The next day, I found the two bands under Bloody Cloud and Shaved Head camped all around a small lake far out on the plains. As soon as I recognized the tepees as those of Comanches, I decided to play a trick on the Indians. I was tired of them rushing out to greet me with their warlike antics, so I decided to charge them instead. They were preparing to leave this camp, and all were somewhat distracted with rounding up horses and packing travois, so they hadn't yet spotted me.

I charged into camp with Jibber barking and Fireball snorting and me screaming a war cry. We scattered women and children and dogs; then reined in and just laughed. Some of the young warriors were angry and strung their bows, but Burnt Belly came over to me and joined my laughter.

"You young fools are lucky it was only Plenty Man, and not a band of *Tejanos* or Apaches. When are you going to learn to guard your village like an eagle?"

Kills Something galloped up to me with a rare expression of surprise. "You have been thinking about my sister. I am glad you have come to join us."

"You misunderstand," I said. "I came for your help. I have a trade to make. It will be a good trade for both of us."

"I do not want to talk about trading. You have come to take my sister. I will go to my father for you and ask what he wants for her."

"No," I said. "I have come for a different reason. I need your help."

"You can tell me about it on the trail," he said. "We are moving today. Come, we have ponies to gather."

Once the horses were gathered, I told Kills Something about the capture of the child. Fears-the-Ground was there as well, and he listened to my story. Shaved Head's band and Bloody Cloud's band were to take different paths today, each going its own way. But when Fears-the-Ground heard my tale, he said he would ride with me if Kills Something would.

"You want my help," Kills Something said in mock anger. "You who tried to kill me the day we met. Why should I help you? You must promise something for me in return; then I will help you."

"What must I promise?"

"Marry my sister, join my band of people, and destroy that fort before the soldiers use it to destroy us."

"That is three things," I said.

"It is three parts of one thing," he argued.

"But the fort is good for us all. We trade there. You bring horses and robes, and I bring iron and tobacco and other good things."

"If you take that girl, you can ride into this camp anytime you want to and trade. You can live among us, help us raid for horses, and then go get the wagons when it is time. You do not need a fort. The fort brings too many white men with too many guns. William Bent is going to trade his other fort—the big fort—to the soldiers. The Cheyennes who live there say it is true. If he trades one, he will trade the other, and then there will be soldiers out here chasing us, as you chased us down today."

"William would have told me if he was going to sell the fort. He said the soldiers would not pay enough, so he won't let them have it."

"I know the soldiers will not buy your little fort if you destroy it. Promise me these things: That you will destroy the fort. That you will marry my sister. That you will live in my village wherever it goes. Promise, and I will help you find the captive."

I sat on Fireball in silence for ten minutes; but Comanches are always patient in counsel or in a trade, so Kills Something and Fears-the-Ground let me think. My first inclination was to agree to everything Kills Something had demanded, for I was hell-bent on getting Julio back to Gabriela. Gradually, however, I began to remember that I was an Indian trader. I would make a deal. Find a compromise.

"Listen," I said. "This is what I have decided. If you come with me and help me ransom back the captive child, I will make a promise to you. After the ransom, I will go back to my fort. If the soldiers come there and try to use the fort, I will destroy it. I built that fort with my own hands. I built it for trade, not for war. If anyone tries to use it to make war against my friends, I will destroy the fort." I tried to leave the girl out of the negotiation, but Kills Something would not have any of that.

"And when you destroy the fort, you will come take my sister into your lodge, and live as my brother. You must promise this, or I will not ride with you for the ransom."

For the first time, I could see Kills Something's logic. It finally dawned on me why he wanted me so badly in his band. He was going to lead this band as chief one day. He was ambitious and brave. He trusted me. He wanted a link with a white trader he could trust. But he wanted the trader to live with him, as a Comanche, to ride for the trade goods only when enough horses and robes had been gathered to make a good haul. I was going to be that trader.

Kills Something had a realistic grasp of the future. He saw more and more white people coming. The rush to California had begun to disrupt game on the Santa Fe Trail. The soldiers from the war had alarmed the Indians and hinted of future incursions into Comanche range. The Texas Rangers were beginning to pursue raiding parties ever farther onto the plains. Kills Something saw all of this. He wanted no fort inside his country to house the soldiers of his enemies. He was a shrewd leader with a view of days to come. He was going to hold these ranges as long as possible, at all cost.

"I promise," I said. "When can we leave to find the captive?"

"As soon as Fears-the-Ground is ready."

"I am always ready."

"When the two villages begin to move, we will move also. We will go west.

I had just enough time to find Burnt Belly and purchase from him the remedies he had already prepared for me.

"I have asked about the captive child," he said, his hand holding my arm, and his eyes searing me from his weathered face. "No one knows anything. Two warriors joined us yesterday from the south. They said the child was not with the band they left. Do not think that west is the only way to ride. The people who took the child could be anywhere. It will not be easy, Plenty Man. I see you in dreams and visions. You are always surrounded by evil, yet you are trying to do good. It is going to get very dangerous."

This was not what I wanted to hear, and I tried dismissing it as the ramblings of a charlatan; but the words burned into the center of my heart. I turned away from Burnt Belly, feeling unexplainably afraid.

I found Kills Something and Fears-the-Ground, and we left. We didn't even bother to tell anyone where we were going. Kills Something said that if they wanted to know badly enough, they could follow us and find out.

FORTY-ONE

There were shallow lakes out there in those days, widely scattered across that infinity of grass. A sojourner who knew how to find the lakes could survive by moving from one to the next—if an isolated dry spell hadn't dried up the lake he had counted on to slake his thirst and water his livestock.

At the first lake we came to out on those vast plains, Fears-the-Ground let his pony drink, then made the animal wade into the lake so that he could scoop water up with his hand and drink without dismounting.

"My friend," I said, when we were again on our way, "I do not understand your medicine. You are brave. Why, then, do you fear the ground?"

"When a warrior goes to seek his vision," he explained, "he hopes to see a powerful spirit talk to him. A bear-spirit, or an elk-spirit. These are powerful. So is buffalo medicine and deer medicine."

"I understand this."

"When a warrior sees the vision of a bear-spirit, he must honor the bear forever, or his own medicine may destroy him. He must never kill or eat a bear. He must not eat the things a bear eats, for that takes food from the bear. And to step upon the track of a bear dishonors the bear-spirit, and so the warrior must be careful to watch for bear tracks all the time."

"Yes, I know about the taboos and the tracks. Do you have bear medicine?"

"Yes. I have all the medicine. In my vision, many spirit-animals spoke to me. Buffalo, deer, elk, bear, mountain lion, antelope. To step on the tracks of any of these could destroy me. These tracks are everywhere. My spirit protectors told me that I could ride a horse, and the horse could step on the tracks, and this would not dishonor them. But still, I try to ride around the tracks if I can."

"But you cannot eat buffalo, or deer, or elk, or bear, or mountain lion, or antelope?"

"This is true."

"Or anything that any of these animals eat?"

"Yes."

"What do you eat?"

"Horse meat. There are plenty of horses, and the mountain lions do not miss one when I eat it."

I felt much better talking to Fears-the-Ground. My burdens seemed light compared to those of a man afraid to step upon the track of an animal across the richest hunting grounds on the continent. Kills Something, too, lightened my mood. While I feared crossing into Apache country, he hoped for a battle with these enemies. He shrugged off the possibility of death, saying, "Who wants to die with gray hair?"

As we rode on, I said, "Teach me how to find the next water."

My two Comanche friends laughed at my ignorance for a while; then we rode on silently. But, at length, Fears-the-Ground drew rein, his finger pointing at something that swept swiftly across the horizon. I recognized the gray streak as a flying dove.

"When Father Sun falls toward the west, the dove flies straight to water," he said.

We changed our course slightly to angle toward the dove's. After riding another hour and a half, we came to a small mesquite switch sticking up above the grass. Kills Something pointed at it and said, "Water is forty arrow shots away."

I had figured the typical Comanche unit of measurement called an arrow shot at about one-eighth of a mile, for a strong warrior with a good bow could easily make an arrow sail that far in a long arch through the air. Forty arrow shots equaled roughly five miles. But I still didn't understand how water five miles away could affect this mesquite switch. Did it have roots reaching five miles underground? Certainly not.

When I asked about this, the Comanches again ridiculed my ignorance.

"You have seen the seeds of the mesquite tree?" Kills Something asked.

"Yes, in pods hanging from the tree limbs."

"The seeds will not grow into a tree without the medicine of the buffalo."

"What do you mean?"

"The buffalo eats the seed and it passes through, taking on the medicine of the buffalo and coming out in the *kwitapu.*"

The polite translation for this, I knew, was excrement.

"Only then will the seed grow."

I considered what Kills Something said. "The buffalo eats the seed of the mesquite," I said. "Then he comes to water. He stays around the water until the grass is gone, dropping much *kwitapu* within an easy walk of the water—forty arrow shots. That is why more mesquites grow near the water."

It was a simple cause-and-effect explanation, but sometimes even a genius misses something under his very nose. As we got closer to the water, I saw more mesquite switches and more buffalo chips. Soon we found the high-plains lake supplied with abundant water. We camped here this night, for my Comanche friends were tired. I chewed the roots of moccasin flower and dogbane, and enjoyed more than four hours of sleep. We rode at dawn.

We rode and rode and rode. I would look back occasionally, and see our trail, straight as a rifle shot. We went west into the third day. Finally, we crossed the trail of a single rider. Following this trail, we found where the rider had moved a buffalo skull so that it would point in the direction of the trail. This was the Comanche way of luring the buffalo-spirits closer to them. We rode hard once we knew we had found the trail of a Comanche rider.

We followed the trail until we came to the breaks of the Pecos River, which the Comanches called "Bitter Water." We found the village of tepees near a spring, and we rode in with an escort of boys who pretended they had discovered us, and took us straightaway to their chief. The band had recently enjoyed a great buffalo hunt, and they fed us lavishly as they told us what they knew about the captive I sought.

Everyone seemed to have heard something, though they might have been talking about any number of captives. Finally, though, one young warrior named Loud Shouter, who had been traveling to different bands in search of a wife, convinced me that he had actually seen Julio. Loud Shouter described how Julio had been captured on the very outskirts of Taos. Every detail seemed to match the facts of Julio's abduction. Loud Shouter said he was owned by the war chief, Bull Bear, who had been camped in the breaks of the Canadian River, three sleeps to the north.

"Will you guide us to this camp?" I asked.

"I am going back there soon," Loud Shouter said. "I have gathered six horses to give to the father of the mother of my children-not-yet-born."

This was luck beyond hope. We had found someone who could take us directly to Julio and help us arrange a ransom. Moreover, Kills Something said he knew Bull Bear, and had no doubt that the chief would sell the captive child to me. We agreed to leave the next morning.

Loud Shouter turned out to be a good hand on the trail, and we traveled northward quickly. With his six-horse dowry, we rode three sleeps until we found the lake where Bull Bear's band had camped in the breaks of the upper Canadian. The grass was used up and the people had moved on. The trail was cold, but Loud Shouter, Kills Something, and Fears-the-Ground said they could follow it to the southeast.

I learned from them. They taught me to look for mounds of horse dung and how to judge from them the age of the trail. They taught me to look for the ruts of the travois. Even though rain and wind had obliterated most of the ruts, an occasional remnant no longer than a snake would point like a compass toward the band's destination. My companions also taught me to look for things missing, like the cropped tips of grasses where the horses had grazed as the village moved. Mainly, they taught me to *feel* the trail rather than trying to strain my eyes so hard to see it. Which way was the good way, the wise way, the best way, the efficient way? Feel the trail. Absorb the sign like the earth soaking in rainfall.

Every day, we would find some trail marker. A stack of rocks. A knotted bundle of grass. Three sticks stuck upright in the dirt. Loud Shouter claimed that these signs had been left for him, for Bull Bear's people expected him to follow with his dowry on the hoof. We rode southeast, through a land of buttes and bluffs, then back out onto the *Llano Estacado*.

"The trail gets fresher," Kills Something said.

"We ride faster than they rode over this same ground, yes?"

"The pole drags go slowly."

"How much faster do *we* ride?" I asked. The question seemed somewhat disturbing to Kills Something, but he formed an answer.

"They ride four sleeps. We ride three over the same ground."

"How many days before us did they leave the last camp?"

This question launched two hours of debate, but finally, the three Comanches settled on the figure of thirteen days. To me, this became an algebraic equation.

"Even if they keep moving," I announced, "we will overtake them before the end of our tenth day of travel from their last camp at the lake. Of course, if they stop, we will overtake them sooner. We have been traveling four days since we left the breaks of the river, so we will find Bull Bear's new camp in no more than six days.

The Comanches looked at me fearfully, as if I were an evil shaman. It was not the Comanche way to figure things out, but to accept whatever happened as the will of the spirits, and react accordingly. By trying to predict the future, I had unknowingly set myself up as a mystic, and tempted the disfavor of their gods. This made them all very nervous, and they refused to talk to me thereafter.

"Count the numbers, and you will see," I said, trying to explain my algebraic calculations in Comanche. "Four is to three as eight is to six as thirteen is to nine and a half, plus half of a half."

Fears-the-Ground covered his ears.

Anyway, they didn't talk to me for six days; but toward the end of that sixth day, we overtook Bull Bear's village out on the plains. The joy of my Comanche friends matched my own. I was elated that we had overtaken the village with whom Julio lived, and they were overjoyed that my prophecy had come true, proving that the spirits looked kindly upon us.

Mounted warriors met us as we overtook the moving village. They recognized Loud Shouter, and welcomed us all.

"Have you been moving since you left the camp in the breaks?" Loud Shouter asked.

"Yes," came the reply.

My three companions looked at me in wonder.

"The spirits talk to Plenty Man," Kills Something said. "They told him we would find you on this day."

"I said if they kept moving. I used the numbers." In my rudimentary Comanche, I continued trying to explain the concept of a variable in an algebraic equation, until Fears-the-Ground covered his ears again, and I decided I would let it go. My real task here was to ransom Julio.

Bull Bear rode to the rear of the column to see what was going on. When he saw me with my three Comanche friends, and heard how I had prophesied the future, he called a halt to the march so we could talk and smoke. I did not mention the ransom right away, nor did my friends. The reason for my journey would be revealed soon enough.

We sat in a circle on the ground, and somebody produced a pipe and some tobacco. Some of the Comanche women

ventured near enough to get a look at me, but I had yet to
see any children at all. Bull Bear lit the pipe, inhaled, patted
the smoke from his mouth onto his chest, and passed the
pipe to me. I have never smoked tobacco, so I declined. The
chief looked at me as if I had insulted him.

"The spirits forbid me to smoke," I said. "I have strange
medicine."

"What kind of medicine?" Bull Bear demanded.

"Moon medicine."

He nodded, as if satisfied by my answer, and the pipe
went on around the circle.

At length, a few children snuck up behind their mothers,
or behind ponies or a travois, and peered at me cautiously.

"Why are they so afraid of me?" I asked Bull Bear.

"They have never seen a white man before," he said.

Now I realized how deep I was into Comanche country.
I was, perhaps, the first white man to venture to these
ranges. This both pleased and amazed me.

After smoking, Bull Bear finally said to Loud Shouter, "I
am happy that you have come to take the girl and make her
a good wife. You have brought friends with you. I am sorry
that my little village does not have wives for all of you."

We all laughed, and I saw my opportunity to announce
the reason for my journey. "My friend, Kills Something,
believes he has already found a wife for me," I said. "I come
for another reason."

"What reason?"

"I come to make trade."

"What trade?"

"I know a man who wishes to pay a ransom for the captive child in your village."

Bull Bear looked over his shoulder. "Wife, bring the
shirt!" he ordered. His wife scurried away, and he looked
back toward me. "Which child?"

"The child was taken near a house at the edge of the
village the Mexicans call San Fernandez de Taos. A boy.
Three winters old."

Bull Bear sat in silence until his wife approached at a trot with a tanned deerskin. She handed it to Bull Bear, and he opened it, revealing, to my astonishment, a Spanish coat of chain mail probably a hundred years old. It was a little corroded in places, but seemed to have been polished recently to a sheen.

"I have already traded the child," Bull Bear said. "I did not want to in the beginning, but look what I got." He held the chain mail up in front of him like a dandy trying on a new vest.

My heart felt like ice in my chest, my high hopes instantly dashed. Still, the trail was warm. I would follow. "Who has the captive now?" I asked.

"I traded him to Lame Deer's band."

Wearily, I sighed. My moon medicine was fading. The dark nights were coming. I felt exhausted. "Who is Lame Deer?"

The words came like a lance point to my vitals: "Do you not know? He shot you in the back with an arrow. Four winters ago, as you crossed the River of Arrowheads. You killed his son, who was dressed as a wolf and was trying to steal your horses. Lame Deer is Mescalero Apache. He is your enemy."

FORTY-TWO

We reached a campsite on a creek they called *Koyah-ah*, which they made me to understand was a reference to the crayfish found in the waters. I set up a shelter made of borrowed lodge poles and a couple of buffalo hides, and went to sleep. For a while, I dreamed fearful nightmares of Julio among the Apaches, and of me trying to ransom or rescue him from my enemies. In these nightmares, something always went wrong with the ransom. Then my sleep became a dark nothingness devoid of any sensation.

When I woke, Kills Something and Fears-the-Ground told me I had slept for almost four days. Bull Bear's people had set up a comfortable village along the stream. They fed me, and I felt refreshed. My moon medicine replenished, I was ready to carry on.

But how? Kills Something and I had both fought hand to hand with Lame Deer's warriors, for they were the Apaches who had attacked Fort Adobe when I rescued Hidden Water. We would not be welcome among them, except perhaps as donors for a scalp dance. We decided that we must find Lame Deer's band without being discovered, and then send Fears-the-Ground in to buy the captive child. He had done no battle with Apaches—at least, none with Lame Deer's band—and perhaps could get away with a trading excursion among them. That my Comanche friends agreed to do this— and even suggested it—astounded me. They seemed filled with fearless faith in my medicine, and their own. I now thought of them as I would Blue Wiggins, or John Hatcher, or William Bent, or Kit Carson. They were friends of the most loyal stripe.

Bull Bear told us where to find Lame Deer's village. Unlike the ever-roaming Comanches, each Apache band camped in one spot throughout the summer to plant corn for autumn harvest. Lame Deer's people would be easy to find. Their village lay ten sleeps south and west, in the Guadalupe Mountains, east of the old Spanish city of El Paso del Norte.

This was a long way away, but at least Lame Deer was camped near El Paso—now an American town, according to the new maps. When I succeeded in ransoming little Julio, I reasoned, I could ride hard for El Paso, and keep the child safe there until a reunion with his mother could be arranged.

Before leaving Bull Bear's band, I made one last request of the newly wedded Loud Shouter. "My friend, will you ride hard through the dangerous land to the north, and carry something to the big fort on the River of Arrowheads,

though your enemies may hunt you for your scalp?" The
way to get a Comanche to do something, I had discovered,
was to make it sound as precarious and as foolhardy as
possible.

"You cannot name a place I fear to ride," he boasted.

I took this as an affirmative reply. I now wrote a letter
with parchment and a pencil I had carried along from Fort
Adobe, while the Comanches looked on with fascination.

"What is he doing?" one old man asked. "Witchcraft?"

"No," Kills Something replied. "I have seen some white
men do this. The signs make the paper talk."

"I do not hear it talk," the old man said.

"It talks only to one who knows the signs. It is strange."

I tried to explain to the Comanches that the signs spoke
to white people the way the trail markers spoke to Comanches.

"Then you will teach me," the old man said.

"It takes much time," I said, trying to figure out how to
explain the concept of the alphabet in my less-than-complete
Comanche vocabulary. "Each sign has a sound that goes
with it. All the sounds strung together make a word, as if a
person spoke it."

This was too much for Fears-the-Ground. He covered his
ears, unwilling to listen to such heresy. The old man waved
his hand at all the nonsense and walked away.

The letter I wrote was addressed to Bent's Fort. I remember it word for word:

To Kit Carson, or whomever may make it his concern:
I am camped with Bull Bear's band of Comanches
somewhere on the Llano Estacado. I am preparing to
ride with two Comanche guides to the Guadalupe
Mountains east of El Paso del Norte, to ransom or
otherwise rescue the child, Julio Zavaleta, aged three-
and-a-half, who is currently being held captive by
Lame Deer's band of Apaches. Assuming I will suc-
ceed, I request escort from El Paso del Norte to San
Fernandez de Taos in order to transport the child

*safely to his home. Any assistance rendered by any
party will be appreciated and rewarded accordingly.*

Signed,
Honoré Greenwood
also known as Plenty Man

I handed the letter over to Loud Shouter and prepared
Fireball for the long ride to the southwest. Jibber was so
excited about the prospect of adventure that he started jumping straight up and down in the air when I grabbed my
saddle. The Comanches thought this was funny, which only
encouraged Jibber, and Bull Bear's people laughed and
laughed as we rode away.

Try to imagine that country in those days. I will do my best
to help you. Let my recollections fire your imagination until
my descriptions play out before your mind's eye like a living work of art, accompanied by all the sounds and smells
and sensations of the wild country.

Imagine your buckskins sticking hot to your skin where
the sun beats down. A gust peppers your eyeballs with grit
and parches your mouth with the dry bitter taste of alkali
dust.

You ride, your saddle pressed hard against your thighs,
the rhythm of your pony's gait a part of your very existence
now. Through your squint, you sweep the horizon in a
never-ending search for something exhilarating or fatal. You
ride all day, day after day, without finding a house, or a
road, or a fence, or even a wisp of cook-fire smoke. All that
you find is wild, from the prairie dogs that perch above their
holes and bark, to the antelopes that stalk you out of curiosity, only to turn and flee at your scent.

You watch a cloud the size of a feudal fiefdom walk past
you on stilts of lightning, an impossible daddy-longlegs spider out for a stroll. You only smell the rain, sweet and
musky, but you appreciate the spider's shadow, for you will

not see a tree large enough to throw shade until you find
running water two days ahead.

Your saddle leather makes a creaking sound you will hear
tonight in your fitful dreams. Your mouth reminds your
hand to touch the canteen, but you know you must not drink
yet. Your pony looks sidewise at a rattling snake that, un-
coiled, would rival a shepherd's staff. You waste no time
with reptiles. You soak in the beauty of the open country
until you cannot hold any more of it. Your senses saturated,
you feel you must scream, or weep, or gallop needlessly, or
go mad. But you just ride on and on and on, and hope for
water, and watch for enemies, and wish for wings. You eat
in the saddle, and laugh a little with friends, and sing songs
under your breath. You ride until you wish you could do
anything but ride, be it float, sail, sleep, sit, dance, crawl,
slide, roll, stumble, or swim. But all you can do is get down
and walk for a while.

You wonder what brought you here.

You began this morning, with the wolves singing and the
stars fading. You will ride until you can no longer see the
ground under your pony's hooves. Then you will listen to
shrieks and howls and hoots of wild creatures. You will ride
again by the rising moon, then by the sun that soars higher
to humble you with its fierce glare. You ride and ride and
ride. Grass gives way to cactus. The coyote skulks in the
distance, an amber-eyed trickster. The hawk dives at twilight, and the young cottontail screams his death song. You
camp at a pond where a flock of redwing blackbirds flies as
if possessed of a single mind, rattling as it plunges at once
into a tangle of reeds and tules. You listen to the low moan
of bullfrogs and contemplate how a frog ever arrived here,
at this isolated pool—perhaps as an egg stuck to the leg of
a heron.

You wake early and ride. Finally, in the distance, like a
great hazy vision, you see the massive purple shoulders of
the Guadalupe Range begin to materialize, and your heart
leaps. You give thanks for your delivery, in spite of the very
real prospects of battle, torture, and death. You have ridden
well and arrived sound.

Now you must accomplish a task that you have come to think of as well-nigh impossible. You will do it, or die.

We camped in a lost canyon Kills Something had visited once returning from a raid down in Mexico. A small seep spring up one of the headers provided just enough water for three men and their animals in a puddle no bigger than a beaver pelt and too shallow to drown a tarantula. After filling our canteens, we had to take the horses to water one at a time, allowing half an hour between them to let the pool refill.

The canyon also afforded three avenues of escape, should enemies discover us here. We made no fire and little noise. From Bull Bear's descriptions, and his maps drawn in the dirt, we knew where to find Lame Deer's Apaches. We were not far away. Just distant enough to stay beyond Lame Deer's guards.

That night, we talked about what would happen when we found the village and sent Fears-the-Ground in to meet the Apaches. I had learned much about my companions through our days of travel, and had concocted a plan. Indians, I had observed, lied well enough when they were setting someone up for a prank. But when it came down to bald-faced dishonesty, they considered lying cowardly. Lying for the sake of intrigue disgusted them. They would rather challenge an enemy to a fight than maneuver him into an ambush with fabrications.

I had come to know that Fears-the-Ground had been hoping for a son, but his young wife had not yet become pregnant, though he insisted he had done his part. "I think she takes stone seed," he had said.

So I suggested this: "Tell Lame Deer the truth. Tell him you come seeking the white child. When he asks why, tell him your wife is unable to have a child. That is all you need say, and it is all the truth."

Fears-the-Ground agreed. He left on foot with the rising

moon, taking great pains to cover his moccasin prints with a branch. He knew the Apaches would attempt to back-trail him. They were highly protective of their summer villages, which they guarded vigilantly against enemy attack.

Kills Something and I waited a day and a night. We planned to rest ourselves and our stock. If Fears-the-Ground succeeded in ransoming Julio, he would bring the child to the canyon. Then we would all ride on fresh mounts before the Apaches could overtake us. We knew they would follow Fears-the-Ground back to this camp to verify his story, and that we would have to outdistance them, or fight them off.

We waited another whole day, and I began to worry. At dusk, Kills Something and I heard a stone rattle below in the canyon, and we stalked cautiously that way to investigate. We knew it wasn't Fears-the-Ground. We had already arranged a signal for him to give upon his approach. We found a good place for an ambush, and waited. We heard a rider coming around a bend, and drew our bows. Slowly, the head of a horse came into view, followed by its rider.

One whiskey trader. Bill Snakehead Jackson.

FORTY-THREE

Snakehead unfolded the letter I had written and hissed with laughter, his brown teeth bared. "It says to whomever may make it his concern. Hell, Kid, I thought that meant me. I owe you one, don't I?"

We were sitting at the tiny puddle of water made by the seep spring in the canyon, and I was watching Snakehead sully the waters with his dirty cupped hand which he used to carry a drink to his mouth. I was thankful that I had recently filled my canteens.

"How did you come by the letter?"

"Kilt the carrier."

I sat feeling stupid and guilty. "Loud Shouter?"

"Was that his name? He shouted loud enough when I stuck him with my knife. I'm pretty sure he was kilt. Maybe he lived."

I wanted to murder Snakehead here and now, and wished I had let him die of cold in that freezing mountain stream. "Where did you run onto Loud Shouter?" I asked, feigning calm.

"At a Comanche camp I was workin' on the Cimarron. He was carryin' your letter to Kit, I reckon. He got so drunk, he decided maybe he could sell me that letter for another swaller. I snatched it from him to read it first, and he got mad and come after me with a war axe. I stuck him, and then it seemed like every one of them drunken bucks decided they wanted to stick me. Damn ungrateful pieces of shit. All hell busted loose about that time, but I fought my way out. I got away with the one keg of whiskey left to me."

"You're not sure if you killed him?"

Snakehead shrugged. "I stuck him deep, but them Comanch' is tough. He may live to drink again."

I looked away from Snakehead, the most repulsive human I have ever known. Everything about him celebrated death, from the string of human fingers he wore around his neck, to his pale killer's eyes. He had a stench about him that made me want to vomit. It wasn't the normal odor of a body too long unbathed. He smelled like carrion.

"You figured out how to git that kid out of Lame Deer's camp?"

"It's being done right now," I claimed. "A Comanche friend of mine, Fears-the-Ground, is bargaining for him today. When he gets here with the boy, we're going to ride as hard as we can for El Paso."

"You sent somebody in? Don't you think they'll back-trail him?"

"He went in on foot and covered his tracks."

"How the hell is he gonna carry the boy if he went in on foot?"

"He's going to trade for a horse, as well."

"It'll never work. They ain't gonna give up the boy that easy. But I'll get him out of there, by God. I've still got one keg of whiskey."

"I'm hoping that won't be necessary."

Snakehead ridiculed me with a foul grunt, and sprawled out in the shade next to the water hole. "I don't savvy all I know about this deal. Somebody must have paid you a hell of a lot of money to risk your scalp away down here."

"The child's grandfather sent me."

"Bernardo Badillo."

I nodded, though I didn't like the fact that Snakehead knew this.

"He's got plenty of land and money. What's he willing to pay?"

"Anything."

"You didn't nail down a ransom?"

"No. He said whatever it took, he'd pay."

"I better go with you to collect, then; otherwise you won't get a goddamn peso."

"He'll pay me."

"The hell he will. I've been knowin' that old bastard for years. He'd cheat his mama out of a day's wages. When we git the boy back to Taos, we'll hold him in the mountains till Badillo pays up what we want."

"Well, the first thing is to get the boy out of Lame Deer's camp." I tried to avoid any talk of a partnership with Snakehead.

"Kid, you don't know the first thing."

I bit my tongue. I was not going to be drawn into an argument with this murderer. "I can do this alone," I said. "You don't owe me anything."

Snakehead just laughed at me and rolled over on his side to go to sleep. I turned my back on him and went to sit out of sight of him. I could see Kills Something on the rim of the canyon, standing guard. The waiting was bad enough, but now Snakehead was here. I could only hope that Fears-the-Ground had succeeded in ransoming little Julio. If so, we could ride for El Paso. Then I could figure out a way to get rid of Snakehead.

Of course, it didn't happen that way. Two hours after dark, after being gone almost forty-eight hours, we heard the call of the great horned owl—the signal we had agreed upon. Kills Something hooted back, and Fears-the-Ground crept carefully down into the canyon. I gave him some water from my canteen. Snakehead, his horse, and the mule he used to carry his whiskey, had depleted the water that pooled in the seep spring at the head of the canyon. After slaking his thirst, Fears-the-Ground told his tale. He spoke in Spanish, so that Snakehead could understand. In the Comanche way, I sat quietly and listened, as if in the council lodge. I knew Fears-the-Ground would have rehearsed this story in his mind, and that it would be most complete, even if it might take him some time to tell it.

"I walked into their camp," he began, "and asked what they had to trade. I thought they were going to kill me at first. They said, 'You have nothing to trade!' I told them I could bring many horses. They brought me to Lame Deer's lodge, and I spoke to him. While we were talking, I saw the captive boy. He was playing with some Apache children, running and laughing. He is well.

"Lame Deer asked if I traveled alone. I told him I did. He sent three trackers to follow my trail, but I was wise, and I knew they could not trail me, for I had walked upon hard places, and brushed away my footprints in the dirt. The sun moved four fists across the sky, and the three trackers came back and said I was alone. They did not want to say that they could not find my trail.

"After a while, I asked Lame Deer about the captive child. I told him I wanted a child because my wife was without a child; and no matter how hard I tried to make her good with my seed, no baby would come. I offered to bring him a horse and some tobacco for the child. He said no. I offered two horses, tobacco, and a gun. He said no. I offered three horses, tobacco, a gun, and much powder. He said no. . . ."

Here, Fears-the-Ground recited the terms of every offer he made to Lame Deer. In the end, he offered twenty horses, two guns, five lodge poles, and a flask of gunpowder.

"Lame Deer said, 'No, I will not trade. Go catch your own boy.' "

There was a silence punctuated by a meteor that raked the sky with its trail from canyon rim to canyon rim.

"That was all?"

"I left their camp. I walked north until I was sure they followed me no more. Then, I came east to this place. That is all. They will not trade the boy."

"Shit!" Snakehead scrambled to his feet.

"What are you doing?"

"Snuggin' my cinch, goddamn it." He began walking toward the horses, and I followed.

"What for?"

"Git them Apaches drunk."

"Then what?"

"Well, I don't know. Let's just find out. Give me the day to get 'em drunk. When the sun sets on Lame Deer's camp tomorrow, and he sees that whiskey start to run low, he'll trade me anything I want, from his favorite wife to his warhorse. Hell, he'll trade me his firstborn daughter. When he gets drunk, a damn Mexican boy won't mean any more to him than a camp dog."

"But—" I started.

"But's ass, Kid." He was picking up his saddle now to throw onto his mount. "You make too many goddamn plans. You just sneak in there about dark tomorrow, and see if you can't carry the boy out without anybody seein' you. Problem is, I ain't got enough whiskey to get *all* of them Apaches stinkin' drunk, and that's just gonna make 'em mad. They could slaughter all our asses. Oh, well, a man's got to die sometime."

I tried to get Snakehead to formulate some kind of plan that would allow for more control of the situation, but he only laughed as he saddled his horse and rode out of the canyon with his pack mule in tow.

After he was gone, I sat down and talked with my two Comanche friends for some time. At first, they looked at me as if my medicine had gone bad, but I told them that I was going into the Apache camp tomorrow after dark because I loved danger.

"The danger I endure proves the power of my spirit-protectors," I said. "Someday I will seek so much danger that it will kill me, but that is better than dying with white hair." This Comanche style of boasting made even me feel better.

We came up with a plan. I would concentrate on rescuing the child. The Comanches would take scalps and steal horses, then ride east with their spoils as a diversion, while I rode west, toward El Paso, with Julio. With incredible luck, I might outdistance the Apaches. Snakehead would take care of himself as he saw fit.

That was the best plan this genius could come up with under the circumstances.

<hr>

The Guadalupe Mountains stand like monuments to survival, rising invitingly from the desert. They reach skyward, gather rain from errant thunderclouds, harbor greenery and water and life. According to Fears-the-Ground, Lame Deer had chosen his camp well. The lodges of his people extended for half a mile along a small creek that collected water in numerous pools, from which the women watered scattered fields of corn. Fears-the-Ground had drawn a map of the village in the dirt floor of our canyon. He had counted thirty lodges in sight. I estimated three warriors per lodge. Ninety enemy warriors. We were outnumbered better than twenty to one, not allowing for the women, who would also fight.

I was prepared to die fighting in Lame Deer's camp. I still held on to a hope of getting Julio out alive, but I would have been foolish not to have addressed the probability of death. Were Julio not the son of Gabriela, whom I knew had to be near insanity from grief, I would have ridden away and let the child grow up with the Apaches. I will be honest. This whole business scared the wits out of me.

We rode as close to Lame Deer's camp as we dared, stopping short of the place where Fears-the-Ground had encountered sentinels on his previous reconnaissance. We rested the remainder of the day in the shade of some ash trees. We talked little. Kills Something chanted. Toward sundown, the Comanches took out their little buckskin bags filled with black war paint made from charcoal and animal fat. Kills Something painted his entire face black. Fears-the-Ground made two streaks on his brow, and three streaks coming down from each eye.

They offered me their paint. I reasoned that it might help conceal my pale face in the night. I thought about what kind of paint I should fashion in accordance with my medicine. Moon medicine. My greatest powers came with the half-moon. The dark of the moon plunged me into exhaustion. The full moon allowed me to stay awake for days, but robbed me of rejuvenating sleep. During the half-moon, I could function almost normally, sleeping a few hours every night.

Accordingly, I painted half my face black. Like a half-moon. I painted the left half, since this side would most likely be turned toward my enemies if I were shooting a rifle or bow. Fears-the-Ground and Kills Something were well pleased.

In the time remaining, I prepared myself for anything I might have to do. I might have to kill. I had not chosen the Apaches as my enemies. It had started when I killed an Apache horse thief dressed like a wolf, four years before, in the Sangre de Cristo Mountains. He should not have attempted stealing my horses. Lame Deer should have traded the captive boy peaceably. This was the way of the plains.

Capture and ransom. He was begging for trouble. Julio deserved to grow up showered by a mother's love. I was prepared to kill for him, and for his mother.

Now I had a long talk with Jibber. My voice was stern, and he sat on his haunches with his head low. I told him that he had better stay close to me and not get himself into any trouble because I would not have time to get him out. We had been together long enough that he knew exactly what I meant.

Before we mounted, I tied an owl feather I had found into Fireball's tail. The owl was the mystical bird of the moon. The feather would grant us the gift of silent flight. I could offer myself no rational explanation why I had begun to believe such things. The sun fell behind the mountains, and we rode cautiously toward Lame Deer's camp.

We found no sentinels. They had all gone to answer the whiskey trader's call. From a distance, we heard drum beats, loud singing, and battle cries. We could tell from the noise that Snakehead had carried through his part of the deal. He would provide the distraction. We had only to find the child, grab him, and ride like whirlwinds.

We waited again. More excruciating waiting. Then twilight fell, and the fluttering trill of a screech owl signaled us ahead. With our blackened faces, we crept forward through yuccas and junipers until we could see the drunken revelry around Snakehead's whiskey keg. He had built a fire up to a white man's roar, and we could see it flickering between the human forms that danced and staggered around it. Then the lines of dancers parted, like curtains on a stage, and I saw the whiskey trader himself, torturing a rattlesnake over the flames as he offered a cup to the highest bidder.

Before the dancers closed ranks again, I saw that Snakehead had amassed quite a pile of weapons in trade for his vile grog. He possessed a diabolical wisdom. He had collected their ability to resist in one pile. He had also set up his whiskey trade well into the canyon, instead of at the canyon mouth, which would have afforded him an easier escape. I thought about why Snakehead had done this. I reasoned that perhaps he had identified the lodge where Julio was being held, and opened his keg beyond that tepee, so that I could rescue the boy and escape without having to ride past the collection of drunken Apaches at the fire.

I got off Fireball at the canyon's mouth and dropped his reins on the ground, knowing he would stay there till I came back, unless a stampede or a brush fire swept him away. I ordered Jibber to stay there with him, the both of them hidden from the camp behind a tangle of agaritas and junipers.

"I am going to stalk closer, until I find the child. When I find him, I will take him, and then you can make your attack, or ride away with your stolen horses."

Kills Something slipped down from his pony. "I will come with you. Fears-the-Ground should stay with the horses until we decide to attack."

Kills Something and I crept through underbrush that skirted the Apache camp, moving like shadowy wolves in the low light that came from a sky the color of slate. Only a couple of stars had begun to show above us. We skulked past eight lodges until we came even with the whiskey trader's fire. The noise from the drunken row was horrible. Some of the warriors were now drunk enough to pick fights or pursue unlucky women or girls into the underbrush. One of them caught a drunken squaw not twelve paces from us, and we had to sneak around them while they scratched and howled like animals, the warrior intent on raping the woman.

Then I saw the boys running around the circle of dancers. They ranged in size, but one was small enough to be Julio. A shaft of firelight shot between two dancers to reveal a face that was dirty, but obviously lighter than the skin of the full-blood Apache children. I knew it was Julio. Even from the distance, in the poor light, I could see his mother's features and virtually feel her blood rushing through his little body.

About that time, a woman came screaming through the camp. She scattered the older children and latched onto Julio's arm. With a switch she carried in her hand, she struck him viciously several times, but he did not cry, though his face showed his pain and fear. This squaw, whom I took for Lame Deer's wife, dragged Julio to a nearby tepee and virtually threw him into it.

I swear I felt every blow Julio took upon his skin, as if it were my own flesh. I seethed with anger to the point that I had to consciously rein in my ire for fear of attacking the whole miserable village. The squaw stepped into the tepee after throwing Julio in, and that put me in the mood for immediate action.

"Go back to the horses," I said to Kills Something. "Attack this village. Leave my horse where he is. I will get the child."

Without answering, Kills Something turned, snuck around the struggle still going on between the drunken rapist and his drunken victim, and stole quickly back toward the horses.

I cannot tell you how sickening it was to wait there alone, listening to the crazed howls, glancing toward the animallike rape scene not far away, worrying about Julio in the lodge with that mean squaw, and catching glimpses of Snakehead's leer as he held another rattlesnake writhing over the flames.

To the approval of the drunken rabble, he chopped the head off the snake, threw it into his open whiskey cask, and dipped out another cup of the foul brew. I watched from ground just high enough that I could see the keg at his feet. I could tell by how far he reached down into the keg that he was almost out of drink with which to bargain.

I watched Snakehead offer the cup to a man ornamented with so many feathers and weapons that I knew he could only be Chief Lame Deer—the Apache who had once sunk an arrow into my shoulder blade while I crossed the Arkansas. Lame Deer reached for the cup, but Snakehead took it back. The whiskey trader gestured toward the lodge with the

vicious squaw in it. I knew they were bargaining for Julio.
I did not like this. I did not want the child in Snakehead's
possession. Something had to happen fast, and it did.

Just as Lame Deer and Snakehead seemed to come to an
agreement, screams rose from the canyon mouth that would
boil the cold blood of a headless rattler. It sounded as if
twenty Comanches were attacking, instead of just two. Lame
Deer grabbed the hilt of his knife, but Snakehead was faster,
drawing a pistol and using it to murder the Apache chief
with a point-blank shot in the face.

I sprang forward, catching glimpses of Fears-the-Ground
and Kills Something charging into the very midst of the
drunken Apaches. As they hacked away with war axes, the
Apaches bolted in every direction, and I reached the lodge
of the vicious squaw. Just as I prepared to throw the door
covering aside and step in, she stepped out. I am not proud
of the fact that I punched a woman in the nose, but I
punched her as hard as I ever punched any man. She fell
limp upon her back, and I stepped into the lodge.

I heard a child's voice say something in a tongue I did
not understand. I went for the sound of the voice, felt the
child, and grabbed him. He bit my arm like a bulldog, just
as I saw the entry open again as Julio scrambled out of the
lodge.

I had grabbed the wrong child! I tossed the Apache child
aside and jumped back out of the lodge. Julio was only a
few steps away. I sprinted forward and grabbed him just as
I felt a warrior descending on me. I turned and drew my
saber. Because the man was naked, I knew he was the rapist.
He came at me with a knife so fast that I didn't have time
to wield my blade. I used my saber hilt to ward off his
ineffectual attempt to stab me. Then I slammed the sword
handle hard into his teeth. I was charged with so much desperate strength that I am sure I broke his jaw and knocked
out half his teeth. He dropped like a shot bird, and I ran
with Julio.

Looking over my shoulder, I saw Fears-the-Ground reaching down from his horse to scalp a warrior he had killed.

Kills Something was darting after fleeing Apaches, with his bow drawn. He could easily have killed two or three, but did not. To one side, I saw Snakehead engaged in a hand-to-hand knife fight with a warrior who had not drunk much whiskey. I turned my back on all of this, and ran toward Fireball.

Little Julio did not fight me. I knew he was petrified with fear, but he had been captured before, and knew the consequences of resistance. He had learned much more than any three-year-old should ever have to. The screams and shouts fell behind me as I reached Fireball and Jibber. I threw the reins over Fireball's neck and mounted him with Julio tucked under my arm. My Comanche friends were galloping out of the canyon now with their scalps.

"I am here!" I shouted, and I joined them as they swooped down upon the Apache horse herd. *"Andale!"* I growled at Fireball, and he seemed to double his speed as I charged around the herd and got in front of it. The stolen horses would follow my lead, and cover my tracks as the Comanches pushed them from behind. We rode a mile south of the canyon mouth, and I heard hard rock under Fireball's hooves. I darted into the herd and cut out three horses, driving them away from the others. I would need a fresh mount or two, and could only hope that these ponies had worn a saddle before. The hard rock would not show our tracks, I reasoned, and perhaps the Apaches would not find my trail at all where it split from the main herd.

We had no time for farewells. Kills Something and Fears-the-Ground simply left me with a pair of war cries as they thundered away with their spoils. I continued southward, driving the three extra mounts through the dark. One hand held the reins, and the other wrapped around Julio to hold him safely in the saddle. I had been unbelievably lucky so far.

I felt a warm tear fall upon the back of my hand. All I knew to do was to keep riding, and sing a passage from *"Juan Charrasceado,"* a Mexican folksong I had learned in San Fernandez de Taos. I thought perhaps the boy had heard it before, and it might comfort him.

FORTY-FOUR

Kills Something had fashioned a map for me the day before. He had drawn it in the sand, using pebbles to represent springs and water holes. He told me about a trail that led from the Guadalupe Mountains to El Paso del Norte. It was part of the old Spanish road between San Antonio de Bexar and El Paso del Norte. Spanish and Mexican soldiers had used the path for over a hundred years, for it passed by numerous springs and water holes—each represented by a pebble on the map Kills Something had wrought for me in the sand. My memory was infallible, but I had to wonder how accurate the map was. When I found the trail under the moonlit peak called El Capitán, then found the first water hole precisely where the map had indicated, my confidence in Kills Something's mapmaking skills soared.

We had ridden at a punishing pace all night, and the horses were tired, but sound. Dawn had come, and the sun was about to rise behind me. As we neared the water, I slipped up on one of the Apache horses and surprised it with a toss of my noose. By this time, Julio was riding behind my cantle, holding tightly to my shirt. This freed my hands for the lasso, and I caught the Apache pony with ease. The pony was tired and did not resist.

I decided to rest just a few minutes at the water hole, which was no more than a catch basin for rain. I let the horses drink. I knew the Apache pony would be easier to handle with a belly full of water.

I filled my canteens and let Julio drink as much as he wanted. *"Cómo esta?"* I asked, but he did not answer. He didn't even look at me. I took Blue Wiggins's gold watch from my pocket. It caught the boy's attention. I smiled and offered it to him. Just as he reached for it, I made it vanish, tucking it into my sleeve with a flourish of my hand. Just as quickly, I made it reappear, and handed it to the boy. His eyes danced, and he glanced at my face briefly, and smiled. Then he sat in the sand by the water hole and played with the watch. Jibber sat near Julio, as if guarding him, but Julio must have been taught by the Indians to ignore dogs, for he made no attempt to befriend Jibber.

It wasn't difficult to get my saddle and bridle on the tired Apache horse. I let him stand awhile so that he might grow accustomed to my saddle. I tinkered with my guns while we rested, preparing them for whatever might come. I had an old musket, a single-shot pistol, and the Colt revolver Colonel Price had given to me. Not much of an arsenal against the whole Mescalero nation. It was better to ride and outrun my enemies, so that I wouldn't have to fight them.

We mounted and continued riding west at a steady trot. When Julio got tired, he would snuggle in my lap and sleep. We skirted a salt flat Kills Something had told me about, and the peaks of the Guadalupe range fell behind us. The road became clearer. For decades, carts had driven to the salt flats to dig up the salt for sale back in El Paso, leaving ruts that would lead us to the old Spanish settlement. Every time the road crossed a high roll in the desert, I looked over my shoulder. I saw no sign of anyone on our trail.

We rode all day at a brisk bounce. The Apache pony proved game, but rode rougher than Fireball. Meanwhile, Fireball seemed to have made it his business to keep the other Apache ponies moving toward El Paso, with Jibber's help. I rarely had to turn a pony back into my little cavvy.

We found the springs and water holes precisely where Kills Something's pebbles had indicated on his map. At dusk, I switched my saddle to the second Apache pony and kept riding until it was too dark to see. Then Julio and Jibber slept curled up on the ground, and even I caught a few winks until the pale light of the rising moon woke me. We ate jerked buffalo meat and rode some more.

By sunup the next day, I was on my third stolen Apache

pony. I found a broad creek valley that had caught some recent rain, for it was dotted with scattered tufts of green grass. I let the ponies graze for half an hour, then moved them on at a walk.

By the third night, Julio had grown to trust me. I finally got him to pet Jibber. At first, he seemed afraid of getting bitten. Before long, however, he was laughing at Jibber's habit of forcing his nose under the nearest human hand, begging to be petted.

By sunrise, I was back on Fireball and riding west. We came to a high point of land in the desert, and I stopped to turn around and look at the trail behind us. About three miles behind us, I saw a tiny plume of dust rising from a moving dot. Someone was riding fast on our trail. I watched just long enough to determine that the rider was alone; then I turned west and urged Fireball into a lope. My heart plummeted into pits of fear.

I rode my horse as hard as I had the heart to ride him, but our pursuer kept closing in on us. I stopped on the next ridge and looked back again. The lone rider was still coming at an all-out gallop. If he overtook me before he rode his horse to death, I would want some cover. Turning west, I spotted a point of rocks that I could use. I decided to stand and fight rather than run my horses to exhaustion. I rode among the rocks, took cover, and waited.

In a few minutes, the rider came galloping over the ridge, whipping his mount. With one look, I recognized Snakehead. He followed my trail toward the gathering of rocks, and pulled rein just beyond rifle range. The exhausted horse he rode heaved for air.

"Kid!" the whiskey trader shouted. "Goddamn, you ride hard!"

I watched him over my rifle irons. I knew the limitations of my weapon. At this range, the old muzzle loader might stand a three-in-five chance of hitting its target, and I didn't like those odds.

"My horse is done in, Kid! I need one of yours so's we

can get the boy to El Paso. Best hurry. I think we'll have company soon."

Consider my options, if you will. I did not trust Snake-head Jackson any more than I could trust a rabid dog. I feared he would try to kill me so that he could claim Julio's ransom. Yet, I could not chance a shot at Snakehead. Should my rifle miss, we would commence a standoff that might allow Apaches to overtake us. In addition, I feared he might stalk me through those rocks and kill me in some unpleasant manner. Make no mistake about it. I was afraid of Snake-head Jackson. I knew that in a fair fight, or especially a fight weighted by deceit and trickery, that he could probably kill me. I calculated the odds in my head and quickly ascertained that my best chance for Julio's survival involved making a pact with Snakehead.

I knew he wouldn't come closer until I showed myself and offered him a horse. Then I would be just as much a target for him as he would be for me. I roped an Apache pony and led him into view. "Come on!" I shouted. "Let's hurry!"

Snakehead urged his mount forward. The poor horse was at the point of collapse when the whiskey trader stripped the saddle from it and threw it on the mount I gave him.

"I didn't think you got out of that camp alive," I said.

"Weren't easy. I fought my way to my horse and tried to catch up to you and them Comanche bucks, but them liquored-up Apaches swarmed me. I had to turn and ride right back through their camp. Turned out they had all their best horses staked in camp. I cut loose a couple of 'em and pushed 'em right up over Guadalupe Pass. I've rode two horses to death catchin' you, and looks like this one's good as dead, too."

"Maybe he'll recover. There's water not too far ahead."

Snakehead had finished cinching his saddle on the Apache pony I gave him. Now he drew his knife. "Recover's ass, Kid." Taking a step toward the exhausted horse, the whiskey trader slashed the animal's jugular with his razor-sharp blade. The horse lurched, took two steps, and collapsed, his blood marking the sand with a horrible black stain as he died.

I could only gasp in horror, and I knew Snakehead would just as soon cut my throat the same way. "Why did you have to do that?" I asked.

"Can't leave that horse for the Apaches to ride."

"He couldn't have carried a rider another mile," I argued.

"You never know what a Indian can get out of a horse. Let's ride."

Snakehead took charge of the two loose horses, pushing them west as if they were his. I had no choice but to ride along, and we pushed our ponies to a lope. We rode for hours without saying much, then stopped to switch mounts again. Fireball rolled in the sand, then sprang back to his feet, and we pressed ever westward.

We rode until dark, then stopped at a water hole the horses found by its smell. It was too dark and the horses too full of water to ride right away, so we rested.

"They'll catch us tomorrow," Snakehead said before falling off into a snoring fit.

Everyone slept but me. I have to admit that I considered murdering Snakehead in his sleep. I felt as if I were back at Saint-Cyr. I could no longer sleep since I had exhausted my supply of dogbane root, and my fears had started to twist themselves into abominations of rational human thought. What thought could be more abominable than the desire to commit murder? In the end, I decided against murdering Snakehead—not because it was wrong, but because I feared he would hear my pistol being pulled from its holster, and kill me before I could kill him—or perhaps roast me to death over a fire, like a rattlesnake. When the moon began to rise, three-quarters full, I roused our whole unlikely party, and we took the trail by moonlight.

By noon the next day, I was switching my saddle back to Fireball. Snakehead had already changed horses and was standing on a high rock, watching our back trail. As I tightened my cinch, I heard the whiskey trader climbing down from the rocks. The next moment, I heard a deafening blast that almost made me jump over my horse. I turned and saw a horse drop to the ground. Now Snakehead swung his muzzle around to the horse I had just finished riding.

"No!" I shouted, reaching for my pistol.

Snakehead was quick enough to kill the horse with a shot to the head and swing his revolver around on me. "Take it easy, Kid. I don't want to have to kill you, too."

"Why are you shooting our horses?" I demanded at the top of my lungs. I could feel the fatigue of the ride and the strain of the whole adventure pushing my nerves to the point of insanity.

"They were done in, and I ain't gonna leave 'em for them Apaches. I just now seen the war party not five miles back. They're comin' fast."

I forced myself to shove the single-shot back into its holster. "How many of them?" I scarcely recognized my own voice.

Snakehead lowered his weapon. "Looked like a dozen or more. We're still fifteen miles from El Paso."

We mounted and made our horses reach. As tired as I was, my mind began making calculations. For an hour, my brain whirled through a storm of numbers, percentages, and odds, figuring our chances of reaching El Paso before the Apaches overtook us. It depended on many things. Were their horses fresher than ours? Would we find help along the way? Would our mounts come up lame? I compared probabilities from the unknown future while the desert seemed to pour out from under me as if we were riding inside an hourglass.

At last my brain settled on the most probable outcome, all things considered. We had a small chance of reaching El Paso before the Apaches. They were going to catch us. Had I not felt so utterly exhausted, I would have given in to paroxysms of terror. But I was so worn down, mentally and physically, that I no longer feared anything. Not even Snakehead.

We had run a little over four miles, the Apaches gaining slowly, when Snakehead's horse began to falter. Finally the pony stumbled, almost pitching the whiskey trader forward before struggling back to his feet. I reined in to slow Fireball. I was holding Julio in front of me. Snakehead had been riding to my left.

"This one's done, Kid," the whiskey trader said, as he dropped from the saddle.

I, too, dismounted, Indian-style, on the off side of Fireball, so that I wouldn't have to turn my back on Snakehead. I clasped Julio in front of me as I stepped down. Now Snakehead and I had the two horses between us. A dozen Apaches were riding fast. My hand was on the grip of my revolver, my pony shielding me. I let Julio drop to the ground behind me and he stood there, disoriented and confused by the entire ordeal.

"We'll make a fight of it," I said. "We'll stand back to back."

"Yeah." Snakehead was watching me hawklike over the back of the exhausted pony, his eyes as pale as the sky behind him, as if they were merely holes that went right through his head. "Like you and Blue Wiggins done on the Little Cimarron."

"Exactly."

We both knew that Snakehead Jackson was no Blue Wiggins. There was no time to maneuver. The Indians were gaining fast. I estimated that the Apaches would overtake us in eight minutes if we continued to stand here. Snakehead knew this as well as I, but his shield was a lame horse, and this gave me my only advantage.

I did not look forward killing that lame pony. It haunts me some to this day, along with all the other hauntings I must endure. But the pony was destined to die of thirst and carnivores, so my shot would be as much of a mercy killing as it was a way to expose Snakehead.

When I showed my pistol barrel, the whiskey trader ducked. I shot the horse in the head, and he dropped in a piteous heap. There was no time to fool around; I had to do it.

I am an excellent marksman, and I knew I could hit

Snakehead, but I had to cock that Colt revolver first, and Snakehead was standing there, ready. He had had his pistol in his hand all along, looking for a chance to shoot me, as I knew he would. He wanted my horse.

Fireball had startled at the sound of my first shot, and his rump was passing in front of me as I thumbed back the hammer and lined the sights on Snakehead where he stood exposed. My pony's tail passed in front of me, and I knew I was dead. Snakehead would not miss me. I could only hope to kill him as he killed me. I turned sideways, like a duelist, to present a narrower target. I prayed Julio would survive among the Apaches. I lamented the grief his mother would know.

I pulled the trigger, felt the pistol buck. Shots rang out like a drum roll, and I stood there, unharmed, watching Snakehead writhe on the ground. I am a genius, but it took me a moment to figure out what had happened. Sometimes—rarely—you can figure the odds, and yet they surprise you with a variable you could not have foreseen. When this happens at the exact moment necessary to save your life, it can only mean that the Great Mystery is looking out for you. There is no other mathematical or scientific explanation.

My bullet had pierced Snakehead's hat just above the brim, slammed into his skull, and glanced upward, probably fracturing his cranium and dooming him to a slow death from brain hemorrhage and shock.

I am sure his bullet would have hit me square in the head, or in the heart, but his revolver had chain-fired, as the old Colts sometimes did. As his bullet passed down the barrel of his Colt, a spark shot out from the crack between the revolving wheel and the breech, igniting the charge of the next load in the chamber, which exploded as the bullet left the muzzle, spoiling Snakehead's aim just enough to make his bullet nick the crown of my hat as the revolver burst in his hand, tearing his fingers, arm, chest, and face with shrapnel.

Yet the whiskey trader lived. He squirmed on the ground

like one of his own headless snakes. I had no time to calculate how long he would live. One way or another, he was
going to die. He rolled over and moaned, his face a mass
of blood and torn flesh caked with dirt. The Apaches were
coming. I cocked my revolver and sent a bullet into his
brain, killing him instantly. Had he survived long enough,
the Apaches eventually would have returned here to torture
him whether he was conscious or not. He did not deserve
my mercy, and I did not enjoy granting it.

Now the quiet of the desert screamed at me in all urgency.
I dropped my revolver right there where I stood. I threw my
hat in one direction and my saber in the other. I whistled
for my horse as I yanked the single-shot pistol from my belt
and tossed it aside. Fireball the Half-Blind came walking
toward me as I pulled my buckskin shirt over my head and
discarded it. I kept only my knife, my buckskin britches,
and my moccasins.

When I reached Fireball, I pulled his bridle off first, cutting one rein, which I used to fashion a war bridle, tying it
fast around Fireball's lower jaw. Next, I loosened and un-
buckled the cinches, letting the whole saddle drop—canteens, rifle, bedroll, saddlebags and all. The only thing I took
from my saddle was my rope, which I wrapped four times,
loosely, around Fireball's barrel, making a Comanche coil.

I jumped onto Fireball's back, rode over to Julio, who
had been standing in one spot through all the killing and
gunfire, and reached down for his hand. He gave it to me,
and I pulled him up and sat him on Fireball's bare back
behind me. Now I slipped my knees tightly under the Comanche coil, fixing myself firmly between the horse and the
rope, and began to ride.

Fireball had caught some wind during our duel. Now,
with his load lightened, we struck an altogether new pace.
I glanced back once on the next high point of land and saw
the Indians milling around the carcasses of Snakehead and
his unfortunate horse, only two miles behind me.

I saw no point in looking back again. We were eleven
miles from El Paso. Fireball had been moving for four days,

with little time to graze. He was running well now, but had
to be nearing the point of fatigue. I just rode. Bareback, I
felt every breath Fireball heaved. He was like a great engine,
carrying us toward salvation.

Ten miles, nine miles . . . Five, four, three . . . Roads and
trails increased. We were close indeed. I looked back now,
and saw the Apaches almost within arrow range. Fireball
was frothed with sweat, yet he tattoed the desert with his
hooves. We neared a rise in the landscape, and he snorted.
He twisted his head in a warning. He had smelled something, and he was telling me about it.

Over the ridge we galloped, charging smack into a party
of nine mounted men, scattering horses and creating a moment of panic. Before I passed among the riders and drew
rein, I recognized faces. Kit Carson. Charlie Autobee. Blue
Wiggins. Tom Boggs. Louis Lescot. Lucien Maxwell. Peg
Leg Smith. Goddamn Murray. And Mariano Zavaleta—Julio's father.

Yes, Julio's father. I knew it the moment I saw his face.
His features were plain in the countenance of little Julio. I
was not Julio's father, and it didn't matter. I still would have
given my life to save the boy for Gabriela.

"Indians!" I shouted.

We could hear the hooves pounding. A rattle of weaponry
commenced, and Kit Carson screamed a war yell. He
charged toward high ground, and the rest of the men surrounded Julio and me. We all followed Kit. The moment
we came in sight of the Mescaleros, they stopped in a spray
of dirt and scattered.

"Goddamn, let's git 'em!" Murray shouted.

"Let them go!" I barked. "Get this boy to the town."

Mariano rode in next to me and reached for Julio. I
handed the boy to his father. Mariano cradled the boy and
wept. Kit Carson fired a shot or two over the heads of the
Indians, and they withdrew farther away. We turned back
toward El Paso and rode at a trot, circling Mariano and Julio
in a protective ring. Through his tears, Mariano looked at
me. *"Gracias, amigo,"* was all he said, but with such ardor

in his voice that he might have spoken a million words of gratitude. As Mariano wrapped himself protectively around Julio, the boy looked at me. He looked me right in the eyes. He was still holding the watch I had given him. I flashed a tired smile at him, and danged if he didn't smile back, a little twinkle in his eyes.

The Mescaleros kept their distance, and refused to pursue us any closer to El Paso, for their ponies were tired and might be easily overtaken.

I was naked from the waist up, hatless, covered with dirt and sweat, overwhelmed with emotion and relief.

"Orn'ry, you sure know how to make an entrance," Blue said.

"*Oui,*" said Louis. "Like the time he rode into Bent's Fort, an arrow between his teeth!"

"Goddamn if he didn't," Maxwell said.

"You wasn't even there," Peg Leg replied.

"Well, goddamn, I heard tell about it!"

I looked at Kit. "How did you know I was coming?"

"That Comanche, Loud Shouter, came and told us. He had a knife wound in his gut where he said Snakehead stuck him, but he came on anyway, half-dead."

"Did he live?"

"He was alive when we left him at the fort. I reckon he's tough enough to pull through."

"Did you see Snakehead out there?" Tom Boggs asked.

We rode on in silence for a few seconds as the saddle leather squeaked out a jolly tune and the hooves clopped in time.

"Snakehead Jackson is dead," I replied. "I killed him not an hour ago." No one ever asked me another thing about it, as long as I lived. It just didn't matter as long as he was dead.

We rode into El Paso as if we had been out for a picnic. Do you know how good a warm bath in a wooden tub can feel? It can feel almost as good as . . . Well, use your imagination.

FORTY-FIVE

Gabriela came to see me at Kit Carson's home in Taos. She came alone.

"Señora Zavaleta is here to see you, *hermano.*" Josefa Carson said. She had taken to calling me "brother."

I had been sitting at a table making, from memory, a map of the country I had traversed while hunting for Julio. I turned in my chair and lay the quill pen down, my heart suddenly pounding. "Will you send her in, please?"

Mrs. Carson nodded. A few moments later, Gabriela stepped into the room, and closed the door behind her.

Her eyes filled with tears and she ran at me, literally colliding with me as she wrapped her arms around me and knocked me back onto the table where I had been drawing. She kissed me all over my face, finally arriving at my mouth. She tore her lips away from mine too soon and just held me, as if I might have been trying to escape.

It was wonderful and terrible all at once. We had come to understand that we could not be together, and that was just that.

"Why do you think it happened this way?" she whispered in my ear.

I shrugged and sighed. "I don't know. Maybe so I could rescue Julio. I don't know."

"You are my hero, *querido*. You are amazing. I love you more than you will ever know."

"I know."

"No, you don't. You could not possibly know."

I wrapped my arms around her tighter. "I believe I do."

We stood there for a long time, holding onto something we had already set free. We said the things that forbidden lovers should say. Though neither of us needed to hear them, it was well that we said them. We sighed and trembled and locked our souls together with lingering stares into each other's eyes. But we both knew she could not stay too long in that room with me.

"Mariano and my father want to throw a big *fiesta* for you."

"Tell them I must decline. I'm going back to the plains. I have things to finish."

She shook her head against her sorrow, and slung tears across her cheeks. We said our good-byes over and over. At last, Gabriela mustered her courage and strength and pulled away from me and walked to the door. She turned. I still remember the sight of her lips whispering words I could not hear. *"Te quiero,"* she said. A more dramatic and passionate creature never existed.

Then she was gone.

I sat back down at my table and picked up my pen. I stared at the page, the hands of fate wringing my heart like an old rag. I heard the door creak, and Josefa Carson said, "Are you alright, *hermano?*"

I turned toward her and forced a smile. "Of course, Josefa. I am just fine."

It was quite a marvelous lie.

FORTY-SIX

I stood on that high roll in the prairie, the seed heads of the grasses tickling my knuckles. Jibber was lying at my feet, biting at a flea on his flank. I wore a brace of new silver-plated Colt revolvers given to me by Don Badillo, Gabriela's father. Fort Adobe was behind me, out of sight.

A crisp, dry snap hung in the autumn air. It was time for

the winter trading to begin. But this year, there would be none of that. When I turned back to the southeast, I was almost startled to see the fort I had built standing there. It was strange, but I finally understood. The damn thing just didn't belong here. I never should have taken part in building it in the first place. As architecture ranked on the frontier, it was a beautiful trading post; but compared to a buffalo-hide lodge, it was an eyesore.

Try to understand. I loved that fort. The walls had taken shape through my very hands. Every dimension remained fused in my memory. But I had built it here in utter ignorance. An ignorant genius is dangerous. I had missed the point. The point was the place itself. The Crossing. The valley. The prairie. The game in the timber and the birds on the wing. The worms among the roots in the soil. The innumerable raindrops seeping, coursing glacierlike through the loam underfoot. To have raised walls upon this place was lunacy. The Red Men had known this since the age when animals spoke, and walked about like two-leggeds.

I sighed and made myself walk with purposeful strides toward the fort. As I approached, I saw William Bent carrying the keg out through the open gates, a cascade of black powder streaming from the open bunghole, leaving a severe black line on the ground. He poured the line all the way to the wagon waiting sixty yards from the gates. The keg empty now, he tossed it aside. He saw me coming and leaned against the back of the wagon.

"I don't blame Frémont," William said, as I came within earshot. "He was only the messenger."

"I'm sure Lieutenant Abert meant no harm, either," I said. "He had his orders."

"Orders. That's what's wrong with the damn army. You can't trust the army and you can't trust the government. They called on my patriotism and, like a fool, I bit. You know, Mr. Greenwood. You rode with me in the Spy Guard. I've lost family and friends out here, warring with Mexico and pacifying the Indians. I risked my life and spent a small fortune on this fort. Frémont swore the army would either purchase it, or reimburse me. Now they act like they don't even know who I am. You understand, don't you? I know you put your sweat and blood into this fort. But I'll be goddamned if I'm just going to turn it over to the army and let them use it. They can build their own damn forts."

"It doesn't belong here, anyway," I said. "I saw that, just now, from the prairie."

He clapped me on the shoulder in appreciation for my understanding. "Do you know what the army offered me for Bent's Fort?"

"No, sir."

"Ten thousand dollars. Ten thousand measly dollars for almost twenty years of work and risk."

"Are you going to take it?"

"Hell, no. After we're finished here, we're going to ride back to Bent's Fort and blow it up, too."

"You could keep the fort."

"The damned government has the right to condemn and steal whatever they want. I won't let them do it. Besides, I won't help the army kill my people. I'm as much Cheyenne as I am white man, by God, and I know you understand that."

"Yes, sir. I've gone about half Comanche myself."

"You should have been here in the old days, but hell, I reckon you were in foldin' britches."

"What was the trade like then?"

"It was a wonder. We made money, but most of all we made peace. We kept things pretty quiet, Mr. Greenwood. Me and Charles and Ceran. We did alright. Before the Texans stirred things up and the army moved in wanting New Mexico, a man could cross these plains if he was careful. Now the Indians are mad, and it takes a party of a dozen armed men to go anywhere. How you survived alone to ransom that Mexican kid is a miracle to me. It's the army's fault. The army don't make peace, it makes war."

"Well," I said, a lump as big as a rifle slug in my throat. "They won't make war from our fort."

"No, they won't, Mr. Greenwood. Not from any of our forts."

Just then, Sol Silver came strolling out through the gates. He reached into his vest pocket and put a crooked cigar in his mouth. It punctuated his smile as he approached us.

"Are they about finished in there?" William said.

"Blue is spreading lamp oil all over the brush roof. I told him we were going to blow the hell out of it anyway, but he said it wasn't going to be such a big explosion."

"It'll be big enough," William said. "What's Murray doing?"

"When I walked out, he was pissing on a scorpion."

"And the rest of them?"

"Just stacking the kegs and spreading the powder from one to the other. They're finished. It's going to blow up like one hell of a bomb."

William looked at me. "You want to take one last look around in there, Mr. Greenwood?"

"No, sir. I've had my last look."

"Well, go get them out of there, Sol, so we can get on with it."

Sol struck a match on the back of the wagon and lit his cigar. "I'll get them out," he said. "Watch this." And he dropped the lighted match onto the end of the trail of black powder. It took off like a sputtering locomotive.

"Oh, shit." William said, a rare grin forming on his face.

Sol Silver began to laugh.

I started to take off at a run so I could kick the powder in front of the flame, but William held me back.

"Mr Bent," I said, "there are twenty kegs of powder in there!"

"Just a few seconds more, Mr. Greenwood. This might be fun."

He waited until the flame was about to enter the gates, then shouted, "Fire in the hole, boys! Run like hell!"

From inside the fort, I could hear Murray yelling, "Blue! Goddamn! Blue! Goddamn!"

Men began to scramble out of the fort. White-haired Thomas Fitzpatrick, laughing Kit Carson, then old John Hatcher outrunning young Tom Boggs. Burly Lucien Maxwell, and long-legged, crazy-as-a-loon Bill Williams, reciting a psalm at the top of his lungs:

". . . They gaped upon me with their mouths as a ravenous and roaring lion. . . ."

French Charlie Autobee and worldly Baptiste Charbonneau, one to either side of Peg Leg Smith, carrying him away as fast as they could run on five good legs.

And finally, young Blue Wiggins wailing, "Whoa-oh-oh-oh," and blasphemous Lucas Murray, shouting, "Goddamn you, Sol Silver!"

The leaders had almost reached the wagon, and the stragglers were halfway there. I put my hands over my ears. I had extrapolated the power of a shotgun blast, and I knew the explosion was going to rock the valley. All I saw were chunks of sunbaked brick hurling past me like grapeshot as the percussion slammed me against the back of the wagon which, in turn, bounced me forward onto the ground. As quickly as I could, I turned and scrambled under the wagon with Sol Silver and William Bent, listening to pieces of my fort rain down on the wagon like hail on a cedar-shake roof.

Through it all, Sol Silver laughed and Goddamn Murray swore. When the danger of falling bricks had passed, Murray pulled Silver out from under the wagon. The cursing, guffawing fistfight deteriorated quickly into a sloppy wrestling match as Murray was too tired from his footrace to give Sol much trouble, though he did bloody Sol's nose.

"Give you somethin' to laugh about, goddamn it!"

"You run like a squaw," Sol managed to say between guffaws.

"You can kiss my goddamn ass and bark at the hole!"

It was only now that I thought to look at the fort. Most of all four walls, and the entire northwest corner had been carried away by the blast. The other three corners had been blasted away to a height of six or eight feet. Bricks and chunks of adobe lay scattered all over the prairie, up to a quarter mile away from the former trading post.

Sol Silver had not quit laughing yet, though some of the men were now pelting him with hard adobe clods. In the end, the laughter became infectious, and every man joined in—even Kit Carson, who had caught a flying brick with the back of his head and lain semiconscious for a minute after the blast; and Charlie Autobee, who had sprained his ankle carrying Peg Leg Smith to safety. In a way, it was funny. I admit that even I laughed at these old warriors acting like schoolboys, though I laughed mostly to keep from crying.

The echo of the blast seemed to ricochet around the valley forever, and I can hear it yet. Sometimes, during the bad nights when the dark of the moon comes on, I dream that the sky is raining bricks left over from the demolition of Fort Adobe, and I just run and run, but the bricks keep pelting me.

Anyway, that was the glorious end of Fort Adobe. It was at once sad and funny. I stood there laughing with the others, my heart broken, my soul ripped open as if from a black-powder blast.

It was hard, but no harder than the things you have done. It eases the hard part when I tell it. I am pleased that you have listened so long.

FORTY-SEVEN

ADOBE WALLS, TEXAS 1927

Listen. Do you hear? That airplane is returning from Albuquerque with the mail. In the dark. Can you imagine? I would like to fly in one of those things. I know they fall from the sky sometimes, but I am ninety-nine years old, for heaven's sake. Those are brave young men who fly those outfits. Listen. It fades away already. It is almost gone. They say that thing has an internal combustion engine with the power of 225 horses. They say it goes over 100 miles per hour. If only it wasn't so loud.

Well, we have had a good, long talk. We have shared a few laughs. A tear or two, as well. If I have horrified you, I beg your forgiveness. I have not told you everything, of course. I know other stories, but they must wait for other tellings. I will tell you this: William Bent did go back to Bent's Fort, and he did blow it sky-high. He built another trading post—a smaller one, of stone, at Big Timbers—and carried on with the Indian trade as long as he could. Some other time, I will tell you about the rest of his life.

I didn't see William blow up Bent's Fort. I left this place, The Crossing, now known as Adobe Walls, and went to find Shaved Head's band out on the *Llano Estacado*. I went Indian. I became a trader and a ransom negotiator. I made war with Apaches against my will. Horrible, bloody war.

Did I marry that Comanche girl, Hidden Water? What would you have done? I cannot start telling that story right now. I know you have other things to do, and I am weary. I will tell you about Hidden Water some other time. Whatever happened to Gabriela? Some other time. I would like to tell you, but now I feel so tired.

No moon will rise tonight. The demons will lurk in these sod walls. But, I have chewed the root of dogbane, drunk the tea of moccasin-flower root, and made a smudge of fir needles. I believe I will be safe. Do not worry about me. I have medicine. *Puha*, as the Comanches called it.

I may sleep a day or two. That is my way. If the rains don't wash away those bricks out there, I will wake to tell you more some other time. But, I am ninety-nine, and my bones hurt, and my heart beats in syncopated rhythm. No man lives forever, and that is well.

But, look. I see a star in the west through that tiny window. The sky clears. The rains will pass. *To sleep, perchance to dream*, the Bard wrote. When you reach my age, you say, "To sleep, perchance to wake."

I like your laughter. Your smile sparkles like a galaxy.

I will share my memories with you again. I know it. My time has not quite come. We will meet again. There is so much left to tell. Much has happened here at The Crossing. Here, at Adobe Walls. Another time, my friend.

I am fading. I must take my leave. I hear voices. The ghosts and visions are coming. I hear Kit. I hear Charles and William. I hear Kills Something and Little Bluff and Burnt Belly. Gabriela sings. I hear them all, chanting. They call me. They long to greet me in the Great Mystery.

We are friends now, you and I. You understand . . . You will forgive me. The moon medicine . *Vaya con Dios* . . . Perhaps another time. Please, visit again. *To sleep* They are calling me. I can hear them. The music sounds so beautiful. . . . *Perchance to dream* . . .

They call me . . . Plenty Man.